SECRET SUMMER

A Mystery set in Detroit and Derbyshire 1966

First Edition

Published by The Nazca Plains Corporation
Las Vegas, Nevada
2010

ISBN: 978-1-61098-029-6
E-book: 978-1-61098-030-2

Published by

The Nazca Plains Corporation ®
4640 Paradise Rd, Suite 141
Las Vegas NV 89109-8000

PUBLISHER'S NOTE
Secret Summer is a work of fiction created wholly by *Narvel Annable's* imagination. All
characters are fictional and any resemblance to any persons living or deceased is purely by
accident. No portion of this book reflects any real person or events.

Art Director, Blake Stephens

SECRET SUMMER

A Mystery set in Detroit and Derbyshire 1966

First Edition

Narvel Annable

For

Paul Hunt and Steve Cole

With gratitude for friendship, encouragement and support

AUTHOR'S NOTE

The secret history to be unfolded in the following pages is largely oral and unwritten. It is a novel inspired by a summer cycling holiday I enjoyed in one of England's most beautiful counties. As a 19-year-old I encountered an interesting selection of some curious and colourful characters which constituted a rich experience. Sadly, most of them are no longer with us. These events took place in real places, in this book peopled by a fictitious cast. Allow me to introduce you to these caricatured composites who are inspired by a selection of the types I met nearly half a century back. However real flesh and blood the original model, who actually ends up on these pages (after being processed through my brain) is very far from being any real person – alive or dead).

CONTENTS

FOREWORD

Life for the gay community is often said to be 'getting better'. We have seen the watershed of Stonewall in the late 1960s, the development of the Gay Rights movement of the 1970s and the spectre of AIDS in the 1980s. In some states in the USA, and in the entire UK, the age of sexual consent for Gay men achieved some equity with the heterosexual majority. As we moved into the new millennium, same sex couples in several countries around the world were afforded the opportunity to marry. The future looks promising!

However, what of our gay forefathers? What of those men and women who had to endure a life far from being liberal; a life significantly torturous and very often closeted? Gay history is not, as is often described, minimal or sparse. It is simply not well recorded or in any great quantity. We did not have the recognition, the freedom, or, indeed, the chance to be ourselves, to be loved and respected for who we are. Nevertheless, gay men and women still met, lived life, loved and eventually lost, just as our straight counterparts did.

History records many events in the way our ancestors would want it to be recounted by future generations. Very often it ignored the sexuality of those who shaped our future. Only relatively recently have we come to recognise those many gay men and women who, over the centuries, would shape our future.

Would we be as technologically advanced if it were not for Alan Turning? Hadrian built Britain's most famous wall. And, let us be honest, only a gay man would have the flair to paint the ceiling of the Sistine Chapel!

Whilst some Gay history is recorded, it needs more recognition. It needs more detail, more realism, to, not least, recount the stories and events of those people who may not have discovered new lands or, indeed, been pioneers in the early days of celluloid. Nevertheless, gay people lived life, despite the hatred, prejudice and fear – as themselves. If we do not make an effort to ensure such stories are recorded – they will be lost – forever.

There are times when you, for whatever reason, pick up a book. Perhaps it's the attraction of the title, the back cover blurb, the author's reputation or – let's be honest – you like the picture on the cover. I picked up *Scruffy Chicken* by Narvel Annable for none of those reasons. It was purely and honestly because my Editor at *Shout!* sent it to me with the usual note, 'please read / review as soon as possible'. I complied; after all, he pays me. Apart from the ASAP, I found the book too good to just quickly read and review. I found myself savouring each chapter. I laughed, I cried and, eventually, I wrote my review. If

I recall correctly, I said the book was '...A tour de force of a read...' It was at the book's conclusion that I made the decision – I had to meet the author....

Several years later, I am proud to say that Narvel, along with his partner Terry, are two of the nicest people you could wish to meet. I am proud to call them friends. Since *Scruffy Chicken*, I have read and thoroughly enjoyed all of Narvel's other titles and was delighted, not only to have this new book dedicated to my partner Steve and myself, but also afforded the honour to write this foreword.

Narvel may not have built any walls in his lifetime or indeed painted colourful ceilings, but he took up his pen and has captured forever more of our history. It can now be told and no longer has to remain what was, without a doubt – a *Secret Summer*... enjoy!

Paul Hunt – Chief Features Writer – *Shout!*
August 2010

CHAPTER 1

Dreams of Derbyshire

Simeon Hogg was homesick. As usual, to ease this chronic misery, he indulged himself by replaying a pleasant memory of cycling along leafy Derbyshire lanes. He selected a recollection from his early teens, a ride from Belper to Wirksworth, a cool bright day in late September. The boy stood hard on pedals. Slowly, very slowly in low gear he pumped up a steep, pretty little lane, up, up to those windswept heights, up into the scent of fern and browning bracken.

This trip was memorable for its beauty, and also for its challenge. Simeon was often stopping to study his precious, cloth-bound, 'one inch' Ordnance Survey map in an effort to carefully navigate through a confusing myriad of many narrow, winding country lanes, all going everywhere. There were lots of crossroads with intriguing signs pointing to odd sounding places – Gorseybank, Shottle, Alderwasley, Alport Height, Idridgehay – all so very strange – all so very Derbyshire.

Illuminated by dazzling autumnal sunshine, brilliant white clouds were chased by the wind across a heavenly vault of deep blue. This same wind roared through a battle-scarred ash tree, danced the bracken, flattened the open meadow but appeared to have no power over a stubborn craggy old hawthorn at the edge of his pretty lane. Tirelessly, it speeded Simeon and moved a million different weeds matured over a long summer, weeds deep green and weeds beautifully brown flashing by as the lane sank into a ravine and then suddenly ascended to reveal magnificent views to the west.

The physical exertion, the physical pleasure, the rhythm of waving trees was consistent with Simeon's own body rhythms. Breaths of sweet fresh air, his increased heart-beat born of ecstatic exercise could never be achieved in a vast ugly conurbation called Detroit.

Here he was home. Here, over a swath of impenetrable prickly gorse he could see forever. Here, on his bicycle, he was on top of the world, could see a view of the whole world endlessly stretching out until it dissolved into a misty distant... and, as the reverie weakened... the scene dissolved and resolved back into the present reality... a grim reality.

These were not the sunlit green hills of Derbyshire in late September 1959. These were the hideous, blighted, flat expanses of an endless, benighted conurbation in early January 1966. A sadder Simeon, barely out of his teens, navigated his car off the I94 Edsel Ford Freeway to join the John Lodge Freeway which would speed him into Downtown Detroit.

Even though his destination was sex, he was still sad owing to a massive complexity of problems, of which, homesickness was just a part. At this moment, on the Lodge Freeway, this unhappy 20 year old, trapped in an alien land, was overwhelmed by a multitude of vague miseries. He was incapable of analysing, unable to untangle the convoluted complications of his present circumstances. No professional gay-friendly counsellors were available – would not be available – for another four decades. Simeon was repressed. Simeon was isolated from friends, family and colleagues by the brick wall of ignorance, bigotry and prejudice which today we refer to as homophobia. Emotionally, he was hiding inside of himself. Effectively, he was an outlaw. He was cut off from all the well-established heterosexual social structures of family support.

Simeon knew that he was queer. He knew it every time he saw a comely face, every time he saw nice butch bulges held snug inside of tight fitting sexy jeans. He also knew that it was wrong to be queer. He accepted received opinion about a certain 'disgusting disorder' which was sometimes treated with electric shock aversion therapy. Still imprisoned inside the primitive peasant values of his working-class family, and, in the absence of educated, enlightened counsel, Simeon Hogg was falling victim to that most dreaded malaise which often infected homosexuals in the mid-20th century – self-hate.

For as long as he could remember, the heterosexual majority had, at every opportunity, reinforced their hard line against queers, perverts, poofs. These ingrained homophobic attitudes, written in stone, written inside his very being, came down from the very top of society often referred to as 'the Establishment'.

When the World Health Organisation was established in 1948, homosexuality was officially classified as a 'severe mental sickness' and remained so until May 17th 1990. This was one of the most important events in Gay History, an event now celebrated annually by Lesbian, Gay, Bisexual and Transgender people as the International Day Against Homophobia [IDAHO].

But Rainbow Flags, Gay Pride Events and gay support groups were still unthinkable, still decades away from the current reality of this sad young Englishman who was trying to survive, trying to make sense of, trying to engage with the illegal, seedy, secret homosexual underworld of North America on this bleak mid-winter evening, January 8th, 1966.

Secret Summer 5

CHAPTER 2

The Windsor Bath House

"Where were ya born?" whined the bored customs officer at the Canadian end of the Detroit-Windsor Tunnel. He was not looking at Simeon Hogg, sitting in his plain and functional Ford Falcon fumbling for his pocketbook to produce the all-important green Alien Card.

"England," responded Simeon, matter-of-fact, disinterested.

The vast majority of travellers would say 'Detroit'. The officer would say 'OK' and the car would move on. 'England' was different. It caused eye-contact and the green card underwent its usual brief examination to make sure the photograph matched the face.

"What's your business in Canada?"

"Shopping," was Simeon's standard reply; a reply which would have been unacceptable in England where nearly every shop closed after 6.00pm. If the customs man asked 'What for?' Simeon had another standard reply – 'For malt vinegar.' Detroit supermarkets had every kind of vinegar for every ethnic taste – except English vinegar.

It would have been impossible to tell the truth.

"What's your business in Canada?"

"Steam bath."

"What!"

"Steam bath. It's called Vesuvio, just this side of Jackson Park."

"Get out of the car!"

"What's wrong?"

It was always a mystery to the Detroit gay community: *how* did Vesuvio manage to remain open? True, it had been raided by the police. They closed it down for several months. Just as suddenly, it had re-opened. There were rumours. 'The cops are being paid off' – it was said. In fact, Vesuvio was the third incarnation for this particular 'den of iniquity'. The first attempt, on Lake Shore Drive, was opened in 1958. Called Etna; it was said to be run by the local 'mob' who were just beginning to exploit the 'pink dollar' on the other side of the river. Gay Americans, taking advantage of a convenient foreign country close by, created a new demand for a relatively safe place to meet for orgiastic sex. One shattering evening, the Law descended and about 50 severely distressed Americans were ordered to dress. It could have been worse, much worse. However, the maximum punishment did not exceed acute embarrassment and immediate deportation of 50 gay Americans. The second attempt on Dougall Avenue was named Stromboli. Eventually, it suffered a similar fate.

Until its demolition in 1964, the Detroit Vernor Baths near Tiger Stadium was never safe from the occasional police raid which involved the horror of arrest, a hefty fine or possible imprisonment not to mention disastrous publicity in the *Detroit News* and / or the *Detroit Free Press*. Canada was not really safe, but Americans *felt* safer, felt it was worth the risk.

And here it was, in the freezing cold, in the black of night, up the proverbial dark ally: 'Vesuvio – Private Health Club'. 'Men Only', proclaimed the grimy sign as Simeon bumped his unloved car around the potholes of the un-lit, un-metalled car park. It had one, never-used, small room; a repository for a few old dumbbells to give the illusion of an establishment visited for the building up of muscles. Members worked very hard at this 24 hour private club – but not with dumbbells.

Simeon faced the peep-hole and, as usual, knocked violently on the vandal-proof, raid-resistant metal door. He was recognised by an obese, malodorous scruff who appeared to be dressed in used clothing, suggesting a period thirty years before, in the depths of the depression. At this slightly stressful moment, he was received in silence by the pale, fat face with its piggy eyes. Pig Face was accustomed to customers who were too ashamed to exchange pleasantries. No membership card was asked for – none existed. Membership was strictly by introduction. Admission, thereafter by recognition, and, of course, the production of a $5 bill. En route along a dingy, dim-lit passageway to the locker room, the familiar musty, dank smell assailed the boy's nostrils. He always supposed it was a miasma of lust, body odour, dirt and damp towels. However, in contrast to the arctic blast of the North American winter in the car park, at least this miasma was nice and warm.

He began to relax. Hot-to-trot, eagerly, he stuffed his thick winter coat into the locker, together with a duffel bag, which contained a large thermos bottle of hot milky tea. Simeon was a Saturday night regular, well known to other regulars as the horny kid who relaxed between orgasms sipping his tea. He checked his watch. It was just after 8.00pm, just about to get busy on this bitterly cold evening, January 8th, 1966.

Like most 20-year-olds, with a sinking heart, Simeon Hogg had received his draft papers. Like most boys his age, he was likely to be sent to Vietnam. On this very day of January 8th, 8,000 US troops attacked a Viet Cong stronghold near Saigon in the biggest American offensive of that dreadful war. That same Saturday, the 'Iron Triangle' was pounded by B-52 heavy bombers and artillery.

Simeon was horrified. Why should he, an Englishman, chronically homesick for the green hills and dales of his native Derbyshire, risk life and limb for the Americans? Why should he be transported to the other side of the globe to harm people who had never harmed him? This is the same Simeon Hogg who would not, could not, defend himself against the merciless cruelty of Mundy Street Boys School just ten years before. The day before, Friday, January 7th, he had obeyed a command to attend the army medical. It was awful! It was a de-humanising routine in which groups of naked boys were barked at, ordered from station to station to be tested, touched, poked and prodded to assess their fitness to serve Uncle Sam. Simeon filled in a form of many questions including one which asked – 'Do you have any homosexual tendencies?' At that time, the United States Army had decided that if anyone answered 'yes' to that question, it did not want that person, even if he had made an untrue statement. The attitude was –

'If, to avoid military service, a man is prepared to make such a statement about himself, to falsely claim that he is a moral 'degenerate': we do not want that man. He is unfit to serve his country.'

Simeon Hogg answered the question about his sexuality, honestly. Accordingly, his initial classification was downgraded from A1 to 1Y. He was overjoyed.

At a gay bath house, bathers tend to fall into two groups: those men who enjoy orgiastic sex and those whose taste and habits are closer to the standard heterosexual model. For the most part, the latter avoid the 'orgy room' – a darkened carpeted chamber, usually full of writhing bodies softly moaning in ecstasy. Private 'rest' rooms are preferred by more selective bathers who are prepared to pay double to enjoy sex with one partner, in private. The 'heterosexual model' never quite suited the kid with the tea who was absolutely one hundred percent gay. He needed a coarse crowd baying for action. He wanted a variety of age and colour. He was excited by a pornographic public exhibition of lewd comments, obscene encouragement and stimulus from many naughty hands and many lascivious tongues. One man in one room was no good to Simeon. The whole experience had to be shocking and shameless.

There was one other public room in that disreputable house where nebulous acts of 'gross indecency' could be observed through a screen of pea-soup boiling fog. In the depths of a raw Detroit winter, Simeon came to life in hot swirls of delicious eroticism. Accordingly, the steam room was his first port of call, where dozens of masculine bodies delighted in the caresses of hot relaxing vapour.

As a courtesy to the others, he began the evening by taking a shower. Hanging up his towel on one of the pegs outside the steam room door, with pleasurable expectation, he noted some three dozen or more other hanging towels patiently waiting for the return of their lewd owners, already within.

He pushed open a metallic door and was assaulted by a hissing haze of severely limited visibility. It rolled over Simeon, thrilling him, warming him with the usual effect on his manhood: a Pavlovian response, a conditioned reflex to the expected delights which were hidden behind that enticing thick curtain of hot gurgling vapour. This room was well designed; a sort of small amphitheatre dimly lit by one, small, amber light. Several ascending deep steps doubled as seats to accommodate an assortment of hungry hunky men – real men. So unlike the sprinkling of highly-visible, effeminate types who inhabited the gay bars. These were the same bars which were off limits to any minor under the age of 21 and, for that matter, would always be off limits the English boy who had an aversion to alcohol.

On this evening, the assortment was typical. Chickens were always in short supply, but Simeon could discern two desirable youths, on the front row, near the door, seated close together in sulky silence. And silence was the general rule in this surreal room of no written rules, no heterosexual conventions, save an evolved custom and practice which forged its own mores. A little further round, a group of thirty-somethings, equally inactive, noted the newcomer who was still peering through the vapours for a good place to settle.

Simeon preferred action. He had little time for the time-consuming cat-and-mouse games which were often played out at his other haunt, the S&C Coffee Bar at

Uptown Detroit. Choosy chickens eyed up each other. They often feigned disinterest before finally deigning to engage in a halting, awkward conversation which, at that late point, might uncover too much sibilance, no common ground and severely disappoint. Similar games were played out in Detroit's Palmer Park: a dangerous late-night lottery of night prowling in which you might win good sex, or be entrapped by the vice squad, or be mugged, or be beaten up by homophobic thugs – or worse. At this early stage of his gay career, Simeon Hogg had learned that steam baths were the best way to meet other gay men.

He had also learned how to read the Vesuvio vapours. The slim, sexy chickens were going to play hard-to-get: time wasters. He had experienced that type before. The thirty-somethings were doing nothing. They were just boring. Less boring were the types who gravitated to the darker end of the circle, opposite the dim light above the door. Those types tended to be older gentlemen, fatter gentlemen, gentlemen of colour, gentlemen of exquisite talent and promiscuous, enthusiastic types who were prepared (nay keen) to perform in front of others. As a rule of thumb, those in the higher, hotter levels were more outrageous in their conduct than those on the lower levels.

And then he saw it… It was not easy to see, but, after a minute of adjustment to poor light, the eye begins to penetrate the fog and make sense of blurred outlines; fuzzy figures engaging in acts of lechery. He climbed up, carefully stepping over the immense Droopy to get a better view of the action. Droopy, so named after his drooping folds of obese flesh, was a skilful Saturday night regular. Simeon was always pleased to see this obscene blob of flowing, thirsty flesh. If no one else was there, the indefatigable Droopy of legendary suction would make the evening a great success. On a continent where fellatio is king, this particular fat man was indeed king of kings. In the course of that evening, Simeon drained every last drop of delicious tea from his thermos bottle, and, in the course of that same evening, Droopy, the vacuum cleaner of the Vesuvio, drained an equal quantity of fresh semen from a multitude of highly satisfied men – young, old, black and white.

Having carefully negotiated the mountain of Droopy's flesh, Simeon was in a position to decipher another puzzling arrangement up on the next level. It appeared to be a contortion of black and white flesh which, on closer inspection, resolved into two kneeling figures. The white end uttered deep groans and sighs of pleasure whilst the black part, a Negroid head, eagerly half buried in white buttocks – seemed very busy indeed. Those arousing moans appeared to be addressed to a pair of feet connected to a stocky man laying flat on his back. He too was exercising an eager muscular tongue. He was searching out exquisite secret places; special, delightful places which resided deep in the fundament of a squatting figure precariously balanced on his heels.

The sight and sounds of this carnal tableau, this confusing tangle of masculine humanity, were mind-blowing to the boy from Derbyshire. Several of that writhing mass became aware of a young, slim, white, desirable observer; an onlooker keen to avail himself of those thrilling, blissful ministrations. After an initial struggle in negotiating a slimy selection of enthusiastic tongues, beckoning fingers, squirming torsos and wriggling legs, Simeon became aware of powerful black hands effortlessly lifting him to a convenient place, a place ergonomically located over a small population of toying tongues.

"Yeah babe," breathed a deep, guttural, Negroid whisper into the white boy's ear. It was a thrilling, soft sound uttered from this mountain of shining black muscle who had just suspended him, offered him, offered his genitalia to an audience of eager thick lips and well lubricated fondling, skilful fingers.

"Yeah babe," again, groaned that big beautiful African head in an effort to be close, very close, caressingly close to the white head, draining every last particle of ecstatic expression, breath, sound which escaped the eyes, nose and mouth of his white property, his white windfall.

Time became irrelevant, but time passed. In the first climax, a powerful spurt anointed and elated several workers. White splashes on black faces. However, they persisted and conscientiously applied themselves to achieve and celebrate the second orgasm. As it happened, it was less spectacular. It was concealed and private inside the mouth of an adept drooler of exquisite technique; a master who just happened to be there at the right place, at the right time.

Two on the trot is enough. The evening was young. Simeon needed to recharge for later. The Giant African felt a pounding heart-beat through his big protective black fingers and noted the Englishman's deep breathing. Sympathetic to this need for rest, he pulled back his chicken, his possession from the suspended location of myriad erotic opportunities. He withdrew the public offering into the cosy protection of his own massive self. Simeon willingly, gratefully, sank into those firm yet comfortable cushions of black muscle. He was deliciously imprisoned by those powerful arms which held its precious white prey in readiness for further sport. With no further opportunity to excite the erogenous zones of young white flesh, no further opportunity to taste white sweat, white dribble or white anus; those lewd labourers melted away – except for one spectator.

The African had made his offering to his own kind. Droopy, the mass of white flesh had been excluded, but had noted the Great African's impressive black tumescence. At full mast, it was very excited during the previous lascivious performance. Like a creeping salivating dog, cautiously, Droopy approached the black 'lazy lob'. The fat man lifted his eyes, sad begging eyes, which met the big round eyes of the African. It was a hard unfeeling stare: an inscrutable giant considering the possible pleasures of a union with a pile of blubber. Now, inches from its objective, a rude tongue stuck out.

"Let him. He's good." whispered Simeon.

Encouragement of widening black legs was, for this fat man, a green light. Simeon was gratified to witness that great black phallus disappear into an experienced throat. He cuddled further into those magnificent firm pectorals, licking, tasting, vicariously taking aural pleasures from deep Negroid purrs and the soft moans of a magnificent black giant in a state of ecstasy. Droopy took his time. But with Droopy, there never was much time at all. He was good. He was the best.

Like an anaconda constricting its prey, great arms tightened their grip around the boy's body which lifted in answer to a spasm. A paroxysm of pleasure had arched the giant's back as he struggled to get more manhood into that fat face, planting his gushing seed deep into that fat throat now grunting to take breath. For Simeon, familiar Droopy grunts were a powerful aphrodisiac.

The Giant African relaxed as he generously allowed his chicken to slide down between his great legs as a gift of gratitude to a servicer whose sad eyes, still begging with open mouthed glistening cavity, revealed that not all had been swallowed. Simeon, although not fully re-charged, notwithstanding, was excited by this erotic device which had a forceful effect. He yielded to the obesity's lewd invitation to enter into a racial mix of further delectation. At the conclusion, the big man pulled back his boy, deep into those massive comfortable arms. Once again, he detected and savoured the post orgasmic chicken heart-beat. Kissing his ear, in a husky, base whisper –

"Yeah, babe. Good? Yeah. Real good."

Having drained man and chicken, Droopy withdrew. He seemed to slide away, to hide away his shameful blubber, loosing focus, dissolving into a warm opaque mist.

This was the quiet time. This was the time of contentment. It was a time when, briefly, Simeon, after good sex, in this alien land, was happy. The Giant African was also, briefly, happy. But only briefly. This was understood. Man and boy were together in this stream room, but they were separated by more than colour, more than race. The big man was nearly 40. It was unacceptable, indeed suspect for a 20-year-old to be socially involved with a man twice his age – even if they were the same colour. To widen the gap, to exacerbate matters, Simeon looked even younger by several years. Like many men at Vesuvio, the big man was married with children. If he gave Simeon a name, it would not be, could not be his own. He could not give out a phone number or an address. Any planned meeting would have to be at the baths or in a public place on neutral ground: difficult, very difficult.

In this brief interlude, boy and man went to sleep. Simeon woke to the slightly sad fact that he was now free, free to escape from those big powerful arms.

CHAPTER 3

Ugly Old Trolls

The Vesuvio rest-area consisted of a motley collection of old, musty sofas and mangy arm-chairs, all of which had seen better days long ago. Simeon picked one of the better ones which had been dignified by a clean, dry towel. Sinking into its creaky, soft, poor support; he unscrewed the cup, poured steaming hot tea from the thermos bottle and cuddled up to the warmth and taste of those first few delicious sips.

Relaxed in an idle reverie, he noticed big bricks forming high walls of a dirty grey. Breeze blocks encompassed this large ugly space in this functional building, possibly a one time factory or warehouse. On his left, he heard falling waters of showers and the distant hiss of steam which angrily increased in volume each time the cheap steam-room door opened with thin metallic clinks. Apart from these signs of life, there was a prevailing hush. Despite the nearby mass of humanity, it was peaceful. Among the bathers in the immediate rest area there were a few murmurs but, on the whole, precious little conversation occurred between the pale heads perched on their soft, uninteresting, under-exercised pale bodies.

A repulsive, stooped skeletal man, covered with age-spots and discolorations, was making a slow, silent progress along a corridor of small private rooms. A familiar character, this was 'Old Father Wrinkles' said to be a –

"Catholic Priest! Really! He is. All of 80. Pays well. Watch the finger. Sometimes he'll coil a $20 bill. Just follow him."

The older, wiser Simeon, looking back, deeply regretted that he never made any attempt to converse with the old Priest, if a Priest he really was. He also regretted not engaging Droopy in conversation. At that moment he too, with short heavy steps, was waddling through the rest area holding a towel in front of his nether regions in a futile attempt to maintain modesty and dignity. The standard Vesuvio towel was far too small to circumnavigate the massive circumference of such blubber. One nasty chicken once remarked to another nasty chicken –

"Why bother? You can see past the towel. What's the point? You can't actually see anything! Whatever he might have, if anything at all, is all hidden under that hideous hanging apron of flesh. That troll is decent even when naked!"

Why did Simeon never speak to these poor men with their sad faces, sad lives? Instinctively, he felt that Droopy and Wrinkles would be more interesting than most of the chickens who were frequently boring. Yet he ignored them. He continued to sip tea, continued to watch them slowly struggle up a crude, wooden stairway, ascending to a gantry which gave on to more private rooms and to the large orgy room. He knew the answer. He avoided social contact because, in the eyes of younger white bathers, social and sexual contact with 'ugly old trolls' and 'ubangis' was, quite simply, unacceptable. A pointless, cruel convention; yet, for many years, Simeon was held in the grip of that convention. Under cover of thick fog in the steam-room and pitch black in the orgy-room, he joyfully transgressed all of these unwritten rules. He gave himself freely to the old, the fat and especially to those with a pigment of ebony which made them completely invisible in the black corners of those very black rooms.

A second visit to the dimly lit steam-room saw more steam and, apparently, fewer people. Visibility was further restricted by the sudden contrast between the brightly lit rest area and the dim amber glow which struggled to penetrate the pea soup of that ever-wet, hot cavern. When Simeon's eyes adjusted, he was able to climb the big steps, to navigate and placed himself in a promising position, next to a large black figure he gladly recognised as the Great African. Almost at the same time, another naked body placed itself on his right – clearly someone had followed him.

 A slight turn to the right revealed the profile of a light skinned young Negro who, after a few seconds, turned a beautiful full face. It was an appraisal, a close-up to confirm his selection for the evening. Here was a boy of stunning good looks fixing Simeon with his considerable power. Here was a chicken-hawk who was accustomed to hunting the chickens of Detroit City – a boy who was accustomed to getting exactly what he wanted – and he wanted Simeon. In those few magical moments, Derbyshire eyes scrutinised Detroit eyes. Both pairs were full of wonder, full of desire. Under pressure of enchantment, each countenance melted, slightly, very slightly into a half smile.

 Simeon was drawn into an alluring face. He supposed that this strapping lad with an Adonis body was about his own age. It was a face of softened Negroid features: not a wide nose: lips not thick, yet temptingly full: coal-black hair, not exactly frizzy, yet, with short tight curls which suggested African ancestry. And big round eyes, yes, beautiful brown eyes, firm of purpose, holding, bayoneting their prey.

 This Englishman was more than ready to surrender to such delectable, unspoken authority when, at that moment, a mighty black hand, descended and firmly claimed his left thigh. The Great African had been observing. He had been reading the script and was determined to change the outcome. Warm fingers of the black man's other hand came over and forced Simeon to look left into a *real* African face: bigger, less sensitive with black eyes. A broad nose complemented beefy, bulky lips, slightly forced apart by the tip of a slowly moving succulent tongue. As planned, such a sight, such a lascivious movement had its immediate effect between widening white thighs. In a trice, the mountain of African muscles swung round to the lower level and a glistening, kneeling slave was about to send Simeon into seventh heaven.

 It was seconds into this delicious succulence when the boy's miasma of pleasure was rudely interrupted by a sharp knock on his right leg. The Great African, conscientiously on course, appeared to be unaware. Simeon was somewhat alarmed and gave his desirable neighbour to the right a quick look. The third party in this minor drama returned a look of horror. And, yes, anger. The light skinned Negro was furious to see a fellow chicken so willingly yielding to such obscene ministrations from the older man.

Bigotry, prejudice and discrimination within the homosexual community had always been a sore disappointment to Simeon Hogg. It made no sense. Here was a minority community, in hiding, suffering disapproval, taking insults, under siege and ever oppressed by a homophobic majority. And yet the very members of that persecuted group formed subgroups who were prepared to accept an unreasonable, unwritten code of conduct. Simeon had learned these rules in the Uptown S&C Coffee Bar for those under 21, too young for the gay bars. There was a rule about kissing – 'chicken shall kiss chicken only'. Permitting the touch of a man over 30 was viewed with disapproval. Sex with a man over 40 was inviting social death. Tolerating the touch of a Negro was seen as bestiality, just plain disgusting.

So what was happening here? He had heard that, within the black population, light skinned Negroes enjoyed a higher social status to those who were jet black. In this case, it was simply unacceptable for Simeon to be disciplined by that sharp blow to his leg on the grounds that a light skinned younger Negro objected to his choice of a coal black older Negro. After all, Vesuvio custom and practice dictated that all were equal in the two orgy areas and a simple threesome should have resolved the problem.

These cogitations were rudely broken by a second, more violent, indeed painful dig into the white boy's side. The Great African, alerted, stopped and took in the situation with a stern glare at his rival. That rival, with a scowl which could kill, held his ground, gripped the arm of his white prey –

"Get the fuck out... NOW!"

At this, the muscle-bound, ebony giant, stood up to a height which was several inches above six foot and, with a half-smile, half sneer, confidently faced down the angry young man below who bravely answered the silent threat.

"Yeah? Anytime, nigger. *Anytime.*"

Storming out in fury, he kicked open the tin door and banged it close with a second mighty kick. It caused a reverberation reminiscent of theatrical, thunderous, sheet-iron sound effects. Sensing trouble, several bathers took flight. They left the steam-room and some left the baths.

Simeon was upset, indeed, distressed. His partner was unruffled by the racial insult, unconcerned by the threat of violence and unmoved by the noisy turbulence. Once again, with his firm black body, he created a delectable prison and enveloped his white property savouring a triumph, expressed in a soothing deep purr –

"Yeah babe, no sweat. Cool. 's goona be OK. Yeah."

CHAPTER 4

Butch as a Brick

Simeon was unsettled. An excellent evening had been spoilt by an ugly incident. Sinking deeper into the sofa, contemplating the bottom of his, now empty, second cup of tea – he felt miserable. His protection, the Great African had been swallowed up into the first floor orgy room and the angry young man... well, *he* had not been seen since that dramatic exit.

Not seen, but thought about. Simeon could not stop thinking about him. Mixed feelings. There was fear. He had been scared by a demonstration of bravery, indeed, an example of recklessness. Also, he was fearful for his own safety. He might well be in Canada, but the reality was Detroit. Detroit was the most dangerous city in the United States. Detroit averaged three murders a day. The vast majority of Vesuvio bathers were Detroiters.

It was quite clear; the angry young man was not well acquainted with disappointment and would brook no rejection. Perhaps Simeon was safe in the baths... but outside? Where was this youth? Outside? Waiting for him? Yet again, he attempted to replay, to analyse this appalling scene. The tough-looking, tough-sounding hood had been humiliated. True, a humiliation of his own making, notwithstanding, the hoodlum had been enraged and may well be intent on revenge.

Hoodlum, yes, but what a *desirable* hoodlum! Back in Derbyshire, Simeon would have been described as a 'bum bandit'. That part of the male anatomy always drew his eyes, always intrigued, always fascinated. He could not delete that recent image, the sensual sight of that beautifully rounded bum as it stomped out of the steam-room in high dudgeon. It had retained something of that firm, upward tilt, so typical of adolescent buttocks, especially protruding Negro buttocks. 'Arse to die for' he whispered to himself. With a jolt, he realised it could end up being the case.

The scene was replayed again, this time concentrating on that ferocious command, that impressive voice. Not as deep as the Great African, but deeper than expected, sonorous and so very macho, so very butch – butch as a brick. At the S&C, 'butch as a brick', a reference to manly qualities, was the highest compliment which could be paid to a gay youth.

It was just after eleven. Vesuvio was still busy and getting busier by an influx from the Detroit gay bars. Horny guys who had failed to score had come to this place where it was difficult to miss. There were a few uninteresting people resting, a few passers-by, thirty-somethings and even more forty-somethings. The odd chicken drifted by including the two choosy chickens he had first seen in the steam-room.

Suddenly he was there! That, angry, magnificent macho youth of light tan. He was still in the building. Confidently, he strode through the rest area, his towel worn in a small, sexy fold just covering the nether regions, barely covering his pouting, muscular bottom. For an instant, he glared at Simeon, quickened his pace and athletically leaped up the stairs to explore the upper level. Simeon was seized by an increased heart-beat! Fear? Perhaps, but fear mingled with the pleasurable sensation of tingle, a delightful quiver of expectation.

Determined to find some sort of resolution, he quickly returned his flask to the locker and, with energy, mounted those steps, two at a time, up to the first floor. Determined to find a resolution? Life can deal us moments when it is difficult to be honest with ourselves. Simeon told himself that he was being brave, facing his danger. Was he? This erstwhile fearful situation had now sweetened into a delicious danger. Simeon had become the prey who wanted to be found, wanted to be consumed in the way he most enjoyed being consumed.

Around a maze of corridors housing small private rooms, the prey prowled like a hunter. Most doors were closed, but he checked the interior of all open doors, rejected several invitations, spoken invitations and the usual silent invitations given in body language. Where did he go? The big orgy-room? Simeon entered the open doorway but remained in the entrance area. Here there was faint light which preceded the promiscuous blackness beyond. This was the depraved, dissolute, darkness he knew so well. It called him, tempted him and teased him with familiar soft sounds of a multitude in ecstasy. On this occasion, he was in no mood to be drawn into the delightful ministrations of the many. He was focused on just one.

And, from behind, just one suddenly appeared. It was a violent attack. He was grabbed, gripped, turned and shaken by a passionate hoodlum who was both asserting his authority and inflicting punishment. In half light, Simeon looked up into that beautiful face of which he had been seeking.

"Are you so cheap? Cheap slut! Givin' it a nigger! Well? Well?"

So shaken, literally shaken, and unprepared; the victim was unable to respond to this fierce reprimand beyond a distressed dumbness and a stand-off of eyes meeting eyes. Stormy eyes met bemused eyes. He was shaken again like a rag doll suffering abuse from a frustrated, enraged child. After another moment of stillness there was indecision. Stormy eyes softened, gave up, seemed to be defeated by some need, some primitive urge. Again Simeon was gripped hard around his arms but, this time, he was forced up to the lips of his assailant.

He was not a rag doll! He objected to be treated as such. Resenting the insulting language, indignant at such unreasonable conduct, he resisted this coerced kiss and began to struggle... But, perhaps, he did not struggle *too* hard.

After a sweet and tender embrace, a special moment he would remember all of his life, the two former combatants looked at each other. They just looked. And the hoodlum looked down at the protrusion, the recent disturbance within Simeon's towel. For the first time, those incensed eyes twinkled; that frosty expression warmed to a half smile.

"So! You *do* like me!"

With a caressing hand, he released that captive tumescence and, within seconds, gently fondled it to an explosion of milky liquid.

"Ooo yeah! You like me a whole lot."

After another, longer embrace, the assertive boy guided his conquest a little way further into the gloomy entrance area which still had benefit of faint light. A pile of large cushions at the edge of a carpeted wall were adjusted for the convenience and comfort of two young bodies. They gladly sank, reclined and proceeded to many mutual pleasures. During these ecstatic minutes, in that public 'free for all', several wandering, groping hands were knocked away by Simeon's new Master. Contrary to orgy-room etiquette, he was not willing to share. But the Master was willing to teach. Silently he guided his pupil to do what had to be done, to bring matters to a satisfactory, if wet, sticky conclusion.

Here and now was the best time with this young man. Here and now was the best time with this hooligan who fascinated, the hooligan now spent, the hooligan now so gentle, so loving. This was the quiet time of mutual relaxation, mutual silence, mutual closeness and mutual stillness. As with the Great African, this was submission sweetly endured. Simeon lay on his side. He faced into blackness, was warmed by the touch, the full length of that young negroid body. He was confined by muscular, lusty arms and thrilled by the thought of no possible escape.

"You're *my* boy now, Booby." exhaled the gaoler in breathy whisper. "Better get used to it."

Booby! His new name? It was a re-Christening intended as a term of affection and accepted as such. Years later Simeon discovered that 'booby' was a reference to a stupid person, a dunce, a dolt. But isn't that part of the definition of 'love'? Isn't love a sort of madness? Isn't it a form of insanity in which the victim is unable to think straight or make rational judgements?

"Whatever 'in love' means," famously spoke Prince Charles in the early stages of a doomed relationship.

This relationship too – was doomed. Perhaps deep down somewhere in the depths of Simeon's psyche, that part which was still objective, still functioning properly; perhaps in that small fragment of grey matter, Simeon knew that he was in the grip of enchantment. But, he did not want to face an unpalatable truth. And why should he?

The truth was grim. This homosexual English boy, always a disappointment to his parents, had never received the same measure of affection or respect apparently allotted to other sons. Unloved and disliked at home, at school, just six years before, it was worse, much worse. In the rough coal-mining town of Heanor he was imprisoned inside a culture of cruelty which drove him to the edge of self-destruction. Mundy Street Boys School was a remnant of Dickensian evil. To a sensitive child it was an unfeeling, ultra-macho hell. At such a school, a boy who would not, could not assert himself with bare knuckles in the Mundy Street playground – that boy was a constant target. He was seen as fair game by some pupils. The Hogg family and working-class mores took the view that bullying was a part of growing up. They were not prepared to interfere with a 'natural process'. No one was there to help that miserable child. On the contrary, a sadistic schoolmaster actually encouraged some of the more savage boys to smell blood, to go in for the kill. It did get physical, but most of the abuse was inflicted in a form of psychological torture which left its mark on Simeon Hogg for the rest of his life.

Snuggling up to that stranger in that dark orgy-room, Simeon wore that invisible mark. Accordingly, damaged, love starved, he was more than ready for this unconditional surrender, this appropriation of ownership, this demand for loyalty and affection. To lay claim; a nameless stranger of so few words had risked coming to blows with a giant of a man. This hunky, gorgeous stranger, so confident, so decisive, so powerful had commandeered not only his body – but had also won his heart.

It was not the venue Simeon had hoped for. In the movies, it was different. In *Kismet*, it was different. The Caliph and his lover were 'strangers in paradise' and paradise was a beautiful garden. This was no garden; this was a seedy homosexual bath house. Even so, Simeon's heart was singing. Simeon was in love.

CHAPTER 5

Menace and Magic

It was just after midnight. Two youths were sitting facing each other. White Tower was a small cheap hamburger joint somewhere in Downtown Detroit. Hard, bright, fluorescent lighting bounced around tacky, shiny, stainless steel surfaces. Finally it lit the face of the English youth, the only white, extra bright face in that soulless joint. After Vesuvio's half shadows, kind amber glows; such cruel illumination did little to improve a mid-winter pale face already ravaged by an evening of over-indulgence and wanton excess.

Biting into his small 12 cent hamburger, tomato ketchup on the corners of his mouth, Simeon was hanging on to every word uttered by his beautiful new friend, the friend of few words who had just disclosed his name.

"Ahmed!"

"Yeah. Ahmed."

"Ahmed? Well... where is that from? I mean, what nationality?"

"It's American, like me. So what's the problem?" asserted that deep, forceful voice, now holding a hint of menace.

"No problem... sorry. It's just... different. I wondered..."

"It's Egyptian. My folks are from Aswan, but I am one hundred percent American. Don't ever forget that, Booby."

So now he knew. The racism was explained. The light skinned Negro was not a Negro at all. He was an Arab. However, the African connection was also explained. Ahmed was a product of the 'dark continent'. His ancestry stemmed from a city very near to the Sudanese border.

"Anyway, what's that accent? Some place East? Boston?"

"England."

"Huh? New England?"

"Old England."

"Booby's an Englishman! Well, I'll be... Like London?"

"Try Nottingham. Nobody's ever heard of Derby, but you've probably heard of Robin Hood."

There was another silence. Very slightly, the two bodies shifted, moved closer together. Knees touched. Faces came very close, too close. Yet again, they looked into each others eyes, searching, desiring, wanting, lusting... loving. Apprehensively, Simeon noticed that their mutual admiration had been spotted by three young Negroes on the opposite counter. Alerted by this sudden change of mood, the Arab tore his eyes away and fixed these teenagers with a belligerent glare. His next move filled Simeon with horror. Ahmed stood up. John Wayne-like, he swaggered over and glowered over the three youths whose disrespectful grin had frozen into alarm and fear.

"You guys want trouble?"

Just four small words, a question softly spoken with confidence. An intimidating question which infused their victims with dread. A question which was answered with a stony silence and, in that silence, the three quietly walked out of the hamburger joint, eyes downcast, with as much face as it was possible to save. This exit left three vacant spaces, sad detritus of half eaten food, paper plates and unfinished milk-shakes. An old Negro who had seen more than his share of 'trouble', slowly moved to the counter with a damp rag to clear and wipe the surfaces. He shook his head, avoided eye contact and shuffled back into the kitchen area.

This perilous episode forced Simeon to the realisation that he knew absolutely nothing about Ahmed. Questions about his home life, his family, his job were side-stepped – 'I get by. I do OK. I make out. I take what I want and I take care of myself and I'll take real good care of you, Booby.' – were typical replies.

Simeon had mixed feelings about being drawn into the role of a gangster's moll. To be 'taken care of' could also mean a spell in hospital recovering from a severe beating. His mind went back to London during the previous summer. Mingling with 'rough trade', he heard talk about a gay criminal, 'a swinger' with an appalling reputation for seediness, shotguns and torture. Ronnie Kray also took 'what he wanted'. He selected boys with 'long lashes with a melting look around the eyes'. They were plied with drink, shown off at the Society Club in Jermyn Street and sometimes taken to Kray's luxury flat in Walthamstow where show business celebrity friends were entertained.

Simeon was rather shocked by rough-and-ready Cockney lads boasting of their connections, their sexual experience with the mobster underworld and certain high profile figures of the Establishment. He was especially revolted by one extremely desirable thug who claimed to have made Lord Boothby –

"... spunk three times! Yeah, straight up. No bovver. Got me tongue in 'is arse 'ole. Moooved it slow... yeah. Nice an steady. Should 'ave 'eard the old geezer, fair squealed with pleasure 'e did. Easy money."

"You rimmed a fat old man!!"

"Leave it out! When did you larrst pocket a tenner for a few minutes work?"

"What were we talking about?" said Ahmed, resuming his seat.

"Robin Hood," said Simeon in some abstraction. "I'm beginning to think that *you* are a hood. Are you?"

"Hey! Listen up, Booby. This is Detroit, not Notting-*ham*. I don't take shit like that. And another thing, if I ever see that big ugly mother-fucker at Vesuvio get his black paws on you again..."

"Not very mature, are you."

This shook Ahmed. He was hurt. He gazed into Simeon's slightly moist eyes and reflected on that comment. A brief reflection which ended with a smile and, surprisingly, a gentle apology.

"OK, Booby. I can't blame that guy. It's just that... you've knocked me over. You're so very special."

"So... I have to be completely faithful to you? No sex with anyone else? For me, especially, for me, that is not going to be easy! I really don't think that I can make that kind of promise."

"My boys don't have to make that promise."

"Well, what exactly do you mean?"

"Shit! I know we can't be like straight kids. In our world there's no woman to put the brakes on. No dame to say no. And it's a horny world out there, Booby. I guess... we have to make our own rules."

"So, tell me about the rules."

"OK. I suppose... Well, I think... I need to be there when you get your rocks off. I need to hold you, to see you, to hear you when it happens. Does that make any sense?"

Simeon made an immediate comparison with the needs, the sexual behaviour of the Great African just hours before. He noted the plural in Ahmed's reference to 'my boys'. Was he to become the latest addition to this Arab's harem? Also, in this tender moment, with careful diplomacy, he remonstrated about Ahmed's inappropriate language, his rabid racism. Using comparisons with the aims of the Civil Rights Movement and the endemic homophobia which had always blighted gay lives, Simeon tried to reach Ahmed's conscience, tried to get him to see how his open bigotry was perpetuating further social injustice.

In this first significant conversation, Simeon discovered another side to this fiery Arab, Ahmed the hoodlum, Ahmed the stud. It became clear that he was reasonably articulate, intelligent and had made good use of a sound education offered by one of the better Detroit High Schools.

"You've got it wrong. Don't be too quick to bad mouth. In your nice white world in nice little England, how can you know what it's like to be me? Listen, kid, I've had to survive in this rat-infested jungle of crime, beatings, shit round every corner. I've had to grow up next door to ubangies, white trash and God knows what uncivilised scum that piss on you – and I do mean piss-on-you. No friendly 'bobbies on bicycles' for us to turn to. Oh no. Hard boiled cops for us. Cops not interested, cops on the take, cops who can hurt you real bad if you get in their way. You got a lot to learn, Booby. It may interest you to know that I am not a racist and I can prove it." He stood up, handed the old Negro a $10 bill with a brief comment. "Here, old timer. That should cover us and those jackasses who didn't pay. Stick close, Booby. We're going for a walk in the most dangerous part of the most dangerous city in the world."

It was late. The streets were almost deserted, but for a few beaten-up cabs crawling around for customers. They walked through Cadillac Square, into Woodward Avenue and made a left into Grand River Avenue. Simeon admired that most potent of American symbols, the skyscraper, of which there were several in the downtown area. One of the oldest intrigued him the most: the Book Building loomed up ahead. Ahmed noted his interest.

"I prefer the Guardian Building. Some sort of Aztec design. Neat." Another left turn took them into a narrow street. He stopped. Simeon stopped. They looked at each other – enjoyed the look when, suddenly, roughly, Ahmed pushed him into a recess, up against a dilapidated doorway and, with arms outstretched leaning on the door, he created a small area of confinement. Simeon was in a trap. It might have been a mugging. They looked at each other. Easy, sweet and slow, the hard strong Arab breathed out a few words.

"You think... I'll lock you in a cage like a little bird, all for myself, a Booby bird?" He smiled, leaned closer and kissed his captive, oh so very gently. "And, if I opened the cage door... would Booby fly away? Would you?"

Simeon was frozen mute by the greatest sexual power he had ever encountered. It was a thrilling combination of menace and magic. He could not run, had no desire to run. Seizing the initiative, with supreme poise and self-assurance, Ahmed continued to weave his enchantment.

"I don't think so. Know why? Because I can get inside you. I can eat you up. I can drain you... and, yes Booby, you'll beg me for it, you'll love me for it. Does my boy love me? Does he?"

As if with a broken spirit, Simeon heard himself whisper an affirmative as Ahmed dropped his arms, descended to a squat, fumbled and concluded his magic spell with physical expression, physical expertise ending in a long, slow, paroxysm of acute pleasure which the English prisoner would remember all his life. He was breathing heavy when that skilled worker returned. Ahmed stood up to his full height and received an enthusiastic embrace of total surrender, unconditional surrender. For this captive it was like the conclusion of some sort of bizarre initiation ceremony in which he had been softened up for entry into an exotic harem. Simeon snuggled his head into Ahmed's chest, pulled down the zip of his bomber jacket, trying to get closer, trying to get inside, trying to get the scent of that butch, solid, Arab body, trying to get warm on that silent, deserted, freezing Detroit street with steam rising from manhole covers.

In these bewitching moments both parties whispered words of love, words of commitment, words which seemed to define future goals with reckless confidence – the optimism of youth – so sure – no doubts.

"Too late now, Booby. I've got you. I'm taking you home. Don't worry; I'll talk to your folks. You'll never look back."

As the embrace continued, Simeon's naughty hands wandered, explored and caressed the beautiful roundness, the tantalising rear he had so admired in the Vesuvio steam. It was a firm, perfect bottom: but now well protected, well-guarded by strong denim. Ahmed responded with a sardonic twinkle, laying down one of his laws.

"Make the best of that, Booby! In case you have any ideas, that is as close as you'll ever get. Nobody goes in there. Nobody goes where the sun never shines. Nobody. But somebody has to deal with this." He took Simeon's hand and moved it to an exciting hardness of impressive proportions. In mute submission, the servant eagerly descended for service below, but, to his surprise was pulled back up to face level.

"Oh no! That's not for your pretty mouth. I need a pro."

Another surprise, Ahmed opened the door behind them and entered. He explained that it was the back entrance to a squalid old bar, a haunt of the low life. A door on the right of a dimly lit passage opened into an equally dark and dingy men's lavatory.

"Now I'm gonna prove how much of a racist I am."

There was an empty urinal, three cubicles, wide open, no doors. In the last one, a slumped stocky Negro appeared to be asleep surrounded by several empty bottles.

"He's an old friend. He's a *nice* coloured guy. Take a good look, Booby," he whispered, "best blow job in the city. Pop is always thirsty." After a gentle touch, the man slowly opened his big round eyes into a big beaming smile. He was clearly delighted to see two young customers. In a groggy, alcoholic, drawl –

"Ahmed! Hey, buddy, it's been too long. How ya doin', Stud?" Silently, without response, no pleasantries, no niceties, the stud unzipped and released his rampant prisoner, no stranger to this long practised master of his art. "Yeah! Hi Hector! You look like you ready to play. You need action."

As 'Hector' disappeared into the warm wet darkness of deepest Africa, Ahmed trembled, rolled his beautiful eyes and pulled his new lover up close.

"Stay with me, Booby," he murmured softly. It was almost pleading, a small, shaky, broken voice trailing off with – "Help me, touch me, tease me... do it... do it..."

CHAPTER 6

The Sultan's Palace

Simeon opened his eyes... and promptly closed them. It was the low level dazzling winter sunshine which spot-lit his face, blinded him. It poured into that large plush bedroom, tastefully finished in conservative dark browns, old golds and any number of similar autumnal tints. The night before he considered it all rather drab, but, now, adjusting to the brilliant illumination after many hours of deep dark sleep, even Simeon had to admire the quality of lavish drapes, swags, and the art of extravagant festoons which framed large windows.

The English boy lay very still in his half of that massive bed, the Imperial sized bed of Ahmed the Arab, Ahmed the lover, Ahmed the sleeper. Ahmed was very proud of his bed. Ten hours before, on entry into this expensive riot of Gothic fantasy –

"What you think, Booby? Hey, bet you never seen such elegance – huh?"

"Well... it... it looks good stuff, pricey. It's interesting."

"Interesting! Is that all you can say? Interesting! A $1000 bed, best bed in Detroit, the acme of culture – and all you say is – *'interesting'!*"

Simeon had never seen such an ugly bed. The ornate headboard, footboard and four corner posts, all dark brown, evoked a mediaeval monstrosity of pointed arches, rib vaulting and flying buttresses which made Ahmed's bed hideous in the extreme. Assorted carved gargoyles gave it an essence of evil, more suited for the boudoir of Dracula.

Indeed, at the inception of this whirlwind romance, the bed was an ill omen. This extraordinary bed was deeply significant. In many ways it represented a profound gulf between the two lovers. They knew it, but, did not dare to speak of it because, to give voice to such a thought would make it real, would make it dangerous. Having found each other, being so excited by each other and besotted by each other; at this early stage they were both determined to make the relationship work.

There was no independent observer to assess the situation, no impartial counsellor to advise these young men. They were alone. They were blundering through a minefield of inexperience and ignorance with scant support from the social skills of diplomacy which have usually been acquired by older people. Half a century on, the older Ahmed and the older Simeon could have counselled their younger selves if, indeed, such counsel would have been heeded.

Simeon's taste was still rooted in the modern, 'contemporary' era of 1959. What could be more modern than 1959 with its simplicity of design, clean straight lines and bold bright colours? Simeon's dream home, his dream bed would have been designed by Frank Lloyd Wright and look more like something to be found in a spaceship, a vision of the future. At a deeper level, Simeon was deeply English. He was ever pining for his homeland, for the Derbyshire Dales, for quaint little villages, for his Ordnance Survey map, bicycle and rucksack. In stark contrast, Ahmed was the quintessential loud, brash American of popular imagination. He rejoiced in a United States which had a 'Manifest Destiny' to rule the world. He considered the world should be grateful to be so ruled. Ahmed was confident and bombastic. His natural element was the bustling American city with its endless 24 hour energy of neon lights, gay bars, gay clubs and the usual homosexual hunting grounds of parks and baths. He would never be happy sitting in an English tea shop, chatting to old ladies, admiring a distant 'green and pleasant' vista. Oddly enough, that Gothic bed became the symbol of these irreconcilable positions.

And, in that giant bed, listening to the regular breathing of his lover, Simeon was now awake and concerned. He was wondering how a boy (yes, in many ways Ahmed was a boy, just as immature as Simeon) could afford to live in such a luxurious city centre apartment. The night before, Ahmed had proudly displayed his personal wealth. In the Vesuvio car park, Simeon's slightly beaten up second-hand 1960 Ford Falcon looked small and sad next to Ahmed's gleaming symbol of power and prosperity. It was the dream of American youth. He owned a 1965 Ford Thunderbird. He commanded a noble beast, an elegant thoroughbred as fine as a steel blade leaving the English boy open-mouthed in awe – a sight which greatly pleased the boastful Arab.

"Yeah! Get a load o' that! Booby's gonna look sooo good in Ahmed's T-Bird. Get in."

"What about my car!"

"No sweat. I'll have it picked up later." Looking puzzled and worried, Simeon stood his ground, a nervous hesitation which irritated his new lover. "Hey listen up, buddy, we're one now with one car – and *this* is the car. I already told ya, you'll get ya clunker back. I mean what I say, and I say what I mean. Understand? So be a good little Booby, loosen up – and get in."

After the brief encounter with Pop, it was already past 1.00am. Simeon, who hated late nights, was very tired after so many erotic exertions. He pleaded for bed and sleep. Accordingly, the magnificent automobile silently floated a few blocks up Woodward Avenue, made a right and darted down into a car park under a tall building of luxury apartments overlooking Palmer Park. Recognising the approaching T-Bird, a smiling, sexy attendant of Middle Eastern appearance ran up to park the car.

"Good morning, Mr Hamah."

"Hi, Calvin. Do something for me." He turned to Simeon. "Keys." The Falcon's keys were passed to the attendant with a $20 bill. "When Chuck relieves you, take a cab to Vesuvio in Windsor. There's a beaten-up red Falcon parked outside. Bring it back here."

"OK, Mr Hamah."

"Keep the change."

"Thank *you*, Sir!"

All very impressive. Even more impressive when they stepped inside a sumptuous reception area panelled in dark mahogany. Another enthusiastic greeting: this time from a uniformed commissionaire who seemed to be guarding four elevators, two each side of an imposing desk of polished granite which seemed to extrude out of a granite floor into pleasing proportions.

"Good morning, Mr Hamah."

"Hello, Ralph."

The far left hand car was an express to the 20th floor and above. Once inside, Simeon expected his rich friend to select 'Penthouse'. However, he touched number 22, eight floors below the top. Perhaps it was not the best accommodation which could be offered by Palmer Heights, but, to the boy who had been raised in a humble miner's cottage (Bog Hole terrace in Horsley Woodhouse) the home of Ahmed Hamah was like entering the palace of a Sultan.

An enormous living room sided by floor-to-ceiling patio windows looked out westward over the blanket darkness of Palmer Park and southwards to the twinkling distant skyscrapers of Downtown Detroit. Woodward Avenue was like a straight line drawn by a giant with a seven mile ruler, the right half glowing with hundreds of bright red rear lights and the left half glowing white from cars approaching. It was beauty in an alien land where this Englishman had seen very little beauty. So far above the frantic noise and stress of American streets, in that quiet palace in the sky, he enjoyed a moment of peace, perhaps a moment of happiness.

Two inches taller, with a larger, more powerful frame, Ahmed came up behind him. Firmly, but tenderly, he embraced his new acquisition. He nuzzled the right ear, appreciating the same far away illuminations which painted the busy city below. A cold Simeon thrilled to the affectionate warmth of his lover's body. Small, sweet whispers into that right ear interspersed gentle kisses –

"Nice? Booby like his new home? Booby not fly away?"

The mood was set. Ahmed had brought other pretty boys up to his luxury home with similar high hopes. But this was a very high hope indeed and he was excited, optimistic for this new hope. Everything seemed so right, so propitious. He had seen into Booby's eyes, looked into his soul, noted his submissive nature and sensed his hunger for love. Ahmed was confident. With sheer force of personality, his beautiful body, his stunning good looks, his recently acquired wealth, a track record of so much success, and, yes, his lust, his city-wide reputation as a powerful tough-guy coupled with his refined professionalism in dispensing exquisite sexual pleasure – with all these attributes this relationship *must* succeed.

During that first Saturday night / Sunday morning in that great bed, Simeon had sampled those legendary exquisite techniques of Ahmed the Master of his Art. And 'Master' was the appropriate word. On one occasion, during the dead of night, the guest was thoughtlessly and rudely shaken to half consciousness out of a deep sleep to satisfy the host's urgent need for an orgasm. Simeon was appalled! The experience left him angry. Only on very few occasions in his life had he ever shared his bed – and it was never a success. Sleep, deep, sound, restful sleep was sacred, was so important to good health. He took the view that a good night's sleep was essential for the quality of the next day. For this sleeper, that quality was compromised even if the other guy moved, let alone touched him. Rumpty-tumpty? Certainly, but afterwards it was a case of 'This is my bed. You sleep in your bed.' However, hated and reviled for its appearance, Ahmed's bed did have one big advantage:

it was big. It was wide enough for two, indeed, wide enough for several and, apart from that one rude interruption, Simeon slept peacefully in splendid isolation.

And the sun still poured through that great eastern window and Ahmed was still sleeping peacefully, snug and foetal, in his half of the Great Gothic Bed. And Simeon was still pondering, still trying to come to terms with his new position after the extraordinary adventures of the previous evening. It was the same question – 'How can a boy, apparently barely out of his teens, live like this?' Reviewing the character of this brash youth, his self-assured audacity, his courage and bare knuckled skill, the name of Ronnie Kray continued to intrude into Simeon's deliberations. But if a thug, a gangster, a racketeer – what racket? Drugs, protection, prostitution? Most likely the latter. Does Ahmed sell himself? Or, is he sold by others who rent out Ahmed? Could it be more sinister still? Young boys? Little boys? In his limited experience on the Detroit gay scene, Simeon had heard the odd hint, whispers of information concerning a thriving and profitable trade in pre-pubescent boys.

At that very moment the bedroom door moved! Simeon sat bolt upright – alert. Silently, it opened a few inches to reveal a very young, peeping pale face which could have easily been pre-pubescent. An intruder? A burglar? Unlikely, a burglar would be less curious and concentrate on the task at hand. Just as silently, the door closed. The child, his sweet, wan, sad face – all gone. Carefully, very carefully, Simeon slid out of bed and donned the expensive silken dressing gown of fantastic lurid dragons presented to him as a wedding gift the night before. With determination, he padded over thick carpet towards the door. The intruder, appearing small, explained Simeon's unusual bravery. Contrasted with the 14th century bedroom, the living room in daylight looked more pristine, more minimal and more modern than ever. He followed a sound which came from a space-age kitchen, severely neat, antiseptic and gleaming.

"Hello."

"Hi," came the rather nervous, weak reply from a diminutive boy who, at first sight, reminded Simeon of Dopey the mute dwarf of Disney fame. "Sorry if I disturbed you. You see... I have to check to see if Mr Hamah is awake... for his coffee... that is..."

"That's OK. Don't worry, I was already awake," replied Simeon in gentle reassuring tones as if addressing his words to a frightened child. "I'm Simeon. What's your name?"

His name was Dale. At second sight, this cute little chicken was quite alluring, bobbing around in his little white shorts. In an interview consisting of cautious questions, slowly, Dale gained confidence imparting information with apparent candour and honesty. His work for Mr Hamah was entirely domestic full time. He arrived at 7.00am each morning and left after the kitchen was in pristine condition (he was proud of his kitchen) usually after 10.00pm. If Mr Hamah was out, which was often, Dale was free to leave, to go home, if all chores were done. He had to be back, to prepare lunch, or dinner, or anytime as instructed. Dale considered that he 'had a very good job' and was 'proud to work for Mr Hamah' who was 'good to him'. When the questions (however tactfully put) strayed from the domestic area of Dale's job description to personal details about his employer, Dale became a closed book.

"I imagine Mr Hamah must have a very good job living in a place like this?"

"Mr Hamah is a busy man. He meets important people. I suppose he does important things – I suppose."

"I expect he has other visitors, like me?"

"Some."

It was these guarded responses which made this cute little servant seem older than his, at first appearance, 12 years of age. His diplomacy, his social skills, his ability to parry an inquisitor in dealing with intrusive enquiries suggested an age more in the area of mid-teens. In brief, Dale had been well instructed, Dale was saying nothing.

"Yes, Mr Hamah has a very good job."

"What does he do – exactly?"

CHAPTER 7

Hate, Anger and Burning Injustice

Breakfast had been fantastic! It was exotic. Simeon raved about the wonderful variety, the strange riot of different morsels which had just electrified his inexperienced, working-class Derbyshire taste-buds. Ahmed explained that they had tucked into one of Dale's specialities. It was a starter consisting of tropical fruits topped with something deliciously tangy, an unknown substance called yoghurt. He listed other items in that bowl which were either little known or completely unknown to his English lover.

"... guava, apricots, papaya, mango, cranberries, kiwi and just wait until you sample Dale's bread. He makes it with millet, poppy seeds..."

"How old is Dale?"

This stopped Ahmed in his tracks. He leaned back in his chair, stroked his mouth and fixed Simeon with a half-smile.

"You like Dale?"

"He's cute, very sweet. We had a nice chat in the kitchen."

"About?"

"Mostly about his work. Don't worry, he told me nothing. But... well... he *is* very young. Surely he should be in school!"

Another pause and more stroking of mouth. But the slight smile started to fade as Ahmed considered his next move. He stood up, went over, crouched behind Simeon's chair and began to embrace his chest by inserting a hand. That warm, sensuous, smooth hand slithered inside the dressing gown producing waves of hypnotic pleasure. As with the previous night, gentle kisses and gentle nibbles were planted on the right ear. It was another mix of menace and magic. It was a difficult moment, but spoken conflict had been diffused by an unspoken physical action – a very successful action. Ahmed was weaving another spell. As expected, they came – the whispered words, gentle words as soft and silky as Simeon's new dressing gown.

"I think, maybe, *Booby* should be in school. And here's your first lesson. Do you know what happened to the cat?" The sitting boy was quite motionless, yet enjoying that Arab tongue toying with his ear and wetting his nape. That naughty hand was still stroking, searching, and having a predictable effect getting closer to erogenous zones down below. Of course, Simeon *did* know what happened to the cat, but he could not answer. Fear had frozen him into silence and that silence persisted to allow more sweet nothings to purr into that right ear. There was something about 'pussy needing morning milk' as Ahmed dipped below the table to do what he did best, what Simeon, even a frightened Simeon, enjoyed best. All this took place in a dining area in front of huge windows overlooking a busy avenue and a public park.

Ten minutes later, lolling on the sofa, the atmosphere was almost completely relaxed. Almost. Simeon, a mixture of conflicting emotions, was settling to a harsh reality which, on continuing reflection, was not really so harsh. Booby must ask no questions. He had pushed his curiosity to the limit and that limit had been tested. The unspoken message delivered with sexy slobbering sweetness was clear – it is better, safer for Booby to be ignorant and obedient – at all times. Stick to the rules and you will be serviced – cared for – at all times. Break the rules and… well, in Detroit it was common knowledge, tacitly understood what happened to people who broke the rules of the criminal underworld.

After all, Simeon was not a complete innocent. For over two years he had learned the rules, survived the secrecy of American gay culture. Like most other cute gay kids in Detroit, he was an occasional visitor to Howard's luxury house in Grosse Pointe overlooking Lake St Clair. Howard Mueller was a retired wealthy industrialist with a taste for teenage boys. To the best of Simeon's knowledge, they were never paid directly but enjoyed parties where food, drink and sex were plentiful. Good behaviour and discipline was imposed by an intimidating bulk called Olga, Howard's 'live in' Lesbian bouncer. An amusing contrast to Olga was the extremely camp and bitchy 'live in' house boy known as Marie. In this environment, it was common knowledge that any careless gossip or indiscretion could expose the transgressor to a lashing from the acid tongue of Marie, a painful punishment. A more serious offence could entail a visit from Olga which would definitely be hazardous to health and sound bones.

But Ahmed was different. Ahmed had hinted at murder. He was involved in something dangerous, and that something was quite unknown to Simeon. The clues were mounting: unlimited money, power to inflict great pain – or great pleasure. There was a young man, an old man and a boy. Calvin, Ralph and Dale had communicated more to Simeon than their respectful words. They had also communicated fear. And, Simeon too; he shared this instinctive primeval dread of the stunning hunk who was relaxing into the long, burnt gold sofa, one of three which formed a great horse-shoe in that living room.

"These sofas are massive!" said Simeon. "You could seat 12 in here!"

"Yeah. We'll have a party. How about inviting your friend?" replied Ahmed. He was holding up a small picture of a beautiful blond youth.

"You've been going through my wallet!"

"Only because I wanted to plant a nice present for my Boy. But hey! *I'm* the one to get the surprise." He slid over to Simeon's side, put an arm around his shoulder and cuddled him close. At the same time, in accusing style, he held up the photograph in his other hand. He looked at the picture and looked at Simeon as if confronting a child with evidence of a wrong-doing. Yet again, in spite of anger, indignation, outrageous invasion of privacy, this guest was melting, quivering in a frisson of pleasurable arousal which caused a movement, a protrusion inside his dressing gown.

"Up again! You'll wear me out. He's put his head up. I guess he wants to play! And, well, we do have to take care of this little guy, don't we?"

And the 'little guy' who became known as 'little Booby', was taken care of, well taken care of – twice. Ahmed, even after his second spurt of vitamins that morning, was greedy. He decided to work for a third. Simeon felt thoroughly drained when his lover, again, picked up and studied the small black and white comely image.

"Mmmm. He is nice. I'd sure like to swing on that. But it's in the rule book – no competition. No sir! Time to say goodbye to your boyfriend."

At this, he crushed the small photograph in his fist, at the same time looking directly into Simeon's eyes to savour the hurt. It was hurt which gave no voice. More and more, he was increasingly silent, increasingly more and more yielding, falling into a whirlpool of wickedness, of fright, of craving for that supreme example of 100% pure masculinity. The English boy was struck dumb, unable to explain himself, unable to defend himself. He was bewitched, infatuated; he was in love. With no voice to put him straight, Ahmed never did discover the identity of the 'competition' who, incidentally, was not Simeon's boyfriend. If only! In England in 1966, there was a certain face, a certain voice and name which was familiar in almost every household: a name which was totally unknown to the American public. No Detroiter had ever seen, or had ever heard of the British pop legend – Billy Fury.

This small but significant act of cruelty created a long sulk – which Ahmed confidently and cheerfully ignored. In that time, they dressed, donned winter thermals and embarked on a brisk walk into an almost deserted Palmer Park. Simeon maintained the silence, but enjoyed the bracing fresh air, brilliant late morning sunshine and dazzling frost.

"We forgot to call your folks." The comment was ignored. For the first time, Ahmed became irritated by the ongoing sulk, the ongoing lack of eye contact. He man-handled his lover. He pushed him hard against a very tall tree and banged the back of his head against the trunk. It did not hurt. The bark of the redwood is very soft, rather like a cushion. Once again, the fiery Arab resorted to violence to solve his problems. It was becoming a standard routine: Simeon pinned up against a wall ready to suffer the force of a tantrum.

"Don't you care about your Mom? your Pa? Where's your respect? Are you so selfish? Out all night. God Almighty, they'll be out of their minds with worry about you!" No answer. He grabbed the boy's jaw and banged his head one more time. "Look at me when I'm talking to you, ya insolent nigger-lovin' cock-sucker." Having forced eye contact, Ahmed softened when he looked directly into young English eyes, hurt and moistened by a hint of tears. His fury turned to frustration, then to resignation, and then to gentleness. "What am I supposed do with you?"

Decades later, Simeon often looked back at that drama played out under that giant redwood. It highlighted the contrast between English and Arab cultural attitudes to family values, parental respect and deference to parental authority. On Saturday nights, Simeon usually returned late but had never before failed to return to his bed. This was noticed with some small concern, but certainly no great alarm. Simeon's Mum and Dad were very reluctant to ask questions – for fear of unwanted answers.

The unwelcome appearance of a homosexual in the working class, coal mining Hogg family had been suspected some ten years before. Jack Hogg proudly presented his son with his first pair of football boots to be used for his first football match at Mundy Street Boys School in the hill-top colliery town of Heanor. For father and son this event was a painful disaster. It left a long shadow which darkened both of their lives: a damaging, humiliating experience showing the boy no mercy. A sadistic schoolmaster encouraged aggressive taunts, brutal insults, screaming jeers reducing Simeon to a very low level of self-esteem. Those boots, used that one time, became symbols of a lifelong hatred of all macho sports.

The boys of Mundy Street, the schoolmaster and Jack Hogg came to realise that Simeon was different. He was different, in the same way the chick in the nest is seen as different – the chick which is thrown *out* of the nest. A civilised society has laws against murder. The Hoggs, unable to evict in such a manner, had no choice but to keep Simeon in the family nest. Accordingly, Simeon Hogg, the unwanted, unloved son, was tolerated under a cloud of quiet contempt. And this persistent contempt was especially pointed, especially vicious from the female side of the family. He suffered years of emotional abuse from two acid-tongued older sisters and an indifferent, frequently absent mother. Simeon the history teacher, looking back, was often reminded of John Knox the 16th century influential Protestant preacher who wrote a book titled *First Blast of the Trumpet Against the Monstrous Regiment of Women.*

In stark contrast, Ahmed Hamah was blessed with a good relationship with his family of two brothers and two sisters. He revered his parents and could not understand Simeon's indifference to Mr and Mrs Hogg and their daughters. Alas, young Simeon was ill-educated and inarticulate. Under that tree, he was unable to make his case effectively. He was unable to describe the regular bouts of family homophobia – the emotional equivalent of being beaten up. The mother tolerated and sometimes encouraged these savage attacks to abase this boy, the family embarrassment, the brother who was, shall we say, 'not quite a *real* man'. Simeon was the 'sissy who had an unnatural aversion to football', the butt of jokes who had to endure endless humiliations. On one occasion, he was shocked by the sudden ferocity, the sudden violence of maternal feminine claws when Mrs Hogg's own sister dared to criticise one of her precious daughters.

The result of these injustices – alienation from working class culture – football, pubs, drink and girls – the result was a profound loneliness.

At this point under that tree in the early days of 1966, Ahmed had no knowledge of his lover's background – the lover who was mute, yet raging inside. Having christened him 'Booby', up to this point, 14 hours after their first meeting, he had not even bothered to ask after his proper name! Notwithstanding, having been reprimanded for displaying a rank lack of motherly / sisterly love, Ahmed had no idea that his Booby was a seething mass of hate, anger and burning injustice.

Booby was damaged.

CHAPTER 8

Love's First Kiss

The mother received her son's phone call with restrained embarrassment. A simple woman of limited intellect, she always tried to suppress the spectre of homosexuality when it forced itself into her neat and tidy homophobic world in the suburban City of Taylor. And, the ugly reality of homosexuality was far more intrusive when Ahmed came on the line!

"Mrs Hogg? Hi. I'm Ahmed, Simeon's new friend. How are you?

"All right," came the unwilling, weak, nervous response. It was cautious and redolent with disapproval.

If Ahmed sensed these feelings he pressed on, unfazed, with his usual confidence. Make no mistake, young Hogg was impressed! Ahmed delivered his eloquent speech with authority, immaculate courtesy and the deference he felt due to a mother whether a princess or a peasant.

"Mrs Hogg, please don't think me presumptuous, but I think your boy needs some help. He's reasonably intelligent but not well educated. He should be in college, not labouring in a steel mill. That whole area around Wyandotte… Great Lakes Steel! It's a terrible place. On some days it stinks even from my place here in Uptown Detroit. What a waste of a life – eight hours a day! The pollution is slowly killing him! I've made a deal with your son. He'll stay with me and I'll pay all the fees to put him through Wayne State University. It's just a few blocks walk from here."

"You'll do that! Are ya sure 'e's clever enough?"

"Don't worry. He is. And, anyway, I know a few people. I can pull a few strings. He'll be fine. I'll take good care of him and we'll come to visit you soon. Be real nice to meet his folks."

Listening to this, Simeon was tempted to revise his estimate of Ahmed's age. Surely such fluent self-assurance must speak of late rather than early 20s? Perhaps, being so gorgeous in the first place, he is just well preserved! Could he be 30? No! Impossible. And, has Ahmed himself graduated from college? A simple idea occurred to him. 'These should not be dangerous questions! I'll ask him.'

Simeon asked his questions. He was relieved to see a gradual smile lighten up that handsome Middle Eastern face as the gorgeous hunk moved over to the settee, clutched his boy and pulled him up to standing position. Again, Booby's face, was forced, pushed, buried into that comfortable human depression between head and shoulders. The strict, strong, left hand at the back of his head was putting pressure, causing difficulty in breathing, but, it mattered not. If he suffocated? So what? Such a great place to die! Simeon savoured the familiar Arab body scent, the familiar taste of Ahmed's neck, the familiar warmth from his torso and that familiar, naughty right hand, a wandering hand at every opportunity, always exploring his bottom. Simeon was a limp doll and was glad to be so. He'd forgotten the questions. Nothing mattered now. He wanted this delicious moment to go on forever.

But that strict hand, the left hand not to be trusted; it moved, it grabbed his hair, it pulled back his head forcing close eye contact – lovely, deep, brown pools. He spoke slowly, low and gently.

"I'm 21. I've never been to college. And... haven't you noticed there's something missing in this room?" He motioned around the room. "No television! I don't watch shit but, I do read." He motioned over to the coffee table which neatly displayed *TIME, US News & World Report* and *Newsweek*. "And so should you."

But their mutual interest was still in each other, still very physical as Ahmed forced a long, lingering wet kiss into the rag doll's eager mouth. This kiss, given willingly to Ahmed, was out of character for Simeon. *His* kisses were given sparingly to boys who had to *be* boys. They had to be butch and had to be beautiful. Consequently, until his first encounter with Ahmed the legendary, stunning icon of Gay Detroit; Simeon had never actually given any boy a passionate kiss. Unlike an act of sex where the male mouth was a frequent delight for this promiscuous youth, a kiss was sacred, a kiss was intimate, an act of love. It was very special and had never happened until the appearance of Prince Charming – and, yes, Ahmed Hamah *was* Prince Charming.

In his early teens, under social pressure to date, Simeon was revolted / repelled by the touch of a young female and utterly sickened by the wet kisses expected by girls. In the Heanor Milk Bar, he often invested a three-penny bit to play a popular record on the juke-box – *('Til) I Kissed You* – by two alluring boys called the Everly Brothers. In 1959, young Simeon could only dream of kissing boys of quality, boys like Phil and Don Everly. Today, melting into the strong arms of his beautiful young lover, Simeon recalled that recurrent refrain, the rolling drum-beat, the sweet thrum of the guitar, the melodic strains of that romantic teenage ballad –

'... never knew what I missed, 'til I kissed you... my life's not the same, since I kissed you...'

That long kiss with Ahmed was the high point of 1966. Simeon's Prince Charming had taken him out of the soul-destroying, filthy steel mill. He had been rescued from the suffocating quagmire of homophobic cruelty, that appalling family home of ignorant Hoggs.

It was now past 2.00pm. After a light lunch they discussed Simeon's future. Gradually, happy dreams of unfocused blissful togetherness re-focused to reveal the problems of harsh reality. What would the new boy study at university? Ahmed's suggestions included the Classics, Music, Literature, Art, Political Science and History. Simeon, aware of his poor spelling, thought he should start with a remedial course in English. He expressed gratitude to his new friend for such generosity and re-stated his genuine love, making it clear that it was the very first time. He had never been in love before, was walking on air! It was an intoxicating incredible feeling. It was exhilarating, a wonderful experience.

However, they needed to be completely honest with each other. Bluntly, Simeon pointed out, as best he could with limited articulation, that he did not really know the guy opposite, the guy he was so crazy about. They were strangers who desired each other and wanted to touch each other – frequently. Simeon asked that they try to get to know each other. He suggested that this was a good opportunity to have a talk, to have a frank exchange of views. Ahmed agreed. He realised that he had been doing all the talking and had heard very little from Simeon himself. He was impressed with this sudden assertiveness, the proposal of sensible aims. He settled himself, snuggled into a corner of the large horseshoe sofa and, significantly, for the first time, addressed his new acquisition by his first name.

"OK, Simeon. Fire away, tell me all about yourself."

Simeon suspected the opulent life-style displayed around him was funded by some sort of criminal enterprise. Accordingly, choosing his words carefully, he started to speak of his own values and moral standards.

"I don't drink. Don't get me wrong, it's not principle. I just hate the taste of alcohol. And hunting: I think it's wicked to go out and shoot innocent animals just for the pleasure of it! They don't always died quick you know. To inflict agony on dumb creatures in the name of sport – well it's monstrous..."

"I don't hunt."

"Good. I suppose really... well, I should really be a vegetarian."

"I'll speak to Dale. What are your views on prostitution?"

"I'm not too keen. I've no strong views. OK – I'll admit to accepting the odd $5 bill when it's offered to me at Vesuvio..."

"$5! Boy! You're *really* cheap! I'll remember that when next I'm hungry. *$5!!* I won't take my shoes off for less than $200!"

"I was about to tell you that it is rather sad when somebody has to buy sex. Those guys who offered, they'd already had it. It was free. I just like sex."

"So I noticed. How about drugs?"

"Never touch them. Don't approve."

"Good for you." His words had the ring of sincerity.

"Ahmed... you live like a millionaire. OK – it's your business and I won't ask you... well... what you do..."

"I won't tell you. And nobody else will."

"Ahmed... we do need to talk about the long term."

"What d'ya mean?"

"Living here will be wonderful. It's a palace. Nobody could ask for more. And college... that's a fantastic gift! I can't tell you how grateful I..."

"So don't try. You'll always be here with me. And I'll always love you. That's all that matters. So what's the problem, Booby?"

"I'm homesick. I don't... I don't think that I could face living in Detroit for ever. Ahmed – at some point, I have to go home, home to Derbyshire... I'm sorry..."

At this, the Arab seemed to freeze to an absolute stillness. His face registered no emotion, just those two enchanting eyes, deep pools of brown which held – and now frightened Simeon. At long last he spoke in a dangerous, soft monotone.

"You are going no place. I'm not a good loser."

As before, an obstacle had blocked the progress of Ahmed Hamah. If he is threatened in any way, if he hears what he does not want to hear, there is a familiar pattern. He approaches, circles his prey, chooses his words before pouncing with that curious mixture of magic and menace. The menace was somehow embodied in his inscrutable expression, perhaps a suggestion of kindly ruthlessness. The magic manifested itself in the gentle way he cuddled up close and held both the hands of his thrilled, frightened lover, the private property he had every intention of keeping. His voice was a purr – deep, smooth, clear, intimidating.

"Don't be scared, Booby. Relax. It's gonna be fine, 's gonna be OK. Listen to me, and listen good. I'll only say this once." He planted a gentle kiss on Simeon's forehead and stroked the side of his cheek. "God! Look at you! You're so beautiful. You could be 16 – just a child. You need looking after, I'd sure hate anything to spoil those pretty sad eyes... What was I saying? Oh, yes. I've lived in this city all my life. I'll die in this city. And so will you. You see... you're the best thing that's ever happened to me. You're beautiful outside and inside. And... it's simple, we'll always be together. This is your home."

His hand, warm and sensuous, dropped onto Simeon's leg, moved up to the groin and gently began to fondle. They both looked at the movement of that hand – and its effect. His purring voice was still soft, still bewitching.

"Try to understand, I can't lose my sweet, pretty Booby. You're my baby. And then, what would I do without my *Little* Booby? Hey! I can feel him!" The mesmerising voice began to become child-like, as if speaking to a child in baby talk. "He's coming up. I'll bet he wants to play with Ahmed's naughty tongue. What'd say Booby? Shall we give Little Booby a good time?"

Little Booby had a great time. And, eventually, showed his appreciation by giving Ahmed yet another milky drink.

The atmosphere for the rest of that Sunday could be described, from Simeon's point of view, as another long sulk. Again it was a sulk totally ignored by his lover. Perhaps, however, this second introspective brood had a slightly different quality. There was no redwood tree to help break the mood. Ahmed continued to be tender, affectionate, attempting occasional small talk; continued to be solicitous and loving.

Simeon was under no doubt that he had been, albeit ever so gently, twice threatened with violence, and, in effect, was now a prisoner in a golden cage. This prisoner, still held by the grip of enchantment, was somewhat resigned to his fate – for the short term. Even in this early stage of virtual abduction, he was pondering a way of escape – and not just an escape to one of the many suburbs of Detroit or, indeed, to any part of the USA. No. Simeon had to flee far away to a part of the world almost beyond Christendom: a place of dark mysterious woods where the mob could never reach him. On that very first day of incarceration, he resolved to escape to the one place he loved dearly – a pagan place of wild beauty, a lonely landscape of weathered limestone crags where cold winds race through lovely dales whipping the tree tops. He dreamed of it everyday. It was a place redolent of ancient legends where rocky precipices weathered into grotesque forms overlooking springs of pure water, deep luxuriant moss and fern. He did not know how, but Simeon resolved to escape from his dangerous lover and hide in a distant remote place, somewhere in the darkest depths of Derbyshire.

CHAPTER 9

A Lad from Huddersfield

Looking over the dinner table that evening, Simeon contemplated his beloved with mixed feelings. It was a nice table. Having sensed the afternoon tension, Dale had taken the trouble to arrange sparkling clean cutlery with precision. He completed the spread with a centrepiece of fresh white hyacinths and miniature daffodils. Ahmed too, was appraising his beloved. Through the continuing fog of silence, he studied the boy's face searching every expression in an effort to read signs of emotion. In many ways, Ahmed was old fashioned. He believed in firm discipline. He expected to get exactly what he wanted. However, if it were at all possible, he preferred a contented Booby to inhabit his golden cage: better still, a happy Booby. But, in any event, he intended to conquer.

Ahmed was feeling confident in his power – with good reason. Just before dinner he showered. Without bothering to dress, he paraded his naked body across the living room into the kitchen to give instructions to Dale regarding engagements for the week ahead. The well-proportioned, strapping body with wafts of expensive cologne seemed indifferent to Simeon's wide-eyed enthusiastic appreciation of the retreating muscular buttocks of perfect proportion. Nonetheless, that lust, that intense desire – it had been noted – and noted well. Ahmed looked smug. It was as if he knew that Little Booby had given a quick flick, a quiver to half inflation.

The murmur of voices, the deeper sound of master and the lighter, more timid sound of servant eventually concluded in silence... a rather long silence. Simeon continued to read – or, at least, tried to give that impression – until he heard the master suddenly exhale and take a quick gulp of breath as if he had been underwater. His panting voice, slightly unsteady, eventually, was able to articulate.
        "Yeah! Nice one, Kid."

Ahmed marched out of that kitchen with commanding steps, wearing a half sneer tilted in Simeon's direction. The conceited Arab was taking contemptuous pleasure in the potent impact of his mind-blowing, erotic condition. Hector! Yes it was Hector, proud as Punch, still glistening with spittle, well serviced, well drained, well satisfied, happy Hector. He was still arrogantly at full mast, now bobbing and swaggering shamelessly with every step of that march back to the bedroom.

Mixed feelings. Yes, mixed feelings on both sides on that Sunday evening across that dinner table. Simeon looked at Ahmed and Ahmed looked back at Simeon who was in a whirl of conflicting, confusing emotions. He was afraid of Ahmed, was angry with Ahmed – and, at the same time, he loved Ahmed. He was jealous of little Dale, sexy young Dale who, apparently, had been groomed up to the required standard of adult oral skills. And yet Simeon was ashamed of his unwarranted, unjustified jealousy because, if he was completely honest with himself, he too desired sweet, sexy little Dale – the innocent child who, after all, had about as much choice in the matter as Simeon. Anyway, common sense told Simeon that he would be sharing Ahmed with a legion of pretty Dales and miscellaneous lovers – so, he may just as well get used to it.

Dale, polite and pleasant as ever was clearing away empty plates after the main course. It had been an exotic tasting dish of red cabbage, sweet potatoes and other tasty vegetables which were quite unknown in a rough Derbyshire coal-mining community. Simeon, feeling tender and sympathetic towards the child-like servant, uttered a few words of appreciation; kind words which were also echoed by Ahmed.

Simeon looked at Ahmed and Ahmed looked back at Simeon. This look held a neutral expression which seemed to say – 'How about a truce?' And so, the boy of many mixed emotions melted. He surrendered as, very slowly, Ahmed defeated him with the onset of a most welcome gradual smile. At that moment, once again he was disarmed. All thoughts of escape to Derbyshire had dissolved as he sat back in the luxury of Sultan's Palace bathed in the sunshine of an affectionate smile from the most stunning young man in the world.

After desert, they retired to sink into the sumptuous sofa to enjoy and celebrate the thaw. Following a few minutes of cuddle, Ahmed picked up and idly flicked through a copy of *US News and World Report*. This intelligent young man enjoyed a comfortable life with plenty of leisure time. Accordingly, he was well read, self-taught with regard to many aspects of current affairs and had a particular interest in news of the world economy. He noticed that his lover had picked up *Time* and was reading an item about Britain's Prime Minister, Harold Wilson.

"There ya go, Booby! He's OK. A poor kid from a crummy background – made good. What a change from that stuffy old Lord Home. That's what Britain needs, a leader who has a regular high school education, can talk to ordinary folks. The English are finally wising up. Is Notting-*ham* near to Huddersfield?"

Simeon was very impressed. He would never expect a Detroiter to have such detailed knowledge of the current PM or to grasp the significance of Huddersfield being a working class location far away from the capital with all its baggage of 'privilege' and the 'establishment'.

But Ahmed had his own agenda. He had a special purpose in the lengthy monologue which was to follow – a lucid critique of mid-20th century Britain. Taking Simeon's hands, he became seriously concerned.

"Listen, Booby, you'll have to get over this homesickness. You can't go back to England – shit, it's a sinking ship! That creakin' old country – why, it's goin' down the tube."

Simeon withdrew his hands. He was proud to be British. He was deeply hurt. With a countenance which had suddenly frozen to stone, he pulled away from the boy he loved and from factual information he did not want to hear. Ahmed geared up to deliver a verbal beating. His voice became hard and cruel.

"Awe no! Not again. More sulks? Listen, kid, there are millions of English peasants working full time for eight pounds a week who would give their right arm to change places with you. I'm offering you an *American* education – the *best* in the world. I know about Harold Wilson, but I'll bet you don't know shit about one – single – American – President. Well? Just give me one fact about one President of the United States. No answer? Just a dumb kid huh?"

Simeon was just about to say that President Johnson came from Texas when Ahmed said –

"I'll make it easy for you. Take Benjamin Disraeli, one of our greatest Presidents. Did he live in the 14th century or the 19th century?"

"It must be the 19th century. America wasn't a proper country until the 19th century."

"Dumb kid." Ahmed slowly shook his head with a contemptuous smile. "Benjamin Disraeli was a Jew. He was the Prime Minister to your Queen Victoria. America is not a country, it's a continent. And another thing, the United States became an independent nation when we won a war against *you* – the War of Independence in 1776 – which was in the *18th* century."

Seeing his victim down cast, defeated, humiliated, Ahmed recognised this as a pyrrhic victory. He considered, softened his tone.

"Ok, you fell into a trap. I needed to make my point. And... alright, you are not dumb. But you *are* uneducated. If you knew all the facts you would not want to go back to England. Booby, listen to me. Your country is in deep doo doo! Not so long back the pound was worth $4.00, now it's down to $2.80. It's dropping like a stone for Christ sakes! Look at the British Motor Corporation. Sick, tired, backward – it's typical. It's in crisis. It's *always* in crisis! Lazy workers riddled with class hatred plus weak, snooty management equals low productivity. Dated restrictive practices, bloody-minded communist led unions, strikes every week! Strikes about tea-breaks and any amount of trivia bringing production to a standstill – and shit quality when it starts up... am I getting through to you?"

Simeon remained silent, but, yes, Ahmed was getting through. In the previous year during a visit to Derbyshire he had, first hand, seen an example of the 'British disease' as it was known in the mid-1960s. In Horsley Woodhouse, several council houses were being painted by a team of council employees. The snail-like progress attracted considerable critical comment in that mining village. Long tea breaks and short work breaks had extended a two day job into a skive which lasted for over two weeks. Simeon had noted that Americans worked harder. There was no slacking at Great Lakes Steel, a private company. The public sector work ethic in Derbyshire was much more leisurely.

"You've made the right move, Booby. You've come to the greatest country in the world. You should be glad – not thinking of going back! Economically we *own* the world. It is ours. Are you listening to me? Heard about the British 'Brain Drain'? A 22% increase between 1962 and 1964. Scientists, professors, engineers and doctors were all leaving the United Kingdom, all clamouring to get into the United States for a better quality of life. You mentioned becoming a teacher. Would you work for $2,000 a year and pay 35% tax to keep an army of shirkers on social security? Here you would start at $7,000 and pay 20% tax. Our rule is simple – no work, no eat. Convinced? Ok – try this: the average Englishman works five weeks to buy the average television; the average American works just *two* weeks for a *colour* television. And another thing…"

"Enough! Please. You're battering me with all this… statistics and stuff. Anyway, you said American telly is shit."

Ahmed smiled. At last Simeon had scored a point. He moved over, hugged his precious Englishman whose eyes became moist pressed into the warmth of the Arab's body coupled with a release of tension. And – something had happened to Ahmed. Some small sound escaped him. It was close to a sob. His grip tightened, emotion welled up into whispered pleading.

"Don't go, Booby. Please don't leave me. This only happens once in a lifetime. I'll never find anybody like you. This has to work. It must work."

CHAPTER 10

A Good Boy

During the next few days, Simeon's new world came into sharper focus. It started when Dale handed him the phone after breakfast.

"Good morning, Simeon. I'm Earl, PA to Mr Hamah."

"PA?"

"Personal Assistant. Could we meet? I need to talk to you about college and a few other things. Calvin will drive you over to my office. See you in… about an hour?"

Simeon was thrilled to be chauffeur driven down Woodward Avenue in the luxury of a floating Lincoln Continental which came to rest in front of Detroit's tallest skyscraper, the 47 storey Penobscot Building. A sole passenger sitting in stately isolation was still fiddling with the handle, trying to exit, when Calvin abruptly opened the door. Very self-conscious on that busy side-walk, slightly uncomfortable, slightly embarrassed, he looked to Calvin for guidance. Instructions were barked out with nothing of the deference previously shown to Mr Hamah.

"Through the main entrance, head on down the hall, second set of elevators on the left. Go up to the 41st Floor and check out the list of wheels."

"Wheels?"

"Big Shots! You're looking for Earl Kureth."

Up high in the sky of Detroit, the swift, smooth elevator announced Simeon's arrival with a melodic chime. He found himself at the end of another impressive, spacious, marble corridor, but his one was quiet and deserted. A short walk brought him to a frosted glass door clearly signed – 'Earl Kureth – Attorney at Law.' During the few moments of hesitation, a young secretary opened the door and reassured him with a friendly smile.

"Mr Hogg? We've been expecting you. Go right in."

A beaming smile from a distinguished, grey, forty-something hit the boy with an even more enthusiastic welcome. With a slight reluctance, he accepted the greeting of an extended, warm, soft hand, but was immediately distracted by the magnificent south easterly view of a giant suspension bridge spanning the Detroit River.

"Isn't she beautiful! D'ya know, Simeon – in the 22 years I've been up here, I never, ever tire of that Ambassador Bridge. Just look at it! What a spectacle! Check out the vast expanse of Ontario beyond."

For a few moments, the boy and the lawyer stood side by side admiring the sun-drenched vista of a misty bridge, slightly unfocused by orange pollutants. The great river which separated two nations, swept away to infinity, a glitter which meandered across a table-top-flat, endless sweep.

The girl, a pretty girl with a pretty smile, entered with a tray of tea.

"Oh, yeah! We've had our instructions. Proper English tea purchased from Canada." said Earl. The secretary placed the tray on a small table between two smart office armchairs. She departed, carefully closing the door behind her. After a few sips and some small talk, Earl leaned back and appraised the young man. His expression and tone was the very essence of diplomacy and immaculate courtesy. His voice was kindly, understanding, gentle – yet – Simeon detected hard professionalism and a steely determination to muster his argument and to make his point. Still wearing the beaming smile, he softened up his subject with compliments.

"My, oh my, oh my! As good as Ahmed said. You're one beautiful kid and that's a fact. And you're one *lucky* kid. Here." Earl handed him a folder. "It's all arranged. It's all in there, classes, times and we got you the best professors. You start at Wayne State University next Monday, January 17th. One week late for the Winter Semester but, I'm assured, it will present no problem. Yes, Sir, lucky, lucky kid! Uncle Sam is sure being good to you."

As usual, this comment caused irritation which Simeon tried to suppress as he opened the folder and examined several sheets of type-written information. For the most part, the selected courses were very attractive, in line with Ahmed's previous suggestions. There was a daily hour with a special private tutor and counsellor who would iron out any remedial difficulties such as Simeon's poor English. Lucky kid? Yes, he was lucky – very lucky. This student was painfully well aware of the usual difficulties of getting into college in the United States. Just months before, he had attempted to register at Henry Ford Community College in Dearborn to undertake a modest load of semester hours. He had scraped up the necessary enrolment and course fees but was defeated by his 'new boy' status. On his all important 'White Card' was a high number. This meant that Simeon was not allowed into the registration hall until the late afternoon, the end of Registration Day when most of the essential classes, the classes he needed, were full. It had all been an appalling waste of time and he had to return to the grime and drudgery of the steel mill. This was the penalty of being a foreign nobody of limited means with no previous track record and no one to advise or help him.

All that had changed overnight. Not only had he been spared the indignity, the clamouring, the pushing and the shoving of Registration Day but, also, the expensive fees of Wayne State University had been paid in full. In addition, the best courses, the best professors and even a private tutor had been obtained. It had all been organised as if he were a foreign prince walking down a red carpet.

"Any questions?"

"I'm grateful. Thank you very much. It's just that… well; you said you were Ahmed's assistant?"

"Right – Personal Assistant – Ahmed's PA."

"But… you're a lawyer!"

"Right! I need to be well qualified to do my job. I talk to people, deal with people and I know the law. See, Simeon, Ahmed is a valuable part of our organisation. I have to see that he's always happy. I take care of any problems he may have. It's like this – a happy guy works well – right?"

At this point, that beaming smile relaxed – just a little. However, Earl was still smiling, still speaking gently when he said –

"Just now, Simeon, you said you were grateful. I hope so. I really do hope so. Because... well frankly, Simeon, you've been causing us some small anxiety."

"What do you mean?"

"Oh, come on now, you know exactly what I mean. You're a big boy. You just have to be a *good* boy."

"A good boy?"

The smile had now all but disappeared. It had been replaced by the countenance of a kindly uncle, slightly hurt, mildly disappointed by his nephew's recent conduct.

"I want you to be a good boy, go to school, keep your head down, work hard and please the folks who have made all that possible. Be a good boy by respecting our rules and not quizzing Dale. Being a good boy makes my job easier by keeping Ahmed happy and a good boy does not ask questions. Got that?"

Simeon sat perfectly still in stunned silence. Earl poured his guest a second cup of tea and continued in a business-like manner.

"Like I was saying, you're a smart kid. We know a lot about you. We know that you've been to Howard's parties. No problem there, Howard Mueller runs a tight ship. He's OK. He told me that you know the facts of life and that you can be discreet." Earl Kureth leaned closer. "See, kid, in this firm there's a great deal of money flying around. We don't take chances and have to be very careful. Your ignorance is your best protection. It's a shield. Don't ever damage that shield. When Ahmed is finally bored with you, ignorance is your safe ticket out of here. If you breach our rules..." He shook his head sadly. "Well... Ahmed can't help you – nobody can help you."

His second cup of tea remained untouched, cold. Earl broke through the tense gloom with a cheerful rush.

"Welcome aboard!"

"Pardon?"

"You're on the team now. Just a few minor items." He reached for a paper with a few scribbled notes. "Like my suit?"

"Of course – immaculate – must be expensive."

"You're looking at a $300 suit! Don't be offended but, well, *you* need to smarten up, Simeon. Calvin is going to take you to Hudsons. We'll make a new man of you – all on the The Firm. You can wave bye-bye to money troubles. I imagine Ahmed is looking after you pretty good – Huh?"

"He put $200 into my wallet." Simeon resisted the temptation to add – 'And in the process he destroyed my precious photograph of Billy Fury.'

"Lucky Kid! Oh, and I have to give you this." Simeon looked puzzled at the five, one hundred, dollar bills just placed in his hand. "Pretty generous, huh? Take that 1960 Falcon to any Used Car Lot and you'd be lucky to get 20 bucks!"

"You sold my car!!"

"We *junked* your car! Do you seriously think we would tolerate the lover of Ahmed Hamah being seen in an old, beaten up Ford Falcon? You don't need a car. You have a chauffeur for Christ sake! And he drives a Lincoln Continental. Calvin's going to look after you from now on."

"Calvin doesn't like me."

"Is that right? Mmm…understandable, I guess." Earl patted his lower lip with two fingers in meditative consideration. "No problem. By the time you get down to your limo, young man, Calvin, who is well paid for what he does, will be very sweet to you. I guarantee it."

And that was indeed the case.

"How did it go, Mr Hogg?" rang out a changed, cheerful Calvin. "We're going to Hudsons. We can have a bite of lunch – if that's what you'd like? They have a nice restaurant on the 14th floor. You got the munchies?"

During the previous 27 months of residence in the United States, Simeon had already picked up most of the American gay lingo. 'Munchies' = hungry. He began to warm to Calvin, albeit his new friendliness was coerced by the firm hand of The Firm – whatever that was. This handsome chauffer, tall and lean, was assessed in his mid-20s. He donned no chauffer uniform but was very well turned out, clearly, perfectly in tune with the latest 'smart-gay-young-man' fashion and fashion accessories. He was no queen, quite butch, tight pants, nice ass, typical of the best which could be found in the Woodward Bar on any evening. As fashion advisor to Simeon, Calvin was well qualified.

And Simeon had learned the Kureth lesson – as had Calvin. In the various departments of Detroit's leading department store, picking and choosing three suits, various items of clothing and shoes, Simeon was also choosing his few spoken words to Calvin with care. Ahmed liked his boys clean cut with a short 'square at the back' hairstyle of the late 1950s. In spite of 'Beatle-mania' which had swept through this conservative 'beer and hamburger' city two years before, the neat 'All American look' was still King. In consequence, precise instructions were given to the manager of the exclusive Hudsons Barber Shop who snapped his fingers for the best stylist.

Simeon did not mind. He admired many aspects of American culture. He considered the 'clean cut look' desirable. He also approved Calvin's choice of clothes. Close fitting pants and expensive body tailored shirts were very acceptable to the young man who, truth be told, had little interest in trendy clothes and was often described as a scruffy chicken. The urban landscape of Detroit was not the natural element for this walker /cyclist who was more comfortable in functional anorak, shorts and boots. This Englishman's body may have been in an industrially blighted corner of the United States, but, his heart was home – and – once again, as the store assistants fussed around him, his spirit was exploring a memory…

It was a memory of dense conifers in a deep Derbyshire Dale. He was cycling fast, fascinated by the effect of sun beams penetrating deep into the gloom of the forest, falling on, and illuminating thick, dark, purple beds of needles. Suddenly there was on old crumbling mill and a very steep, densely wooded hill to the north. The lane narrowed and took him, as it seemed, into another world. Like entering the 'secret garden', Simeon had been transported into a beautiful secluded deep valley, shut in by rocks and woods, the first of a chain of lovely limestone ravines.

The world became cooler on that warm summer afternoon, more tranquil with a totally different atmosphere – save for a rush of water to his left which required investigation. Smooth, clear, polished water, slow at first, and then bending, dipping, just before getting cloudy and agitated as it tumbled over a rocky fall.

There was a feeling of safety in the comfortable seclusion of this 'Shangri-La', this deep ravine; a serene, silent world of enchantment, steep rocks painted with lichen and moss giving a protective shield against modern noise.

Rocks and trees everywhere. He looked upwards, following interesting craggy forms which became ruined castles – crooked medieval castles. Unexpectedly, above the natural finials, above the high foliage – a solitary hawk was hovering high in the distant blue.

The warmth of the afternoon reacted with the cold of rocks, water and shade to create sudden gusts which stirred up willows. Zephyrs flashed the underside silver of leaves making a stark, bright effect, which travelled along the riverside, waving in waves and swathes, rippling, swaying, bowing and beckoning – before subsiding and returning the foliage back to green.

Ubiquitous ferns with their distinctive smell covered the banks, sometimes marestails pushed out of the mud and sometimes a delightful patch of forget-me-nots turned the riverside blue. The water had mood changes. When it was slow it showed shimmering reflections of ash and sycamore. Sunshine glistened, sparkled and twinkled off the river surface – a surface often broken by the quick leap of a fish catching a hapless fly.

Limestone had a multitude of tints from a flash of white to grey and occasional black. Above and beyond, right at the top, smooth, bright, green fields closely cropped by grazing sheep, were occasionally scarred by eruptions of ancient weather worn rocks.

The boy was entertained by sinister grotesque shapes of long dead trees, still majestic in death as in life: living ivy feeding on the rotting wood. Here he joyfully scared himself with ugly goblins, old hags and monsters which looked like some of the crooked old queers he had met, the old men who inhabited public lavatories of Derbyshire. Dense foliage formed mysterious tunnels and caves, darkened and obliterated with cascading ivy, lots of ivy, harbouring more unknown horrors…

"You look like a million dollars!" said Calvin, breaking into his day-dream. This comment signalled the completion of Simeon's transformation from a Derbyshire scruffy chicken to the privileged, newly Americanised lover of Ahmed Hamah.

CHAPTER 11

A Party of Chickens

The new luxurious life-style settled into a comfortable routine. A docile and obedient Simeon enjoyed his lover's huge appetite for carnal pleasure and never complained when the great, ugly, medieval bed had somehow managed to acquire an extra occupant by first light. Indeed, why complain? These sexy teenage acquisitions were always very desirable, often beautiful and, after The Master had had his fill, always available for the delectation of Simeon. It was OK. It was sanctioned by 'the rule book'. Providing that Ahmed was close by, could watch, could touch and could join the activities at any moment – Booby was permitted to help himself. Indeed, the young guest was just as much obliged to satisfy Ahmed's lover as he was to service Ahmed himself.

Gradually, he learned how these nocturnal acquisitions had been acquired. Some were innocent lads who had responded to an invitation. Some were 'street-wise' professionals. Some were self-employed hustlers who could be dialled from the nearest telephone. Some were boys obtained from the stable of a pimp. Simeon suspected that the majority were probably supplied by The Firm. And then there was 'rough trade'. These were the ultra butch types, often petty criminals who gratified Ahmed's predatory instinct: tough, feral heterosexuals who were hunted down by the horny Arab when in sexual aggressive mood. Simeon was never quite sure, but gathered that such butch numbers had been persuaded to yield by the 'stick and carrot' approach. The stick being the threat of violence and the carrot was usually a $50 bill. In 1966, this was about half the average weekly wage.

This carnal conveyer belt of humanity was deeply unsettling, somewhat disturbing to the Englishman who, gradually, very gradually, began to accept Ahmed's apartment as his own home. He had to be honest. He enjoyed the sex, but, ever hanging in the air was a brutal aura of force and passion which somehow connected with Simeon's dark side. He had long suspected that the savage years at Mundy Street Boys School 1955 – 1958 had left him emotionally damaged. There were unpleasant parallels between the horrors of that, often erotic, culture of cruelty a decade before, and the lascivious regime at Palmer Heights. Unlike a majority of the Heanor juniors, Ahmed's choices were all post-pubescent – but some – only just.

And then there was that extraordinary contrast between Ahmed's dark side and the power of his genuine love for Booby. That iron hand in that velvet glove could be – oh – so – very gentle, so tender and so very sweet. Ahmed often sailed close to the wind and Simeon always feared being confronted with some situation which would morally outrage and be totally unacceptable. However, the charm would be turned on and turned up. Those big brown gorgeous eyes were hypnotic; those benign arms were merciful in their gentle embrace into that wonderful, warm upholstery of firm, butch, pectorals, and, as ever, Booby was defeated. He was lost – lost in paradise.

January 17th was Simeon's first day at Wayne State University.

"I'll walk," said Simeon, just after his wake-up cuddle. "It's only five miles down Woodward Avenue to Warren Avenue. Should do it easy inside of 90 minutes."

"The hell you will!" said Ahmed, snuggling up, still fondling one cheek of his lover's rump.

"I need the exercise. It'll do me good."

"It may kill you! *Nobody* in their right mind *walks* down Woodward. Know how many vagrants, winos, muggers or any number of scum you can meet walking around here? You need exercise? *I'll* give you exercise – work out on this."

On that first day, Ahmed himself drove his precious Booby all the way to his new school. They were met by a young, well-built Negro, who announced himself as Laurent, a member of the office staff with a special responsibility to look after the new student. He guided them through a labyrinth of corners and corridors to the office of Simeon's personal tutor / counsellor. Alfred greeted them with cordial warmth and kind assurances. Following a short interval of hand-shakes and pleasantries, Ahmed left and Laurent escorted Simeon to his first class. After an hour, Laurent was waiting at the door to take him to the next class – and so on. That same youth met the new student in the afternoon after his final class and carefully escorted him to a waiting limo. Calvin drove him home. The same watchful scenario occurred day after day: Calvin chauffeured him to the university in the morning and chauffeured him back to Palmer Heights at the end of the day. Laurent, a sexy number, very easy on the eye, met Simeon at the end of every class and always escorted him to the following class.

Being of similar age, over the next few weeks the two boys, although exchanging few words, seemed to be content with a friendly silence. Laurent's duties were mutually understood but never discussed until Thursday March 3rd. At the lunch table, Simeon was reading an item in his *US News and World Report* announcing that BBC Television would start experimental broadcasts in colour sometime in the following year. Vaguely listening to the Chiffons singing *Sweet Talking Guy* and idly playing with the few peas left on his plate, his minder, Laurent, was seized by a weak moment. He breathed out a lustful whisper, an indecent comment.

"Bet you got a sweet dick!"

Simeon looked up and into Laurent's eyes which held their gaze for a few seconds before dissolving into a lovely smile to ease the embarrassment.

"Sorry, you didn't hear that."

But Simeon *had* heard it. He had more than adequate access to oral sex from his lover and a multitude of visitors. All such guests were of the highest quality, but all were selected by Ahmed, and all were strictly white. Visits to the Windsor bath house, Vesuvio, had been strictly forbidden and were becoming a distant memory. Simeon was missing the excitement of talented chocolate. This unexpected utterance from the silent, black stud was temptation indeed. His charge nodded over to the men's room.

"Why not try a taste?"

"No man! No way! Mr Hamah! Why, he'd kill me!" The smile was wiped in an instant by genuine dread leaving Laurent quite distressed.

"Just forget it man. I can't touch you. *You* know that."

But Simeon wanted to be touched and intended to seize the moment. He pointed out that, in the university, Laurent was his only watcher and only they would know what had happened. Gradually, he yielded to Simeon's gentle reassurances, his titillating persuasion.

"... and you've put me on a horse – I need the ride."

Capitulation, when it came, was unmistakable, silent and succulent. A hard steady stare was broken when thick lips were slowly parted by an exciting, protruding tip of stealthy tongue. Five minutes later, in secure seclusion, a gasping student was standing in front of his seated guard who had withdrawn at just the wrong moment. He looked up with smiling surprise, wide black nose and black cheeks contrasting with thick white blobs which had suddenly decorated that African countenance. Simeon panted out an urgent, embarrassed, whispered apology. The response, equally urgent, equally as sincere, came back swiftly.

"No sweat, man! It's OK. Yeah, man. It's really *very* OK."

To further re-assure, Laurent stood up. Simeon fumbled for a handkerchief and gently wiped clean that handsome black face now several inches above his own. A tender embrace followed, and then, more fumbling as the spent student sat down to attended to the needs of his big horny guard.

That tender moment brought the guard and his charge closer together. They talked more. It came as a surprise to learn that Laurent the Negro admired and respected Ahmed the racist.

"He's a star! For us gay folks, well, it's like the Black Panthers for us black folks. Mr Hamah, well, he sure is tough. And, know what? He looks after us, know what a mean?"

Simeon and Laurent became closer, but not close enough to allay their mutual dread of The Firm. One day, Simeon complained about being a prisoner, albeit a prisoner in a golden cage.

"Hey man! You button up! Don't you be goin' telling me nothin' a shouldn't hear!"

This incident unsettled Simeon. It emboldened him to remonstrate with his young Lord and Master over dinner.

"Why am I watched all the time?"

"You know why! You might run away, back to England."

"Seems pointless buying me all those new clothes if I can't go anywhere. I'm missing my old friends."

"What friends?"

"I used to enjoy Howard's parties. Earl said Howard was OK. I got to know a few of the regulars. They'll be wondering what happened to me. Couldn't we go, just once in a while? You'd be there, watching. Will you take me to Grosse Pointe? Please?"

Much to Simeon's relief, Ahmed responded in his usual physical way when feeling generous. He got up, came over, kissed and embraced his lover as if a child entrusted to his care.

"Is my Booby missing his little friends? Well... I guess it can't do no harm."

This was a first. Ahmed was proud to display his Booby at Howard Mueller's regular Saturday evening chicken party just two days later. They were relaxing in a spacious, sumptuous living room with views over an immaculate lawn which swept down to the shores of Lake St Clair. This immensity of grass was framed by occasional trees and illuminated by concealed lights which penetrated the freezing winter darkness all the way to the water. It all made for a comfortable contrast between an opulent warm interior and a hostile North American expanse just beyond the huge modern floor-to-ceiling windows.

By a large fireplace of crackling logs, Ahmed chatted to Howard. They were huddled together in the manner of two old friends who had not spoken for sometime. Front of house, Marie, the elegantly dressed effeminate house boy was making himself agreeable, circulating, posing, sweet-talking, serving drinks. Out of sight, Howard's principal domestic and feared bodyguard was busy preparing 'the munchies' in her ultra modern kitchen. Simeon found the marked contrast between the morose, formidable Olga and the ever babbling Marie quite hilarious.

At this moment, more interested in the impressive stretch of landscaped garden, he chose to locate in the corner of a vast six-seater settee which was situated for the enjoyment of that very aspect. For a few minutes he had it all to himself, until a familiar blond youth abruptly dropped down at his side.

"Hi, stranger!"

"Gary! Oh, it's *so* great to see you."

Simeon had not met, Tab Hunter lookalike, Gary Mackenzie since Howard's New Year party. The first meeting with this cute 17 year old took place just over two years before. It was at a pre-Christmas gathering in the more modest home of another chicken hawk known as Finkle Joe who lived on Finkle Avenue. Initial sexual attraction soon evaporated leaving more enduring foundations for a lasting friendship. Unlike the awkward, unstable and fractious chemistry between Simeon and Ahmed, the chemistry between Simeon and Gary Mackenzie was fun, smooth and characterised by playful banter. From the very beginning they engaged in the current tittle-tattle about their fellow chickens and thoroughly enjoyed each others company. And, yes, they *had* missed each other.

"I'll bet you were wondering what had happened to me?" said Simeon.

"We all *know* what happened to you." A few seconds passed as Gary's smile faded into an expression of concern. "Do you love him?" he said softly.

"Yes... very much so. And... I'm surprised to hear myself saying that... considering.

"Considering you're a captive?"

"What do you know about this guy, Gary?" said Simeon in a whisper, and, in some agitation having just discovered that his predicament was common knowledge.

"What do we *all* know about Ahmed!" hissed Gary, barely audible. "Look back there – into the group. What do you notice?"

"Well... 20 or 30 guys. About usual."

"No, not numbers. What about the atmosphere? Is it the same?"

Simeon considered. Above the scintillating strains of *I Hear a Symphony* by The Supremes, it was a touch on the quiet side. Underneath the surface frivolity, the smiles and silly comments, he noted a change in the usual ambience. There was a hint of subtle restraint and, perhaps, a feeling of caution seemed to hang in the air.

"They're all scared of him aren't they?" whispered Simeon, acknowledging the grim reality.

"Too right." said Gary. "How the hell did you get into this shit?"

Simeon spent the following few minutes giving his street-wise friend an outline of his adventure at the Windsor bath house and the subsequent consequences – a forced change of address, the forced sale of his car for $500, the gift of $200, his new student status, the night visitors and the subtle threats from Ahmed following confessions of homesickness and his vague plans for escape into deepest, darkest Derbyshire. He also mentioned Dale, Calvin, Earl and Laurent.

Gary sank into a deep gloom and regarded his naive buddy with a dour expression. Suddenly, he seemed to make up his mind and reached for a large coffee table book. It was an expensive heavy tome consisting of glossy, garish photographs of Michigan.

"We need to talk – but we have to talk *safely*. I'll point to things in these pictures. It'll be like we're talking about all this stuff. If anybody comes near, start asking questions."

"Bad as that?" said Simeon, pointing to the Capital Building in Lansing.

"It looks OK to me, but I hear tell it's supposed to be the ugliest dome in the world!" said Gary, as a thin boy walked over to the large window. "It's life and death." answered Gary when the boy was out of earshot. "Trust *nobody*. When it comes to The Mob – trust nobody at all. Be extra careful with the chauffer, the house boy, hustlers, heavies and anyone on the payroll. Be on your guard here with *these* guys. Be very careful, because, my friend, you are cuddling up to dynamite."

"I just can't believe that Ahmed would ever... *could* ever hurt me!"

"Don't count on that, Simeon. I know one kid who crossed him: he isn't here anymore. Another one told the cops. He lost his front teeth in an accident. Three guys, friends of mine, saw what happened to a guy one night in Palmer Park..."

"Well? What *did* happen?"

"The jerk tried to mug Ahmed! Bad choice! Bad, bad choice! Know what? I'm really surprised he's gone a bundle on *you*."

"Thanks a lot."

"Well... it's like this, I've known Ahmed much longer than I've known you."

"You never mentioned him?"

"People don't. It's safer that way. Anyway, I know what he likes and he likes them young – *very* young. You passed the 'Big Two' last year and Ahmed is usually looking at 16 – or less. He likes very tender meat."

"He knows my age. If I'm too old why the hell am I banged up at Palmer Heights guarded round the clock?"

Gary looked at his friend in mild amusement.

"To start with, you could still, at a pinch, just about get away with 16 with the light behind you. The zits have gone. We used to call you the 'spotty chicken'. And... anyway, it's more complicated than that. It always is. This has never happened to Ahmed before. Not like this. I guess he's tapped into something he needed, something special.

There must be something about you that's got at him, churned him up." Gary paused and looked searchingly at his friend. "It must be your sad eyes."

They both collapsed into a fit of giggles as the heavy book fell on the floor. Simeon had not laughed like that for a long time. He retrieved the book and began to explain about the difficulty of communication with Ahmed.

"We don't find the same things funny... can't talk to each other. There are big gaps, long silences when I don't know what to say to him – and he doesn't know what to say to me. We can't really enjoy each other. The sex – oh God, yes, the sex – it's fantastic. He only has to touch me – wow! I just melt. I can cum for ever. He's magic."

"Naturally! Like I said, I know what Ahmed likes and I know what *you* like and what you like is what Ahmed excels in, is renowned for. I've heard young kids scream with pleasure. Of course the sex is great – it would be," said Gary with a smirk and a twinkle.

This last sardonic comment was a thinly veiled reference to the cultural sexual differences between Britain and the United States in the mid-20th century. During his Derbyshire cycling holiday the previous year, Simeon set out to discover an English gay scene he had never known. By American standards, he found it very primitive. Homosexuals referred to each other as 'queer' and a frequent question was – 'Are you butch or bitch?' In Detroit 'butch' simply described a guy who behaved in a manly way as opposed to being effeminate. In Derby and Nottingham, 'butch' informed that you 'gave it' as opposed to being passive in anal sex. Simeon found both possibilities appalling and was quickly labelled as a useless case of bad acne. Hearing a full account of all this sent Gary into fits of hysterical laughter. He took malicious pleasure in the fact that his English buddy was just as sexually useless in his homeland as was Gary on *his* own patch. It also fuelled in him a strong desire to escape the US oral culture and visit the United Kingdom in order to take full advantage of that same rampant anal culture. This handsome blond had suffered too many humiliating comments along the lines of – 'Gary Mackenzie! Forget it, he hits the *dirt* road.' Up to the previous Christmas, both friends had been planning an English cycling vacation for 1966. Gary was still speaking –

"Everybody knows it, Ahmed is the best. He's the Prince of Detroit, the Prince of Pleasure." Gary leaned closer to Simeon's ear. "All right, so this jam don't look too good. On the other hand, I'll bet ya half the kids in this room would be glad to change places with you."

"But the danger! A golden cage is still a cage."

"Danger? Sure, don't you ever forget it, but, that Arab is one ravishing hunk. Oh – yes – please – ass to drive ya crazy, hung like a stud..."

"How do *you* know that?" cried Simeon feeling a twinge of jealousy.

"We *all* know that! I told you, that beautiful guy is legendary! He's had everybody worth having – and now he's having you. Don't get too depressed about it. Hey, listen up. One horny afternoon in 1961, Ahmed Hamah walked into the locker room of Lincoln Gardens High School, looked around and took his pick. He picked me!! He dragged me into the janitors office and gave me a rim and blow job which blew my mind with a first ever orgasm and *whacked* me right into seventh heaven. I was doing cartwheels and summersaults all the way home.

"You must be joking!"

"I kid you not. OK, later I discovered that the janitor had me sussed out and was probably paid off. He figured I wouldn't struggle too hard – and I didn't. He gambled that I wouldn't blab. I didn't. I wanted more! It was the 9th Grade and I was 13 years old. Ahmed, already a gorgeous hunk at 16, was a well-known hood in gay Detroit but unknown in the straight suburbs. He still takes what he wants, always has done. Still want to escape?" concluded Gary with an ironic smile.

"Escape to where?" demanded Ahmed, in deep menacing tones looming over them.

CHAPTER 12

Chains of Enchantment

"Hi, Ahmed! How ya doin'?" asked Gary jumping up, standing to attention to show deference for a senior officer of The Firm. "It's been too long, we never see you here," he added, expressing sincere disappointment with all the skill and control of a consummate actor. It was a very convincing performance. Inside, Gary was panic stricken.

"Well, you know me, Gary. I like my chicken fresh, natural, unpolluted by the artificial affectation of 'the scene' – and Howard's soirees, nice as they may be for you, are certainly a part of that sickening 'scene'. Too many nancys in this place. Glad to see that my Booby's had the good sense to keep away from them." Again, Simeon was impressed with his lover's mastery of words, his lucid command of vocabulary.

"Booby?" asked Gary, puzzled.

"Yeah, right there, *my* boy, the guy you've been monopolising for the last half hour."

"Hey, Ahmed! Come on now! Get real. Next to you? What kind of competition am I? I've known Simeon a long time and…"

"Escape to where, Gary?"

"Escape? Oh that." He picked up the big book which was open at Mackinac Bridge and Mackinac Island. "My English buddy here hasn't really seen very much of America and nothing of northern Michigan. I was suggesting an escape into the past. Automobiles are banned on Mackinac Island. It's all bicycles, horse and buggy. You should take him out more. Show him the Porcupine Mountains; he'd love that. It would stop him forever winging about Derbyshire. All I ever hear is nostalgia about Derbyshire's hills and dales. What do you say?"

The good looking blond stepped back anxiously as Ahmed suddenly raised his hand up to Gary's face, but only touched his nose with the tip of a finger.

"I never could resist that turned-up nose." murmured Ahmed. "You're making me wet already. It *has* been too long." He addressed his lover, "Olga's been asking about you, Booby. Go into the kitchen and talk to her." He cupped Gary's backside and gently pushed him into the direction of the nearest bedroom.

Obediently, and with some relief, Simeon went in search of Olga. Truth to tell, the ritual chat with this unusual woman was always the best part of a 'Howard evening'. Considering all the baggage – Simeon's negative experiences with the opposite sex, ongoing hostility from his mother and sisters – he seemed to communicate quite well with Olga. She came across as somewhat sad, unfulfilled behind the up-beat cheery façade.

"Howya doin', Kiddo? How's married life treating you?"

Simeon steeled himself. Olga was different, a big strapping fearless woman who spoke her mind. He decided to break the rules and ask her blunt questions.

"It scares me, Olga. That's how it treats me." She stopped her culinary activities, put down a utensil and gave him a stern look. "I'm in trouble, Olga. I need help. Is Howard part of The Firm?"

"Howard? Nah! He's just a side show. These kids are no good to The Firm. Most of them are too camp, too socialised into 'the scene'. Ahmed gets the quality, the 'Real Thing'. The Firm needs 'em rough, natural. That's where the money is, Kiddo. Get real!"

"Is that what Ahmed does? Is that his job – procuring boys?"

"Who the hell knows for sure what Ahmed does – but – yeah, I guess that's part of it."

"What's the other part?"

"Ahmed has to do what all run-of-the-mill mobsters do. He's tough. He's a 'hard man', enforces discipline, punishment beatings when necessary and... Hey kid! What gives?"

Simeon, quite pale, was swaying on his feet, visibly distressed. This was the confirmation he had dreaded. Concerned and solicitous, she gently guided him into an adjoining room. This was a privilege; entry into Olga's inner-sanctum was granted to just a few favoured visitors in special circumstances such as this one. It was a comforting space of two easy chairs, an office / work area and home to her dog, a pure white Spitz called Angel who was occasionally fussed and cuddled by the boys at Howard's open nights.

"Hey, girl; put down ya toys. Look whose come to see you! Don't you remember Simeon?"

They sat down. For a few moments they were silent whilst the guest soothed himself by burying his hands into an impressive dense, beautiful coat. Angel responded with unconditional affection which is characteristic of all dogs. At last, when Olga spoke, her voice held a tenderness he had never heard before.

"Listen, Simeon if you want out, you'll have to plan it *real* careful. You must do it the *right* way."

"How? Go to the police?"

"Police!! You have to be joking! The cop you talk to – he may be on the take! On the Mafioso payroll. If you are ever branded as a traitor, you might just as well bolt to the top of the Penobscot Building and make like a bird in the sky. It will be quicker and less painful."

Simeon was reminded that Olga herself was sometimes referred to as 'Momma Mafia'.

"I don't know *how* you'll get free. It has to be possible. I'll think about it." She looked at Simeon. "I hear tell that you really love this guy?"

"Chains of enchantment, I suppose. I'm under his spell," uttered Simeon with an edge of contempt.

"For what it's worth, from a bull dyke, I think Ahmed is one of the better class heavies. He's intelligent. He talks smart. He *is* smart. Did you ever ask yourself why Negroes have done good and we haven't? It's because we're seen as sissies – soft targets.

The Firm has proved that is *not* the case. Stick with us, Kiddo. We're changing the world!"

Briefly, Olga paused to check the effect on her listener. At this point she was wearing two hats. Employed by Howard Mueller, this bodyguard had a responsibility to The Firm, to keep the wheels well oiled. At the same time, she had a modicum of motherly compassion for the distressed youth before her.

"It can't be *all* that bad Kiddo? You're well fed! You're cosseted, chauffeured around in a fancy car and milked like a cow according to the gossip! I'll tell ya – most guys here tonight – oh boy – they'd sure like to be on tap for Ahmed Hamah's daily vitamin count."

Simeon responded with a feeble smile.

"What is he *really* like, Olga?"

"Ahmed?" She considered. "Well, I guess he's a charmer. I think he's OK. Even a criminal has principles. He won't touch drugs or cigarettes and drinks hardly at all. Sure, he has had his infatuations – but *you* are different, Kiddo. He likes you. He likes you a whole lot and he intends to keep you. That's what makes 'escape' so difficult. Ahmed keeps a tight grip on his chattels.

"And another thing: have you considered the danger of Ahmed getting badly injured or even killed? In our world, life is cheap. It can be all too short and that spells big danger to *you*, Kiddo. Right now you have cast iron protection. You're Ahmed's boy. You are number one in the harem. You're untouchable. No member of the gang would be so stupid as to harm one hair of your pretty head. Believe me, Ahmed has a fearsome reputation. We *all* know that. So what happens if that protection disappears? Well, Kiddo, I can tell you straight, some folks are envious of you, especially some of the thugs in this outfit. Words of wisdom, Simeon! Take it from an experienced bull dyke."

Simeon was shocked. He was also slightly shocked when Olga referred to herself as a 'bull dyke'. Apart from the occasional reference to Momma Mafia, she was always Olga, never a dyke or even a lesbian. Nobody would dare. But this was one lesbian Simeon had always liked, indeed, the only lesbian he had ever really known. There seemed to be a parallel between gay Negroes and gay women. It was the same ongoing social apartheid Simeon had observed – an injustice within the homosexual minority which was already under siege from a disapproving heterosexual majority. He considered it sad. The boys and girls shared the same problems, had so much in common, yet, there persisted an unspoken indifference, lack of interest and lack of effort. He took the view that all gay people were diminished and socially impoverished by such discrimination and prejudice.

Olga encouraged Simeon to talk through his fears and anxieties.

"It was when you said 'punishment beatings'. That got to me. I shouldn't be surprised. I knew. His work hours! The phone rings and he goes out at anytime of day or night. He may be gone for anything from an hour to 24 hours. You never know, he doesn't say. I guess *he* doesn't know. If he *has* hurt somebody, he comes back to me, declares undying love... and is just the sweetest, most gentle guy in the world."

"And he really is, all the world to you, isn't he?" she said with feeling.

"Right, Olga. I'm demented over this beautiful boy, absolutely smitten. He comes home, grabs me, holds me close and I want that incredible moment to last forever. When he's nasty to me, I plan a break-out, an escape back to England. Right now he's probably screwing Gary. That's not too bad, I can cope with it, but, in truth, I *am* jealous..."

"And if *you* went off with another guy, and closed the bed room door on *Ahmed*... Oh boy! BIG SPARKS would fly – right?"

"Right. But that's not the worst of it. We... we don't seem to like the same things. How can I put it? You remember last Fall. I told you and Marie all about my cycling vacation in England. You seemed interested?"

"Interested! We were both *fascinated*. You'd stumbled on an alien world back in the Old Country. It couldn't have been more different from Detroit. Like a fairy story – a *freak show* for Christ sakes! What was it – goblins, gnomes, old hags, crones, toads inhabiting caves, ravines, public latrines in old Victorian back alleys... Are you telling me that Ahmed wasn't interested in your exciting adventures last summer?"

"He wouldn't even listen! Hated the sound of it all. Just called them all creeps, deformities, monsters. I tried to explain. Of *course* they are all those things. That wasn't the point. Just being gay, being hated, being afraid, isolated, hiding from the mainstream – that is precisely what warped these odd bods. They *mutated* into a thing like 'the Belper Goblin' or Guzzly Granddad or Toby Jug. He didn't want to know. Told me to change the subject."

"Ahmed surrounds himself with beauty. I guess he has a horror of gay grotesques," said Olga, thoughtfully. "He dreads getting old, like so many young gay guys. Marie's the same, takes hours and hours with his creams, lotions and cosmetics."

"Marie wears make-up!"

"Oh sure! You can hardly tell. It's applied with great skill, turns the clock back. Do you know, Simeon, years ago when I was 19, Marie was 23. But when I turned 30 Marie was *still* 27! Why yes, he actually overtook me. Even more miraculous, I'm 42 and Marie has yet to hit 30! Talk about slowing the clock! That painted queen is something else!"

"You don't look 42," said Simeon, kindly, if mendaciously, avoiding eye contact as he caressed and straightened out Angel's impressive, pure white curled tail.

"Born in 1924 on the same day as Lauren Bacall."

"But... hang on... I always thought that Marie was 20 something. Are you telling me that Marie is *40* something! It's unbelievable!"

"Believe it. Marie tells the chickens he's a war baby. Quite true, but he don't say *which* war. It's the *First* World War – not the Second. Good to see you laughing again, Kiddo.

"Cooee in there! Yoo-hoo! Sexy sweet Simeon! Here comes my body!" The subject of the discussion suddenly sailed through the kitchen and came to rest in the inner-sanctum. After a quick stoop and affectionate acknowledgement of Angel's luxurious white tail, Marie rushed into a mock remonstration.

"Bitch! For the last five years, I've been flashing my big beautiful eyes at Ahmed the he-man – with what result? Zilch, honey, zilch! *You* come along and clean up! Bitch!"

"Sorry, Marie."

"That's OK, honey. I guess I never really was his type," replied Marie with sudden saccharine. He broke into a mischievous big smile, toyed with the buttons of Simeon's shirt and allowed his forefinger to slip inside touching the bare flesh within. "Mmmm, so nice; real nice."

"Get real, Sugar," Olga's pet name for Marie. "Of the fruit of *this* tree, thou shalt *not* eat! Unless, of course, you want to risk any sudden, drastic facial re-organisation."

And the sardonic banter continued between this unusual couple, much as it had done over the many years they had known each other. Simeon was fascinated by this entertaining exchange, this bizarre fluidity of gender between an effeminate queen and a masculine woman. They had been in the service of Howard Mueller for more than two decades sharing responsibilities and work load. The conversation meandered around several subjects including a small dispute over domestic duties.

"Well *I* did the two hours of pen pushing! And it was *your* turn to clean the office." argued Marie.

"That's hardly the point! You knew this place would be filled with kids tonight. You should have locked it up. You should check and lock all the 'no go' rooms. Don't always leave everything to me." replied Olga. She explained the problem to Simeon. "Howard keeps *far* too much cash in this house."

"Cash necessary for services rendered," added Marie, in sweet, snide tones for Simeon's benefit.

"Point being," carried on Olga, "that one of these days one of those chickens is going to wander into that office and help himself in a *big* way."

"I take it that you are Howard's personal private secretary, Marie?" asked Simeon.

"We both are," said Olga. "We take turns at being chauffer, chef, butler, housekeeper, cleaner... I guess I tend to do more of the heavy stuff."

"Looks like you're required for heavy stuff right now!" said Marie as an angry Howard marched into the room.

"Get rid of that acid tongued red head. I want him out *now!*" snapped Howard, to Olga. He turned to address Simeon. "And you'd better get back in there, young man. Ahmed is looking for you."

As Howard stormed out, Olga gave Simeon a parting hug.

"Hang in there, Kiddo. We may not see each other for a while, but, well, we'll sure keep in touch. Looks like somebody has upset the boss. I'll have to take care of it."

CHAPTER 13

Plan of Escape

"That Gary Mackenzie! Boy! He is sure one wild kid in bed," boasted Ahmed to Simeon sitting in the limo on the return trip home. "I got him hollerin' an wailin' like an alley cat. You should have seen…"

"Don't. Please don't," pleaded Simeon, somewhat distressed.

"Hey, baby! Lighten up. Mackenzie's a slut. He was beggin' for it. You know I would never hurt *you* like that. Come on now." He drew his lover close and planted several gentle kisses on his face. "Did I ever try that back alley stuff with you? Did I? Did I? Anyway, I'm empty. So what!" More kisses and now gropes together with a impish conspiratorial whisper, playful, childlike… "Bet ya if Ahmed looks around here he'll find something *really* nice. Bet ya Ahmed can find a mischievous Little Booby who is *not* empty, a Little Booby who likes to hide in Ahmed's nice warm mouth…"

It became clear that Gary's suggestion of travel had taken root. Ahmed said a vacation was a good idea. It would be romantic, do them both good and take Booby's mind off England. There was just one small point; if a student was doing well at university, his studies should not be interrupted. Accordingly, Simeon would have to wait until the end of the Winter Semester on April 22nd when he would have a clear week free before the start of the Spring Semester on May 2nd. On this issue, Ahmed was adamant. Like a strict Victorian father, albeit this dad was just one year older than his son, he took his responsibilities seriously and pointed out that Booby's education had been carefully planned and was expensive. It was not just the cost of tuition, but also the full time cost of Alfred, the private tutor / counsellor, Laurent the guard and Calvin the chauffer. Simeon resisted the temptation to pass comment about 'paying the gaoler'. Ahmed was delighted with the steady flow of excellent reports from Alfred who liaised with Booby's professors and, like a good parent, Ahmed questioned the student about his day at school and encouraged him to express opinions.

When there was something to talk about, Ahmed and Simeon talked freely and plenty. The latter enjoyed his studies and was stimulated by the interest of his intelligent, well read lover. As with sex, this aspect of the relationship was a success. Indeed, this unequal partnership appeared to be sound at all times when Ahmed was in a good mood, which was probably more than half of the time. The other half could be divided into two quarters –

neutral mood and bad mood. Simeon was not allowed any moods at all. He learned to be in good humour, responding appropriately to the current temper of his Lord and Master. If he was not actually mad, because love *is* a form of madness, this state of affairs might be more tolerable. Occasionally, Booby would misjudge the disposition and receive a sudden and painful whack. Once, during a quiet and tender moment, he put his face very close to Ahmed's face inviting a kiss. Sadistically, that handsome face abruptly turned away. Another time he tried to display affection by returning a little of Ahmed's 'baby talk' which he found so comforting and erotically arousing. Very rarely did Ahmed address Simeon by actually calling him 'Simeon'. He was utterly stunned by the cruel response.

"What the hell is *that* supposed to mean? When are you going to grow up, Simeon?"

And then there were flash points which could trigger a mood. References to England were reasonably safe, but references to Derbyshire which could invoke the ugly spectre of homesickness, were not safe at all. At an early stage, Simeon learned to avoid a certain type of impersonation. Ahmed was not overly fond of Booby's frequent funny 'voices' which were an artistic expression of his sense of humour. Marie had been bitching about one of Howard's friends who, like Marie, had been making a cosmetic effort to 'turn back the clock'. Thinking it highly amusing, Simeon gave a performance of Marie's nasty comment.

"Who does that old fossil think he's fooling? That pathetic queen with the *rug* on his head! He should watch out. I like to pull *hair* when I'm excited."

Simeon found Marie hilarious and thought his little show quite clever: clever, that is, until he saw Ahmed's grim and menacing scowl which caused the blood to drain from his own face. The reaction was violent. An indignant Arab grabbed Simeon's shoulders and shook him. The reprimand was reinforced by a shaking forefinger in his face.

"Don't *do* that! Don't you *ever* do that again! What are you – a boy or a screaming faggot?"

With a supreme effort to overcome fear, gently, Simeon moved the finger which was inches from his moist eyes. He struggled to find a small, shaky voice in his dry throat.

"What are *you*, Ahmed?"

"What am I? I am *not* a homosexual. I am *not* a fairy and neither are you. You are a *real* boy. You walk like a real boy and you will *never, ever* behave like that again. You are *my* boy. You have a responsibility to live up to *my* standards, *my* image." The jabbing finger returned to emphasise the next line which held a tacit threat. "Do you understand me, Simeon?"

"I understand. It won't happen again."

Ahmed accepted this defeated response as a meek apology, a capitulation to a greater power. It meant something quite different to Simeon. He took the view that he could never really be himself with this tough guy who had a different sense of humour. Perhaps the tough guy had brutally trampled over his lover's feelings... just once too often. Simeon recalled the boys in London who spoke of Ronnie Kray. He wooed his carefully selected pretty boys with 'long lashes and a melting look around the eyes' – but they all had to be butch. With cockney contempt, Kray insisted –

"I'm a homosexual, not a pansy, not a poof."

After the wounding Marie incident, some of the hope was gone. A part of Booby died.

Throughout March and into April, the captive was permitted to attend several of Howard's Saturday evening chicken parties. Some were with Ahmed. Some were in his absence when the eagle-eyed Calvin stood in as chaperone to ensure that Booby adhered to his Boss's rules. These social gatherings were Simeon's only social outlet. He was not allowed to mingle with fellow students and forbidden to enter any gay bars. As a non-drinker, this was not a problem. He *did* miss the Windsor Bath House, and the hunky, horny Negroes within. Laurent, however, from time to time, took some of the edge of that particular longing.

After the initial gift of $200, Simeon received no money; neither did he ask for any. Everything was provided. And, after all, he did have a total of $727.62 which came from the original $200 gift, the $500 from his compulsory car purchase and the $27.62 which was already in his wallet on January 8th, the night of his abduction.

Money acquired a new significance during a serious, secretive conversation at Grosse Pointe. On that occasion, the pampered prisoner opened his heart to Gary Mackenzie. Simeon could cope with the near future, but he was developing a dread of the middle future – the summer followed by the Fall. The middle future would be more tolerable if there was, in place, a plan of escape back to the United Kingdom. He confessed the turmoil of his mixed feelings to Gary. He admitted that he was imprisoned in his golden cage by restraints which were not just physical in the form of Laurent and Calvin, but also emotional restraints constructed by Ahmed himself. Ahmed had once said – 'I can get inside you' – and Ahmed *was* inside of Simeon. Simeon was bewitched by this magnificent, beautiful, mesmerising Arab in much the same way that a cobra has a hypnotic effect on his victim. Little Booby became ecstatic inside that succulent mouth and there were moments when *big* Booby wanted to be consumed in the same way. Such a ravishing hunk: his smile, his deep voice, the fragrance of his masculine body and just one touch from that sensitive pleasure-giving hand was enough to turn the rational Simeon into a defeated, enchanted Booby. There were times when he never wanted to be apart from Ahmed and times when he was seriously afraid for his very life. Indeed, his life *had* been threatened on three occasions and his moral fibre was under constant threat from the dark unknown of some sort of underground, underage sex trade.

Simeon explained to Gary that he had worked out a plan for a sudden get away. As a form of insurance, he needed to take his street-wise friend into his confidence. Gary may see flaws in this design which were invisible to an English boy of limited experience with the Detroit underworld. It was like Oliver Twist consulting the Dodger. Mackenzie had not been known long. He was three years younger than Simeon and, on a few occasions, his integrity had been found wanting. This risk, however, had to be taken.

     The scheme was revealed. Simeon would use a time when Ahmed was absent all night – usually about once a week. He would pack a suitcase. He'd tell Calvin that the suitcase contained materials for a class presentation. A few minutes after Laurent had escorted him to his first morning lecture; he would exit the building, grab a taxi to Detroit Metropolitan Airport and buy a ticket for London via New York. As there were frequent flights each day, he would be hundreds of miles away by the time that Laurent could give the alarm. After buying his air ticket, he would land in London with about £200. This was more than enough to get to, and disappear into the North Derbyshire wilderness for several months. No element of the American Mafia could possibly find or touch him.

"What do you think?"

Gary was thoughtful, silent for a few moments before he gave his tactful reply.

"It's OK, until you get to the airport."

"Why?"

"That's where they'll be waiting for you." He made a cut-throat gesture with his forefinger. Gary leaned closer. "Listen, friend, first thing – you have to really *want* to escape. I predict that you will – eventually – but, only after something nasty has happened which will really shake you up. I know you! You'll be real upset and ready to go. When you *are* ready, when you've *really* made up your mind, call me at home the morning before from a university call box. Mom will answer and take a message if I'm not there. Even if you are speaking to me direct, you will say exactly the same thing – 'Tell Gary, Ahmed said that's just fine. He'll know what it's all about.' Remember those words."

"Tell Gary, Ahmed said that's just fine. He'll know what it's all about." repeated Simeon, slowly and carefully.

"Good. The next day, we use your plan right up to when you're standing outside the Main Office hoping to find a taxi. A taxi *will* be there – with me in the back seat *not* bound for the main airport. As for the rest, well, you'll just have to trust me. And another thing – you'll need a whole lot more than $700. You can leave that to me."

"You have money!"

"I'm one hell of a good stud! And a busy hustler! Sure I have bread. Didn't you know how good I was?"

Simeon did not know. He knew that Gary hustled from time to time, but was slightly shocked to learn that he had been exploiting his personality, his skill and drive so efficiently as to make prostitution pay, and pay well enough to accumulate capital. Years later Simeon recalled that significant conversation and appreciated how he, Gary and other friends enjoyed one of the benefits of the gay world. The 17 year old Gary Mackenzie had, effectively, been matured by his social and business associations with older, educated homosexuals. The relaxed, after-sex chats with his clients were civilising and instructive. As with so many young gay men who were instinctively isolated from the heterosexual majority, Gary had nothing in common with his ignorant boorish brothers and, like Simeon, he was a disappointment to his 'beer and hamburger', baseball-mad, homophobic father.

After Gary's assurances and with 'the plan' firmly in his armoury, Simeon was able to face the middle future with more confidence.

CHAPTER 14

Naughty Boys up a Tree

On the Tuesday evening of March 15th, Calvin chauffeured Ahmed and Simeon over to Taylor in the suburbs to visit Mr and Mrs Hogg. Ahmed conducted himself as a perfect gentleman. Although he was formal and very correct he was also friendly, ultra respectful and demanded that Simeon should honour his parents with a similar show of equal veneration. Ahmed did not approve of Simeon's cool, indifferent attitude to his mother and father. He had no knowledge of his lover's traumatic and damaging experiences at Mundy Street Boys School ten years before which had influenced that negative attitude. Ingrained in that culture of cruelty was a cardinal rule that the victim, especially 'the Hogg', must never 'tell tales', never complain about any class mates. To 'tell' a master would give licence to vicious bullies to bring down upon 'the grassing Hogg,' further unbearable hazing humiliations. Not wishing to appear a soft target, it would be another 40 years before Simeon revealed the full truth of Mundy Street Church of England Boys School.

The visit was prompted by Ahmed's sense of duty, his curiosity and desire to meet the Hoggs. It was also prompted by Simeon's desire to retrieve, to once again hear and enjoy his gramophone records, a treasured collection of 45s dating from 1958. Ahmed, a lover of classical music, had purchased a good quality phonograph for Booby's exclusive use. That such 45s be played upon Ahmed's cherished $2000 High Fidelity equipment, with its two enormous Gothic speakers resembling cathedral towers, was simply not open for discussion.

This meeting was not a success. It was the first time Mum and Dad had seen or heard of their son in more than two months, yet there was no warmth or pleasure to be observed in this reunion. For all Ahmed's courtesy, his valiant efforts with pleasantries and small talk; the Hoggs were awkward, taciturn and deeply uncomfortable with the unspoken spectre of homosexuality hanging in the air. Ahmed the Arab, in the flesh, was alien and unwelcome. He represented confirmation of their worst fears of the son who had brought shame upon the family. Making conversation with these uneducated homophobes was hard going, like swimming in molasses. There came a point when Ahmed gave up. He rose and Simeon rose. Mr and Mrs Hogg remained seated. There was not much to be thanked for, however, very politely; the Hoggs *were* thanked for receiving their guests into their home.

Nevertheless, time was pressing and other matters needed attention. Simeon picked up the suitcase full of his records and they showed themselves out of the house. At the end of the drive, Calvin, reading a book, was surprised to see them so soon. He jumped out and opened the door. Just before entering, Ahmed looked back at the house and noted that the couple were not at the door to give a wave of farewell.

The two lovers sat in silence, Simeon resigned to what had always been normal and Ahmed thoughtful and slightly disturbed. Minutes later the limo was speeding along the I 94 Freeway towards Detroit. Simeon broke the silence to explain that, in Derbyshire working class culture, it was not the custom to rise when visitors are taking their leave, or, to escort those visitors to the door and wave them goodbye. Ahmed slid over, cuddled his boy with quiet tenderness and, once again, his boy felt that warm reassuring love within those strong arms from the only human being who had ever really loved him. He felt safe. To obtain more safety and more love, he snuggled further inside Ahmed's light jacket and, as ever, unconsciously conditioned himself to a familiar body scent and a familiar heart-beat. Several peaceful minutes passed until, this time, Ahmed broke the silence.
    "Know, Booby," he said, in a gentle meditative tone, "I wanted it to go so well with your folks." Awkwardly, like a young adolescent, he looked down to their two hands which were still embraced within a loving clasp. "Kind of... well, like I wanted to do the *right* thing."
    "I know," whispered Simeon.
    "I guess... I wanted them to know that we had the *real* thing. Cus, I guess, that's what we got."
    "I know," whispered Simeon, as he snuggled in some more.

The next day Ahmed took Simeon to visit *his* family. The experience was quite different. As with all other venues, Ahmed was received with great respect. He was treated like a prince. They were proud of Ahmed. Simeon looked at the smiling friendly faces and tried to see behind the smiles. Did they know what he did for a living? If, deep down, common sense confronted them with the inescapable reality that no young man of 21 could possibly command an income which supported the opulent lifestyle of a film star; *if* this was indeed the case, then the collective Hamah self-deception was well established at an advanced level.
    At one point, Simeon was able to chat to Ahmed's sister and make an occasional reference to her brother's good job, ritzy apartment and millionaire status. She was candid and sincere. She responded with enthusiasm about his meteoric success, his great kindness, his generosity to the family. She commended his knowledge on world affairs and spoke of his immense value to The Firm and a handsome salary which, in her view, manifestly reflected that value. Significantly, she added that Simeon's 'friendship' had been a source of strength to her brother and that 'all of us are so very pleased that you are both so very happy together.' He found this element of the self-deception very touching and reassuring after a lifetime of blatant hostility from Derbyshire working class culture. Clearly, here was a major contrast to his own background. The Hamahs were middle class. They were an intelligent and reasonably well educated family. He looked into the clear brown eyes of this sister who seemed to have found an inner peace. It was a serenity Simeon was unable to find.

Howard's party had somehow influenced Ahmed into trusting Simeon – giving him a little more freedom – just a little. April saw the arrival of a few warm weekends. Occasionally, when he was not required by The Firm, Ahmed took his Booby out to Belle Isle where they hired bicycles and explored the meandering bridle paths of that wooded island in the Detroit River. It was romantic, especially in the quiet glades where, so near to Downtown Detroit, it was possible to feel remote, private and very boyish.

They dismounted, explored a beach which ended in a playful race where the dominant boy outran and caught the weaker. His prey was quickly brought down and pinned down on the sand in delicious submission. Simeon was ready to accept a punishment of sensuous tickles and naughty gropes. Eventually, this frisky conduct subsided, melted into tenderness, into many gentle kisses at a point when the victim gave up his struggle, lay still, was totally beaten. He became totally compliant, yielding up his body to the required pleasures of a beast in heat.

Back to the bicycles, they remounted and set out seeking further adventures which included a stand of tall trees. Simeon was starry-eyed watching his hero show off well-toned muscles. Ahmed used his favourite boyhood tree as a gym, energetically leaping around the branches until, triumphantly; he reached the very top and demanded that Booby join him. This large beech was not so very different from the Derbyshire trees he had previously scaled. Albeit with less speed, strength and agility; Simeon eventually ascended, somewhat out of breath, to join his vigorous and erotically charged lover. In nostalgic reflection, Ahmed boasted of numerous boyhood conquests and described how desirable youths had been deflowered on that very same bough. To demonstrate, he suddenly became hard, he became stern and rough. The hunter seized and uncovered his prey who – in that precarious situation 140 foot off the ground – was in no position to argue or resist. Using convenient branches, the quarry was rudely positioned for an oral attack between the buttocks which afforded a few minutes of pure ecstasy. Never was a naughty tongue so titillating or fingers so clever, so fondling: until, eventually, one panting Booby hung limp, satiated, after the desired result had been achieved.

And then there followed one of those many quiet moments, golden moments which, in retrospect, would be cherished in later years. Only for a short time, yet it was so wonderful, so very precious. Simeon could look back on his great love and savour these fleeting minutes when the relationship *did* work and *did* prosper. Here was the creation of one such memory. Ahmed's eyes mellowed to a half smile; divine, deep brown pools of pure love communicating an unspoken promise for a life-time of conscientious care and unstinting protection in a harsh urban environment. During that moment, Simeon also became aware of Ahmed's sexual generosity, his frequent willingness to give pleasure and not require reciprocation. Success, and, in this case, the novelty of venue was its own reward. High up in that beech tree, a dominant primate was wearing an exultant expression, an equivalent of beating his chest. He had captured, conquered and drained a lesser primate of the booby variety.

Minutes passed. Further into that quiet moment of quality silence, still up in that tree, Ahmed leaned over and whispered into the ear of his lover –

"License my roving hands, and let them go,
Behind, before, above, between, below.
O my America, my new found land."

Simeon received these rather obtuse, erotic words in puzzled silence. He assumed it was a quotation and waited for Ahmed to elucidate.

"Like that, Booby? Like poetry?"

"Is that what it was? Oh! Well... I've never really understood poems; they don't seem to touch me. Did *you* write it?"

Ahmed threw back his head and let rip a loud guffaw. He seized the weaker boy, still precariously balanced, and forcefully inflicted kisses, interspersed with insults.

"Oh my sweet, stupid, ignorant Booby! You need your college education real bad. Those words are 400 years old! It's the timeless work of an eminent English poet – *my* poet. Hey, listen up – poems are profound – they live forever. What can I tell you? Hear this – some king in India had a lover. She died. He was grief stricken. He built a mausoleum to honour her memory. You *have* heard of the Taj Mahal?"

"Of course I have! It's beautiful."

"Sure, but it won't last," continued Ahmed. "The elements will get to it – eventually. It *will* crumble. That king would have been better to have commissioned a good poem which would last forever.

"Hear this, Booby – my poet... correction, *our* poet – was writing about *us*. In just a few words he summed up our love, our pain, our pleasure and all our contradictions. Can't you understand that?"

Ahmed clutched his lover closer, forcing Simeon's head into firm chest muscles – a place where that head was happy to be. Breathing in body scent, listening to a heartbeat and viewing a mass of young, green foliage which had just brightened due to a sudden sunburst; he soaked up more of the secret world of poetry. And those sexy deep throated words of the lusty Arab were now being spoken, more softly, delivered with gentleness and understanding.

"Pretty boy, I know it's tough. But we *have* to keep working at it. Don't ever give up on us, Booby. I won't. This Englishman now, this poet – hear him. He's telling us that love is the *Big Chaos!* A mental hiccup. Love *is* chaos – OK? It has the potential to disrupt *all* our lives. It's the chaos unleashed upon the one we love. It has fall-out for all the people around us."

Ahmed shuffled to change his position on that bough and guided his lover to face him. Balancing, with sincere earnest expression, he faced Simeon, cupped his face with warm hands and continued in tender mode –

"Listen, Booby – that chaos, we call love, the *big* chaos – it's magic! It's worth the risk. It's an enterprise worth embarking on. We can die by it, if not live by love. And if unfit for tombs and hearse, our legend be, it will be fit for verse."

Again Simeon was puzzled. He followed Ahmed's words, gleaning some small meaning, but doubted that the last were his own. Also, those last words were frightening. '*We can die by it, if not live by love.*' What did Ahmed mean by that? Simeon felt threatened.

Years later in the next century, Old Simeon recalled that extraordinary conversation which took place somewhere inside the mass of foliage of that great beech tree somewhere in Belle Isle. He reflected on the effects of a mixture of the Big Chaos with the insidious homophobia which had blighted his life. Take Big Chaos, add gay hating parents, gay hating sisters and terrorism at a brutal junior school – result; the victim sustains permanent damage. Those miserable injuries cause their target to limp through life, hiding his true face, hoping to be invisible. The wounds fester into a terrible rage which eats away at the body. It's one of many bodies trying to survive in a dysfunctional, closeted homosexual society which, under pressure, often turns on itself and attacks its own kind.

For the most part, the onset of spring had tended to sweeten Ahmed's moody nature. Accordingly, at breakfast on the last day of the Spring Semester, Friday, April 22nd, Simeon plucked up the courage to ask about his promised vacation.

"Well, here we are. I have nine days off school. Are we having that holiday you promised? Will you be able to get the time off?"

"Will *you* be able to get the time off? Alfred is going to get me your exam results on Monday. If they're OK – sure, we'll go some place nice. Are you confident of good results?"

"I think so."

"Anyway, best suit tonight, Booby. We're going to an important party. I'll be able to introduce you to my colleagues."

"Colleagues!"

"Colleagues." Ahmed sat back in his chair, with a neutral expression, observing the effect on his very curious lover.

Simeon was chauffeured to this gathering with an entourage of pre-conceived ideas of bad guys, 'blood and greed' moral codes, all absorbed from several classic film noir gangster movies he had seen years before. An older Simeon would have expected real life to be rather different, which, of course, it was.

It was a party of suits held in a luxury suite at Detroit's principal hotel, the Sheraton Cadillac on Washington Boulevard, the City's answer to Fifth Avenue. There were about two dozen dark, smart suits. Ahmed was the youngest and one guy was well into his fifties. Simeon assessed the others in their 20s and 30s with two who might be in their early 40s. Taking care not to be observed, he studied this assembly. From their body language and faces, he tried to gauge a possible level of wickedness. Some seemed to have cruel eyes, some had a powerful build and at least one *did* fit the Lee Van Cleef model; a wicked type dreaded by the English boy who had always been far too sensitive for his own good. Others were just chatting, smiling and could have blended into any gathering of legitimate businessmen. There was absolutely nothing about these macho guys to suggest that this mysterious organization catered for gay men. With the occasional nocturnal appearance of a desirable youth in the mighty, marital bed, Simeon had overwhelming evidence that homosexual prostitution was certainly a part of this illicit corporation. But what of other criminal sins associated with gangsters – narcotics, gambling, protection rackets and orgies of blood? He simply did not know and nobody was willing to tell him.

"Hi, Simeon. Has he abandoned you already?" said one of the 40 somethings. It was Earl Kureth, PA to his lover.

"Sorry, Earl. I didn't recognise you."

"Let me introduce you to Barney."

As his name suggested, Barney, a slightly stocky muscular type, had the friendly soft round features of a St Bernard dog. He was the other 40 something and was about to interview Simeon as he relaxed into one of the two facing armchairs in the corner of that sumptuous venue. Patently, the new boyfriend of Ahmed, now four months down the line, was being given the once-over. Who *was* this relaxed Barney of supreme poise and deep brown voice? Was he an old-school Mafia don with the power of life and death? After initial pleasantries, the probe began with a reference to Simeon's drink.

"What *is* that?"

"It's orange juice. I don't drink."

"Right. I was told you're a clean livin' kid. Good match for our flagship golden boy. He's *squeaky* clean, worth a million dollars." He leaned forward and changed gear. "We don't want anything to go wrong, do we?"

In that last sentence, a subtle change in the man's voice caused the boy to look up sharply. A large, warm, strong hand was placed on his knee. "You mustn't judge us too harshly, Simeon," said the big man.

"Who's judging? How can *I* judge? I don't know anything about any of you guys," remonstrated the interviewee, somewhat alarmed and nervous.

"Wise kid," smiled the man who removed his hand, sat back and was now stroking his square jaw. "London's a great city, a beautiful city. We do business there," he added significantly.

"I've only been there a few times. I'm from Derbyshire, about 120 miles north."

"I know. Robin Hood Country. I know all about you, Simeon. Ahmed and I talk every day." He looked at Simeon. Simeon remained silent. "Do you know what an outlaw is?"

"Some kind of criminal in the old days?"

"Right, but an outlaw is a criminal who has been declared as 'outside the protection of the law'. That means that you can do anything you want to an outlaw and get away with it. You can torture him, you can kill him. The authorities don't care. That happened in the medieval period. In most civilised societies today – countries like the US and the United Kingdom – *everybody*, no matter how heinous the deed, everybody is subject to the protection of the law. Well, that, at least, is the theory. My point being, Simeon, that gay people, like us, are *still* outlaws. If a homosexual is beaten up, Joe Public or the cops are likely to look the other way. Outside on the streets of this city, right now, you can be a thief, a thug or a murderer and be afforded more respect than a faggot."

Simeon was startled by the stark truth of this statement. Old humiliations had inflicted long lasting damage and he had suffered painful examples of the gay-hate which would eventually be coined 'homophobia' in the following century. Indeed, for some of these villains, such homophobia was seen as a badge of honour. In the macho, football-crazy, working-class, coal mining culture of Derbyshire, several distressing incidents had taught Simeon Hogg that the local dishonest 'village rogue' or the violent 'town thug' enjoyed higher esteem that any gentle, kind, honest poofter. This explained why many boys like Simeon made a dash for an unhappy marriage and hid inside a dark, well locked closet for the rest of their lives.

Barney was still speaking.

"Let me put it like this; a gay guy in a restroom makes a play for the wrong man, another guy who is straight. The gay guy is knocked to the ground, kicked unconscious and left in a pool of blood. The general verdict would be – 'Guilty! The pansy had it coming. Serve him right. Should have killed the bastard.' Am I getting through to you, Simeon?"

"Yes. Yes you are, Barney." He spoke slowly in a weary defeated voice. "I know all this. I know it only too well."

"And yet, you look at all the men in this room and you see 'illegal', 'mob', 'gangster'. Right?" No answer. Simeon appeared to be trying to find the exact centre of his orange juice. "The gay world is illegal anyway. *You* are illegal every time you sexually touch another boy. OK, Kid?" The large, warm hand returned to rest upon his knee.

"OK, Barney," was the weak reply as if responding to a headmaster who had just delivered a stern reprimand.

"Well, I like 'em much younger." His big face suddenly broke out into an honest, big, sunny smile. The smile became slightly less honest, slightly lascivious as a wanton tongue made a brief appearance between full lips. "But, then again, you *look* much younger. Let's give it a try, Kid."

Simeon was surprised. Suddenly he was being led through this large reception room into an equally splendid bedroom. En route, he caught sight of Ahmed in conversation with three other colleagues. In this den of criminal characters with its hierarchy, its chain of command; fleeting eye-contact did not appear to unsettle his lover who continued to smile, continued to enjoy a light hearted conference. Both lovers knew that neither had any choice in this matter. Both accepted the situation with equanimity.

CHAPTER 15

Hung up on Morals

Simeon was entirely happy with this situation. Barney, hairy and over-weight, was as cosy and cuddly as the big dog he resembled. His sexual prowess and long practiced expertise was second to none as was often the case with such older voluptuous types. Like Barney, Simeon too 'preferred them younger' – much younger. However, erotic ecstasies delivered with the skills of a butch, bear-like, mature hunk such as this one, created blissful memories which would endure long after the average encounter with the average chicken. There was something perverse, something deep in Simeon's carnal psyche which responded enthusiastically to a fleshy bulk like Barney. It was so sensual. Those 30 minutes of grunting and slobbering around the boy's genitalia were rewarded by three consecutive orgasms.

At long last both combatants in the struggle for mutual pleasure lay side by side, exhausted, replete – completely relaxed. He was no longer a mob boss; he was just friendly 'Barney'. Simeon was off his guard and, temporarily, had forgotten about dons and godfathers. He liked this big man, not only physically, but he also liked the man's reasoning and was yielding to his gentle persuasion.

"Oh, God! You are really, so very very good," whispered the grateful receiver of so much pleasure.

"Better than the average bidet," acknowledged Barney in a Yogi Bear impression. Since he did not know what it was, the significance of 'bidet' was lost on this working class lad. "Did you see those impressive architectural sculptures on the front of this great hotel?"

"No," replied Simeon.

"Ahmed should do more to excite you're interested in this great city. He tells me that you admire our magnificent automobiles."

"Oh yes! Love them. They float. Dreams on wheels."

"In that case he should have drawn your attention to those statues. One was of a Frenchman called Cadillac and next to him was an Indian Chief called Pontiac. He should also have told you that when this hotel was completed in 1924, it was the tallest building in the world." Simeon looked sceptical. "Absolutely correct. This is just one of 1136 rooms."

"Oh. Well... I suppose he just forgot to tell me."

"Love that accent!" said the big man now with another big smile suddenly planting a powerful kiss on the boy's cheek. "And I know you're missing Vesuvio." Simeon broke eye-contact. He was embarrassed. "Hey! No sweat, Kid. It's in the nature of most gay guys to enjoy orgiastic sex. Perfectly natural. I've told Ahmed to take you to the big baths of New York. You'll love it! In time, you'll come to love the United States and, maybe... you'll come to love – *us*."

Momentarily eye-contact was resumed. In those young eyes, Barney saw a profound sadness, a sort of helplessness, a mixture of bad conscience and chronic pining for the hills and dales of Derbyshire in springtime. Gently, a large left hand fixed Simeon's chin whilst a warm right hand tenderly stroked his cheek. Barney's gaze reflected confidence and determination, but his voice was soft and benign.

"Don't get hung up over morals, Simeon. We're in the oldest and the most profitable business in the world – supplying illicit pleasures to guys who can afford to pay our prices. We're not cheap. We are very expensive. We are not evil people with horns. All our boys are well paid and well treated even years later when they are no longer boys. We are educated, articulate, cultured, reasonable – but most of all – we are very successful. You're a nice kid. I know what's troubling you. You're right. Sometimes our organisation is threatened. From time to time, it can get unpleasant. We are not gratuitously violent or cruel but, just occasionally; we have to take care of a problem.

"Give it time, Simeon. Give Ahmed time. He's infatuated, terrified of losing you. That's why you're watched and fettered with those golden chains. Give it time and you'll be trusted, you'll be vacationing in England with the most desirable stud in Detroit – in style! Isn't that better than living and teaching there for $40.00 a week! You could earn three times that amount right here in this hotel as a *cleaner*."

Simeon was alarmed to discover that Barney knew all about his desire to return to England and become a teacher. He was surprised and yet not surprised. From time to time he had been chatting to Dale, Calvin, Laurent and originally Ahmed himself about his hopes and dreams for the future. All had instructions to report any significant information. Laurent had warned him of this fact, as did Gary.

This well informed senior executive of The Firm expounded economic criticisms of a Britain in terminal decline. He started by attacking Wilson's Socialist Government, socialism in general and linked it with the decline of Rolls Royce, a once fine automobile – no longer 'the best car in the world'. He spoke of archaic industry, low productivity, weak arrogant management, unrealistic wage demands, the looming threat of runaway inflation, wild cat strikes and made a depressing contrast with the current vibrant economy of Germany – that same Germany which *lost* the war! Barney constructed an unanswerable cast iron case. He ended up on a line the Englishman had heard before, a line which was just as irritating as before.

"Kids like you back in Derbyshire, why they'd give their right arm to have the chance to live right here in America."

Simeon was not as articulate as Ahmed or Barney, yet, he did feel there *was* a case to answer and seized on a term which seemed to suit his needs – 'quality of life'. Haltingly, struggling to obtain the right words, he drew attention to those intangible aspects of a Derbyshire existence which are impossible to measure on an economic scale. He recalled to the big man, scenes and senses from his younger days in Belper. As an eight year old,

Simeon spent long days wandering around exploring that old mill town. He told Barney about one special, beautiful, sunny morning. It would have been late May, 1954. He sauntered away from his home under the cool brilliance of a perfect blue sky. He often did this. Nobody missed him. Nobody cared.

On this day he rambled rather too far. He was lost, but not distressed. On the contrary, it was rather fun to be in strange territory. At some point he emerged out of a jitty on to a long street of terraced houses. He progressed down what seemed like an endless brick wall on both sides until a narrow gap on the left revealed a steep descent down to a brook. Water was always nice. This water was especially nice because large rocks made the fast flowing water perform interesting effects and, also, they formed a dam creating a home for several ducks. The brook chased down a narrow valley overlooked by backs of houses attached to their long narrow gardens reaching down all the way to the stream. Simeon was envious. If *he* lived in one of those tall thin homes, all joined together, he would be able to play in the water with the ducks all day long!

He continued to follow the path now narrower, closed in by hawthorn, redolent with the sweet scent of brilliant white may flower gleaming in the sunshine. Climbing steeply up, he was tempted by a stile on the right which invited an exit into an open field. Exhilarated by this sudden expanse of space, he ran across grassland, so fast, it was almost like flying. There were views of houses rising on the right and the vast meadow on the left appeared to rise into infinity. Simeon was attracted to the direction in which he was going. Straight ahead, in the middle distance, there were lots of big trees.

Being lost was even more fun in this ancient woodland known as The Parks. The big trees changed everything. Holly, oak, ash, beech, silver birch and some specimens so strange, so twisted, so bent that they inspired enchantment worthy of Grimm. It became darker and cooler. Bright sunlight had been fragmented into artistic mottles which illuminated a strange blue haze nestling on the ground. This boy had discovered the cool, damp tranquillity of bluebells under a canopy of sweet, clean birdsong. He pressed on; the forest became darker still. His imagination was fired by mysterious dark cavities formed by exposed root-systems, dragonflies which morphed into fairies, nymphs, naiads, dryads and old gnarled trunks which suggested ugly goblins.

In this narrative of recollected images long past, Simeon was presenting Barney with a Derbyshire view of 'quality of life'. The presentation, however sincere, quaint and charming, failed to convince the battle-scarred businessman. He challenged such a sentimental view of life.

"We can't get back to the innocence of childhood. Belper sounds like a nice place, but, unless you make it big as an acclaimed poet, bluebells are never likely to pay your bills. They won't give you a standard of living to which, Simeon – thanks to *us* – you have already become accustomed."

Simeon was delighted with Alfred's report on the following Monday morning, April 25th – all A's and B's with supporting comments to match. Ahmed was overjoyed. He expressed pride and encouraged his lover with sincere high praise. Such praise was well received, but this student of average ability took a realistic, modest and balanced view of his speedy progress. It owed a great deal to his hard work, but also to perfect conditions for study. Since January, he had lived in an atmosphere of luxury with few distractions. The average scholar might have to share basic lodgings with other youngsters and perform time-consuming domestic duties – not to mention the necessity of holding down a part-time job.

Due to Ahmed's restrictions, there was no television and few social commitments to tempt this student away from his essential writing, reading and research.

His main concern had been the possible cost of interrupted sleep from strangers appearing in his Master's bed. Simeon had always been very conscientious about obtaining a wholesome eight hours and once suggested to Ahmed, in the interests of diligent learning, the possibility of being granted his own bed room – one of the two guest rooms. This suggestion was met with the equivalent of a solid brick wall – and an angry brick wall at that.

"You have to be kidding! How dare you! Booby's place is in *my* bed every night. I'm real proud of my beautiful boy. I want these kids to see just what I've got. Anyway, you're a sound sleeper. What's the beef? Most times you sleep right through. Most times you don't even *know* I've had an overnight chicken. *And,* I do seem to recall that when the fun rouses you out of deep slumber – you *never* refuse! Oh no! You're mighty quick to join in the action. *And* you sleep all the better afterwards."

Simeon had to acknowledge the lascivious truth of this remonstrance. His real saviour, and aid to quality sleep, was the sheer size of that great, spacious, gothic bed which comfortably provided roomy accommodation for two lovers and several sexy chickens.

CHAPTER 16

Manhattan – An Isle of Joy

The promised holiday materialised on Tuesday, April 26th when Calvin chauffeured Ahmed and Simeon to Detroit Metropolitan Airport.

"I took Barney's advice. We'll do the New York tubs."

"Tubs?"

"Gay steam baths of New York. We're well matched, Booby! We're a marriage made in heaven. Did you know that? Sure! We don't like noisy, smoky bars or clubs. We want to be where the *real* action is! The Big Apple is the best place in the world to gorge yourself on all that delectable sweet meat.

Apart from a glimpse after disembarkation from the SS Queen Elizabeth some three years before, Simeon had never explored New York City. It sounded exciting. Even so, if he *had* a choice (and Booby almost never had a choice) he would have chosen the more rural destination of Northern Michigan suggested by Gary Mackenzie.

All the same, it was first class all the way; first class flight on American Airlines, first class hotel situated at the lower end of Manhattan Island in a suite overlooking Central Park. That week was filled with romantic activities and Simeon's head was filled with the evocative lyrics of Lorenz Hart, the music of Richard Rodgers and the legendary voice of Ella Fitzgerald singing *Manhattan*. Just Manhattan, there was no time for the Bronx and Staten Island too, but they did visit Coney and eat baloney on a roll. And yes, in Central Park, because they were two guys, 'a kiss they stole', and it certainly was – 'soul to soul'. Ahmed overheard his Booby softly humming this familiar refrain and, in a surprisingly good singing voice, broke in with –

"The great big city's a wondrous toy, just made for a boy and boy. We'll turn Manhattan, into an isle of joy."

At that very special moment, sensitive, solicitous and warm, they looked into each others eyes, moist, glittering under the sun – very emotional. Ahmed reached out to repair a slight dishevelment in Booby's parting, a small, tender gesture, full of significance on that nice day. It *was* a nice day. If breezes were not exactly balmy, in a quiet area of Central Park, Ahmed was emboldened to take his lover's hand – and – for just a short way – hand in hand they strolled.

Reputation had it marked as a deadly fist, but the sudden touch of that wonderful warm Arab hand never failed to thrill, never failed to send electric shock waves of pleasurable anticipation to the very core of Simeon's psyche. He was surprised and disappointed when the brief interlude of enchantment came to an end. Those loving fingers loosened their grip. 'Gently gliding by', a few ambling onlookers had noticed the same-sex, romantic coupling – and clearly showed disapproval.

"Know what, Booby? It's a real shame. Some folks just don't like to see two boys holding hands. Perhaps they'd rather see us holding guns."

They did all the usual things people do in New York. They explored the skyscraper jungle around Wall Street; they strolled along Fifth Avenue, Times Square, Broadway, 42nd Street with its glaring lights, frenzied pace of the neurotic and the avant-garde – but nothing had actually changed between Ahmed and Simeon. The two personalities continued to be at odds, the chemistry simply did not work and the problem of communication persisted. A typical barrier was a sense of humour which could not be shared. Simeon was 100% British to his very core. He had been brought up with Tony Hancock, Kenneth Williams, Jimmy Edwards and a whole parade of pure English iconography which never successfully transferred to the United States.

Nevertheless, they genuinely loved each other and took nourishment from this city renowned for love and sex. Simeon was never bored with the ever impressive Ahmed who radiated not only sexual, but also intellectual energy which often fired his lover's interest. This fracture in the 'spirit of community'; this condition of no humour, no fun, no spark – all so essential to a good relationship – manifested itself in long silences between the two young men. But each silence can vary, it can have different qualities. Some silences were uncomfortable in which the two vacationers became aware of the unpalatable truth – fundamentally, they had very little in common. Neither could bring themselves to acknowledge this appalling threat to the future and, consequently, nothing was ever said. As Ahmed once pleaded –

"We have to make this work, Booby. It's *got* to work."

Other silences were neutral. Conversation was not required, so nothing was said. On the other hand, this love affair took sustenance from the contentment of the occasional *good* silence, the silence of quality which usually followed a carnal moment such as the quickie on the top of the Empire State Building and another naughty quickie on the spiral staircase which leads to the observation platform in the crown of the Statue of Liberty. This was Ahmed's sport. It was an opportunity for him to assert his power, authority and dominance. Yes, the sex – it was fantastic. They both knew that. Just so long as Booby could kiss, cuddle and play with Hector until he spent splattering his seed everywhere – just so long as Little Booby could keep recharging himself for the nourishment of the lusty Arab – just so long as that master could continue to inflict lashings of ecstasy on his willing slave – so the relationship was safe – would overcome all the problems – would last forever.

On the third day they stood in front of an impressive Romanesque façade of huge round arches on West 28th Street. Ahmed looked at his Booby with an inscrutable expression.

"Well, there it is – the Main Attraction."

"It looks like a church!" said Simeon.

"It *was* a church until 1888 when a man called Everard turned it into a rather grand Turkish Bath House. It was a real classy, gracious gentleman's club – but not now. Now they call it Ever Hard or the Old Dirty Foot because it smells of sweat and Lysol.

Welcome to skid row." His enthusiasm rose to a crescendo. "You'll love it, Booby! It's Windsor Baths to the power of ten! Your eyes will pop when you see those erotic, dim lit, mind-blowing tableaux. Hades, one guy said, but for me, oh yes! – more like heaven. You'll meet joy boys on the make and be pleasured by the fat, the aged and the perverted. There are hundreds of them, all faceless, nameless bodies in a massive shadowy steam room with benches where the steam hisses through leaky pipes which – like some of those old guys – are 78 years old. This is the Big Apple at its most bizarre, its very best!"

Ahmed had revealed that he was well acquainted with this run down, seedy, depraved establishment. His words were contemptuous but the tone indicated a certain perverse erotic excitement. In this, the two lovers shared common ground best described as deviant as they passed under the imposing and lofty portico with indecent haste.

"Wow! Just like the Derby Turkish Baths, only much bigger," commented Simeon standing in a dingy lobby which still held something of its former majestic glory.

"Moorish arches finished in marble. Yeah, the whole outfit is pretty impressive. Sure hope those Derby folks make good use of that public bath house. I hear tell the English are real smelly."

Simeon found this comment hurtful, yet he could not deny the problems of infrequent bathing in mid-20th century Derbyshire where some homes still lacked a bathroom and very few had the luxury of a shower. In the previous year on holiday, he had re-discovered the enduring working class culture of his boyhood – 'Friday night is bath night'. It was a culture which made American promiscuity (the culture of the quickie) if not impossible, certainly not very inviting. When they had stripped, save for a white towel, Ahmed read Booby the riot act.

"Usual rules: we stick together; share everything, no screwing – *no* niggers."

What a pity! This palace of pleasure was full of magnificent macho black men with big full lips and big round eyes which appeared to be focused on Simeon's sensuous white erogenous zones. He took solace in being reunited with Laurent after the vacation.

Something made him think of Laurent on the Monday morning of May 2nd, his first day back for the Spring Semester. As usual, Dale gently resuscitated him with pleasantries and a large stein of tea, but *unusually*, he became conscious of being alone in the Great Bed.

"Mr Hamah sends his apologies. Urgent business has called him away for a few days."

Simeon was uneasy. Something in Dale's tone was a little off-key. It would have been no use asking him any questions. The little servant could hold his tongue but could not conceal what was in his heart – and his heart was certainly troubled. Yes, it was unusual for Ahmed to leave his bed in the night without a word of explanation, but it *had* happened on at least two previous occasions. So why worry? On the drive to the University, Calvin was just the same. He never said very much anyway. Routinely, he was perfectly correct when he opened the door for his passenger to alight. With some eagerness, the student jumped out expecting to see his alluring black guard. He was keen to tell Laurent – ever chatty, friendly Laurent – all about his wild vacation in New York. But the sexy Negro was not there? He was always there! It was so odd. It was uncomfortable for this prisoner being suddenly bereft of his desirable, well-built gaoler. Simeon looked a question at Calvin who was about to drive off. He simply nodded in the direction of a man standing nearby, a dark suit, an older man, equally well built, in fact, a hulk.

Simeon froze. His colour drained and his mouth dried up in seconds. The man in the dark suit; it was the menacing 'Lee Van Cleef' character last seen at the party of suits in the Sheraton Cadillac Hotel. This stern hulk took a few steps up to his new charge. In those few moments this prisoner felt the full force of villainous dominion: it was the essence of the gangster's power, his psychological skill to intimidate. He recalled the London rent boy who had socialised with Ronnie Kray, the criminal who once remarked – 'happiness is fear'. The darkest hour at Mundy Street Boys School also came to mind when only self-destruction could free the victim from the grip of intolerable bullies.

Dour, uncompromising, wearing a sardonic sneer; the tough-guy slowly shook his head. It was a big head, well secured to a thick, powerful neck. He spoke in a sluggish, throaty drawl.

"You are getting forgetful. You seem to have forgotten you are Ahmed's boy! Bad move, kid – stickin ya dick in a nigger's maw! Bad move for you, worse for the nigger – much worse."

The last two words were very quiet, very frightening. They held the unspeakable horror of a cruel man who had witnesses an act of iniquity, so appalling, that even a hard type such as he was moved to feel some pity.

With head bowed, Simeon was escorted to his first class. He sat like a zombie hearing not one word the professor said. He could think only of Laurent. Poor Laurent! What had happened to him? How was it possible? How had they been rumbled? They had been so very careful! Assignations had always been very discreet, in a quiet restroom, in a quiet block, on a quiet floor at a quiet time of day. True, as confidence grew, the frequency of their delightful carnal couplings had increased from once a week to once a day. Eventually, Simeon, ever horny, made the greedy suggestion of upping to twice a day but, wisely, Laurent had pointed out the danger. Ahmed would certainly detect smaller ejaculations which came *his* way – and draw the obvious conclusion.

And then there was guilt. Was Simeon effectively responsible for the murder of his illicit black beau? Much the same age, but more mature, it was Laurent who had always been the one to urge caution in all things. He was the more experienced partner having mastered his sensual skills as a pre-pubescent in the Detroit ghetto more than ten years before. From being a small boy, Laurent knew all about The Firm. Everybody knew about the good money which could be made. Harsh penalties inflicted on transgressors: it was common knowledge in the ghetto. After each encounter, it was Laurent who checked for drops of semen on Simeon's clothes. It was Laurent who checked for any stray frizzy, African hairs in Simeon's underpants; hairs which could be difficult to explain should they come to light.

Half way through the next class, still in a turbulence of thought, still conscience stricken, the professor's voice continued to be an ongoing background drone. Wayne State University was a community of thousands, but how many students arrived in a Lincoln Continental Limousine and were continually chaperoned throughout the day by an impressive body guard? Nobody *appeared* to take much notice, but Simeon would certainly be high profile to the run-of-the-mill student who, at some point, may have witnessed and reported the indiscretion.

But what now? Grief for a fallen lover was giving way to thoughts of self-preservation. And those concerns led on to panic. Ahmed called away? Was it possible that he needed to distance himself from a planned punishment? A beating? Worse? It was time to hit the panic button! He checked his watch: about half an hour to the bell. Simeon did what he often did for meetings with Laurent. He simply walked out of the room in the hope that Van Cleef was not guarding the door. All was well, but the hulk would certainly return minutes before the end of that class. He had no time to lose and not far to walk. In an age before the cell phone, there were plenty of pay phones in any corridor. Fumbling for a tiny dime, his hand shook.

"Gary! Thank God it's you. I've forgotten that stupid code. I'm all to pieces. Trust me, this is a deserted corridor. *Nobody* can over-hear me. Let me explain…"

In disjointed agitation, Simeon gave his friend an incoherent account which was interrupted with –

"Stop there! You have to get back to that class. I've got the main outline. As planned, be there in the morning with a *small* suitcase, your passport and that money you told me about. *Not* the main entrance. Go to the north end of the Humanities Block. Go there when you're about halfway through your first class – about 9.30?

"I'll be there."

"This is no time for bull shit. These gorillas don't mess about – but, if it helps you, it's looking like nothing will happen until Ahmed gets back. In any event, you have no choice. Just one thing: I'm watching my own back. You won't see me, but I'll see you. If it's safe, *then* you'll see me. Courage friend… I'm out."

Gary Mackenzie had hung up.

CHAPTER 17

Monsters from the Id

That night, in that luxury apartment, up high in Palmer Heights, Simeon was alone. He was so very alone in the isolated splendour of Sultan's Palace, the sole diner at The Sultan's Great Table. The silence, so intense, was broken only by small sounds coming from the kitchen. As usual, Dale was very correct in his professional duties, indeed, he was hiding behind the mask of the perfect servant. Dale was afraid. According to routine, he cleared away, left a pristine kitchen and the apartment just after 10.00pm. Simeon went on to the balcony and watched the sad, small figure, far below exit the building. He made his usual progress down Woodward Avenue, presumably towards home. Poor boy! All this time, and he still knew nothing about this cute little chicken who, like Simeon, was isolated by the dread of an unspoken rulebook, enforced by chronic apprehension. After all this time, he still knew very little about Ahmed Hamah. Apart from being an over-sexed, gorgeous stallion – the dream of every gay boy – who exactly *was* he? Many would see him as a rich, loud braggart. To British sensitivities, Ahmed exhibited the worst traits of the typical brash American. What of the dark side? Was he really capable of wickedness? On the other hand he was certainly intelligent, knowledgeable and he could be tender… loving…

Simeon closed his eyes in an effort to suppress a welling up of tears triggered by a paroxysm of despair and grief. Salty liquid blurred and smeared the distant city lights and illuminations of automobiles endlessly on the move. It was cold on that balcony. He used his handkerchief, took a grip on himself and went inside.

Simeon was alone, so very alone in that Great Bed. It seemed larger than ever. His mind, ever searching for answers, raced through all the ramifications of the recent appearance and foreboding words of Van Cleef. Just past midnight, in a fury of mixed feelings, he decided that sleep was never going to happen this night. He jumped out of bed, stood for an anguished moment and decided to pack his suitcase. Halfway through that task, again, he was seized by that same sudden grief. Yes, it *was* effectively – grief. Effectively, he had lost Ahmed. Simeon was bereaved. We all deal with grief in our own way. Something drew him to his lover's wardrobe. He reached out to touch one of his shirts and then noticed the bomber jacket Ahmed wore on the night of first meeting. He lifted it off the hanger and held it close. As on that night, Simeon cuddled his face up into the inside lining in an effort to draw in some spirit, some actuality, some essence of the man he loved. It

was there, in the fabric; the familiar warm body scent. It seemed to whisper his name –
Booby – a name which was only ever uttered in an aura of gentle affection. Overwhelmed
by a multiplicity of problems, a yearning for that lost love, the lost security together with
an appalling mess of conflicting emotions – it was all too much. His tears flooded back
with redoubled force. He fell on the bed and gave way to a seizure of heavy sobs which
shook a nerve-racked body at the very edge of despair.

The sobs subsided leaving him in a bleak state of emptiness, deep gloom and
melancholy. In this sad condition it is difficult for anybody to be completely rational,
but the mind never gives up. The thought process is always trying to make sense of life,
and so it was with Simeon Hogg in the middle of this long, dark, sleepless night. For this
miserable young homosexual in the homophobic world of 1966, it was even more difficult
to analyse his predicament. This particular Hogg was an isolated Hogg. Another Hogg
would never have been in this difficulty in the first place. A *normal* boy would have found
a nice girl and that relationship would have been approved by all the other Hoggs and
all other heterosexuals in the wider community. Approval and support would have been
demonstrated by smiles, nodding heads and polite enquiries. If the relationship ran into
any difficulties, friendly advice would be offered by family, friends and colleagues. The
world at large would bless and encourage the union of Simeon and his girlfriend in the
form of weddings, family morals, numerous films and the general media ever pushing and
promoting heterosexual values.

The older Simeon sometimes looked back at Simeon the boy. Alas, like millions of
other gay boys, he felt the suffocating weight of heterosexual reproach and rejection. To
compound problems, he was inarticulate. He was too callow and too young to mount an
effective challenge to all the perverted brainwashing of the previous 20 years. It is not
easy coming to terms with being different. That particular form of education is sometimes
a bitter experience. Take an example which occurred many years after this unhappy dark
night. Take the teacher who was given tragic news, the sudden death of her mother. She
collapsed into a flood of tears, was inconsolable and had to leave her duties immediately.
She was helped out of the staffroom and taken home. All other colleagues were distressed,
rushed over to be supportive, kind and sympathetic. As a witness to this event, Simeon
was also distressed – but not in the same way. He was distressed at his own extraordinary
response to this upsetting scene. He did *not* feel sorry for the poor woman! On the
contrary, he resented her. Why? Simeon knew that he was 'damaged goods', but he was
no psychoanalyst. He was unable to probe the Freudian darkness, to examine the monsters
that lurked inside his own id. Was the hostile reflex connected with a comparison? Let us
assume that Simeon receives similar bad news – his long standing partner has died. Dare
he weep? Dare he show pain, as *she* did and risk admitting to a 'degenerate' relationship,
an unnatural, illegal closeness?

Perhaps the callous reaction was linked to envy. A close maternal bond existed between
the teacher and her mother. That incident of a grief stricken daughter caused him to
reflect upon his own response to the passing of his own mum and dad in 1972 and 1993
respectively. Nothing! Nothing was felt. Not one tear was ever shed. Yet, in the small
hours of that dark Tuesday morning, May 3rd, 1966 – to use a Derbyshire expression –
'buckets' were shed for the sudden loss of his lover, Ahmed Hamah.

The young man's heart may have been broken, but his natural instinct for survival was intact. As that dark night progressed, rational thoughts gradually superseded his lamentations. He took stock of his situation. He had become entangled with a criminal gang and broken one of the rules. It was Ahmed's rule for his Booby – no sexual liaison should take place unless his Master was present and no carnal contact was permitted with any member of the black race. If Simeon believed the rule racist, unfair and unjust – this was beside the point. He had cheated on the lover who had cared for him. He had betrayed the lover who had been absolutely clear on this sexual matter right from the beginning. Ahmed, Earl, Barney, Olga, Gary and even Laurent himself had all alluded to, and implied severe punishment – even threat of death – for any misbehaviour within this criminal community. Simeon had been warned. Now Gary, a good friend, at considerable risk had offered him a life-line. To renege on the arrangement, 'the plan of escape', could involve grievous bodily harm, disfigurement, or a fatality. Simeon continued to pack his suitcase.

For Simeon, a rucksack was standard, but the whole plan hinged on that suitcase. It had to be accepted as containing material for a class presentation. It was put to the test the following morning.

"What's that for?"

"Charts, graphs, maps, photographs, lists. I'm doing a…"

"OK."

Calvin did not want to know. He was easily turned off by anything connected with 'book stuff'. Van Cleef never asked, but did speak.

"Hi."

Simeon did not answer. They walked in silence down the corridor. In the elevator, the silence persisted and became oppressive. They reached the eighth floor and were approaching the student's first class when the guard spoke a second time.

"They call me Teddy." No response. "Suit ya self, kid." Teddy Van Cleef walked away to kill time until the next class.

Thirty minutes later, Simeon had just arrived at the agreed place when Gary Mackenzie pulled up in an impressive 1960 Chevrolet Impala, the model with the famous distinctive rear gull wings.

"Where did this come from?" asked Simeon.

"Don't be fooled. It's real cheap – 'Save a week's pay at Gene Merola Chevrolet'. $10.00 down and $10.00 a week. Anyway, it's not my car. Meet Sam," replied Gary, indicating the back seat with his thumb. Simeon saw a small dark chicken, barely noticeable, barely old enough to own a car, nestling in the off-side corner who uttered a weak –

"Hi."

"Hi," returned Simeon.

Hurtling down the I 94 Freeway, the escapee became concerned when the exit for Detroit Metropolitan Airport was ignored.

"No sweat. We're heading for an airport, but not *that* one. Get real! The Big One – no way! It's the first place they'll look."

An instinct told the runaway not to ask questions. The smooth silent Impala cruised along, ever westwards, well above the speed limit eating up the miles. A worrying thought crept into the boy's head. This elaborate plan of escape, these careful precautions – and yet – could it all be undermined by Simeon's own enthusiasm for his Derbyshire collection of freaky friends? He so enjoyed narrating his 'Grimm's fairy story' 1965 adventures to listeners within Ahmed's sphere. How much did he tell Ahmed about Mr Toad, or the goblin, or the gnome, or about the snobs who ran the gay scene? He could not remember – or, for that matter – would Ahmed remember, or would he even care? But, if Ahmed, or any of the others *did* recall any facts; could such intelligence be used to track down and locate Simeon?

Gary turned on the radio. Simeon immersed himself in the delicious strains of The Ronettes singing *Do I Love You*. Sharing tender moments, he and Ahmed had often cuddled to that record. That single, beautiful, vibrato voice; it thrilled him. It cut through his sorrowing soul like a sharp orgasmic knife –
        '*And would I die, if you should ever go away…* '
In embarrassment of welling tears, he turned his head away from the driver to study the disappointing, scrubby countryside flashing by. Directly from Motown's famous 'wall of sound', the car was filled with a thrum of double bass, bass guitar and deep drums which, in pleasurable sadness, resonated with his prevailing mood of sweet melancholia. The lyrics of every record played, to some extent, seemed to echo his own heartrending emotions.

More than an hour had passed and they had already reached the middle of the vast, flat emptiness of the great Midwest. To Derbyshire eyes it was an ugly expanse of nothing going nowhere with not a single feature or word of conversation to break the endless monotony. It was sometime back when they had passed a sign for Ann Arbor and now another sign announced the approach of Battle Creek – but they never saw Battle Creek. Gary slowed to exit the Freeway and took a minor road to the south.
        "You'll need to direct me from here, Sam," said the driver.
        "Go straight on," responded the taciturn Sam.
        "I think you mean 'gaily forward'," corrected Gary.

A few miles down that road, a wind-sock proclaimed a small, lonely air field to the left. They entered and were confronted by a solitary private aeroplane which stood at the end of a single runway. A man who had just emerged from the only hangar approached rapidly with enthusiasm. Gary and his fugitive friend alighted.
        "Hey there, Gary! What ya knowin'?"
        "Not much. Here's your parcel."
        "My oh *my*! So *this* is what you've been hiding from me. Hello, Englishman, sure wish we had the time to become better acquainted." The Englishman was looking at pleasant rounded features, a beaming, bronzed, freckled face, clearly still short of 30 – quite easy on the eye. "Hey, security's so tight here; I'm not even allowed to know your name! I'll call you Englishman and you can call me Pilot. How does that sound?"
        Bemused by all this cloak and dagger paraphernalia, Simeon was trying to think of a sensible reply when he noticed the departing 'gull wings' of the lovingly cared for Impala leaving the air field! Shy Sam had gone without a word of goodbye, or, for that matter, any other word. The big surprise was to see Gary heaving *two* suitcases into the luggage area of this four-seater Cessna.

"What's this? Is he coming with us? Surely this small plane can't fly all the way to England?"

"No, but it can you get all the way to Buffalo. And yes, Gary is coming too." At that point, Gary had rejoined them.

"You know I always wanted to get the hell out of Detroit and see Europe. This is my big chance! I can keep an eye on you at the same time. You don't mind... ?"

"No... I'm just mixed up... look, *where* is Buffalo and *why* are we going there. I need to get to England. England is in the east. I have to go *home*. I need some answers," pleaded Simeon, becoming perturbed, losing patience in the endless fog of mystery.

"Calm down, Englishman," said the pilot. "You'll be in the air in minutes, heading eastwards, in the general direction of Great Britain. I kid you not." Gary decided it was time to supply further details.

"Look, my friend, this is an old buddy of mine. He's given up a full day of his valuable time to help you out of a tight spot. Everything's been carefully planned to get you away from the mob as safely as possible. The less you know the better. Like I said, Ahmed's gang should never be underestimated. They have top cops and even some politicians in their pockets. Right now they may be checking Detroit Metro and maybe even O'Hare in Chicago."

"Buffalo is pretty close to Niagara Falls. It's about three and a half hours from here and is not the first city to spring to the mafia mind," assured the pilot.

"Neither will Allegheny Airlines who run old turboprops from Buffalo to New York. And from New York we can squeeze into a similar old crate which will take us to Reykjavik," said Gary.

"Where?"

"No sweat. It's in Iceland – and it's cheap. From Reykjavik we can get a flight to Prestwick in Scotland. If they look in New York, they'll be checking BOAC lists."

"And if any of their agents in the UK are sniffing around, they'll be sniffing at Heathrow in London," added the pilot.

"I cannot believe that I'm – so – bloody – important!"

"You're not!" said Gary. "Those crooks would squash you as look at you."

"Ahmed, in person, will want to do the squashing, Englishman," warned the pilot. "Trust me, I know this guy. He's dangerous; a bad looser. He'll demand that you're tracked down. It'll be a matter of honour. He's like one of the old-time slave owners; he's set the dogs on absconding kids before. My advice – hide yourself in some wilderness and keep your head down for as long as you can."

"I'll be damned if I'm going to change my name! But... anyway, thank you, Mr Pilot, for all your trouble and planning." Suddenly, for the first time, Simeon thought about money and fumbled for his wallet. "I don't know how much..."

"Put it away," said the pilot firmly. "You'll need all that *and* a lot more. In any case, I owe this horny scallywag." He suddenly grabbed Gary's blond hair, roughly yanked him over and playfully shook him. "Yep, we go back a few years don't we, Buddy. And, along the way, he's brought me quite a few nice presents, some real juicy stuff."

For Simeon Hogg, life had recently become a long, steep learning curve. At first meeting, Gary Mackenzie came across as a regular, clean cut, wholesome all-American-boy-next-door. If not an actual member of The Firm, he now seemed to be right up to his neck in a miasma of sexual sleaze. The evidence pointed to a freelance hustler who played a lone hand and operated outside the circles of which Simeon was presently attempting to escape.

Notwithstanding, this absconder was very grateful for the assistance of a good friend, albeit that friend was turning out to be a precocious street-wise-city-rat.

CHAPTER 18

Excitement of Adventure

Very kindly, Gary allowed his friend to sit up front next to the pilot for maximum view and exhilaration. It was Simeon's first ever flight in a light aircraft. A roar of engine, rapid acceleration and sensation of leaving the earth; all this temporarily jettisoned the effects of his current heartache. As Simeon's spirits were lifted, so all were lifted high above that same bleak landscape now heading in the opposite direction, due east, the direction of Derbyshire. It seemed that just minutes had passed when the airborne truant was studying the City of Detroit, attempting to locate the Downtown area and the Detroit River – all of which were soon behind them. Ahead of them was the great expanse of Lake Erie, diminishing into a point at their destination. As a treat, the pilot made a detour, swooped over and around Niagara Falls before landing at Greater Buffalo International Airport at a little after 2.30pm.

Gary's pocket book was very impressive! When opened to buy tickets to New York, Simeon was goggle-eyed to see it packed to capacity with $100 bills.

"My God! You *have* been a busy boy haven't you!" Gary ignored this remark and concentrated on financial logistics.

"We'll keep this simple. I'll pay for everything up until we get to... Where *are* we going when we get over there?" Both boys realised that they had not given much thought to accommodation in the Peak District.

"Well... '*we*' is now something of a complication," responded Simeon. "I was vaguely thinking about pitching a tent in some remote northern Derbyshire Dale which is not marked on any American Mafia map."

"No tents for me, buddy boy, no way! I've been saving for this trip for a long time. That is, since you told me all about those horny, butch English guys. And I do mean butch as in the British meaning of that word. On the other hand, no sense wasting bread. Can't we stay with Aunty Joyce?"

"No. Absolutely not. Joyce is a shy, repressed, sensitive spinster. She's nervous enough of me as it is. What with your bulging basket and that 'come-and-get-it' arse, she'll pick up on you right away! You'll scare her to death. Would you consider dossing with one of the odd bods I met last year?"

"One of your freaks? I'm not sure. Which one did you have in mind?"

"We have to consider security from the heavy mob and think about who is likely to put us up. Or, more to the point, who will put *up* with *us*. The best security would be Nobby the Gnome, because he's in a different home every night. Teddy Van Cleef would never find us! It would also be very entertaining. Nobby is lots of fun."

"Mmmm. I think we'll give Nobby a miss. It would be kind of crowded – the three of us – in a WC cubicle in a public lavatory. Ok, funny guy; let's get on this plane and then we can consider some *sensible* suggestions."

After months of luxury, Simeon suffered the shock of travelling economy class. The American Airlines flight of the recent vacation had been smooth, quiet and quick with lots of room in first class. The old turboprop tourist class of Allegheny Airlines to New York was rough, noisy and cramped. Icelandic Airways had much the same type of basic accommodation; limited comfort, but at least the connections had been fortuitous. They managed to get a flight which left Buffalo at 4.00pm and landed in New York at 5.15pm. At 7.00pm a flight to Scotland departed Kennedy Airport calling at Reykjavik for the sole purpose of re-fuelling. Two very tired young friends landed at Prestwick at 12.00 noon British Summer Time on Wednesday, May 4th. Their body time was actually 7.00am but, in spite of severe vibration, they did have the benefit of some poor quality sleep. Simeon was sufficiently awake to inform his friend that Elvis Presley had never visited England, but, had briefly set foot on Scottish soil, at Prestwick, some six years before.

Gary was more interested in a map which showed that they would need to trek 30 miles out of their way north-bound to Glasgow in order to catch a fast mainline train south to Derbyshire. He estimated the distance of a car journey from Prestwick to Buxton to be about 250 miles and suggested the possibility of obtaining a long haul taxi. Buying or hiring a car was mooted and quickly rejected on the grounds of security, various complications and practicality. On the map, Simeon noticed the nearness of the seaside resort of Ayr. He pleaded for a proper bed and plenty of rest prior to any further travel. Unlike Gary, he did not take kindly to the stress and excitement of adventure.

It may have been Scotland, but a short taxi ride brought Simeon into a scene which set alight every Derbyshire nerve in his very essence. Clogged with the busy detritus of tiny cars, vans and bicycles, they made poor progress through narrow medieval streets. Under the cool, sparkling sunshine of early May, the newcomers were dazzled by an excellent view of old crooked buildings and two ancient castellated foot-bridges which crossed the ice cold River Ayr. The azure skyline was punctuated with several ornate gothic spires thrusting upwards, leaving far behind all the confusion below. One high steeple, a magnificent example, sported turrets incorporating tall slender windows. Even here – in the heart of Robert Burns country with sightings of the Twa Brigs bridges and the Tam O' Shanter Museum – Simeon was thrilled to be reunited with his ancient homeland. They turned a corner into an attractive fishing harbour and the friendly driver said he could recommend a small comfortable hotel which overlooked a sandy beach. At the entrance, he mentioned a figure in British currency. The driver's speech was unintelligible to the American with a wallet excessively pregnant with dollar bills of high denomination. Simeon produced a five dollar bill which more than covered the fare. A delighted taxi driver drove off with enthusiastic wishes for a good holiday.

After lunch they set out to explore the nooks and crannies of this quaint little town and, once again, tackled the thorny problem of where to stay in Derbyshire. Gary thought through Simeon's extraordinary fairytale adventures of the previous summer.

"Claud Hoadley's place sounds nice. A devoted servant, bay windows giving on to massive trees and a dreamy view of the park – that's my first choice," said Gary.

"Snooty Hoadley wouldn't touch us with a barge pole," replied Simeon. "I think you're expecting too much. Gay Americans may tremble and buckle at the sight of a willing sexy chicken, but professional gays in England are extremely cautious – especially the Derby Camp. It'll be just the same with Tommy and Martin in Nottingham. And, in any case, I wouldn't put on their generosity. Not to mention one small point – we're supposed to be in hiding. We need to be in the countryside away from large towns."

Gary was about to suggest residence with the Belper Goblin – the rotting old crone who lived up a dirt road under ancient twisted trees filled with the din of raucous crows – until he remembered that ugly old Jasper's medieval cottage had a sunken roof and was about to fall in. It was an 18th century hovel with no gas or electricity; used a well for water and the call of nature had to be answered by a visit to an outside earth closet!

"What about that old man, that old 'Granddad' who lives in... Chichester?"

"Chesterfield. No good. You'll recall that Guzzly Granddad did a runner when the police started to nose around at the end of my vacation."

"I guess we're out of options," said Gary, rather gloomily.

"Not quite," replied Simeon, slowly, choosing his words carefully. "There *is* a possibility of comfortable free accommodation *if* you are prepared to pay the price."

"Free? Paying the price? You speak in riddles!" replied Gary, noticing that his friend was attempting to suppress a sudden attack of the giggles – and, suddenly seeing the light – "Oh no! Not that vile 'Mr Toad' with his foul breath? NO WAY!"

"It is the *only* way, as far as I can see at the moment. He's child-like, quite harmless, and he loves people staying with him. Becksitch Lane kinks and winds up one of Belper's more obscure steep hillsides. It's a challenge for anyone to find Crow's Hole, the home of Mr Toad. Strangers from a distant land of straight flat roads wouldn't have a hope."

"Mr Toad! What's his real name?"

"His proper name is almost as daft: Aubrey Pod. Listen, Gary, you're going to have to bite the bullet with this one. Apart from being an outrageous, over-wound sex maniac; Toad is famed – well, let's say notorious – for his big dick and his expert ability to use it to your advantage! Really! In some of those cottages, I've heard kids cry with pleasure and beg for more. Perhaps grotesque, but Toad *is* a legend in his own lifetime."

Something in this last line incited a sinful desire deep within Gary's sensitive fundament which, temporarily, dispersed all horrors of toadal touches. He assessed the total picture, all the pros and cons –

"Well... I suppose... After all," reasoned the horny youth more to himself than to Simeon, "I don't actually have to *look* at the reptile – do I?"

"Of course not, Gary," said Simeon with a half grin and more than a touch of sardonic mischief. "Anyway, you and Mr Toad would be facing the same way – wouldn't you?"

At this point the subliminal teasing broke to the surface with open roguery and mock violence. The blond raised his hand and rained blows upon his roguish friend, an enjoyable attack which eventually subsided in a fit of mutual giggles which lasted until they both staggered up to the local taxi office.

"Yes." said the rather cautious lady to the youths before her, clearly in high spirits. "Please pay in advance. A car is available tomorrow morning, Friday, May 6th to take you all the way down to Belper."

It was a fascinating accent of careful clear enunciation which could be cut with a knife. Gary made a quick calculation and fumbled with his fat wad of green-backs to settle the account. Once again, American currency was very acceptable at this time when the British pound was falling like a stone.

"We really should be settling up, Gary. And flashing all that cash! It's making me nervous. You'd never do it in Detroit."

"You're darned right I wouldn't! Look, there's a bank over the road. Let's get it sorted."

Simeon's $727 barely made £250. Gary never disclosed the figure of his total wealth and was careful to conceal the change of currency.

"It would be stupid to change it all," he said. "The dollar gets more valuable every day that passes. Hey, ya know what? I've got more bulk now than before! These things are the biggest bills they have."

With youthful boasting he brandished a bundle of £10 notes before stuffing them into a pocket in his rucksack. Simeon estimated that bundle to be worth about £500 and was thankful the small town of Ayr was unlikely to have any observant opportunistic muggers. He took out his own smaller ball of rolled £10 notes and began to peel off the estimated amount of his debt owed to Gary.

"No, buddy. Put it away. Put it safe. Now it's *my* turn to play Prince Ahmed. When Mr Toad gets tired of us, and throw's us out… well, that's all you have in the world. Right? Listen, when the well runs dry, I can always use my body to make dough. But I don't think you have it in you – do you? Right?

Simeon knew Gary was right. He looked at his friend with gratitude and wondered at what *was* in Gary. What *was* the nature of that kind of talent which makes for a successful prostitute who can acquire so much cash? But Gary was quite right about Simeon's woeful credentials as a hustler. He recalled Ahmed's scornful laugh when a man gave him a $5 bill at the baths and went on to say – 'I won't take off my shoes for less than $200!' Simeon had no strong moral objection to the sale of sex. It just seemed to him so sad that money had to change hands in an essentially friendly situation where physical pleasure is exchanged. He was especially sensitive to critical attitudes from his contemporary chickens. They took the view that Simeon was breaking the rules – 'He *gives* it away, *and* to old trolls who can afford to pay!'

Simeon studied Gary's profile and tried to see his physical assets as a punter might see them. He failed to find any hardness which is associated with the raunchy life-style of a street boy. Diffused Scottish sunlight softened by high cloud caught soft down on his chin, sparkled the delicate hairs of his eyebrows and gently lit a comely lightly tanned complexion of peaches and cream. The whole, including his well-proportioned body which bulged in all the right places, was an alluring package of which any gay man would wish to take delivery. Gary enjoyed two other attributes which were valued in the homosexual world. His demeanour was masculine and that masculinity was buttressed by the quality of being totally natural with a manlike walk combined with an occasional quick smile and seductive boyish charm. Seventeen he was, but, in certain situations, this flaxen youth could easily be 15 or even younger than that. Simeon's conclusion – Gary had formed an accurate assessment of his own worth. Together with confidence, knowledge of the market and good business sense, he had clearly built up a viable and prospering concern around his youthful body and bubbling personality.

As the walk around Ayr continued, Simeon himself was feeling much more confident about the future. All the adventure, travel and change had been a beneficial distraction. It was good to be back home in Britain. Everything was worth looking at. Everything seemed pretty and attractive. Everything was smaller, including small cars and small people who were thinner, perhaps slightly scruffier than the people of Detroit, but the British were more craggy and more interesting. The threat of danger from a criminal gang, an ocean away in a distant country, seemed to be like a bad dream – totally unreal. Or so he hoped.

CHAPTER 19

The Movie Changes to Colour

It had taken all day to travel all the way from Scotland to Belper. On the last leg, Friday afternoon, congestion through Bakewell and Matlock seemed to be especially bad. 'Tea time traffic' thought Simeon, as he affectionately recalled one of the many quaint expressions used by Mr Toad. Having passed the sign announcing 'Belper', the driver left the main road and concentrated on Simeon's tangled directions, as he navigated the taxi up Cow Hill and around a steep, knotty labyrinth situated on a westerly facing hillside. It was an ugly little car at the foot of a long, steep and overgrown garden which announced their arrival at Crow's Hole. Toad's home was known to the gay community as Toad Hall. Gary was utterly repelled by both the house name and this strange vehicle which was shaped like a slug.

"What is *that*?"

"I'm told it's known as the toadmobile," replied Simeon.

"My God! It offends every bone in my Motor City body!" Gary harboured the unspoken dread that the toadmobile was but a prelude to meeting the hideous deformity just a little way above; a deformity who might require his rent paid in kind.

The two friends wished the driver a safe journey back to his distant homeland. He departed and struggled to escape the maze of kinky, narrow lanes in search of the north-bound A6 main road. Weighed down by bags and baggage, with a heavy heart, his passengers set foot up the mossy garden steps, scaling the long climb to the sinister front door of Mr Toad, high above, only just visible through gaps in the light green spring foliage.

"Oh my God!" said Gary. "Up there! Why it looks just like the house of Norman Bates in *Psycho*. You *did* say that Toad's mom was safely dead?"

"Nelly Pod is long dead," laughed Simeon. "An appalling harridan; she was the terror of shop assistants in King Street, but, I can assure you, her spirit does *not* live on in Aubrey Pod. He's a perfectly safe, nice little toad."

"Just the same, I'll skip the shower."

"Shower! Count yourself lucky to have access to a *bathroom*. Most of the nearby terraced cottages still use a tin bath hanging up outside. Crow's Hole is posh by comparison. In its day, this was one of the more substantial houses up here on Cow Hill. According to Aubrey, his mom was a miserable old miser. She'd never spend a penny if a ha'penny would do. The result: as you see, it's pretty run down."

"Why can't toad maintain it?"

"Because he's Toad of the Toilets! He's obsessed with clocking up sexual conquests. Doesn't take much interest in anything else – not even in his work. He's a music master at the local grammar school – quite a talented musician really. Anyway, if he'll have us, it'll be interesting staying up there for a while. I *like* a spooky old house! It's interesting. Not many homes can boast a tower. On top of 'Toad's Tower', you can see Matlock *and* Derby."

The trudge up the steps was a chore for Gary, but Simeon was overjoyed by the view of the lush Derwent Valley. It was like balm, soothing, slowly seeping into and healing his Derbyshire starved soul. Distant green fields of the high Chevin surmounted the deeper green quarried woodland of Firestone Hill. Down below, far below, numerous waterside alders sporting new foliage tantalisingly obscured the River Derwent, but for a few short, shimmering stretches.

Half way up, Gary begged a break.

"I must be out of condition," he gasped out. "A few weeks in Derbyshire and I'll have muscles like Cassius Clay." Gary sat on his suitcase, caught his breath and took a long look at the twisting, interlacing muddle of the precipitous, long, neglected garden. "Just look at that! It's a jungle. Nothing could get through that tangle."

"And it's been tangling for at least 30 years," said Simeon, smiling. He was thinking of a young toad who once amused himself by playing nasty pranks on a long serving gardener. On one dreadful day, before the war, he had had enough! The poor old chap downed tools, never to return to his duties. "But it goes with the house, don't you think? I *like* this garden. *You* see it as dark and creepy. I see it... No – I *feel* enchantment. You're wrong, Gary. It's not *Psycho*, it's more *Sleeping Beauty*."

"I can buy that," responded Gary, philosophically, as he looked up at the old house. "It's easy to imagine that nobody's been here for the last 100 years. Look at those bedroom windows. They're half covered by ivy and... I think the other stuff is Virginia Creeper. And that tower top – it's sprouting weeds!"

"Pretty weeds, though. It's buddleia. Smells nice."

"Tell you what, if you can find the energy, when we finally get up there; give Mr Toad a kiss. He may turn into Prince Charming!"

This last hit the Englishman with a sharp pain like a knife through the heart. He did not need to kiss the toad. He had already met his Prince Charming. And now, he had abandoned his Prince Charming. Ahmed was 4000 miles away. He reigned in a foreign land, in a different world, but Simeon could clearly see his beautiful deep, brown eyes, his sweet smile and feel the strength of his arms and the caress of his gentle touch. The anguish was extreme. His heart was breaking in a miasma of conflicting / confusing attempts to assess how he had come to this point; the point of giving up the most wonderful boy he has ever met. To escape this sudden misery, this intrusive onset of grief, he concentrated on, and took comfort from the enchanted garden. He cast his eyes over this kingdom of thorns, the thick snarl of bramble, the flowering dog roses, the bindweed, ragwort, bluebells and various long grasses at the edges. Elder, hawthorn and hazel left mysterious cavities of gloom fit only for a few brave ferns and wild bracken. They could hear the inhabitants – foraging blackbirds dutifully scratching up food for hungry chicks that will eventually emerge into this very safe garden.

Puffing and panting, the visitors eventually reached the summit and stood before the brooding Victorian residence which, covered with foliage, looked much older than a 100 years. In spite of the late afternoon chill, the front door of mock Early English design was wide open. It revealed a dingy hall which had not been decorated in decades.

"HELLO!" called Simeon. "Are you home, Aubrey?"

The response was almost instant. A small stocky man came hurrying out of the living room to investigate. On seeing two young men on his doorstep, his exuberant bulging eyes bulged even wider with childlike delight. The first sight of Aubrey Pod was usually a shock – and Gary *was* shocked. He had to restrain himself from saying 'No – no – please – *NO!*' He had to resist the impulse to turn, to run, and to affect an escape from the hideous toadal presence. The reptilian eye balls seemed to be set wide apart over a tight mouth which was more like a crack in a pie.

"Simeon! Simeon you've come back!" squeaked Mr Toad in an ecstasy of excitement.

"What the hell! I *will* kiss a toad."

Breaking the rules of chicken etiquette, Simeon warmly embraced the formless little creature and hugged his repulsive, soft, slug-like body. Nothing supernatural happened during that moment of physical contact, yet in other ways, it was a magical moment. It was a confirmation that the lad from Derbyshire had truly re-established himself with the very essence of old fashioned Englishness in its purist form. Aubrey was a bundle of fun, a barrel of laughs, as vulgar as a seaside postcard, an amusing character in caricature and perhaps the last of his type. In these few seconds of touching the toad, Simeon saw the light! He saw the true reason for being torn away from Prince Charming, his opulent, comfortable palace and cosy life-style. In fear for his very life and *still* miserably in love with Ahmed – even so – Simeon had never accepted the endless flat expanse of tar and cement which called itself Detroit. He *had* to escape from Detroit. In the previous year, as a spotty chicken, he had returned to his homeland and discovered toads, gnomes, goblins, fairies and a whole Derbyshire world of quirky characters who inhabited a secret homosexual underworld. This would be the battleground – Prince Charming *or* the world of Mr Toad – he could not have both.

Twelve months before, Simeon had formed an affection for Aubrey. The unlovely little music master was despised for his common accent and promiscuous reputation by other homosexuals of the professional classes. This self-styled superior group divided themselves into the Derby Camp and the Nottingham Camp: both snobbish, both very exclusive.

The welcoming cuddle had lasted a few bare seconds when naughty toadal paws began to clutch at Simeon's bottom. Not a problem: he recalled that this toad loved to be tickled. Thus the embrace was neatly concluded when chicken fingers dug deep into soft slug-like flesh causing Aubrey to wriggle and collapse into an ecstatic fit of squealing giggles.

It was an opportunity to introduce Gary, who quickly stepped back in alarm at the sight of gloating, reptilian eyeballs sticking out like bayonets. Worse still, podgy paws were rapidly approaching the American's crotch.

"Glad to know you, Mr Pod," parried the young 'cowboy' in his most menacing, masculine, no-nonsense voice. "BUT – make no mistake; if I stay here you'll need to keep those paws to *yourself*!" Pod was gently, but firmly pushed back about three feet. "Now don't you take offence, ya hear! But, young guys like me from the US of A, well; they need personal space."

"Aubrey," interjected Simeon in some anxiety, "Perhaps I should have written to you about this, but, well, it would be really helpful if we could stay with you for a few days before moving on."

"Of course, if that is *not* convenient, I'll call a cab and we can leave right now," added Gary in cheerful finality.

"Call a cab?" asked Aubrey, still smarting from Gary's reprimand.

"He means telephone a taxi," said Simeon. "Gary doesn't know that most of us on this side of the pond have yet to enjoy the luxury of a private phone."

In the moment which followed, Aubrey Pod decided to be rational. If the gorgeous Gary refused to play, Toad took comfort from the fact that Simeon happily obliged last year. Very likely he would make himself available yet again during this visit. Accordingly, Aubrey took a deep breath, swallowed his anger and irritation born of American rejection. He decided to be a gracious host.

"Of course you can stay. You *must* stay," said the odd little fellow with arms up to shoulder level, fingers waggling in excitement. "I've three guest bedrooms which haven't been used in years. Mavis could do with the money from a few extra hours."

Mavis was the grumpy housekeeper. She had looked after the Pods ever since Aubrey was an odious child who made her life a misery when she first started as a teenage maid. Grudgingly, with sour face, she had been trudging up Cow Hill to 'muck out' this (in her view) obnoxious family of nasty mother and deviant son since the death of Mr Pod the local Bank Manager back in 1934. Mavis took the view that the money was good. Furthermore, the old witch and her repulsive reptile had always seemed indifferent to Mavis's caustic sarcasm. They were quite prepared to suffer her barely civil attitude, best described as thinly veiled chronic hostility.

Simeon stood back and soaked up the comforting scene before him: a musty hall of faded quality, filled with life by his funny little toad who was jumping about, chatting nineteen to the dozen about plans of entertainment for the next few days. Like the year before, the movie had changed from black and white to colour. It was like – 'I've a feeling we are not in Kansas anymore!' And this was certainly not Detroit. This was genuine Derbyshire and the excited toad was there to prove it. Gone were the young, desirable, all-American, butch clean-cut types. Aubrey inhabited a different world. He was one of several homosexual freaks who lurked in and around the dark corners of Peak District public lavatories.

Simeon was as exhilarated as the toad and just a voluble. He fired out questions about acquaintances and characters encountered during the previous vacation. How was little fat Dolly getting on? Still ferrying people around in his Morris 1000, doing his 'tours of old queens' and drag shows in sleazy, ramshackle back-street pubs? Was Jasper the Belper Goblin still offering sensual massage for the desperate? Was the old crone still busy chiselling out holes between one WC cubicle and the next? Did he still dedicate six half days of the week to sitting in his favourite cottages in Heanor, Ilkeston, Matlock, Ripley, Chesterfield and Derby Bus Station? What of Nobby, the funny little Gnome who danced for pennies and performed conjuring tricks? Was he still homeless? Was he still living in a different gentlemen's toilet every night? And what of that dusty old antique known as Toby Jug who had sat in a Buxton lavatory for half a century? Was that cantankerous old devil still defending his territory by attacking rivals? Did the hideous old drag queen Becksitch Betty ever turn up from his sudden disappearance at the Derby Turkish Bath? And what about that smelly mountain of ancient flesh who had to get out of Chesterfield when the police were closing in? Has Guzzly Granddad turned up in a new location? Did he take those horrible feral boys Monks and Muckles with him? Where they still procuring young lads, taking them back as 'food for Granddad', back to some other decrepit slum? And that funny little queen: did he still live with them: the one who went into a trance to communicate with the dead?

Aubrey could hardly keep up with this instant demand for so much information, so he shouted up the stairs and barked out an order for refreshments to welcome his new guests. Five minutes later they were in an antiquated, fusty living room of many covers which had all the Victorian taste of Nelly Pod and all the indifferent neglect of a toad who had dedicated his life to the service of others – mainly servicing other gentlemen who loitered in various gentlemen's latrines.

A sour, sulky Mavis appeared with a large try of tea. It was dropped with contempt on a side table, disturbing the dust on an ancient aspidistra.

"Thank you, Mavis. You'll remember my American friend Simeon?"

"I remember 'im," sniffed the God-fearing, 'chapel-every-Sunday', deeply homophobic Mavis, avoiding eye contact with both boys.

"Well, this is his friend Gary. They'll be staying for a few days. I hope that won't put you out too much?"

"Extra hours, Mr Pod." stabbed out the grim servant in cutting response.

"Of course, Mavis! That goes without saying."

And without saying anything, Mavis turned and stomped out of the room.

"You mustn't mind Mavis. She's one of the 'old school'. She can be a bit abrupt and waspish, but she's faithful, slops me out every morning, looks after me very well."

"Slops you out?" enquired Gary.

"She empties out his chamber pot," explained Simeon. "It's a ceramic pot kept under Aubrey's bed – for convenience. The two proper loos are down here – one inside and one outside."

"Oh my God!" said Gary.

"Anyway," replied Aubrey, ignoring this criticism of primitive conditions, "just make sure that you keep your rooms tidy or you'll get the sharp edge of her tongue!

"I think I've heard of your Mavis," said Gary. "Is she a Mrs Danvers?"

"No," said Aubrey. "It's Mavis Plunket."

Aubrey Pod was quite well read in the classics, but Gary's sardonic comment was completely lost on both toad and chicken.

CHAPTER 20

Sneering Snobs

As it was Friday, Simeon's enquiries turned to the upper echelons of Derbyshire's gay society. The year before he had been taken to a weekly gathering of elite homosexuals who were known as the Derby Camp. These 'gentlemen of quality' assembled in a dimly lit bar inside an old hotel called The Friary, situated in a smart Georgian area called Friar Gate. For nearly half a century it had become an institution – Friday Night at the Friary. Simeon had dubbed these servile types 'nodding heads' because of their endless obsequious agreement with the boss. It was sickening to see the slavish, sycophantic worship of their leader, a certain Claud Hoadley, who seemed to have authority, seemed to exert power.

"Don't talk to me about that artificial, affected ponce!" spat out Aubrey with bitterness. Toad of the Toilets had never been received into that privileged clique in spite of his university degree and status as a schoolmaster. Apart from Pod's appalling reputation, his outrageous promiscuous conduct, Claud Hoadley would not tolerate such an ugly effeminate man in his inner circle and certainly not a man who spoke like a peasant. In the Derby Camp, careful enunciation was all important. All vowels had to be perfectly rounded and highly polished in an attempt to reach the majesty of Hoadley's own Royal Diction – the Gold Standard in this privileged community of homosexuals in the professional classes. The closed 'U' and occasional dropped 'H' of a common toad could never be acceptable in The Friary.

"Well, it *is* Friday night. Let's go to The Friary." said Simeon with a mischievous grin.

"NO!" shouted Aubrey. "I refuse to be humiliated again. I tried it once. Nobody spoke to me, nobody cared…" said the little fellow as his voice trailed off attracting Simeon's sympathy. He was young, but able to appreciate all the negative experiences over the years which had warped this unpopular and disturbed individual.

"Hypocrites!" responded Simeon. "And half of them devout Anglicans sitting, kneeling and standing at Derby Cathedral every Sunday. Listen, Aubrey, The Friary is a *public* place. We'll go there tonight just to irritate them. They can't keep us out."

"That's where you're wrong. They can keep *you* out. There's a strict dress code. They'll say you're not properly dressed. You've to wear a suit. As I recall, everybody called you the 'scruffy chicken' last year – anoraks, shorts, boots, rucksack and the rest. You haven't got a suit."

"Actually, Aubrey, this year, I *do* have a suit. And we are going to The Friary. We'll march right up to snooty Hoadley and force him to acknowledge you. We'll rub his face in it!"

Later that evening, Gary and Simeon had somehow shoehorned themselves into the uncomfortable toadmobile. Aubrey, excited and frantic as ever, was hunched over the wheel, tooting at other road users who had the temerity to be on the same road. Eventually, they entered the Georgian splendour of Friar Gate in Derby. Like a dodgem, the 'pregnant roller-skate' (as Gary called it) made several agitated turns before coming to rest in a picturesque retreat of cobbles and old lime trees. Aubrey bounced out like an over-wound toy and, more slowly, his passengers prised themselves out of that little tin box. They took a few seconds to admire several classical columns supporting an impressive porch – the grand entrance to a dignified 18th century mansion which had become the Friary Hotel.

The soft silence, dim lighting and faded grandeur of the public bar was just as Simeon remembered it: dark and fusty. The very fabric of ancient drapes, worn carpets and leather chairs seemed to have absorbed decades of snobbery emanating from snooty, stuffy old men in dingy suits. The leader of the rival Nottingham Camp, Martin Harcourt QC had described it as –

"A temple of theatrical affectation – a platform for the power structure of Hoadley's sneering disciples – an empire built on the fear of exposure. Indeed, an empire still feeding on the Victorian myth that insanity and homosexuality are seen as caused by moral weakness. Beware, young man! Hoadley has Derby tied up tight. If you fall under his influence, he will subtly undermine your confidence. Your dreams of becoming a teacher – or anything else worthwhile – will end up in the dustbin!"

And there they were – the nodding heads – all fawning, all kowtowing, all murmuring agreement, all clustered around the First Homosexual of Derbyshire. It was that same group of shadowy, dark, smart, grey gentlemen – the same tableau which had been on show for decades. Hoadley, the quintessence of good taste and excellent grooming was just as impressive as ever from the top of his perfectly combed hair down to his highly polished expensive shoes. The exulted reputation of Hoadley and members of his retinue was further buttressed by a regular presence at Derby Cathedral. Membership of the Church of England ensured that this self-proclaimed elite were seen as 'gentlemen'.

Nobody *appeared* to notice the entrance of two chickens and one toad because, as usual, Hoadley was holding court passing comment on current affairs. After a brief observation of the appropriate sentence just passed for the iniquitous crimes of Brady and Hindley, he applauded the recently deceased Evelyn Waugh for refusing to have a radio or television in his home.

"Not that I particularly admire his work. Of course, we could do worse in our choice of reading, but, we should aim higher and cultivate taste befitting a gentleman of true quality."

"Quite right, Claud," droned a big, soft, pappy, nodding queen.

"Hilary Raymond Hawley," whispered Simeon into the ear of Gary. "He's Hoadley's number two, known as HRH to the Nottingham Camp. Completely unreal! An ideal target for piss taking."

"Of course I've written to *The Times*," continued the pedant, who had now moved to a different subject. "I'm horrified the BBC should regard a foul-mouthed, lowborn bigot as a fit subject for humour. The script writer went too far in describing Mr Heath as 'a grammar school twit.' I shall also…"

Hoadley came to a full stop when the three strangers had stealthily shuffled so close to his august presence, they were now impossible to ignore. In sharp tones, he addressed them directly.

"You there! Did you want something?"

For a few moments all three were cowed by the majestic reprimand so carefully enunciated, it clearly relegated the trio to a place in the lower orders. Simeon felt as if he were a dustman who had blundered into the wrong entrance looking for bins. He was the first to speak.

"Sorry, Mr Hoadley. I do beg your pardon. I assumed that you had recognised me. David Bond presented me last year but… well; I don't seem to see him here," asserted Simeon, with a satirical hint of bravado and cheek.

"Mr Bond is not here," said Hoadley maintaining an edge to his voice. In the poor light available, he studied the young man. "Yes, I have a dim memory of receiving you. Your name?"

"Hogg, Simeon Hogg."

"Are you not the cyclist from the colonies, originating from a colliery village?"

"Horsley Woodhouse," said Simeon, slowly, carefully sounding both H's.

"Quite. You must excuse me for a few minutes, gentlemen. This young person is in need of… suitable advice."

Hoadley detached himself from the group and escorted Simeon to the bar. Leaderless, the nodding heads began to mill around, chatting with each other like pupils who enjoy the sudden absence of a stern schoolmaster. Gary was quickly approached by a thin, tall man with a macabre grin. Ghastly skin stretched tight across facial bones gave his head the appearance of a skull. Aubrey Pod was approached by no one at all.

In that short walk, Simeon noted Hoadley's bolt-upright, straight-as-pole posture which added to that indefinable air of authority. Close up, the sharp handsome features suggested a man in his mid-fifties more than a decade short of his 68 years. However, those shrewd, cold, grey eyes and cruel lips were poised to bring this common boy to heel. A few minutes into this rather tense conference, it became clear that the former schoolmaster's memory of the previous meeting with the cyclist was not so dim after all.

"Good to see that you have decided to dress *appropriately* on this occasion – and, I perceive – minus the acne!"

"David advised me to sunbathe."

"Indeed. I don't wish to appear rude, Simeon, but I feel that you and your friends would be more in place, shall we say, more *comfortable* at the alternative venue for members of 'our society'."

The 'alternative venue' was a clear reference to the Corporation Hotel in the Cattle Market. Even in that seedy establishment, homosexuals were tolerated in the crowded passageway only, but it was usually lined with friendly faces amid the hum of jolly banter. Rough trade, rent boys and a notorious urinal in the yard gave made the Corporation very attractive to (as Hoadley would put it) the lower orders. These were members of the Third Camp, a dustbin for homosexuals who were excluded from the elite gatherings known as the Derby Camp and the Nottingham Camp.

As the dialogue progressed, Simeon sensed that, behind the formal mask of authority and rectitude, Hoadley found this working-class youth alluring and was content to keep the conversation going. At one point, he enquired about Simeon's adventures on the other side of the Atlantic, and visibly sneered at the mention of a university in Detroit. All things American were despised by this Victorian arch-anglophile.

"It's gratifying to hear that you feel you did well at... that college. Notwithstanding, surely you must be aware that academic standards in the United States are *far* below our own, and therefore, your high marks should be treated with caution. David showed me a letter that you had written to him, the one in which you outlined your plans to train as a teacher in this country. Please don't be offended, young man, but your English leaves much to be desired. Your grammar, spelling and general syntax are at a level more consistent with junior school, let alone the rigorous entry requirements of *our* teacher training colleges. Of course, I appreciate it's quite natural for you to desire to re-settle in your homeland – but you *must* be realistic. Forget higher education. The economy is vibrant. At the present time the newspapers are full of jobs. I noticed that Spondon Power Station is recruiting craft apprentices." Against his will, the listener was impressed by the number of Rs inserted into that one word 'crrrarrrwft'. The speaker prepared his closing line. "Of course, if you prefer a cleaner environment – perhaps shop work?"

Simeon listened to this demeaning lecture in stony silence. Even so, perhaps because he believed Claud Hoadley to be essentially a 'wise man' who could proffer good advice, he remained open to further questions and, ultimately, revealed the full story of his painful and failed love affair with Ahmed. The older man listened in respectful silence but with reproving thin lips pressed tightly together. At the conclusion, he lifted an imperious finger to summon the barman who raced over to the Great Man. The drinks arrived. Hoadley examined his glass for any offending smears and took a sip before responding.

"I disapprove of homosexual love affairs. They never work. It is in our nature to stray. We are disposed to be promiscuous. Love? Don't be stupid, boy. You were never in love. You were – in *lust*. You allowed yourself to be mesmerised by a comely lad of powerful personality who abused that power. But most of all, Simeon, I am *appalled* that you have allowed yourself to fall into the grip of *criminals!*"

"Have you been listening to me? I didn't have much choice!"

"I can assure you that I have listened to your woeful tale with the utmost attention and, of *course* you had a choice. You should have chosen to turn your face away from evil. As we speak, in our own capital city, a monstrous homosexual is corrupting and seducing boys, boys younger than yourself. He and his twin brother have built up a powerful crime syndicate which punishes disloyalty with unspeakable torture and death. It seems to me that *you* have found the depravity of your brash, loud-mouthed lover acceptable because, in your eyes, it is done with *style*. The opulence of his home and flashy suits has covered a multitude of sins. Wake up, boy! Open your eyes to the parallels! It's just the same as Ronnie Kray. The unpleasant nature of *his* career is disguised by his adherence to old-time East End virtues of family solidarity and by the reflected glory of the irresponsible showbiz company he keeps. Like you, those dreadful celebrities do not enquire too deeply into how such a lavish lifestyle is funded."

At that moment, Hoadley noticed the effect of his heartless castigation. Staring hard at some focal point far beyond the Friary Hotel, Simeon was silent, holding himself very still with deep, unsteady breathing. Glistening eyes suggested a tremendous effort to keep back tears. A small part of this pompous pedant could still communicate with the one-time teenage Hoadley and recall an intense love affair with a soldier of the First World War. It was this part which was touched by the human failings of the boy before him. Accordingly, his hard features softened and, when he spoke, his voice held an uncharacteristic gentleness.

"I know you've hated me for this... brutal scolding. It's difficult being a young man in love. It's even more difficult and painful when homosexuality complicates matters – as it always does. For what it's worth, I don't think you need fear this distant criminal or 'The Firm' as they call themselves. It's unlikely their senior management will be prepared to invest the time and sums necessary to locate and snatch you back to satisfy the hurt pride of the young man you describe. Articulate and intelligent he may be, but – do not be deceived by his personal magnetism – he is a thug, and an American thug at that. People of that class have a high sex drive and will quickly find a replacement. The idea that you need to hide with the toad is fanciful. Just get on with your life."

CHAPTER 21

The Wolfenden Report

Hoadley looked at the boy who appeared to be rather miserable in his current miasma of mixed and confused feelings. For a moment, the pedant, still inclined to gentleness, unsure of his next line, seized on an opportunity when he noticed Simeon had an empty glass.

"You hardly look old enough to be in here. Notwithstanding, I suppose you'd better have another orange juice." Again, Hoadley raised a commanding finger. At the double, an obsequious waiter slightly out of breath was at their side. Embarrassed, Simeon muttered his thanks.

"Well at lease you'll be spared the liver failure which struck down young Jeremy Wolfenden last year," said Hoadley in a deliberate attempt to change the subject.

"Another chicken?" asked Simeon.

"Apart from homosexuality, you and Wolfenden have almost *nothing* in common. If it's any comfort, actually, I find you more likeable."

"What do you mean – 'struck down'?"

"Liver failure is the result of excessive drinking, young man. Ah! Here is your orange juice."

"Thank you, Mr Hoadley."

"Not at all," replied Hoadley, as he motioned for the hovering waiter to depart. As if making a speech, he resumed. "Of course, it was *claimed* that Wolfenden fainted and hit his head on a washbasin. A likely story! And at 31, we can hardly accord to our Jeremy the status of 'chicken'. 'Suspicious circumstances': that's how the *Daily Telegraph* put it. *You* should be reading a broadsheet of quality, young man. I can recommend the *Daily Telegraph*. It is the preferred choice of Our Gracious Lady, Queen Elizabeth. Now where was I?"

"Something about The Queen?" suggested Simeon.

"*Nothing* about The Queen you ignorant youth!" I was *not* referring to The Monarch. I was referring to her mother. To be perceived as someone of worth you should always mention the Sovereign simply as 'The Queen'. To gentle people who move in superior circles, Her Mother is always 'Queen Elizabeth', *not* The Queen Mother and *never* The Queen Mum!"

"What about this Jeremy Wool-thing-done?"

"Ah! Of course, Wolfenden. He was in Washington at the time of his death as a Foreign Correspondent – but he had other fish to fry," added Hoadley with an edge of contempt.

"Why don't we have anything in common... me and this Jeremy Wool-thing-done? And what's fish got to do with it?"

"You must forgive me. I speak in riddles. Jeremy Wolfenden was educated at Eton and went on to Oxford where he received a first class honours degree in Philosophy, Politics and Economics." [Lots of Rs stuffed inside the tiny word of class] "He was known as the cleverest young man in England."

Hoadley came to a significant pause and looked down his nose at the working class boy before him.

"David Bond tells me that you hail from a family of coal miners and attended a Secondary Modern School in... *Heanor*, I believe he said?"

"That's right," said Simeon, bridling and bristling up to his full five foot, nine inches. "*I* was the cleverest boy in Mrs Cook's class!"

"*Indeed!* I'm gratified to hear it." replied Hoadley, with a smile responding to Simeon's sardonic tone. They both smiled and both enjoyed the joke. "As to fish," he continued, "I regret to inform you that Jeremy Wolfenden was a spy. Most of the time he lived in Moscow and was a friend of Guy Burgess. Of course, nobody's quite sure which side he was on. Probably *both* sides."

"A double agent," mused Simeon. "Why is it that gay people are so traitorous? Could it be something to do with gay men being already, well, sort of... separated from mainstream society? I mean, perhaps they feel isolated and have no real feeling for Queen and Country."

"A good question – well answered. Full marks to Mrs Cook for encouraging you to think. But, dear boy, *this* is England. In this country we're quite content with the word 'queer' as an alternative to homosexual. The Derby Camp does *not* approve of vulgar Americanisms."

"*Queer* is vulgar. It's insulting. Gay comes from Good-As-You and homosexual sounds like a disease!" asserted Simeon with rising confidence.

"How quaint, but your American university really should have helped you more with *correct* pronunciation. When *you* say homosexual it sounds more like a popular washing powder much beloved by our dowdy fish-wife population. Dreadful common women! They keep popping up on commercial television – the channel of plebeians."

"What's pebble – beans?"

"The common herd, boy! Plebeians are the people outside of our society, peasants cluttering the street beyond these hallowed doors. They are the coarse and the crude. You will find, Simeon, people of quality, those of us who circulate in *higher* circles know the difference between Latin and Greek. The word homosexual is from the Greek – homo meaning the same pronounced as 'hom – o'. It is *not* from the Latin – homo meaning man pronounced as 'home – o'".

Hoadley allowed a few moments to pass whilst his pupil absorbed this refined knowledge.

"As Lady Britomart said – 'Nobody can say a word against Greek: it stamps a man at once as an educated gentleman.'"

"Who is Lady Britomart when she's at home?" asked the pupil.

"A woman from one of Shaw's more socialist plays. I disapprove of socialism," replied Hoadley with the finality of tightly closed lips.

Simeon was sadly mulling over his ignorance of Shaw and socialism when the pedant broke into his thoughts.

"Returning to your question, it was said that young Wolfenden was recruited by our SIS."

"SIS?"

"Secret Intelligence Service. They seek out superior homosexuals as spies because homosexuals are not generally encumbered with the usual baggage of wives or children. And many have already been disowned by close relatives by the end of their formal education."

"So I wasn't far wrong," said Simeon with a touch of bitterness. The two men looked at each other.

"No Simeon." Hoadley spoke solemnly with sincerity. "You are correct and have spoken well. Jeremy was honest and open with his father when he confessed his homosexuality. But he should have remained silent like the rest of us. It broke poor Sir John's heart."

"The hell with *poor* Sir John's heart!" spat out Simeon. "Why should anyone 'confess' to what is natural? Would your precious Sir John admit his disgusting heterosexuality to his son and be ashamed to have those feelings for the opposite sex! Can't you see that it's people like *you* who have always…"

Simeon came to an abrupt halt. His argument had collapsed in a tantrum seething with anger and injustice. The Master of the Friary kept a tight grip on his dignity, remained composed and took a few moments to muster his response. In spite of his establishment views, innate snobbery and rank pomposity, Hoadley harboured a small sympathy for the frustration boiling over before him and had empathy with a passionate youngster who had a good case but was unable to articulate that case. Accordingly, when Hoadley's response came, it was far less acid than if the attack had been delivered by an equal. His tone was measured, calm and slightly nonchalant as he picked a speck from the arm of his immaculate suit.

"I take your point, but you know Simeon, I wouldn't be too hard on Sir John Wolfenden. He's rather like me. He's on your side. He's on *our* side."

"What's that suppose to mean?" responded a sullen Simeon, temporarily reverting to his one-time Heanor rudeness.

"It means that I'll be posting a strong letter to the Chancellor of your American university."

"What!"

"Don't be alarmed, boy. *His* conduct and standards will be called into question, not yours. You told me that your courses included a survey of 20th Century British Social History. Yet, the honourable name of Wolfenden meant nothing at all to you!" Continuing, Claud Hoadley stiffened and mounted his soapbox. "John Wolfenden was an Oxford Don, a former headmaster of two quality schools and eventually became Vice Chancellor of Reading University. Quite rightly, he was knighted by Her Majesty in recognition of his services to the nation in chairing the Wolfenden Committee. This was a mixed group of 'the great and the good' who were charged with the responsibility of examining laws which apply to homosexuality. In other words – should men who are caught with their trousers down having sex with *other* men with *their* trousers down – should those naughty men be punished? Should they be thrown into prison?"

"No," said Simeon.

"That is what Jeremy said to his father. The Wolfenden Report was published in 1957 – only nine years ago." Hoadley stepped down from the soapbox and looked at a bemused Simeon. And he waited.

"I had hoped, young man," he said in a more persuading, personable voice, "that you would ask me about the *findings* of Sir John's report."

"What were the findings of Sir John's report?" said Simeon mechanically.

"The Wolfenden Committee urged that public statutes should avoid the attempt to legislate morality. It said that private homosexual liaisons between consenting adults over the age of 21 be removed from the domain of the criminal law."

"What a mouth full! Does that mean that we'll be able to have sex just so long as nobody can actually see us?" said Simeon.

"Would that it was so simple!" smiled Hoadley. "I've studied the Wolfenden Report. If its recommendations are *ever* accepted, *if* that is ever the case, then homosexuality will *still* be illegal unless it takes place within carefully defined circumstances."

"So we *can't* have sex!"

"You would be able to have sex with a man in a private house providing a third man is not in another part of that house. Sex in a hotel or in a car would remain illegal. Entrenched attitudes will *never* change. Heterosexuals will always be able to 'chat up' each other, as the current lingo has it. In this establishment, for example, 'chatting up' would be seen as soliciting for an immoral purpose."

"Doesn't sound very hopeful," muttered Simeon.

"On the contrary, I am very hopeful. The very existence of the Wolfenden Report is evidence of progress. During my lifetime, we have seen no progress at all. A word of advice, young man: be patient, tread carefully to advance effectively. *Example* is our most potent weapon. I move in the highest circles of Derby and am always treated with the greatest respect. People are not stupid. Take this hotel, the staff and management, they *know* but do *not* wish to be told. Mrs Patrick Campbell put it very well when she urged good behaviour and discretion. It's what she meant when she said 'don't frighten the horses'. And one other item," he looked over to Gary and the toad, "*your* position, young man, will *not* improve keeping company with toads, goblins, gnomes and other assorted low life. Don't forget, you are judged by the company you keep."

To rest and allow his words of wisdom to percolate into the youthful mind, Hoadley took a few more sips of his drink.

"I wonder? Will you profit by my counsel?" Since the meaning of this question was not entirely clear to this particular youthful mind, the pedant took advantage of the hesitation and put a different question. "If it will be of any assistance or encouragement, I'll deign to follow your progress. I assume you have a card? Most Americans do."

"A card? What sort of card?"

"Like this."

From his inside pocket, he produced a small white card beautifully inscribed thus –
Claud Hoadley Esq.
Darley Towers,
Darley Park,
Darley Abbey,
Derby.

Simeon looked at this impressive crisp card which was in mint condition.

"Note the omission of the 'e'.

"Pardon?"

"My Christian name. It is spelt without the usual 'e'"

"Oh." replied the boy who would not have been able to spell Claud anyway. Simeon dug into his fat wallet, rummaged around and eventually pulled out a roughly cut card, one of several, upon which he had carefully printed his name and an address at Bog Hole Row in Horsley Woodhouse. Aunty Joyce had given this permission for a postal address.

"What is *that*?" cried Hoadley in some alarm.

"Well it might not be as posh as yours but..."

"No, boy! *That!!*" Rudely, he thrust his hand into Simeon's wallet and removed another card upon which was printed a list of names, addresses and a few telephone numbers. Equally as rudely, Simeon snatched back his card of contact details.

There followed a rather severe reprimand from the older man who was extremely angry.

"Have you any idea how dangerous it is for those unfortunate people on that confounded list!"

Simeon was stunned into a hurtful silence. The Great Man was in a fury. The scolding increased in its severity as he spat out each word which comprised a painful castigation.

"When you are being dragged around stinking latrines by that disgusting toad or – God knows what public urinals known only to that vile vagrant the Gnome – at any time, lad, at *any* time, you could be, probably *will* be, entrapped by the CID! They are plain clothed police officers known as *agents provocateur* – policemen who are trained to tempt homosexuals into committing a crime of lewd conduct, a crime of gross indecency. You will make your move, and then they will arrest you. They will also arrest the toad, or the Gnome or that obese Dolly or whatever cesspit-slime you happen to be with. Oh yes," he nodded, "David Bond has informed me of the sickening circles in which you move. Officers of the Law will then escort you to the police station and promise leniency if you agree to tell all. They will write down every sordid detail of the activities involving the ill-fated men on that appalling list. *You* may escape, but *all* on your nasty little list will go to prison. The men *you* denounce will suffer. Make no mistake about that, boy!"

Simeon could not reply. Wounded, choked with emotion, he stood frozen before the Master with moist eyes. The older Simeon of four decades on would always remember that painful moment. When the new century arrived some 34 years later, he had long forgiven Hoadley for his robust reaction to that infamous list. This was a wiser Simeon who had, by that time, enjoyed the benefit of the Wolfenden Report. Ten years after publication, its recommendations were finally accepted by the Wilson Government in 1967. At long last, homosexuality had been de-criminalised and gay address books had lost much of their terror.

Simeon and Claud – here was a clash of cultures, a clash of times. Essentially, Hoadley was a Victorian. He had seen terrible affliction to his people from the endemic scourge of ignorance, discrimination and bigotry which had stalked English homosexual society during his lifetime. Claud Hoadley did not have a word to describe such rabid prejudice against the gay community. Homophobia was that word. It had yet to be coined.

The angry castigator took a hold, calmed down, collected himself and resumed his straight-as-a-pole posture. He avoided eye contact with Simeon. The sharp edge of his voice had disappeared when he spoke a few measured words to conclude his 'suitable advice'.

"I've found this interview instructive and interesting." He looked over to the group which was now humming with conversation. "Your well-proportioned American friend seems to be quite popular with our gathering. Extremely popular! Yes, quite so. We'll be pleased to see you both here... from time to time. However," his tone was now commanding and slightly sardonic, "I beseech you, Simeon – *do not* on any future occasion desecrate the sanctity of the Friary Hotel with the appearance of a lowly, common toad!"

That same toad felt totally humiliated. He had had quite enough of standing around and being ignored. He was frantically gesticulating to Simeon and rattling his keys, a familiar signal which meant 'I WANT TO LEAVE NOW'. Simeon left Hoadley without a word and ploughed through the thick knot around Gary.

"Toad's throwing a tantrum! He's about to leave with, or without us," said Simeon with some urgency to his popular friend. Gary pulled him aside to impart secretive news.

"You go back with your spoilt little reptile. I'm staying," whispered Gary. "I've discovered something *really* exciting. Here in Derbyshire! You'd never believe it! I want to learn more from the professor."

"Professor? The one you've been chatting with? Tall, hideous, looks like death warmed over, head like a skull?"

"And prepared to pay my price. No time to explain now. Tell you at Toad Hall on Sunday. I'm going back with him – for the weekend. It's the information I'm really interested in. Hey! What gives? Are you OK?"

"Course, I am!"

"Sure?"

"Yeah."

"You look like you've been crying!"

"No."

"OK. Speak soon."

CHAPTER 22

Martin Harcourt QC

After breakfast on the following morning, Aubrey vented his frustration, disappointment and anger regarding the 'rude conduct' of his American guest.

"Going off like that! And with… did you see him?"

"Yes, Aubrey. Not a pretty sight," mumbled a groggy Simeon through a mouth full of toast, still struggling to full consciousness after deep sleep.

"Not a pretty sight! It was the ugliest thing which ever broke bread! Did you see his face? Haggard, dirty yellow, sunken and stained with age! Gary goes off with that emaciated old cadaver and has the cheek to refuse *me*! Me!! A youthful, virile 36 year old!"

"Yes, Aubrey," muttered a bleary-eyed Simeon pouring himself a third cup of tea.

"Of course, I could refuse to have him back. That would teach him! Why should I provide accommodation for the ungrateful? I am *not* the Salvation Army!"

"No, Aubrey."

"And if he likes what you say he likes, I could do something for him – and do it well. He should be grateful. It wouldn't hurt him to let me have a poke, would it?"

"No, Aubrey."

"I'm *good* at it. I'm well equipped," ranted the boasting toad, warming to his subject, leaning nearer over the remains and rubble of breakfast with a lascivious leer. "After I'd done that rough hippie in Canning Circus cottage last week, I said to him 'Was that all right then?' and he replied, '*You're* all right where it *counts*!' Another satisfied customer. You should have been there, Simeon. They were all looking at us! We were going at it like billy-oh! Him bent over, head in the urinal, *loving* it – ornamental chains dangling round his dirty neck, strings o' beads, necklaces and stuff all swinging to and fro, banging away, rattling away like there was no tomorrow. If a copper had walked in at that moment, we wouldn't stop. No. He would have had to wait until we'd finished. And another thing, you know what Dolly always says…"

"Yes, Aubrey," said the weary, harangued guest in an attempt to stem the endless bombast. "We all know what a big boy you are. You've told me many times what Dolly always says – 'You were on the front row when they were given out.' Anyway, if this old guy is still a professor at some university, he must be under retirement age."

"A professor!"

"Yes. He professes to desire Gary and is prepared to pay."

"Gary charges for sex?"

"Yes. And a lot more than the ten bob you gave to that scruffy road sweeper in Ripley cottage last year."

"How much would he want then? Would he do it for a pound?" pleaded the eager toad, keen eyes bulging and mouth salivating in the hope that he may yet lay his lewd, lecherous hands on the ravishing Gary Mackenzie.

"He charges the going rate in Detroit – $20 minimum. That's about £7. Sorry, Aubrey, but in *your* case, I'm afraid it would be a lot more. That death's head professor will be paying through the nose if I know my friend." Aubrey was visibly gobsmacked by these sums. Simeon added – "Don't forget, wages are three to four times higher in the States. Manufactured goods are cheaper, but *services* are much more expensive. I pay $2, that's fourteen shillings just for a haircut, and it's at least $20 to visit the doctor."

Aubrey Pod sank back in his chair to ponder the implications of this new intelligence. He reached for a pencil and asked questions about Gary's business habits.

"Well, let me see," said Simeon. "I reckon, on average, he turns two tricks a night – shall we say – about five days a week?"

"That's $200 a week," said Aubrey, now scribbling in the margin of his *Derby Evening Telegraph.* It was next to an item which had caught his attention; an unfortunate vicar arrested for gross indecency. "How many weeks holiday will Gary give himself?"

"My friend is an opportunist," smiled Simeon. "He'll work on vacation if the occasional skull-headed professor turns up with an offer. I suggest you multiply the $200 by 50 weeks per year. Gary will celebrate his 18th birthday this September and I'm certain he's been hustling at this rate for the last three years."

"Eleven thousand pounds – eleven times my net income!" said Aubrey, concluding his calculations with incredulity.

"And tax free," added Simeon.

"Would he have put it in a bank? Would his parents know?"

"I wish I knew. I expect his parents, like mine, know, but don't *want* to know about his activities. Banks? Well, on this holiday he carries around a great deal of cash in large denominations. In Scotland he changed about $1500 into sterling and then found it very bulky. I can't say how much he still has in dollars here, or back in the States. I suspect it's a very large amount! It's all guess work and, frankly, none of our business."

Simeon looked over the breakfast table at his friend who, at a loss in this brief silence, seemed younger and vulnerable. Contrasted with the machinations and hard realities of Detroit, the toad, an already damaged little man, was very much a creature of his own Derbyshire and of his own time. It was a more innocent time, if anything, more pre-war than post-war. Suddenly, Simeon became aware of the possible danger to his defenceless friend.

"You know, Aubrey, I've been thinking. It might be better for you if we *both* moved on and found alternative accommodation." At this, the toad shot out of his seat in alarm, came round the table and pleaded with his guest.

"No, no, don't go Simeon! I've offended you haven't I? I apologise. I really do. Gary can stay. You can both stay as long as you like."

Overcome with affection and compassion for his funny little friend, Simeon stood up and gave the toad his second hug, a longer hug – and *still* he failed to turn into a handsome prince.

"My poor, poor little Aubrey," he whispered into the toadal ear. "You've completely misunderstood me." At the conclusion of the embrace, they went into Mr Pod's private study and sank into comfortable armchairs where Simeon decided to trust his ugly little friend with all the information he had already imparted to Claud Hoadley on the previous evening. Aubrey listened to his guest's extraordinary saga of abduction and resulting adventures with bated breath.

"So you see, Aubrey, staying here could put you in danger. We *must* go."

After the style of Sherlock Holmes with fingertips pressed together, the host sat back and stared through the window up to the high Chevin Hills nicely lit by morning sunshine. Apart from the bad-tempered sound of Mavis clattering pots in the kitchen, all was silent. Aubrey was mulling over, considering and analysing the implications of this new intelligence to his personal safety. Eventually, he burst into excitement, sat up straight and eagerly leaned towards Simeon.

"You will stay! Both of you for as long as you like. This is the safest place. Anyway, Hoadley is quite right. The mafia, if it is the proper mafia, won't take the time and trouble to scour England, turning every stone, seeking out the likes of you two. It sounds as if this Arab has a good choice of stuff already. He's only to cast out his local net and pull in as many chickens as he wants. You stay with me."

Just to be on the safe side, feeling the need for the best possible advice, the best *legal* advice, Simeon decided to consult his friend Martin Harcourt QC in Nottingham. But after this important conference, there was an improvement in the general atmosphere. Aubrey became bouncy and cheerful at the prospect of having two frisky young lads around the place to balance the po-faced, strait-laced and generally dour Mavis. He suspected that he would see little of the mercurial Gary Mackenzie, but Simeon was a different matter. He was more stay-at-home, more pliable, and, in this year, actually more affectionate.

Simeon suggested that the 'extra hours' and other additional expenses should be covered by a weekly payment for board and lodgings.

"How much do you think?" asked Simeon.

"Don't trouble yourself about that for a few weeks," said Aubrey, gently, kindly – but with ogling toadal eyes getting larger and a wanton toadal paw landing on the boy's leg. "I'm sure we can come to some satisfactory arrangement," purred the vile, mouth-watering little reptile, now crouching, wanting, fumbling with zipper and willing to receive his boarder's first milky instalment of rent. Simeon was embarrassed and ashamed. He had a dark side which wanted to be ravished by a monster. As with the previous year in a cave near Bridlington, he had to acknowledge that deep in his sexual psyche there was a perverse desire to be tasted by that clever toadal tongue slobbering and slurping with succulent sounds. And below, those naughty fingers, busy fingers, sticky with drool, searching and sliding around the nooks and crannies of bliss. It became too much; overwhelming – toadal touches, tickles and titillations of a thousand thrills – until he spent. He deposited his ecstatic first instalment deep into the dark depths of the talented toad – ugly Toad of Toad Hall.

As it was a sunny Saturday afternoon, Aubrey invited his friend to join him on a tour of the cottages. If it was a rainy Saturday afternoon, the Derby Turkish Bath would call. Simeon politely declined, but asked for a lift to the village of Horsley Woodhouse. He decided to visit Nottingham. For this, and to get around generally, he would need the bicycle he had bought the year before. It was still where he parked it, the safest possible place, leaning up against the wall in the hallway of Aunty Joyce. This shy spinster of limited experience was surprised to see her nephew turn up out of the blue. After the usual routine of gentle fussing and wittering, she was a little hurt to learn that that he was staying elsewhere.

"Is it that man who come to see ya?"

"What man?" asked Simeon, suddenly very alert and cautious. Joyce became puzzled and somewhat confused.

"Well... he didn't give a name." said Joyce, slowly, bovine as ever. "You've so many friends. It were yesterday, just before teatime. He'd got a car! He was nicely spoken with nice manners and well dressed. Ya grandma used to say 'If they've got a clean handkerchief and polished shoes, there's nowt much wrong with 'em.'"

"Did he have an American accent?"

"What?"

"Think, Joyce, this could be important. This man – did he sound *foreign* in any way?"

"No. Don't think so. Just talked nice to me."

"Could you tell if the car was English? Was it a very big car.?"

"Well it was... sort of... a *nice* car."

Cycling to Nottingham, Simeon did his best with this meagre information. In the previous year he had given Aunty Joyce abridged accounts of his friends but, for obvious reasons involving homosexual secrecy, she had never actually met them. The mysterious caller could have been any one of several acquaintances from the previous year – or, he could be somebody enquiring on behalf of The Firm in Detroit. He thanked his aunt for keeping the bicycle for him. On departure, for security, he stooped to mendacity. He mentioned staying at a hotel in Derby for a few days. As vague as possible, he explained the holiday would consist of cycling around the country, staying at cheap bed and breakfast places and the occasional youth hostel.

Joyce Hogg was just the same, never changing; not very bright, but neither was she simple. However, the unwelcome experience of a strange man calling at her door had been unsettling and the tone of her voice held a hint of disapproval. Over the years, this narrow spinster had absorbed some of the ongoing unspoken undercurrent of family homophobia directed towards Simeon. Be that as it may, aunt and nephew had always got on well together. Indeed, they were held together as victims of family scorn and shame. In common, they both suffered a degree of working class opprobrium heaped upon a woman who had never married, and also heaped upon a youth who was never seen with a girlfriend.

A brief call from a public phone box established that Martin Harcourt QC was available and would be delighted to see Simeon. It took about an hour and a half to cycle the thirteen miles to Nottingham Castle and arrive at the exclusive, leafy residential area adjacent called The Park. As with his first visit, the cyclist was in awe of the size and splendour of the portico. He was a touch embarrassed standing with a humble bicycle before the

large black door with its highly-polished brasses. Two powerful knocks summoned the
same young, exotic American Negro who had excited considerable lust on the first visit.
There was a marked disparity between the informality of an enthusiastic beaming smile of
welcome and the dignified hush of an elegant old house known as The Court.

"Hey, Simeon! What's cookin', sweet meat," said a row of beautiful gleaming
white teeth. "Bring it right in, man."

"Hello, Butch. Good to see you're still here – and, as ever, still bulging in all
the right places!"

Boy and bike were admitted into a richly-panelled reception area. The latter
enjoyed the splendour of a parking-place in stark contrast to its more familiar place of rest
in a miner's terrace cottage. Simeon was showed into the library where Martin Harcourt
QC jumped up and greeted his guest with a warm embrace. A large antique desk top was
scattered with open tomes and legal papers. They spoke of important work in progress.
However, with exquisite courtesy, the marque of a true gentleman, the barrister brushed
aside hurried and earnest apologies for the interruption.

"Nonsense! You were quite right to phone. I was glad of an excuse to stop work.
Tommy will be sorry to have missed you."

In the upper echelons of the Nottingham Camp, references to Martin Harcourt QC were
usually expresses as simply 'Tommy and Martin'. Tommy Sperry, a highly-placed, highly-
paid executive of a major, multi-national company, had been 'the affair' [partner] of Martin
for 19 years.

"What will it be? Still a tea drinker? OK, Butch, a tray of nice tea and perhaps
something to nibble on."

Butch disappeared into the kitchen, just ahead of his mesmerising, mouth-
watering bottom. The gracious host directed his guest to a comfortable pair of armchairs in
the cove of a splendid gothic bay window. Through stone mullions there was a panoramic
view of an old garden framed by mature trees. It all fell away rapidly to much lower levels
and the effect warmed Simeon's pantheistic heart. An afternoon sun highlighted the blood-
red tops of copper beech and red maples which, in a light breeze, danced and twinkled like
rubies. After an exchange of pleasantries, the visitor quickly came to the point.

"I'm in trouble!"

"Yes, Simeon, I know you are."

"You know! How?"

"In our world, a precarious and private world, I make it my business to know as
much as possible. Information received suggests that at least two private detectives are
trying to find you, sniffing out where you're staying. No mistake, these are professionals
and professionals are expensive. Ergo, you must be in *big* trouble if somebody wealthy
is tracking you down with all speed. Of course, they've been clever. That's part of
the job – appearing like an ordinary bloke on the scene chatting casually. One of them
was circulating in the Flying Horse. He posed as one of your friends when speaking to
Edward, and in conversation with Tommy. He was supposed to be an acquaintance with
an important letter to give you. The other private investigator was hanging around the
Corporation Hotel in the Derby Cattle Market. I'm told that he was attempting to ferret
out your movements in that rather grotty dive. I think, young man, that you had better tell
me all about it."

Over tea and delicious hot buttered cinnamon tea cakes, Simeon gave Martin
a full account of his activities and troubles from his first meeting of Ahmed to his recent

alarming interview with Aunty Joyce. For the most part, the boy's narrative flowed without interruption, save for an occasional question to clarify a point. At the conclusion, counsel took a moment to organise his thoughts.

"For a few days, no more, that eerie old place in Belper is a fairly safe house – *if* this Gary Mackenzie has had the good sense to keep his mouth shut. For a start, toad's residence stuck up there in that mountainous labyrinth would be the very devil to find. And you have to find Belper first – no easy task. And then there is the advantage of anonymity; few people know toad's real name. They call him 'Toad of the Toilets'. He's seldom out of them. Give the man credit; he's taken good care of himself. He plays safe, gives people the impression that he lives in Nottingham and rarely takes anyone back to his home. I gather you've already encountered that horrendous woman who 'does for him'? She's not likely to give male visitors a warm reception I shouldn't think. You, of course, a close friend of Pod... are an exception."

Diplomatically, Martin resisted the temptation to elaborate. It was unheard of for a youngster of pleasing appearance to yield to intimate toadal ministrations. Due to Aubrey's triumphant boasting, Simeon's heinous faux pas of 1965 was now common knowledge on the Derby – Nottingham gay social circuit. Accordingly, this damaged his opportunities to 'know' (in the Biblical sense) similar, more choosey chickens.

"Well what am I to do?" wailed Simeon.

"It will do no good at all to get upset or to worry yourself to death!" said the lawyer, firmly, as if to a client. "I will make the following observations. Criminal gangs in organised crime are poorly understood and vary greatly from gang to gang and family to family. We don't know much about them simply because they *are* criminal and – by necessity – secretive. Does that sound familiar to you, Simeon?"

"I don't think I understand?"

"Don't you? I take it you are aware that homosexuality is illegal and, no doubt, you break the Law of the Land on a regular basis."

"As regular as possible," replied Simeon with a weak smile.

"Quite so," said the barrister employing his professional skills. "Returning to my thesis on secrecy – you and I – in fact, all homosexuals have much in common with the Mafioso. Like them, we need to be secret to hide our shame. In some countries, people like us need to hide for their very lives. Like the rest of us, *you* will continue to hide. I'm relatively successful, but need to be very quiet about my private life. It's a case of colleagues not asking, and me not telling. A secret society: that's the way it's always been for our people."

"I'm not sure... look here; I don't think I *like* your comparison with racketeers! Crooks are ruffians, violent people. I'm not wicked and I'll be damned if I feel any shame for what comes natural to me. I *like* giving pleasure to others. I *like* sex with other guys. I do *not* feel any shame! So there!!"

"And stuff that under ya wig!" laughed Martin Harcourt QC. "Well spoken, young sir. But you should have listened more carefully to what was said. The reality is unchanged. To protect ourselves we live in a secret society to hide a lifestyle which is shameful to the heterosexual majority. That is a simple fact of life. If you tell Aunty Joyce the truth about your good times in the Derby Turkish Baths, she may well disown you – or faint on the spot. If you solicit the sympathy of one of your Heanor mates with regard to the recent painful love affair with Ahmed, he'll probably be horrified, consider you mentally ill – or – he may just thump you! If I tell the judge or a fellow barrister that I have a desire to enter a man's bottom, my career in law would end up in a similar dark place. Of course, it's perfectly OK to make ribald comments about an usher's big tits or her nice bum. That earns brownie points, makes you one of the lads.

"Back to your current problem," continued Martin, "it's difficult to assess the risk. I've heard of the existence of the, so called, 'pink mafia' in the United States."

"Pardon!"

"I have precious little comfort to offer you, Simeon, but, as I told you before, criminal gangs vary. Your ex-lover appears to be involved with organised homosexual prostitution and, quite rightly, you fear the brutality and disapprove of the immorality such activity will certainly entail. I suspect that the *degree* of brutality and immorality will depend upon the level of risk and the level of risk will largely depend upon the age of the boys concerned. You speak of 'teenage boys', but there's a big difference between 13 and 19. When we last met, *you* were 19! Even so, I was not morally outraged when you outlined your colourful adventures of last year. Had you been 13, I would have been troubled and very concerned for your safety – not to mention my own safety! You mentioned the little servant of uncertain age."

"Dale. Nobody would tell me his age. I *still* don't know how old he is – or for that matter, anything at all about him! What's your point, Martin?"

"Simply this: for a Mafia type of operation to exist there has to be a demand for 'forbidden fruit'. That huge, illicit demand has made The Firm wealthy, but some people – police, politicians, bankers etc – will have to be paid off. It's a sort of modern slave trade, but younger slaves will raise the stakes and strict discipline is essential for all concerned. I don't have to remind you that enforcement and unconditional obedience is maintained by fear and intimidation and the necessity to inflict occasional punishment – or worse. You've spoken of this Ahmed and, as I understand, fear a second abduction?

"Yes... Martin, what are you getting at?"

"Has it not occurred to you, Simeon," warned Martin in deepening voice, wearing a grim expression, "that this matter of your absconding has already taken the matter *out* of the hands of that beautiful young man? After all, he is just a cog in a large criminal organisation. Has it not occurred to you that a top level decision has already been taken?"

"Decision? What decision?" gasped Simeon in alarm. "I don't know *anything*! They told me nothing – for my own safety. I made *sure* of not knowing anything."

"And, to save you, it's entirely possible that Ahmed has convinced his superiors of that very fact. Nevertheless, Simeon, it's now time to grow up, to think the unthinkable. If I'm to help you, we must assume and prepare for the worst. You have been at the heart of this syndicate since January – that's over four months! Top management may see you as a danger, a cancer which, to be on the safe side, must be cut out. I'm sorry to sound dramatic, but these sleuths could just possibly be assassins – contract killers. I don't know. I could be wrong – but you need to make plans."

"What plans?" said Simeon in despair, his voice muffled by his face buried in his hands. "Tell me what to do," he uttered in mournful misery.

The older man came round and cradled the boy in his hands. He spoke gently.

"The first thing is not to go to pieces. Go back to Mr Toad. Stay with him tonight and tomorrow night. On Monday, announce that you've decided to cycle around the country, just as you told Joyce, staying at B&B and Youth Hostels and sign in with a different name."

"Like a fictional name?"

"Of course! And especially use a false name when chatting to homosexuals."

"I'll call myself Sam Clifton," said Simeon, pleased with his quick thinking.

"Anything but Simeon Hogg," replied Martin.

Sam Clifton was not such a clever kneejerk choice. Samuel was his middle name.

Martin Harcourt continued.

"It will be the same as last year. Take as much as you can in your saddle bag. Be gone by mid-week, don't risk it any longer. Don't tell anybody you've been here. Tell Gary *nothing*. Just disappear. Do you have enough money?"

"Yes, over £200."

"Good. That should last for a month or two. Phone me every week from a public telephone box so I'll know you're OK. And you *will* be OK because, an itinerant boy on bicycle meandering around the country lanes of England will be almost impossible to locate. That will be even safer than getting you police protection." Martin stroked his chin in a few moments of brown study. "On balance... I suggest that you cycle *north*. Yes, north. It's more gritty, craggy, primitive communications. It'll slow them down; make detection more difficult than in the civilised south. And, as the weeks drag by, that could prove *very* expensive – even for The Firm – as you call it. We'll give it about three months, after that, I'll take advice and we'll reassess the situation."

"Advice?"

"I have friends who can help."

"A Nottingham mafia?" enquired Simeon. Martin roared with laughter; an occurrence which nicely broke into the dour atmosphere.

"The nearest thing to a Nottingham mafia is me and Tommy! No, my boy. Queer we may be, but we are firmly on the right side of the law in all other respects. I have powerful friends in the police, the judiciary and even in the Special Branch. If it comes to it, the most drastic protective remedy would be a complete change of identity. In that event, Simeon Hogg – well, he would cease to exist.

CHAPTER 23

Hades Under High Tor

It was a stuffy malodorous air which assailed the nostrils of the cool and detached Mavis as she entered the gloomy, untidy, brothel-like bedroom of Aubrey Pod on the Sunday morning of May 8th. Treading over crumpled clothes which had been carelessly thrown down the previous night, she opened the curtains and briefly took some comfort from the effervescent and glistening westward view over the river valley and on up to the Chevin Hills. The reflected brightness stabbed the unwholesome room and brought a low grunt from the blobby, slobby, screwed up bundle in the bed. This was followed by a moan and slight movement, as the heedless servant made her quick exit – chamber pot in hand – at the very distant end of a fully extended arm. A few minutes later she returned and sharply deposited a large mug of hot sugary milky tea, with a thud, on his bedside table. Her 'Mornin' Mr Pod' hit hard, sounding more like a reprimand than a greeting. The music master moved, gradually opened unwilling, squinting eyes which, at this time of the day were more like piggy eyes than toad eyes. He made his third inarticulate sound by way of a groan. Mavis stood back, well back, safe from an assault of foul breath and made a bee-line to the refuge of the kitchen and the call of the frying pan. As Aubrey dragged his shapeless form to the reviving tea, he became aware of a soft drone coming from the living room below. These were the voices of Gary and Simeon, tête-à-tête in earnest conversation, a conference which had started nearly an hour before.

Before the hour of nine, Gary had jumped out of a taxi, eager to tell Simeon all about his exciting weekend adventures. The first one took place at the home of the cadaverous professor who was 'entertained' by, not only his American guest, but also a couple of rough chickens, rent boys with an appalling reputation. Simeon had encountered these feral boys, Monks and Muckles the previous year. This was an unholy duo of doubtful provenance and doubtful age, generally assessed as about mid-teens. Indeed, Monks and Muckles did not know their own age; had no knowledge of parents, family or place of birth. It was said that their present 'keeper / guardian' – an ancient pile of human blubber infamously known as Guzzly Granddad – had first acquired them some ten years before. Simeon met the old man in Chesterfield during his last visit to England.

The emaciated professor, who always paid well, was known as 'the professor' to willing yobs in the lower orders. To his equals in the ranks of the nodding heads, he was referred to as 'Aggie'. As with so many homosexual gentlemen in the professions, his true name was never known. And like so many in his class, he was prepared to pay for coarse, masculine youths, hard types who were adept at creating erotic situations which were none too gentle but could be extremely exciting. Rumour had it that the punctilious Claud Hoadley, no less, had employed the services of Monks and Muckles for the delectation of their 'Fantasy Sex Sessions'. On one nerve-shattering occasion, the strict schoolmaster had been found on the kitchen floor, naked, reeking of urine secured by a collar and lead. Like a dog, he was tied to the leg of a heavy Victorian table. According to Gary, the deaths-head don was excited by a similar humiliation.

"Oh God! In his birthday suit! It was like a freak show. Victim of starvation; I don't know how else to describe it. Those guys were so cruel. They made him do it *all* – and I mean *all* on pain of the cane. He had to crawl round the room riming us, licking us, all three of us, one after another. But, he loved it, baby! He sure did. We drained him. You should have been there."

"No, Gary. I should *not* have been there. I met those two last year. They are atrocious. I'm disappointed that you're prepared to sink as low as consorting with, of all people, Monks and Muckles – the scum of Derbyshire. It's just awful! They're a blot on the gay landscape."

"Hey! What gives? You're upset! What's happened? Has toad been misbehaving?"

"No. Aubrey's fine. I... I had a dream about Laurent last night... I suppose..."

"Don't worry, my friend." Uncharacteristically, Gary showed concern. His voice was mild and kind. "I should have realised what you've been through. It's bound to take a long time to get back to normal. I guess it's like grief. Ya know something, if *you* love Ahmed Hamah, can he really be *all* bad? Maybe Laurent just got his ass kicked. We don't know. Maybe he just got fired. Happens all the time."

Simeon wanted to be honest with his friend about the appearance of possible killers asking questions, but he recalled Martin's strict advice.

"I need to be on my own. I've decided to get on the bike and just go somewhere."

"Where?"

"Doesn't matter. I'll do a hostel tour around the country."

"OK, buddy. No sweat," said Gary, scrutinising his friend's face, trying to read the problem.

Gary sensed there *was* a problem. He assumed the problem was connected with the aftermath of the dramatic and heartrending break with Ahmed. The younger friend had many commendable qualities for one so young. He was sensitive enough to be mindful of the emotional differences between himself and his older friend. Gary saw himself as tough, but assessed Simeon as vulnerable and rather weak. Correspondingly, and still in solicitous mode, he attempted a few words of comfort.

"Ya know, buddy, in a way, I'm envious of you. Really! What you had was the best hunk in Detroit – wow! Were you the cat with the cream! What you had, the memories, the experience – you should treasure. Treasure it – don't forget it. I *never* had it. Probably never will because, well, I don't have in *me* what you have inside *you*. It was the thing which Ahmed saw and needed. He was the only one allowed to call you 'Booby'... nobody else. And, ya know, some people live a long life – and die – and they never fell in love the way *you* fell in love. I saw the way you looked at him. I could feel the magic." His voice faded, became softer as Simeon turned his head away, urgently, to study an old sepia photograph of assembled Victorian Pods. "Well... all I can say is... keep the good memories in your heart."

During that tense moment, a misquoted line from Tennyson floated past the Englishman's consciousness –
    'And he loved him, with a love which was his doom.'

Gary rose, walked around the room and gazed out of the window. It gave Simeon a chance to compose himself. Returning to his seat, he resumed in a cheery up-beat manner.
    "Before you go bicycling around, will you come with me to the caves on High Tor?"
    "You want to go to Matlock? Caves? Why?"
    With great excitement, Gary sprung out of his 1930s armchair and launched himself towards Simeon seated in the opposite 1930s armchair. To lend emphasis to a thrilling announcement, the kneeling teenager placed his hands on opposite knees, still covered by pyjama bottoms. Animated eyes fixed the sad eyes of the cyclist.
    "I wanted to tell you all about it at that snobby bar. Simeon! Simeon, my friend, listen to me and listen good. The professor told me about some naughty caves on the top of a cliff in a place called Matlock Bath. These dark cavities are full of horny chickens – *gay* chickens! Yes! It's true. That's where they go, where they meet. They get it on with *wild* action, baby!"
    It took a few seconds for this extraordinary intelligence to percolate into Simeon's consciousness.
    "Gary," responded an incredulous Simeon, remaining calm with a touch of cynicism, "I suspect the skull has been winding you up. He's been taking advantage of your over-active erotic imagination! Sure, you'll always find a few lads playing around those rocky places on High Tor. I heard about it from school friends who used to cycle to Matlock Bath and explore old Roman mine workings. Strictly speaking, they're not caves at all. They're roofless. Sort of narrow deep ravines: you go down, it gets dark, comes to an end and then you come back."
    "You don't believe me! I can't believe that you don't believe me. What's the matter with you? The Prof knows his stuff. The feral boys are always there – with a lot more of the same type. Listen, they're called the Fern and Roman Caves and you're wrong. It's years since *you* were there. Caves change. They're limestone. It dissolves with constant rainfall. It's always raining around here so they get bigger. You go down to the dark part – then you *turn right*! There's a small entrance into a larger cave system. I hear tell that it's a gap which has got bigger in the last few years."
    Reluctantly, a sceptical Simeon had to acknowledge the accuracy of Gary's information. These caves (or old mine workings) were indeed referred to as the Fern and Roman Caves. It was possible that erosion, no doubt assisted by some youthful rock breaking, had formed a link with other virgin caves.
    "You said it yourself, Simeon – many times. You're always ranting about 'Mysterious Derbyshire' being on top of a honeycomb of underground caverns, a magical world of stalactites and stalagmites. Why do you think I'm here? You've sold it good! And now *I'm* the one to tell you all about an underground kingdom – and you won't believe me. Will you let me prove it?"
    "Have you been there?"
    "No. Not yet. We'll get toad to take us in that hideous contraption."

"Lots of gay chickens? Really! Is there a king of this underground kingdom?"

"Yes there is," said Gary with a smirk. "You'll love this one – Guzzly Granddad!"

"Guzzly Granddad! You must be joking! He could probably roll *down* that steep hill but it would take ten healthy chickens to pull him up. Gary, this nonsense is fast descending into farce."

"So – prove me wrong. Let's investigate."

"If there is something going on there, and, I repeat *if* – what exactly are we talking about? These dark spaces deep beneath the earth, is it like a gay steam bath, or an active cottage or just a private club which doesn't have to worry about rates or bills for the electric light?"

"I don't know – and that's a fact. It's something to do with it being safe – very safe. That's the great thing about it. It's a whole maze of complicated passage ways, tunnels and paths in total darkness. There are rules – no flashlights. If a flashlight is seen, everybody knows that it's an intruder – could be the cops – and they all beat it – real fast. As I said – *safe*.

"So nobody can see anybody else. Right. OK. How can you tell a chicken from – let's say, for example – Nobby the Gnome?"

"Oh, I think I could feel the difference between a firm teenager and a soft old fossil," said Gary with a touch of disdain. "I'm not even sure that I should be telling you all this!"

"Why?"

"Well… it's supposed to be a big secret, for teenagers only. You've turned 20. Right?

"I'm over the hill already. I see. Tell me, young Gary, how does our old friend the skull, Mr Death-Warmed-Over, how does *he* get admitted to the teenage caves of High Tor?"

They both roared with spontaneous laughter. In this topic, there was growing absurdity and endless possibilities of biting wit. After a period of silly small talk, Gary returned to the fact that, in truth, he knew very little about this bizarre homosexual venue.

"But it has to be the usual stuff – doesn't it? You know, something along the lines of selling and buying. Right?"

"You mean hustlers and punters?" responded Simeon. "Or, in Derbyshire terms, rent boys and freaks. On the other hand, you'd love to get your hands on a few nice young boys. Right?"

"Too right! And why not?"

"Why not? Because, in case you've forgotten, so soon, Gary, we have just taken flight from big trouble in Detroit. We've escaped from prostitution, possibly involving young boys, pimps and all the dangerous baggage which goes with that seedy life style. *You* are in this with *me*. It was your choice, and you are right up to your neck in it! Should we *really* be getting mixed up with the likes of Guzzly Granddad, Monks and Muckles and the rest of all that shit?"

"Monks and Muckles were OK with me. They were good. Oh, boy, real good!" said Gary in recent erotic recollection, with feeling. "You are just the same as you were in Detroit – afraid to take a grip on life."

"What's that supposed to mean?" retorted Simeon. "I'm just saying this: *why* in God's name should we put our heads on the block? Why put our heads into that murky, dangerous world of those caves and risk a whole bunch of trouble? Answer that."

Gary resumed his seat and sat back with an air of contemplation considering his next move. He had read the 'book of life', considered himself to be wiser and was determined to impress this fact on Simeon Hogg.

"Don't be offended. Please don't go cool on me but – ya know, Simeon, life is passing you by. Do you want to end up an old maid like Aunty Joyce? Know your trouble? You've been watching too many Doris Day movies. Such a nice world! A world where everybody is nice and everybody is heterosexual. Get real! It's a fantasy. Life is not like that. But life *is* like a movie and real life is a tough movie to watch. This is not Bambi, this is real life and we should grab it. Here is a chance to meet cute guys, butch, horny guys. If Monks and Muckles are anything to go by the other boys will be top quality – hard and rough! Here is a chance to overdose on rocky chambers which echo with the moans of young studs and here is a chance to make bread – maybe lots of bread." The sad cycling eyes continued to hold their hard scepticism and stern disapproval. "For God's sake... let me try to appeal to your sense of adventure. There is a *lake* down there! Try a little excitement. Let's live a little. Let's go for it!"

Simeon was both impressed and amused by the eloquence of such a powerful pitch. Yet, in contrast, this boyish enthusiasm was showing Gary for exactly what he was – a 17 year old.

"Wow! We've gone from Doris Day to the rough wild orgies of Hades," said Simeon.

"Hades? What's that?"

"It's where *we* could end up! Listen, mush, if that place is one tenth of what you say it is; us two could end up in really big trouble. Greek mythology; it was a course. I took it at Wayne State. Hades was the underworld, sort of – home of the dead. Ideal for the skull. No wonder he's so keen to get down there! *You* paint a picture of heaven. Well, I've news for you, Gary; Hades was the Greek idea of *hell*. For the likes of us queers, prison really is hell. And now we have a lake! A deep, dark lake and no light to see where that lake is! That does *not* appeal to *my* sense of adventure. No, sir. It sounds like a sure quick way to get wet, cold and very soon dead if we don't get arrested first. And that reminds me – in Hades there is *also* water – the River Styx, across which the souls of the *dead* were ferried. Maybe our deathly corpse-like Professor is the ferryman when he's not nodding in the Friary."

"I should get real? No, Gary, *you* get real. Once the Derbyshire police get as much as a sniff of the underage enjoying an underground overdose of gross indecency... well, it'll all end in tears, horrible embarrassment and possible prison with a bunch of queer bashers. This is England. In England you can't bribe politicians and you can't buy cops."

"Can't you?" parried Gary, lightly, in a tone of unnerving confidence. He leaned forward with a smug expression of self-assurance. "I seem to recall you telling me about a man in London known to cockney chickens as – now, let's see, what was it? Oh yes – His Lordship."

CHAPTER 24

A Horror of Great Darkness Came Upon Me

Simeon had to acknowledge the truth in Gary's reference to London's homosexual criminal underworld. However, in his heart, he still held that England, especially Derbyshire, was a much less corrupt environment. Before Gary could return fire with citations including Lord Boothby, Ronnie Kray and the rough chickens of Walthamstow's Dog Track, he was interrupted by the sudden explosion of an energised toad.

"So! The wanderer returns! And what rude mischief have *you* been getting up to, you *naughty* little boy? Come on now – tell all."

And Aubrey did hear it all – including wild tales about Matlock Bath, apparently, the new gay capital of the Midlands. Always on the look-out for new venues of carnal gratification, Pod was very excited. He was keen to get stuck into these chasms as soon as possible. On the other hand, the more sensible part of Pod – Pod the music master – he considered the possible *cost* of such an unknown and novel pornographic gold mine. He leaned forward, bulging toadal eyes agog, shooting out questions.

"What do *you* think about all this, Simeon? Can it be true? Would it be safe?"

"My instinct is to keep well clear. As I understand it, the only non-teens allowed into this maze are Guzzly Granddad and anybody else who is prepared to pay. Granddad would have difficulty squeezing in there anyway – with or without his teeth. We had this discussion last year. Who actually *does* run the rent boys in south Derbyshire? They all said it was Granddad! Some folks, including Martin Harcourt, believe there's a mysterious Mr Big pulling the strings."

"I always suspected that ugly drag act, Becksitch Betty," said Aubrey, "but he's completely disappeared."

"My money would go on an intelligent bloke, somebody with a bit of clout like Claud Hoadley – or one of his nodding heads," said Simeon.

"Or one of the Nottingham Camp," said Gary grinning. "Somebody like an eminent lawyer who wears a wig."

"No, not Martin," replied Simeon, "he's too idealistic. He dreams of the day we become legal, the day every town has an official support service for all gay people. He's got it all planned out. Meeting in a comfortable setting... well... like a sort of public house. And he *doesn't* mean a pub. He means a respectable clean place where you can enjoy a nice cup of tea and be with helpers, advisors who encourage us to talk through our problems."

"Doesn't sound very exciting!" said Aubrey.

"I'll second that," added Gary with a sneer of cynicism.

"And *I'd* like to know when I'm supposed to cook a breakfast!" said an irritated Mavis who had just burst into the room.

After lunch, after much cogitation, Aubrey laid down the law. He would provide the transport to Matlock Bath on condition that Gary entered the black hole and return to the surface with a nice chicken. And said chicken must yield to toadal fondles costing no more than one pound. Gary quickly agreed to this obscene demand with absolutely no intention of fulfilling a contractual obligation to such a detestable little man who was as hideous as he was cheap. Aubrey had decided that, on such a nice sunny afternoon, he would probably enjoy scaling the woodlands up to High Tor. There were qualms, but, even so, High Tor was a public place – a respectable schoolmaster showing his American visitors around the wonders of Derbyshire – what was wrong with that? Just one mention of Monks and Muckles was enough put him off from actually entering the caves. Toad of the Toilets was resolved to remain in the open, to enjoy the light and fresh air. He would keep well away from those nasty feral boys who had humiliated him so many times, in so many public lavatories.

The comical toad was hunched over his steering wheel, en-route, tootling north along the A6. In between the occasional toot at other cars, he was holding forth on the evils of an organised vice ring.

"I don't like it! Too much like Fagin's kitchen if you ask me!"

"We didn't," muttered Gary on the back seat.

"It's more honest to go into a proper cottage," continued Aubrey, "and wave a ten bob note under the nose of the chicken of your choice. Anyway, what's the point of buying what can't be seen? Total darkness! It's ridiculous."

"Yes, Aubrey," murmured Simeon who was wondering about the mysteries of these strange fissures in the earth. As an early teenager, he had occasionally investigated the secrets of the western wooded hills of Matlock Bath which climbed up to the Heights of Abraham. In this impressive 'Switzerland of England', for a small fee, it was possible to be guided through the Great Masson Cavern or the Great Rutland Cavern, in perfect safety, and enjoy a cup of tea in an alpine café at the end of the walk. The giant crag of High Tor which crowned the more creepy, darker woods to the east of the River Derwent – that was a different matter. On High Tor there were no friendly guides to steer you around dangerous bottomless holes half hidden by centuries of accumulated foliage. You were on your own! There were traitorous chasms and sudden sheer drops of hundreds of feet down to the river below.

At the northern end of Matlock Bath, the car was parked. By a process of trial and error they located the bridge which crossed the River Derwent. After some small confusion, much worrying, wittering and fussing from Mr Toad, eventually, Simeon found the correct track. Here was the entrance to the woodland grounds, the rough path which zigzagged all the way up to the very top of High Tor crag. Immediately the trail became very steep and quite difficult for the unfit podgy Pod after his misspent lifetime of despising exercise and stuffing himself with sugary cakes. Hard and painful progress slowly led them up into a darkness which was rather like a cave in itself. On both sides they were enclosed by impenetrable stands of oak, maple, beech and bits of holly which brought a coolness to match the dimness. On top, leafy canopies interlocked to form a roof producing the effect of an arboreal cathedral.

After ten minutes of hard labour, Aubrey's incessant, stumbling, panting, gasping and grumbling brought forth from an exasperated Gary a furious retort.

"For God's sake!" he said through hissing, snarling teeth. "Shut the fuck up you stupid – irritating – ugly – freak!"

The irksome little fellow had no resources left for any defensive response. He just collapsed onto the prostrate trunk of a fallen tree, a sight which inspired a wave of sympathy from Simeon who joined him.

"Perhaps we should take a few minutes to catch our breath, Gary? Aubrey's not used to a climb like this." He put an arm around the little reptile and gave him a quick squeeze of encouragement and affection. Moments later, Aubrey recovered a weak whisper.

"I'm not having that! That rogue can pack his bags when we get back. I want him *out* of *my* house."

"As you like, Aubrey. He wouldn't have stayed long anyway. Gary's always on the move. For the present, just try and enjoy these beautiful woods."

"Beautiful? They're sinister! It was sunny when we started. We're in deep gloom. You can't even see the sky."

"Look for the good, Aubrey. This is a magical place. Put your nose into this sweet white blossom. It's rowan. Witches used it. There! Look, over there." Simeon was pointing into the shadows under bramble. "Did you see that?"

"What?"

"It's gone now. I've never actually seen one before, only on a farthing. It was a jenny wren, quick as lightening with its cute cocked tail. Listen to it. This wood is full of birdsong... and that dank smell." He breathed deeply. Suddenly, he noticed the log upon which they were sitting. It was remarkably comfortable, smooth, and in good condition for a fallen limb. He stood up and looked at it. It was not a fallen tree at all! They had been sitting on a fat, healthy, living root. It was the lower part of a massive beech tree, towering above them, exploding in all directions in mammoth branches and lesser sub-branches.

"Stand up, Aubrey! Look up there. Look into that vast expanse of foliage and tell me you don't like it." The little man obeyed, craned his neck and gazed up into a luxuriant world illuminated in lime green. Toad was right, the sky could not be seen – however – it was replaced by a lovely verdant glow which could never be described, as sinister.

Simeon studied the giant root which had provided a seat. It was part of a considerable root system uncovered and cleaned by years of erosion. For decades, enormous tentacles had dug in with determination in a continual effort to keep ahead of a natural process of undermining. He admired these immense legs. They extended along a bank, grasping at rocks, searching out deep cracks, exploring long fissures to firmly anchor the colossal living beech above. In so doing, they had produced mysterious cavities into the hillside. Gloomy hollows were begging to be explored. Enchanted places had always fascinated Simeon Hogg who was now mesmerised into an idle and pleasant contemplation. The reverie was broken by an excited Gary running towards them.

"Hey, guys! Come and see what I've found."

They ran over a dark ground-cover of creeping ivy. Pushing through a curtain of scraggy yew, a flapping blackbird screamed out his complaint and terrified the toad just before they emerged into brilliant light and the gentle spring warmth of English sunshine.

"Careful!" shouted Gary. "It seems like we're a mile up in the sky."

In sudden horror, Aubrey stepped back, well back. Somewhere between heaven and earth, they were standing on a high rocky ledge and were only inches from a sheer drop into the canopies of distant trees and the River Derwent far below. Gingerly, for a view to die for, Simeon steadied himself by grasping the slim trunk of a young ash tree. Somehow it had rooted itself into a crack in the vertical limestone cliff. Ignoring urgent protestations from the others, he trusted to the strength of that baby ash and leaned out to take in the full view of that famous High Tor rock face – now looking like the north face of the Eiger. He estimated that they were still only about half way up.

The instinct for self-preservation prevented Aubrey and Gary from sharing this aerial enthusiasm of their friend.

"Look at those cars down on the road! They're like Dinky Toys. We might be in an aeroplane," said Simeon. He turned his head from left to right beholding a magnificent panorama of a lovely valley edged by wood and moors. Looking southwards, the Lovers' Walks followed the shimmering river. Tiny visitors enjoying this pretty resort moved around riverside gardens and paraded along dignified Georgian and Victorian facades. The road and river curved westwards until they were out of sight, blending into the deep, green gorge. High to the east, above the dense woodland, there was an expanse of open fields. Higher still and further distant, emerging from very dark woods were the dramatic crags of Black Rocks.

With the support of the young ash, Simeon had given himself a birds-eye view looking directly down a sheer rocky drop on to the tops of a few terraced, three-storey, stone cottages, far below. Other scattered dwellings, humble old cottages, half hidden in foliage, were climbing up the opposite side of the valley; so far away, so small, they seemed like models. Eventually, the slope levelled slightly to support a saddle of meadow before, again, steepening into a further sylvan delight.

The trio plunged back into a verdant murk of tangle to continue their difficult ascent. After a while, things got better. The thickets gave way to more agreeable glades, allowing for an explosion of colour. Bluebells, anemone and celandine were highlighted by mottled sunshine. The walking became easier over a natural paving of smoothed stone and worn spreading tree roots. Gary was activated. He has seen something and ran ahead to inspect, what appeared to be, a solid rock wall partly obscured by falling ivy. This obstacle threatened to block all further progress.

"This is it!" he called in excitement.

"The end!" said Simeon, unable to understand such enthusiasm.

"No – the beginning," answered Gary. "Monks gave me good directions. This is the beginning of Giddy Edge. To get to the crag top, we need to follow this rocky lip, to the right, around the cliff face... if we can ever find it... here! Here it is."

He pushed through bushes, shrubs and squeezed behind the ivy curtain hard up against the rock to emerge onto a narrow verge which, after a few cautious steps, afforded intermittent views of the world far below.

"One thing about these infernal caves," panted Aubrey. "You'll not have to worry about too many groping old fogies haunting the nooks and crannies. Only the bravest, youngest and fittest could possibly complete *this* obstacle course. That's for certain. All this adventure! I feel like a character in *King Solomon's Mines!*"

"And guess who's playing Gagool?" quipped Gary.

Giddy Edge lived up to its name. The narrow cliff edge rendered the explorers inches away from a sheer fall of hundreds of feet. This induced in Simeon some unsteadiness and inflicted upon the nervous toad a distinct dizziness. Most of the time, any fall could have been stopped by a frantic grasp at several stunted hawthorn bushes – small comfort for the three adventurers. Eventually, the path appeared to come to an abrupt halt, suggesting that the walker would soon be walking on thin air. To the rescue came a welcome rail firmly anchored into the dark grey rock face. It protected against a dangerous narrowing foot-hold which took the climbers to the brink of a sheer drop to oblivion. Against a cool biting wind at that altitude, the intrepid mountaineers made slow and careful progress. The appearance of a brave weather-beaten ash tree, half strangled by creeping ivy, indicated the end of this frightening ordeal.

Suddenly, it was all brilliant sunshine! An unexpected emergence into an open, sloping space, carpeted by moss, interspersed with a natural paving of sparkling grit stone, was familiar to Simeon. He had seen these special effects before from gemstones admired in countless Peak District nick-knack shops. The sun picked out specks of translucent rocks. There were fluorspars, calcites, barites – the ground was all a glitter.

In triumph, the two boys made a dash over this cheerful adornment to the peak of this famous tor. It raised its naked head straight from the valley floor, a sheer height of 350ft from river to summit. With elation, they were standing over the giant 'face in the rock' which had always intrigued Simeon. Carefully, he approached that famous edge to take in that famous view. To the north, Matlock town spread up the hillside. Many miles beyond those hills, the dim outline of Kinder Scout – the roof of Derbyshire – was just visible. The ruined walls of Riber Castle crowned the hill to the east. To the west, Victoria Tower poked out of the aerial woodlands of the Heights of Abraham. Directly below, the River Derwent sparkled through gaps in the foliage as it meandered southwards through the ravine. Aubrey, exhausted and gasping, finally caught up and let out a shriek, warning Simeon to step back to safety.

"Have you got *any* sense? A freak gust of wind could have whisked you straight to that big cottage in the sky!" He spat out his next barb to the American. "And what horrors have you planned for us next?"

Very near to his objective, Gary was excited. He explained that had been instructed to place his back to the top crag edge and walk in-land, several paces, towards a shallow depression in a grove of windswept trees. And there it was! As if split asunder by an ancient earthquake, a great yawning crack, deep in the earth was dramatically speared by a shaft of sunlight. All three were electrified by this spectacle. It surpassed the excitement generated by a more typical cave entrance. The youths took a few steps towards this curious chasm.

"I'm looking for a secret entrance further down on the right," whispered Gary in a slightly conspiratorial manner. "Come with me until I get to check it out. Then you'd better get back to the toad. For God's sake try to keep that ugly bastard out! Sit him down on that flat rock. This is strictly chicken territory."

"No sweat! He's had enough as it is," replied Simeon, somewhat aggrieved that his friend felt it necessary to treat their host in such a hateful manner. He raised his voice and called out, "We won't be long, Aubrey."

As they began to descend, Simeon experienced a sudden silence and a sudden chill. He recalled that caves were always cold. They maintained the same temperature summer and winter. The entrance of this ravine was beautiful, richly decorated with shrubs and stunted trees which became smaller and more stunted further down as the chasm narrowed. Eventually, deeper, such adventurous vegetation gave up the struggle for light and more simple plants, fleshy weeds and ferns grimly clung to the rock edges. A determined dark yew struggling out of a crevice was grasping at a brief moment of sunshine. Indeed, the narrow beam of sunlight was still there, still impressive providing brilliant illumination not only on Gary's golden head, but also further down deeper, some 20 to 30 feet into a bottomless black hole of immense mystery. But the sun is ever moving. The depths of this strange world received only a few valuable minutes of life-giving light, at a certain angle, on a daily basis. Those precious minutes were dwindling. Gary's limelight was fast fading, as was his striking good looks. His hair became dark. His peaches and cream complexion changed into a hard silhouette against a limestone face which had barely enough light to support an occasional dab of moss.

Underfoot it became muddy. For reassurance, Simeon looked up to the outside world to discern a jagged crack of mostly bright blue and sections of leafy green.

"This is it!" whispered Gary in excitement. Sure enough, on the right was a black space which made them both feel much cooler. "I need to get my bearings, maybe locate some of the guys. Give me about... say, half an hour? It's just to feel my way around and I'll be able to give you the lowdown. Get back to that reptile. Wish me luck!"

Gary had gone. He had been swallowed up by the blackness. Simeon pushed his head into that rocky entrance and was suddenly seized by a mortal panic as he heard himself speak the words several seconds too late.

"Good luck." Simeon's utterance, in a weak voice nearly broke. It was consumed into that vast, cold, dark emptiness as completely as the friend he had just lost. For a moment he felt bitterness against the heterosexual world which prospered, existed easily under the warm sunshine on the surface. At the same time he recalled a memorable line from *The Time Machine* – 'A horror of this great darkness came upon me. The cold, that smote my marrow, and the pain...'

"Is that it?" he thought. Have we been driven to a subterranean Under-world like the sinister Morlocks?"

CHAPTER 25

Lost in a Labyrinth

Walking slowly back, Simeon found Aubrey in the grove, in a sunny spot, seated on the suggested rock. For a rock, it was quite comfortable.

"I don't like your friend."

"No, Aubrey. And don't expect him to pull any chickens out of that hole for you. He won't. Let's check out that wonderful view again."

Once again, Simeon approached the cliff top and surveyed the scene. Again, following close behind, Aubrey urged extreme caution. During a few moments of silence, the younger man dreamily cast his eyes south west, noting curling smoke escaping from half-hidden chimneys, indicating the hamlet of Upperwood. Just a few homes nestling in mature woods. Years before, it was a thriving mining village. The silence became a little tense. It was broken when Simeon felt compelled to rationalise his friend's negative attitude to an older, unattractive gay man.

"Try to understand, Aubrey; in some ways Gary is mature for his years, but, in other ways, he comes across as exactly what he really is – a tactless teenager and quite often selfish."

As best he could, Simeon tried to explain the uncaring, ruthless chicken culture of Detroit and how that unfeeling social environment had shaped Gary's hard-nosed approach to life. He spoke of the young men in Detroit's Uptown S&C Coffee Bar.

"Of course, they dread getting old. *Thirty* is old to those guys. They didn't seem to be interested in you or any of my English adventures last year. Meeting all those unusual characters, struggling to cope in a hostile straight world; well, I felt I'd experienced something quite unique, quite precious. Gary is typical of the S&C boys. He values youth, beauty and survival. That's what he is. That's how the world has made him. He calls my English friends freaks."

"Which, of course, includes *me*."

"Yes, Aubrey. I'm afraid so. But, know what? We're *all* victims in this game."

"What's that supposed to mean?"

"I wish you hadn't sneered at Martin's ideas about gay support services. It's the way forward. I know it is. If we could just pull together instead of this endless bitchiness and self hate which pulls us apart, destroys us."

"Martin Harcourt QC has never shown me any kindness at all." Aubrey stood up, bent his knees and gesticulated in typical toad style. He looked Simeon straight in the face. "The Nottingham Camp is an exclusive club which has *always* excluded *me*. Your friend Martin should practice what he preaches!"

"I know he should, and, what's more, *he* knows he should. He told me that last year. He said – 'Some people see things and say why? I see things that never were – and say – why not?'"

"Martin Harcourt said that?" Grudgingly, Aubrey was impressed. Simeon returned with a sad smile. "No. I think he was quoting President Kennedy. But, hear this, Aubrey – Martin's vision is still valid – is still good – is still worth aspiring to."

"Why?"

"Why? Look at it this way. You are Mr Toad, the despised toad. The Derby and Nottingham snobs look down on you and chickens make fun of you because you are odd and, in their view, much worse – old! In queer pubs and Turkish baths you are seen as quirky and regarded with contempt. In a gay support group that would not be tolerated. All the people in that small community would be *required* to treat you with respect. You're an educated man for God's sake – quite knowledgeable in the classics and in literature. Organised social activities would bring out your qualities and people would see you in a different light. They'd learn to appreciate you."

Simeon looked at Aubrey. He had now resumed his seat and was processing this information, considering his response.

"I know you mean well," said toad, with a sigh, in an air of resignation. "But you're young, idealistic and a bit off-key. Let Martin Harcourt get on with his social engineering. I wish him luck, but he can't change human nature. Too much hypocrisy, that's what I say. All that sitting around in pubs looking at each other. Silly games! I want an orgy – me. *Instant* sex, that's me." To emphasise his point, the ugly toadal face jutted out, was pushed up hard into the other face. "Why waste time? *Get stuck in!* That's me. I'm a chicken farmer – and a practicing homosexual to boot – and I need all the practice I can get."

"Is it *ever* possible to reach you?" said Simeon with frustration. "Unlike *you*, Martin is well informed about current affairs and homosexual progress. He reads the papers. He tells me there's good reason to be optimistic about a new law which will make gay sex legal."

"What *I* want to do will *never* be legal! Arse hole after arse hole after arsehole. I'll soon need a remould on my tongue."

"I give up."

Simeon stomped away from the infuriating little man towards the chasm entrance – which was very quiet. Desperately, he tried to suppress the anger and frustration the defiant toadal attitude often stirred. Simeon was determined not to fall out with Aubrey, a damaged man, who at the same time, inspired affection. He recalled his own words – 'we are all victims' and calmed himself with the thought that the toad was also one of the many victims of endemic homophobia. He recalled the previous year when Mr Toad triumphantly bounced out of a Nottingham Police Station shortly after being arrested for 'importuning'. Simeon admired the resilience and fighting spirit of Aubrey Pod the 'unsinkable toad'.

And time passed. Simeon was uneasy. Aubrey was angry. Toad and chicken continued to watch the entrance of the chasm, continued to think about Gary Mackenzie. Nearly an hour had passed when Simeon consulted his watch for the umpteenth time.

"He said he'd come up after about a half hour."

"If he's found something nice down there, he'll not be worrying about the likes of us. Anyway, I'm not waiting here all day. He can find his own way back to Belper and then – *out* – he – goes!"

"I'm going in there."

"Don't be a fool!" said Aubrey, quite alarmed, clearly concerned.

"I must. Oh, I know you think he's not worth it... but somebody has to take responsibility. You're probably quite right; he'll be in there, on-the-job, getting his oats. When he's found, I'll give him a good bollocking for his thoughtlessness, mucking us about and wasting our time. But listen here, Aubrey, Gary could be in trouble! It's like what I've been talking about. There's a gay boy down there. He's cut off from all the usual protection a straight boy has."

"Here we go again! More of Harcourt's ideology," sneered toad.

"You know exactly what I mean. What if he doesn't come out? We wouldn't dare call the police for help – would we? He's foreign. He has no family who care about him, even if he was near home. I never told you about Gary's family did I – horribly religious, rabidly anti-gay."

"Are they fundamentalists?" asked toad, suddenly animated and interested. "Or perhaps, Jehovah's Witnesses? Jehovah's Witnesses are *poison* to queers! I had a friend who was brainwashed into being celibate... it was terrible. He was changed... like a zombie."

Unexpectedly, Aubrey's voice cracked and attracted Simeon's attention. He choked back a sob, took a deep breath and managed to continue. "We enjoyed friendship and fun; we were good for each other, but his sister described us as... degenerate. She worked on him, well, they *all* did. Indoctrination – no other word for it. Eventually he... well, he just cut himself off from all his queer friends... even me. That was a long time ago. Last year he became dangerously ill. His family..." Aubrey hesitated, became bitter and began to spit out his words. "That vile family, they were primitive, prejudiced and cruel to the very last! They refused to let any of his queer friends visit him... not even to say goodbye."

At this point Aubrey Pod completely broke down, gave way to a flood of tears as Simeon, embarrassed, but more disturbed, rushed forward to offer his poor little friend a hug and a comforting shoulder where he continued to whimper for a few moments. After fumbling for a handkerchief, after a few blows and snuffles, a short silence was followed by further revelations regarding this one-time, painful love affair.

"He died last August. He was a lonely, sad, sick, broken man – the end of an unnatural, wasted, mangled life."

Deeply touched by this emotional revelation, Simeon guided his friend back to the comfortable rock and spoke kindly.

"I'm not sure about the Mackenzie religion; it could well be the one you describe. His brothers are boorish but have certainly been bible bashed. I can tell you this – if Gary comes to some harm in any part of our twilight world – his family will say he's been punished by God. If he's found dead, drowned in that subterranean lake, they'll say it's a fitting end to a sinful life. They'll say that the devil has taken him. You're quite right, Aubrey, these bigots are evil people... and that's why I must at least try. Right now, he has nobody else who cares. I *must* go in there."

Aubrey Pod protested vehemently and was only persuaded, consoled when Simeon spelled out the precautions he would take.

"This is a promise, Aubrey; I'll not be distracted by any exciting action which may, or may not be happening in those naughty catacombs. As soon as I'm satisfied that Gary's OK – I'm out! And, I'll not go beyond a point where you can't see the light of the cave entrance. As long as I can see that light, I know the way out. Don't worry, I'm no hero. With me it's 'Simeon first' – count on it."

He went back down the great crack into the earth. Again, he felt the cold and noted the increasing paucity of vegetation until the black entrance on the right ominously presented itself. 'Bible black,' thought Simeon, in an ironic link with the recent conversation. In a further link, he recalled Ahmed's tongue-in-cheek comment when Simeon suggested a return to the Vesuvio Bath House.

"Too dangerous, Booby. Sure, it's a fun place, but too much like Sodom and Gomorrah. And you know what happened to those guys!"

In this somewhat satirical mode of thought, Simeon passed through the invisible curtain of bible blackness in search of the friend who had yielded to the temptations of an abomination. He conjured up a picture of a lusting population in perpetual darkness with outstretched arms beseeching Gary –

"Step forward, young foreigner. Yea, come forth that we may know you better and taste strange flesh. Lo, enter deeper in to our carnal cave. Give yourself over to much sweet lasciviousness and fornication."

"GARY! GARY!" called Simeon, seriously, propelling his voice at full volume into the void after dismissing his religious reverie. There was a hollowness of sound, but an expected echo did not return from any part of this stygian emptiness. Neither did he hear any other sound of life. Gingerly, he located a wet, cold wall to his right and took several careful steps in this land of the blind, continually making sure the wet, cold wall was still there. Turning round to check, he was comforted by the light at the entrance. It could have been a better light, but for the deep ravine and foliage above. However, it *was* a light – evidence of the outside world. Also, Simeon was careful to, as far as possible, follow a level path. Up or down, were risky complications he could do without. After more steps, perhaps thirty to forty foot, again, he turned round to check for the life-giving light. It was still there. As expected, it was further away but somehow different. If anything, it was brighter than before! He assumed this effect could be due to his eyes having now adjusted to the total darkness.

Total darkness. Out of a miasma of emotions including fear – bitterness returned. The Morlocks returned to threaten him. Mentally he revisited Martin Harcourt. On one occasion, in full flow, he inveighed against injustice heaped upon injustice when, abruptly, he stopped and, for a moment became abstracted. When he spoke, he spoke a few words which stayed with Simeon all his life.

"These privileged, ignorant bigots, these so called 'normal' people who live in the light...they haven't a bloody clue. They haven't the first idea of what it is like to be us – we who live in darkness..."

Suddenly, Simeon was seized by a horror of an abyss to his left! He turned his head in that direction, tried and completely failed to get a sense of the dreaded bottomless space beyond. He knelt down and lightly ran his fingertips over the ground area for any stones large or small – of which there were none. It was as silent as the grave. The sound of a falling stone would have been useful to locate any perils in this dreadful, cold nothingness. He cursed his appalling lack of preparation. The rules had forbidden light of any kind. The hell with rules! What a fool he had been! Simeon Hogg was now terrified for his very life.

An evil thought intruded. Could all this be part of a trap? Harcourt had instructed him to keep Gary in the dark with respect to a possible hit man on their tail. So Gary, who had not been warned, was, consequently, not forearmed! What if The Firm had somehow communicated with the Guzzly Granddad syndicate? Surely this is the perfect place for a murder: a place deep in Hell where a body would never be found.

He resolved to move a little way further and make one last call out into the darkness. This was done with all the volume he could muster – to no avail.
    "That's it, I've had it, I'm going back." He shouted this defiantly into this endless night of no stars. He turned round to face the life-giving light – *but the light was gone!*

At all costs, he must not panic. The light *had* to be in the direction in which he was facing. It was probably hidden by a small curve in the wall which was now on his left. He was certain that he had not ascended or descended, but, perhaps, he had veered slightly to the right. The light would return if he moved forward. He walked a few steps. Not far enough, all was still darkness. He walked on and on into continuing gloom, into a dismal growing sense of despair. He must not panic. He had not gone far. The world was nearby. It *had* to be. He was cold, very cold. In the upper world it had been a sunny day of reasonable warmth for an English spring. Appropriately, he had donned small white cycling shorts and a small rucksack containing a light jacket. Putting on the jacket helped to keep him warm and, more important, kept him occupied. He was *doing* something. If only he had a few stones as a tester. His purse! There would be coins and pennies in his purse to use to test for safety. As that small hope was born, it died. He realised that he had given it to Aubrey for safe keeping. It was a well observed rule – never take money into an active gay venue.

To relieve tension, he stood up very straight with his back to the wall, a wall which did not exist until it was touched. How could he have gone wrong? He had followed the wall of rock almost all the time. Almost! Was it possible that he had missed a part? He must not panic. He recalled the previous year on top of Snowdon when he wandered off the main path. A dense mist descended. He trusted to his sense of direction to return to safety, only to find that instinct had failed him. The going got very rough, he was completely disorientated. How did he get out of that? Voices! He heard a group of other walkers who, of course, were on the correct path near the summit.
    He must do the same here. He must listen for footsteps. What else was there to do? Surely others would be cruising these caves? Cruising: the American term for walking around a gay location in the hope of meeting other gays. He preferred 'cruising' to the English equivalent of 'trolling' which, like so many English gay terms sounded effeminate. English gays referred to each other as 'queer', a word he found so insulting. Same with the word 'packet'. 'Basket' sounded more masculine. *He must not panic.* Should he try to move on? Would things get worse? *Could* they get worse?
    "GARY! GARY! GARY!"

Was that a sound? Or was it his echo? Somewhere far below, now to the right, where his instinct had suggested an abyss; a distant sound from the bottom of a great hole floated up. Beyond the fact that it was human, possibly several humans, he could say no more. It was not laughter – just a sound of a voice or voices. Another sound! This time the unmistakeable plunge of a boulder hitting still water from, what seemed like, miles below followed by the same profound silence as before. Simeon now had the answer no stone or penny could possibly have supplied. He appeared to be on a ledge overlooking a subterranean lake or river, about as far down as the River Derwent looking from High Tor. He suddenly grasped the appalling horror of his present predicament – inches from a dark death in a hollow mountain! He compared it with other precarious gay adventures within his personal experience, such as nocturnal visits to Hampstead Heath or Palmer Park. Always the fear of an arrest from the police or an attack from hoods – but this! And those places had one major advantage – stick around and eventually it would get light again. In this tomb, it will *never* be light!

It was no good, he had to *do* something. He had to move. He still had a rough sense of the direction of the light and resolved to keep that bearing, aiming on target. This trajectory also had the advantage of moving him away from the horrific abyss. Alas, he sensed that this progress was taking him down, further down. Worse still, he reached out for the security of the cold, wet wall of rock only to discover it had now forsaken him! The wall was gone.

   "Perhaps this is a good time to panic," he said aloud, into the blackness, in an attempt to throw a little humour into a desperate situation. He continued to put one foot in front of another in such a way as to carefully test firm ground with every step. He continued to descend, and that descent was steepening. The same intuition which had identified an abyss, or a massive chasm, now told Simeon that any walls were a long way off. He sensed that he was walking down something akin to a steepening open field and his heart sank with every step. Abruptly, the oppressive silence was broken by a sound of dripping water somewhere to his left. At least that was something, an improvement on the endless nothing. He reasoned that water coming in might point to a way out. He turned left. The path became rocky and, eventually, he was impeded by stones and boulders which would have been so useful a little while back when they were not available. For insurance he put a few in his rucksack. The atmosphere seemed to feel wetter as the dripping sound became closer. Smooth limestone paving, once again, returned underfoot. That which he had feared came to pass: one foot expecting firm ground found empty space! With a brief utterance, Simeon expelled a prayer of thanks to his pantheistic gods, the Old Gods of Derbyshire, invoked by unbelievers in times of extreme peril.

He found himself on another ledge which overhung the grim and black River Styx below. But, he reasoned, not so far below as the lake of death which lurked deep in the abyss. He groped for the largest rock in his rucksack and tossed it over the subterranean cliff. Silently, the missile left his hand and continued to progress in total silence. As the quiet, heavy rock sank through thin air to its oblivion for the longest time, so did his spirits. It seemed like a long time, but, perhaps it was just a few seconds before a distant splash was heard. What was that? Did he hear a human voice make some response to the splash? Or was it another audio mirage, a distorted echo bouncing around the Halls of Hades. Simeon realised that he should call out, and cry out, more often, if he was ever to communicate with another living soul.

"HELLO! HELLO, THERE! I'M LOST, I NEED HELP. PLEASE HELP ME. IS ANYBODY THERE? ANYBODY AT ALL?"

Nothing, absolutely nothing. Which way? Left or right? He decided left towards the direction of dripping water. Making a snail-like, advance, and in an effort to stave off complete madness, he conjured up the image of the emaciated Professor, a member of the nodding heads. Simeon cast him as the grim ferryman conveying the souls of the dead across the River Styx. In his mind's eye he saw the skeletal fingers closing around a large coin...

Shock horror! Somebody – or something had grabbed at his arm!

CHAPTER 26

Secret Silence of Sodom

No. It was not a skeletal hand. It was human. It was a warm hand attached to a living person. In a burst of pent-up emotion, relief and gratitude; Simeon broke one of the unwritten rules of anonymous meetings in naughty locations. He spoke.

"Thank God!" he gasped, heart going nineteen to the dozen. "Oh, thank you so much. Just lead me out of here. I have to get out of this place." There was no response. In a moment of panic, Simeon grabbed at the stranger in an effort to make sure he would not escape into the inky nothingness. "Please! Please guide me out. I have a friend waiting for me on High Tor. I've kept him waiting for ages. He'll be going out of his mind with worry. Won't you…"

But it was too late. The person gave a jerk to free himself – and was gone. This invisible human being, who briefly existed in the sense of touch alone, had chosen to disappear back into that confounded, cold, ebony void. After the warm touch of that welcome hand, Simeon was colder than ever, but he had no more clothes to put on. There was nothing in his rucksack but a few dismal stones.

For a while, in utter misery, he stood still facing the direction in which (he assumed) the young man had fled. He had begged this man for help, but help had been brutally refused. So much for the Good Gay Samaritan. As bad as things were, he tried to swallow his acrimony and make sense of this man's callous conduct. He began to reason. If Simeon was ever going to get out of this horrible hole, he must use his brain; he must use his guile and his knowledge of what makes a gay boy tick. His bid for freedom failed because he spoke. In any anonymous physical encounter, you *never* address the other guy. In all secretive, sexual fumbles, speech is regarded as threatening at worse and blighting at best. 'Compliments to the chief' were never appropriate on such a sensitive occasion. He recalled an amusing quip from the outrageous Simon Tonks. The little queen was applying his well-honed oral skills to the private parts of a lad called Monks, gratefully receiving considerable ecstasy.

"Ooo that's *GRAND*, lass! Aye it's rate good. Ya've got a *lovely* tongue," moaned the recumbent young Monks.

"Shut oop!" responded Tonks in some irritation. "Ya spoilin' t' lewd atmosphere."

On a more serious level, a stranger begging for help would certainly be a big turn-off to Simeon's mysterious arm grabber. To a teenager surviving in that loose, covert web of tenuous acquaintances, the sheer panic and urgency of another teenager in danger would be intimidating. Again, Simeon was forced to confront the harsh realities of his secretive, illegal, immoral existence. This way of life had created a world in which one homosexual would, in certain circumstances, walk away from another homosexual who was in desperate need of assistance.

Meditating on these sad matters, wearily, he continued on in the direction of the dripping water for several long minutes – a trudge which rewarded him with another life-line – more human sounds. These sounds were rather muffled, not exactly speech but somewhat familiar. These were the sounds of sex. He advanced to reach a point where the activity was obviously just inches away. Simeon stretched out to touch, finding himself exploring the torso of a firm, well-built guy, patently close to an orgasm. The extra hand was one of several hands already very busy and, from ecstatic vocals – the international language of love – that extra hand was very welcome.

Simeon had learned his lesson. He resisted the urge to address this industrious gathering, and did not enquire after the nearest exit. However, less than a minute later, he was pulled away from this group of strangers by another stranger who came up behind him. The clink of a metal buckle hitting the ground indicated somebody dead keen, somebody with a youthful, impetuous disposition.

Since entering this void of darkness, the sighted Simeon had learned something of blindness and the skills of those who exist in eternal darkness. This silent stranger was employing those same skills of touch to 'know' Simeon in as much detail as possible, and Simeon was applying similar techniques to form a picture of the guy before him. They were feeling each other – but with what results? First and foremost the stranger was young. His body had nothing of the softness associated with the wrong side of 30, or, the slimy, scented smoothness so typical of an effeminate queen. No 'love handles' here, neither was he too thin. He had a flat, solid stomach and – very important to the ass loving Simeon – prominent buttocks of lust inspiring curvature. Feeling the stranger's face, with inexperienced fingertips, confirmed neither beauty, nor, any definite ugliness. A trace of grease did suggest a boy, possibly in his mid-teens. One hand exploring a tumescence of average proportions, bursting to escape the confines of underpants, confirmed that this certainly *was* a male. Simeon's other hand delved into a healthy shock of shaggy hair giving an estimated height of near to six foot.

The stranger crouched down. He warmed Simeon's cold limbs with his warm hands in an investigation driven by a fascination of muscular cycling legs and an alluring special interest in the crucial place where those legs met. After the examination was completed to the examiner's satisfaction, he fiddled with the button and zip of Simeon's shorts: an exciting action which had a powerful effect on his blood flow. There were other indications that this guy was a desirable, butch, working-class youth. There was the sound of regular sniffles, plus a certain roughness, impatience in the way he yanked down underpants and eagerly tasted the nooks and crannies of newly exposed secret places.

Little good had come from the investigation of this cave, but this particular moment was good. It was very good and, in spite of his recent distress, Simeon was able to rise to this occasion, enjoying these delightful ministrations. A difficult interval arrived when the stranger returned to his full height and, in very English style, came round his partner's back. Perhaps a slight tenseness was communicated to the stranger letting him know that, in this individual, the back passage was a 'no-go' area. Fortunately, this guy showed an unexpected tolerance. His thrusting lust dissolved into a non-threatening boy on boy embrace as his manhood slipped easily between Simeon's legs. This action effectively combined animal ardour with a more gentle emotion, akin to the affection of a lover. So it was that both boys locked in passionate embrace, almost as one entity, were now facing the same direction and, presently, they both ejaculated in that same dark direction. The precious seconds following this completion were extended whilst the coarse, grunting youth of hot blood continued clutching the cold cyclist; a cyclist who eagerly soaked up delicious life-giving warmth, willingly receiving a deluge of wet kisses in, and around his neck.

Now was the time to ask for help. It was always acceptable to speak after sex. When the boy spoke, as expected, it was rough, common and terse. There was a nasal tone and his disjointed, abrupt delivery was constantly interspersed with sniffles. Simeon offered him his handkerchief which was accepted without comment or ceremony. These few words uttered, with apparent matter-of-fact indifference, amounted to a curious contrast to the physical act of love which had just taken place. In a second significant and tender moment, the nameless stranger, gently, but firmly, took hold of the lost lad's hand to guide him out of that cave. It was a warm, secure hold for which he was most grateful.

Eventually, Simeon discerned a glimmer of light. Not much, but a faint greyness which turned out to be the reflected gloom on glistening rock face from an exit obscured by shrubs already dimmed by more mature trees above. A few more steps and he was dazzled – and he was free! He stood on a ledge and savoured the fresh air and sudden warmth of the sunny outside world. The oppressive silence of the deathly void had been replaced by birdsong. There was a hum of distant traffic and the low murmur of human kind – the folks who wander around the enchanting nooks and crannies of Matlock Bath. Matlock Bath! What an amazing change from, what seemed like hours, incarcerated in the secret silence of an underworld City of Sodom.

Oddly, unwilling to see the face of his unknown, underworld lover, Simeon looked down at the strong, warm hand which had yet to release its affectionate grip. It was a freckled hand. The arm had hairs which glowed with an orange tinge. Face looked into face with no expression save for a silent, mutual curiosity. This was no Morlock! He was ginger. His bright red mop of shaggy hair was still mussed up from the earlier examination. Simeon's eyes searched this face with almost the same conscientious effort as his fingers had investigated it in the pitch black of night. But fingers cannot identify light eyebrows or eyelashes rendered almost invisible by the sunlight of early May. And fingers could never convey the youthfulness of freckles, the roundness of sparkling eyes or describe a child-like nose which had developed little from its original button-like charm.

That deep adolescent voice should have told him. It *was* faintly familiar. He had met Muckles the previous year. This was the infamous Muckles of 'Monks and Muckles', a terrible duo – wild boys of no known origin who lived with Guzzly Granddad in a grotty little backstreet terrace in Chesterfield.

    "Muckles!" exclaimed Simeon.

    "What of it?" responded Muckles, in sullen defiance, breaking contact with Simeon's hand.

    "Just surprised, that's all. Do you remember me?"

"Yeah."

He seemed embarrassed. Perhaps he recalled the circumstances of the last time they met in that darkened, dreary room which was as musty as a brothel. Muckles was standing at a urinal – but – it was *not* a urinal, although the function was similar. The lusty youth was relieving himself by using his Granddad, giving the fat old man what he needed, his morning cream. Muckles with flame red hair, arrogant as ever, leaning backwards, pleased as Punch was sticking it out and giving it out. Hard faced Muckles, grinning at Simeon from ear to ear, was delighted to be 'on show' at that triumphant moment. He was so proud during those few seconds: arching back, rude tongue sticking right out signalling his instant of ecstasy to an audience of one. And that solitary voyeur, excited as hell, was galvanised by such a lascivious sight and sound of that final, long, cavernous groan of pleasure rumbling from somewhere deep within the blubbery caverns of Guzzly Granddad.

Simeon had judged Monks and Muckles harshly. He had heard about their mischief, yobbish behaviour and personally witnessed one particularly cruel example. Many in that secretive Derbyshire society knew of 'Muckles the Knuckles' who could well look after himself. If the tearaway before him was sullen with embarrassment, at least that was evidence of some small contrition. Should Simeon also consider what had just passed? Last year, this flame red ruffian had come across as immature, selfish and self-centred. Such conduct did not square with the recent erotic encounter. It showed consideration, tenderness and concluded with kindness.

"Down there… can ya see? Ya go down that path. Can ya do it?"

Simeon could see a rough, barely discernable, steep track through dense foliage which did not look easy.

"I'll be OK," said Simeon with considerable doubt. "See ya," he added, in a forced, breezy manner. He stretched up to plant a quick, goodbye kiss on the ruffian's full red lips. However, after making sweet contact, the other refused to accept either 'quick' or 'goodbye'. With strong arms, Muckles held firm to his recent discovery for a duration which lasted through luscious moments of mutual re-erections and more gropes. When the redhead released his quarry, he stood back and beamed a warm, loving smile which, briefly, transformed him into a real beauty. It was a total contrast from the hard countenance so familiar the summer before. He spoke a few of his rare words. He persuaded Simeon to be escorted along that difficult path which, eventually, would merge into one of the pretty Lover's Walks. Thoughtfully, he further suggested that Simeon might enjoy tea and cakes at one of Matlock Bath's many quaint Victorian style cafes. This was declined on the grounds that the all important purse had been given to Mr Toad for safekeeping – and the toad would now be long gone. Muckles smiled a harder, less pleasant smile which seemed to say 'no problem.' He produced a £5 note earned earlier from one of the older ghosts who haunted the Halls of Hades.

This reference to 'rent' was an opening to mention Gary. There was no point asking if Muckles had *seen* a blond kid, so, his enquiry concerned a new voice with an American accent. No, no new voices, no accents. There had been much activity that afternoon, but precious little conversation. It seemed that Gary had been swallowed up inside the dark bowels of Derbyshire.

It was well passed 6.00pm and most of Matlock Bath had already closed up. However, one quaint establishment, opposite the Petrifying Well, was still welcoming customers for tea and refreshments. After an anxious afternoon, the slightly decayed, cosy ambience of a Victorian tea shop was both nostalgic and comforting to a homesick English boy. He relished the faint aroma of toasted teacake, the time-worn willow tree china, the cracked teapots and the approaching ladylike figure with her gracious smile and wispy grey hair which completed the picture.

Sipping a fresh brew was also an opportunity to get to know this mysterious companion much better. Simeon reasoned that if he freely talked about himself, this might loosen the cautious tongue of Muckles. Consequently, he volunteered information and encouraged questions about the USA in general terms. Few questions came. The illiterate youth sitting in front of him had never been to school. Beyond an innate animal cunning in protecting his own, and his lair, he seemed to possess rather limited intelligence. When questions were asked about the chaotic world of Muckles, Simeon picked his words with care. For the most part, attempts to extract data failed.

"How is Guzzly Granddad? Are you still living with him?"

"Granddad's all right. Keeps dodging t' rozzers. We all do."

"Was he in the caves?"

"Try an keep 'im out! Thee all in there this year. Good place."

"I was told that you don't know how old you are, or where you came from. Is that true?"

"Am 16."

"If we're guessing, I'd say 17 is nearer the mark," said Simeon, with a twinkle.

"Suite ya self."

"Have you absolutely *no* idea of where you came from? There must be a few hazy memories when you were a small boy. I have them. Have you no memory of a mum or dad – where you lived – anything?"

Muckles was more willing to disclose recollections of his childhood. Indeed, he was intrigued with his early memories of a place inhabited with men and lots of other boys. He spoke of a large, dark-stoned building which frightened him. It was surrounded by a sort of fence made with sharp spears. He remembered big trees with no leaves which bent in the cold wind. It was always cold. Everybody had a cold. As the narrative continued, Simeon was beginning to get a picture of a Dickensian nightmare.

"Those men; were they good to you? Or were they nasty or cruel?"

Muckles found the question somewhat strange. With limited articulation he explained that the men were neither good nor cruel. They were just there; shadowy adults who wandered around gloomy halls in the big building. The boys had enough to eat, but not much else. Was it a workhouse? He had heard of 'a workhouse' but was not sure of what it was. Simeon suggested a school of some type? Perhaps it was a 'ragged school' for the destitute? No, not a school, but, with an effort, hazy recollections began to appear.

"There were a big kitchen an wash-room with a big mangle an fire to 'ot t' water an pigs an pig-sty… an t' pig 'ole."

On these last words of 'pig hole', that rather unpleasant smile, more of a lewd leer, reminiscent of the Guzzly Granddad episode, began to spread across the freckled face of Muckles. Simeon was alerted by a subtle, salacious change of voice which could almost be described as threatening, aggressive. This lecherous look suggested a sudden turn to the erotic. He interrogated this one-time waif about the difference between the pig-sty and the 'pig *hole*'. As expected, the pig-sty was a home for the pigs. Little Muckles and the other urchins enjoyed feeding them on a daily basis. He said the pig hole was for t' dotty lads' (dirty lads). Simeon was horrified! He steeled himself to hear about some unspeakable, medieval punishment. Conversely, Muckles assured him that the pig hole was an enjoyable experience for all the rogues who were judged to be 'dotty' –

"Cus thee ant wiped thee booms propa" (Because they had not wiped their bottoms properly).

Further questions threw light into this dark corner of the boy's distant memory. Selected dirty boys were taken into a dingy room and instructed to remove their britches (trousers). They were then guided over a dark hole – the pig hole. He said that pig grunts emanated from the deep blackness below – grunts, not from pigs – grunts from two men. To give this story extra colour, extra life, Muckles began to grunt at Simeon like a pig.

This caused him great distress. It was not so much because he was disgusted by a filthy narrative, or fear of where such an appalling story was going. These sound effects were excruciating for Simeon Hogg. He was taken back to the most painful period of his life, a time when he considered ending that life. At Mundy Street Boys School he was known as 'the hog' and the hog had to suffer for being different, had to be punished regularly by the chanting of pig grunts in the playground. Muckles was surprised and disappointed to see such a shadow of agony suddenly twist the features of his guest's face.

"Don't ya like to 'ave ya boom licked? Why not? It's nice. We loved it! What's oop with ya?"

Simeon was unable to speak to this boy about the horrors of Mundy Street and could not explain his apparent disapproval. Instead he tiptoed around the situation and, with careful diplomacy, attempted to voice his concern about young children being manipulated by powerful adults. Muckles was miffed. The pig hole men gave him and his mates pleasure. He objected to Simeon's moralising tone. He saw no problem with sex at any age. He had experienced a happy childhood. If these men were inducing little boys into a taste for erotic games – so what! It also became apparent that Muckles the Knuckles was no Simeon Hogg. Whatever or wherever this hellish place was, this tough youth with the red hair was never going to endure the humiliations which had damaged Simeon's life. A harrowing daily routine of psychological torture in that Church of England school began with prayers and hymns and ended with a desire for death.

Many years later, Simeon often looked back on that conversation in the Matlock Bath tea shop. He tried to make sense of the confusing ethics arising. His sadistic schoolmaster was innocent of any sexual misconduct, but, he enjoyed engineering situations which inflicted agony on a defenceless boy he saw as a sissy. That adult was without pity, and some cruel boys under his evil control, had nearly broken Simeon Hogg. Yet *their* conduct was seen as 'normal' – a part of growing up. They had committed no crime and all went on to prosper. On the other hand, the men in the pig hole were a different matter. If *they* had been brought to a court of law, they would have been incarcerated for many years.

CHAPTER 27

Wealthy Hedgehogs

"With no money, how did you get back to Belper?" barked the exasperated toad who had been thoroughly irritated by the whole shambolic afternoon.

"I hitch-hiked. Is Gary here?"

"No, he is *not* here. When he deigns to turn up – *out* he goes! He's brought nothing but disaster to this house. You're too late for dinner, so don't ask. Mavis has gone."

After a few words of mollification, Aubrey and Simeon settled themselves in the comfort and safety of 'the lounge' where the latter narrated his long, underground adventure, including his eventual deliverance, courtesy of Muckles.

"I wouldn't trust *him* as far as I could throw him! You've got yourself mixed up with a right lot haven't you! Muckles! My God! And *don't* start telling me that *he's* a victim as well. I'd seal up that cave. Yes! I'd get builders in! I'd have them seal up every entrance with bricks. That'd get shut of all that scum in one go. That's what I'd do. Yes! I'd…"

The toad ranted on with enthusiasm. He set out his plans of revenge on a gay community which had always excluded him, had always held him in contempt. He had a special hatred for the upper-middle class homosexuals who moved in the professional circles; those who were known as the elite Camps of Derby and Nottingham. Accordingly, the diatribe took on a menacing, softer tone, when he turned his wrath on the self-styled 'people of quality', the sneering snobs of Nottingham and Derby.

"I have already arranged a *special* punishment for them!" Big, round, toadal eyes bulged and gloated as an evil grin spread across the unpleasant features of an already ugly face. Podgy hands came up to nipple level and fingers began waggling with dastardly excitement.

"Aubrey! You nasty, horrible, little toad. What have you done now?" cried Simeon in genuine alarm.

But the toad was unable to reply. His repulsive, shapeless little body started to shake and writhe in malicious pleasure to accompany his high pitched spiteful giggles. A few moments after regaining composure, Aubrey explained his wicked plan with malicious pleasure.

"I have made a new will! It names people who will be required to attend a short film show in order to benefit. You know them. There'll be the stuck-up Claud Hoadley and the high and mighty Hilary Raymond Hawley who looks at me as a vile piece of slime crawling across the floor. From the Nottingham Camp, I'll invite those condescending, arrogant bastards Tommy and Martin and that white-faced, pretentious, affected prat, Clarence Soames."

"What about his affair, Bob Philips?"

"He's not quite so bad. I don't mind Bob, at least he speaks. He's civil to me in the cottages. Last winter, he did me a kindness. He removed a light bulb I couldn't quite reach in that lavatory opposite the Police Station on Queen's Drive. It was *marvellous* after that. We all got stuck in!"

"Quite. But tell me this – these are all people who've been unkind and spiteful to you – right?

"Correct."

"Then why should they believe that you, of all people, have left them any money?"

"Because," here the evil grin returned, "my solicitor will say in the letter that Mr Pod, on his deathbed, underwent a religious experience and wanted to make his peace with those he had grievously offended by his appalling behaviour. Hoadley and Hawley will be informed that a substantial sum is to be divided between them and their precious, pious Derby Cathedral."

"But... do you have a lot of money?"

"Enough to retire at 50 and escape from those horrible girls at school who are making my life a misery. Yes, my investments from father and miserly mother are, shall we say, *considerable*. In that letter, the total amount of my estate will be disclosed to temp them. No fear; my enemies will be *sure* to attend. They'll be there – and they'll fall into my trap."

"All this, of course, is assuming that you die first."

"If I outlive them, I can dance and piss on their graves! If not, well, the only snag is that I'll miss seeing the look on their smug faces when they hear my malicious message from the grave." He was seized by a crescendo of more spiteful giggles which pierced the Pod parlour.

"When this dastardly film begins to flicker, what are you going to say to this unfortunate audience of five?"

"Correction, it will be an audience of 25. Each of the five victims will be required to designate four friends or, colleagues who must be professional gentlemen. They will receive £1000 each. They'll get my money, *providing* that the said victim remains in his seat until the end of the film. That will insure that they attend, and that each victim suffers the full extent of my carefully rehearsed insults. I expect those extras will be the eight 'nodding heads' from Hoadley's Derby Camp and twelve snobbish, Flying Horse disciples from Tommy and Martin's Nottingham lot."

"And... the nature of these... 'insults'?"

"I have yet to complete the script," hissed the iniquitous toad, slowly, softly, as his unpleasant features morphed further into something akin to the depravity of a medieval torturer. "First, I'll greet each target in turn," he hissed, "then I'll share with the gathering a few damaging and humiliating anecdotes I've been gathering from my spies. That will inflict *maximum* embarrassment."

"Such as?"

"Oh no! You're not going to wheedle it *all* out of me. But, I'll give you one example. Last January on a frosty evening, that big soft ponce, Hilary Raymond Hawley

was enjoying a short walk through Derby with his lord and master Claud Hoadley.
Answering the call of nature, Hawley deigned to enter that decrepit, whiffy old Derby Fish
Market cottage. Of course, he's a wimp. He's led a very sheltered life and doesn't really
cottage as such. Anyway, there was one other man at that stinking urinal who happened to
be my bum chum, Albert Birkin. He was in there for the 'long haul'. Albert's a friendly
sort. He said to HRH, 'Cold isn't it?' Hawley, superior as ever, just ignored Albert treating
him like a fag end in the latrine gutter. Naturally it irritated Albert. He's a rough old
bugger, so, suddenly, he brandished his massive 'milk bottle' weapon and shouted – 'Ear
are, lass, warm ya 'ands on this fooker!'"

"Oh dear!" said Simeon, grinning from ear to ear. "And *did* he warm his hands?"

"He did not! Hawley fled! She's a lady! Never seen anything so big. Never
experienced anything so insulting or rude! HRH left that piss corner so fast his feet hardly
touched the ground." Aubrey broke off for a moment to allow a spiteful, high pitched
shriek of giggles to subside. He was in tears of laughter having difficulty completing his
tale. "Hawley shot out and went straight, bang, smack into a horrified Hoadley. Both had
to be calmed down in the nearest pub with Hilary's tipple – a 'white lady'.
"That is just *one* example. I've got the goods on all of them, and at the very end, when
they are all thoroughly dishonoured and disgraced, I'll tell them where my money is *really*
going."

"Yes?" said Simeon, "I'm all agog! *Who* gets the money?"

"My capital goes to those who have given me pleasure, to those dear little
creatures who have never done me any harm. I'm leaving everything to the hedgehogs!"

"*Hedgehogs!*"

"Every penny to the British Hedgehog Society and you Simeon, as my dear
friend, must promise not to tell anybody – and spoil it all."

"I promise, if I can be invited to enjoy the show."

"You can enjoy the show sooner than you think! I'm to be filmed next week
and it should be ready for projection before the end of this month. Ooo! If *only* I could
be there! It would be worth faking my own death to see *their* smarmy faces looking up
at *my* face – close up – looking into my venomous face – distorted with rancour, spewing
out nasty..."

"Alas, Aubrey, truth to tell; I'm not at all sure that I'll be back before the end of
the month to see the film of your distorted, venomous, rancorous face."

"Back from where?" cried Aubrey in alarm.

It was in a flash. It was in his voice. During such moments, this nasty, warped little man
showed a nicer side. At that instant, his tone indicated vulnerability and affection towards
the young man of whom he had become very fond. Aubrey had come to hope that Simeon
would stay with him forever. Simeon knew this. He remonstrated over a note sent to the
headmaster – 'too ill to work' – would be back on Wednesday. Aubrey was desperate
to have as much time with his chicken as possible. Accordingly, Simeon decided to be
gentle with the little fellow, explaining how it was necessary to cycle around the country
to mitigate the possible threat to his life. Toad threw a small tantrum and demanded to
know exactly where his friend would go – without result. Aubrey protested – in vain.
Eventually he was somewhat calmed and appeased when Simeon solemnly promised to
send a postcard, about once a week, just before he moved on to a new town or village. It
was essential that the blabbering toad could not tell anyone where his chicken was located.

This precipitated a raid on the toadal stamp bank. Twenty stamps were foisted on the cyclist for exclusive use for Pod cards.

Simeon was concerned for the safety of his friend Gary Mackenzie. He would like to know that Gary had returned to Toad Hall, if only to be refused and immediately ejected onto one of the byways of Belper. But the toad had no phone and direct communication was impossible due to the need for strict security.

CHAPTER 28

Sheffield Sam

The dawning of a fresh, sunny Monday, May 9th was auspicious for a cycle ride to the north, but dulled by Simeon's concern for Gary Mackenzie and Aubrey's concern regarding the imminent departure of the house guest he had come to care for.

"At least you should stay until your friend comes back to remove himself! *And* all his ill-gotten cash! Mavis is as honest as the day is long, but I don't like the idea of temptation laying about my home. If Gary's been bragging to such villains as Monks and Muckles about his immoral earnings, I'm quite likely to be burgled in the middle of the night!"

"But not raped? Sorry! Look, if I stay… let's say until Wednesday, and if Gary still hasn't shown up… I don't suppose there's any point suggesting we go to the police?" asked Simeon, without much hope, playing with his toast.

"*Are you mad?* Do you know what they do to people like me in prison?"

"OK. It's the horrible injustice of it all. A friend in need and we can't ask for help. It's – so – bloody – awful."

After breakfast, a decision was taken to jointly enter Gary's room and investigate the suspected large sum of cash. The bedroom was untidy: one suitcase, one rucksack, several shirts, socks, shoes and sundry items littered the floor. It was so depressing, the vacuum and the total absence of a cheerful, bubbly personality which had once filled the room. A life force which had been so very full of life, now gone, made it all seem so heartbreaking. Gary had been generous and kind. In the circumstances – dark caves, feral boys, and so much danger – Simeon was sure that his friend would have sent word by now. A telegram, a note via taxi, anything to reassure that he was OK – if, indeed, he *was* OK.

With an air of poignant helplessness, he checked in the usual spots including shoes and socks. The cash, however, was discovered in a more obvious place. It was concealed inside the semi-secret lid of his rucksack. Aubrey thrust forward his ugly face, and, eagerly watched Simeon count out 23 ten pound notes.

"Two hundred and thirty pounds," said Simeon, slowly, thoughtfully with concern. "That squares with the $1500 he changed into sterling back in Scotland. It would have made about £500. He will have already spent some of it, and has probably carried the balance with him in his wallet."

"For the record," said Aubrey, "you can struggle up that step ladder with me and watch me hide this confounded rucksack up in the loft."

Simeon witnessed the sad rucksack being buried underneath a musty pile of Nelly Pod's winter coats and old hats clearly dating to the 1920s.

Aubrey followed Simeon around like a miserable dog, anxiously watching him pack his saddle bag with three changes of socks, shirts and underwear. He took an interest in the obscure and circuitous route being planned from a close study of the Ordnance Survey map. This was a cyclist who took his time – time to enjoy all the unusual nooks and crannies England had to offer – and there were plenty of those. His path avoided busy roads, cities and towns. It was a path which favoured quiet, rural, kinking roads. Simeon was happy to meet the challenge of frequent map reading and steep hills which were not a problem, if you simply dismounted and turned yourself into a pedestrian.

Again, in his pushy way, Aubrey lunged over and watched his chicken jot down a rough itinerary leading to the north – Shottle, Wirksworth, Via Gellia, Winster, Elton, Youlgreave, Over Haddon, Ashford and on to the heights of Great Hucklow. On the reference to Castleton Youth Hostel, typically, toad butted in with a toad-like bark.

"Is that your first overnight stay? Is it? You must write to me from there to say you're alright! You will won't you?"

Simeon gave appropriate assurances and the notated tour continued with Hope, Thornhill, Ladybower Dam turning east on the A57, first left turn up to Strines Moor (near Lost Lad) and then down to Dale Dyke Dam...

"Why have you stopped!" snapped the forceful toad of jutting head.

"Because that's as much as you're going to get," replied Simeon, slightly irritated by Aubrey's assertiveness and bad breath.

Mindful of Martin's instructions regarding secrecy, Simeon decided that a route beyond Dale Dyke Dam was more than he was prepared to disclose.

"What's this Dale Dyke Dam? It sounds like a horrible place! Why go there?" demanded the toad.

"It *was* a horrible place! And if you were nicer to Nobby the Gnome, you might know something about it. In 1864 it showed no mercy. It killed 300 people!

Simeon had first laid eyes on that legendary institution, the intriguing Nobby the Gnome the previous year. At first sight he was just an odd little man skipping about entertaining a small audience for pennies – but Nobby was much more than that.

Larger than a dwarf, not quite so shrivelled as a very old man, but certainly a small old man of uncertain age. Yes, definitely a gnome. Nobby had a nice simple face reflecting a kindly nature which made him popular with children – popular with almost everybody – except Aubrey Pod and the snobs of the Nottingham Camp and the Derby Camp. Claud Hoadley had an acute horror of this lowly, common gnome. And, yes, there was an air, a suggestion of the supernatural about old Nobby under his funny little beaten-up cap, clad and shod in medieval attire. There was something timeless, something 100% Derbyshire about this strange little fellow who belonged in the dales, in the woods, on the moors, alongside the canals, the rivers and would not be out of place in deep ravines or in the entrance of a cave.

Like others, Simeon had been absorbed by the strange spectacle of Nobby's funny little jig. He was mesmerised by its hops, its spins and whirls. It was magical in its effect and was entirely wholesome in contrast to the evil 'dance of delight' from Aubrey Pod. This toadal 'dance of delight' was quite a talking point! It was most frequently seen when one of his enemies, the 'gentlemen of quality', had met with some misfortune. Simeon saw this extraordinary phenomenon for the first time on his last visit. The terrible toad had just read in the *Derby Evening Telegraph* that a high ranking member of the Derby Camp, a professional man close to Hoadley, had been entrapped and arrested in the notorious Chester Green cottage on a charge of lewd conduct with intent to commit an act of gross indecency.

That article, a tragedy for a homosexual man, had the monstrous effect of inducing a rising cascade of shrieking giggles in another homosexual who was clearly warped. In his sinful excitement, the toad jumped up and, for a few seconds, was seized by a compulsion to dance! He joyfully skipped his 'dance of delight'; a cruel caper, a perverted prance which horrified, mesmerised and yet, amused Simeon. At the time, he formed the impression that he had somehow stumbled into a scene from one of Grimm's fairy tales.

"What's Nobby the Gnome got to do with Devil's Dyke?" insisted the toad.

"Not Devil. I said *Dale* Dyke. But you're not far wrong. Apart from one devilish evening about a hundred years back, Nobby told me it's a nice place to visit. It's peaceful and pretty."

"Is there a good cottage there?" enquired Aubrey getting excited. "Nobby *lives* in lavatories."

Aubrey Pod had made a simple statement of fact. Within living memory up through the 1960s, Nobby the Gnome had been a living legend with his little jig, his magic tricks and his itinerant lifestyle of overnight sleeping in public toilets. By such means, he could be, on hand, to dispense pleasure to those who were glad to receive it. Such delightful ministrations in remote parts of the Peak District where were few and far between. As the famous Dolly of Derby once told Simeon –

"Old men sitting for hours on end in Victorian lavatories is an ancient Derbyshire tradition."

Aubrey pressed Simeon further on the connection between his arch rival in the cottages, Nobby the Gnome, and a beauty spot located up in the moors to the north west of Sheffield. It transpired that, amongst his many other talents, this old curiosity was also a repository of folklore and local knowledge. In previous cycling expeditions through Derbyshire, Simeon had come across Nobby on several very enjoyable occasions. At each instance (on completion of the important business) this chatty old soul was always pleased to pass the time of day with Simeon the cyclist. The old sage shared traditional stories and local gay gossip, some of which had been passed down by word of mouth for several generations.

Nobby's knowledge went back more than 100 years. He spoke of a notorious queer, a rough, tough, randy navvy known as Sheffield Sam who had been working on the construction of a new dam in the 1860s. The rapidly expanding steel industry of Sheffield in the mid Victorian period, together with the resulting expansion of population, had put great strain on the Sheffield Waterworks Company. It needed more reservoirs for more fresh water to combat outbreaks of cholera and typhoid. Sam was one of a small army of labourers who found employment constructing a dam on Dale Dyke, a remote stream which drains the high moorland near the border of Derbyshire and Yorkshire. Eventually, much lower down, it becomes the River Loxley. Running lower still, the River Loxley joins the River Don which flows through the centre of Sheffield.

After many months of heavy digging, hard graft and, according to Nobby, quite a bit of groping; Sam and his mates had completed Dale Dyke Dam in the early days of March 1864. There was an atmosphere of celebration on the night of March 11th when Sam persuaded two strapping teenage youths to share his bed at his digs. Nothing posh, it was a small, simple room upstairs in a pub called The Barrel. This was located in a hamlet called Damflask about three miles down the picturesque Loxley Valley.

Nobby talked Simeon through the social complications, the 'rough and tumble' culture of ill-educated, common working men. He clarified the apparent contradiction between the familiar macho condemnation of queer activity and the unexpected tolerance of a sexually active character like Sheffield Sam. Over the months of work, sexy Sam, a likeable chap with a strong but naughty hand – feel by feel, fumble by fumble – gradually cultivated popularity with his mates. His quick wit, coupled with the occasional crafty caress, gradually won over several comely lads in his gang of labourers.

When it came to 'scoring' with crude, butch blokes, the Gnome was interested in no other type, he explained to Simeon the secret of his skills. These techniques were used by Sheffield Sam and commended by Nobby as best practice. Yet, Simeon already knew this secret! At Mundy Street Boys School in Heanor between 1955 and 1958 he had been brought low by a well-established cruel regime of pain and terror which turned him into an obedient zombie, a sexual object for the exclusive pleasure of some sadistic youths. Simeon Hogg had no choice at Mundy Street. By contrast, William Howitt Secondary Modern School, a culture of kindness, gave Simeon a lot of choice to have a lot of sex with a lot of boys in 1959 and 1960 – the best years of his life. Like Sheffield Sam he had come to know the value of confidentiality, discretion and tact. *That* was the secret! That was the secret of having regular erotic encounters with a harem of boys on an equal, mutual, regular basis. There was no speech. Each incident came with the unspoken assurance that nothing would ever be said. Each incident was accompanied by opportunity and a suitable venue – the toilet, the cloak-room / sports changing room, a book cupboard, a corner of the playground or, indeed, almost anywhere. Like a good scout, Simeon was 'prepared'. He never wore underpants and always had a useful hole in his trouser pocket – as did a few of his regular partners. After four years of sexual slavery at Mundy Street, the members of Simeon's harem at Howitt were guaranteed an experience of quality. It was good, safe and quick. At the age of 13 to 14 it can be very quick indeed!

So long as he played by the rules – after gas lighting, open fires and the grim Dickensian reality of Mundy Street – life at Howitt was sheer joy.

Life for Sheffield Sam, often brutal and hard, also had occasional hours of joy. Tragically that life was cut short during one of those joyful hours, in one of the early hours of March 12th 1864.

It took several days for the high Dale Dyke rivulet to back up against the new dam which flooded Bradfield Dale. This created a new reservoir for the folks of Sheffield far below. Eventually, the dam was full to within 2ft of the crest of the overflow weir. On the evening of March 11th, all appeared to be well as darkness approached. All that afternoon, raging winds had conjured up a fearful tempest over the high roof of Derbyshire, creating great waves across that large body of water which had recently changed the map. Sheffield Sam and his horny boys, bouncing happily between those semen stained sheets, were oblivious to the driving storms and heavy rain hitting the high moors above them. The peat and heather could soak up only so much of that terrible drenching and were about to hurl down the valley a wall of water which was 50ft high in places. At 8.30pm, construction workers, still on duty, noticed a horizontal crack about 10ft below the top of the dam. As the hours passed, as the storm increased in strength, so the crack widened to weaken the dam. At 11.00pm, a deluge of water broke over the top of the wall creating an effect below of Niagara proportions.

On horseback and on foot, people rushed down the valley to warn the population of impending death and destruction. Many heeded this threat of imminent annihilation – but some did not. The wife of the publican of The Barrel, rushed up the stairs, burst into the room of Sheffield Sam intent on dragging him out of deep sleep to save his life. She shouted urgent pleas to the navvy. She begged him to get out – immediately! She yelled for him to make a dash to higher ground – to save himself. However, these frenzied words died on her lips when she was frozen by the shock of the lewd, noisy scene before her.

Although naked, parts of Sheffield Sam's well-toned, muscular body where obscured by parts of two other bodies – equally desirable, younger, equally naked. She was looking at a carnal complexity which, at first sight, seemed to the landlady to be an alien creature from hell grunting and moaning. It appeared to have six flaying arms and six writhing legs. This terrifying fiend took no account of her rude entry and hysterics but, in little more than a few seconds, she had sorted out the puzzle and resolved the monster into three bodies. Groaning, grinning and contorted in ecstatic mischief, the two visible faces were strangers. It told her that the recumbent body of obscured face must belong to her guest. Sam's head seemed to be buried in the buttocks of the first youth who was obscenely squatting over his mouth. This lewd squatter was facing a second squatter whose disgusting crouch had consumed Sam's substantial, well inflated length. Just for a few bizarre moments, in spite of herself, in spite of the shock, she was galvanized by what appeared to be two naughty boys, laughing and shouting obscenities at each other, enjoying a sexual see-saw. But it was only a few moments before the instinct of self-preservation kicked in and overruled her mixed feelings at that filthy scene. The landlady took her own advice and ran for her very life.

At midnight, the stricken dam lost the last vestige of any strength at all to hold back its millions of gallons of captured water. Consequently, a gigantic tsunami, inexorably, thundered down the Loxley Valley sweeping away all before it. This dreadful deluge destroyed cottages, bridges, watermills, riverside forges, paper mills and a hamlet called Little Matlock was wiped from the map. Eventually the torrent arrived in Sheffield and wreaked havoc with wire mills, steel mills and inflicted considerable damage on furnaces and other buildings.

Continuing his oral history, Nobby the Gnome told Simeon that this, the worst man-made disaster to hit Britain, has a special place in homosexual history. Minutes after midnight, Sheffield Sam and his boys were carried away on a wave of erotic ecstasy shortly before they, like Little Matlock, were removed from the secretive map of gay life. Of the 300 plus souls who were taken, Sam and his nameless chums who existed in a twilight world of Victorian social concealment, were counted among the 27 bodies which were never found.

At this stage, the Gnome made a profound observation.

"If it hadn't been for the local vicar, we would have never known anything at all about Sheffield Sam! Now then!"

This landlady had good intentions. On the other hand, it has been said that the devil is at his most dangerous when he becomes respectable. After missing death by inches, this ignorant, narrow and bigoted fishwife told her homophobic story to the world. Aghast, there was nothing in her limited experience in such rural remoteness which had prepared her for a sight which shocked and sickened. Traumatised by the calamity, she seized an opportunity to proclaim righteous indignation about perverts in the community who had richly deserved the Wrath of the Lord. The vicar and other preachers were quick to make the contrast between her divine salvation and the imminent execution of the lascivious and the wicked.

In the weeks and months which followed, the pulpits and halls around Sheffield resounded with cries from the virtuous who blamed Sam for the debacle which had devastated life, property and industry. It was claimed that the many had been punished by a vengeful God for the secret sins of the few – especially the sins of Sam. An account in the local press suggested that his poor workmanship and general inattention had *also* been a main cause of the fatal breach. It was concluded that too much horseplay and groping had corrupted and distracted younger labourers.

Nobby was not an educated man. Yet, he had in him enough enterprise and zest to research, to dig out the truth behind this destructive event. The records revealed that Sheffield Sam was one of hundreds of unskilled labourers who, for small reward, undertook heavy digging for long, hard hours.

"It was nothing at all to do with Sheffield Sam," remonstrated Nobby with indignation. "An *engineer* designs and builds a dam. Quality and reliability – that's the *gaffer's* responsibility! Blaming poor Sam! He and his mates did as they were *told* to do. Like all working men. They did the *hard* work. They did the *spade* work. John Towlerton Leather – what a mouth full! *He* was the engineer. *He* was responsible for the reservoirs of the Sheffield Waterworks Company – not Sam. Not only that; Leather also built the Bilberry Dam at Holmfirth a few years before. Now then!"

"Now then what? What happened to *that* dam?" asked Simeon.

"It fell down! That's what happened!"

CHAPTER 29

Old Nottingham

The conversation about Nobby the Gnome and his oral histories had drained several pots of tea and eaten up the best part of the morning. Indeed, it was nearly lunch time.

"You should, at least, stay for lunch before setting off on your epic cycle journey to the far north," said the toad, with a certain smug satisfaction. Aubrey tried to capitalize on Simeon's enthusiasm for homosexual history. He encouraged him to keep talking, hoping to squeeze an extra day of having him close by.

"Of course, you're quite right." said Aubrey, three hours later, after a long leisurely lunch. "If I were on better terms with Nobby I'd be better informed. But do try to understand, Simeon; cottaging can be *very* competitive. It can even get hostile when an attractive young chicken is at stake. I've had few nasty punch ups with the Gnome when there's been something nice we've *both* wanted. Verbal, of course. We never get violent – just an exchange of bitchy insults. Monks and Muckles! Now *they* are the ones to watch. Terrible! I've had flaming newspapers pushed underneath to smoke me out. It's true! They know I'm in there all day. And then there was that time when they pinched poor old Jasper's teeth! No respect for the old. No respect at all.

"Anyway," continued, Mr Toad, keeping it going, "it was very decent of Nobby to do his research. Sheffield Sam! He sounds all right. Just my sort. I don't know about that dam, but, if *I* ever get a rough navvy on the other side of *my* glory hole – he be as well drained as any busted dam! He'd be one satisfied, empty Sam by the time I'd done with him! That evil bitch dishonoured his memory. It's just not on! I'd had slapped her bloody chops and...

"But it needs to be written down!" cried Simeon. "If it's not documented soon, it'll all be lost. He's not young."

"Well over 80, at least," said the malicious toad, nonchalantly chomping into his cheese and biscuits.

"Nothing like! I'd put Nobby in his early 70s. And all that hiking up hill and down dale – wow! I'll tell you this, Aubrey; that old timer has a well-proportioned, firm body. I've seen it at the Turkish Baths. It's as fit as mine. I'll bet he can out-walk me any day – and you as well," added Simeon, looking at Aubrey's shapeless, toad-like form; the result of too many rich puddings, such as the two helpings he had just consumed.

"Well I'm not exactly the rucksack, shorts and boots type like old Nobby," said the slug-like toad cutting more cheese.

"And *I'm* not your average historian, but *somebody* should be talking to the likes of the Gnome, *and* that old fossil in Buxton they call Toby Jug *and* the Goblin, that ancient horror who advertises massage.

"What a good idea!" exclaimed Aubrey, suddenly aroused in excitement. "Forget cycling. You should stay here, interview all the Jurassic queens and write up a history of homosexuals.

"Don't know about a book! But I should at least get some notes down for posterity for somebody else to use. Anyway, look at the time! Not much point leaving now."

"No," said Aubrey.

"First thing in the morning," insisted Simeon.

"They've given out heavy rain for tomorrow. You should get started on your history book."

"It'll never get written if I'm dead!"

As these words left his lips, he found them dramatic and unbelievable. Yet, each time he examined the evidence – strangers making enquiries, disappearance of Gary Mackenzie, concerns and warnings from Martin Harcourt QC – a very credible figure – the result was the same. Simeon was in danger and he should heed the advice of a respected barrister. The cyclist was instructed to be, effectively, incommunicado, on a cycling tour, no later than Tuesday. Martin considered that mafia agents could well locate him at 'Toad Hall' by Wednesday.

After dinner and especially after his recent exhausting adventures in the High Tor caves with its fear and frights; Simeon was beginning to feel the benefit of having passed a lazy day with an amusing toad. Aubrey was old fashioned and comfortable to be with.

The conversation became philosophical. It was one of those occasions when the usually funny, foolish toad demonstrated an intelligent logical mind. The subject in question turned to the unusual nature of many secretive homosexual men. There was a common link – mystery – a complete lack of history – a total absence of any background and a dearth of provenance. They discussed Sheffield Sam and the mysterious, obese Dolly of Derby. They talked about the hideous goblin, Toby Jug, Monks and Muckles who were not sure how old they were. And then, Aubrey asked a question.

"What about Nobby the Gnome? How did *he* end up being a tramp sleeping in lavatories?"

"Nobby's had a hard life."

"He's never done any hard work!" sneered Aubrey.

Having spoken at length to Nobby, Simeon was in a position to enlighten his friend. Since the old vagrant was so closely associated with the Derbyshire countryside, Aubrey was surprised to learn that he originated from an area of ill repute in a rough part of Nottingham. As with Monks and Muckles, Nobby the Gnome was not sure of his age. Simeon outlined the old man's boyhood descriptions of slum streets in the Meadows, south of the Nottingham Canal, north of the River Trent.

"Rows of old terraced houses, two up, two down, gas lit, open coal fires, all rented, all grotty with tin baths hanging up outside. Nobby said it's much the same today."

"It is," replied Aubrey with rising enthusiasm and gathering speed. "I remember it *exactly* like that when I used to take chickens back to Old Louie who lived on Northcote

Terrace. Terrible place! All scrubbers! You could *see* them 'at it' in the back alleys. It was near to clapped-out steam trains which rattled over a viaduct. A right ramshackle slum! No loo, you had to piss in the sink near a pile of unwashed pots. I could never fancy a cup of Louie's tea. A right old slut was Old Louie."

"Who is Old Louie?" asked Simeon.

"Ask, who *was* Old Louie. He died in 1950. Ugly bugger! A sleazy, shabby, shambling chap with a sing-song voice. You could always take stuff back providing *he* got his smackers round it *first*. 'Share and share alike,' he used to sing out." At this point, Aubrey 'took off' Louie in one of his amusing caricatures. "He always said the same thing when you turned up on the door step with something nice – 'Surprise, Surprise'! And Old Louie is the only man I know who was actually proud to return from his holiday paler than when he went."

"How is that?" asked Simeon.

"Arr, well you see; *that* was the proof that he'd done well. He'd had a great time! It was the evidence that he'd spent most of his holiday inside his digs, his B&B bedroom, lying down on his stomach all day. That was Louie. Always bragging. The bigger the better, the more the merrier. The only sound louder that Louie's orgasm was that clattering engine ever puffing over that rickety bridge. I expect he was shagged to death in the end – but, I digress. Back to Nobby. It's hard to believe that an ancient fossil like that was ever young. Where in the Meadows did the Gnome live?"

Simeon explained that his whimsical old friend lived in many homes in the twisted complication of streets in the Meadows area. He had no memory of his 'mam or dad'. He was shared by Aunty Sally, Aunty Lil, Aunty Nellie, Aunty Fanny, Aunty Gertie, Aunty May and Aunty Edna. By inclination a happy child, the little gnome recalled these women as having hearts of gold. If one of them was his mother, it was never disclosed. They called him Nobby due to his small stature. He looked like a gnome. His cute little face had a turned up nose with round eyes like two marbles rather too close together. 'Nobby's no oil painting isn't Nobby,' was his common catchphrase.

He was dubbed 'the gnome' not long after he began to toddle up and down the row. It was a distinctive odd way of toddling, an invisible signature in the air which would identify the little chap for the rest of his life. The hops and skips of this unusual gait, indicated the friskiness and fun in his personality. The spring in his step suggested a caper, a mischievous frolic which characterise his funny little dance.

Aunty May, small, sweet, pretty and simpering was the seamstress for most of the aunts and the much loved little sprite. This woman of creative skill and imagination had been struck by Nobby's funny face. It had a suggestion of the medieval period. Accordingly, she crafted a capuchin, a long pointed cowl with cloak which gave the gnome a picturesque look of a hooded peasant working the land. Years after the death of Aunty May, content with his fairy tale image, the Gnome continued the tradition with needle and thread making a crude capuchin to ward off the Derbyshire chill.

This good natured fellow had a good start in life. In those idyllic Victorian days of the late 1890s and the early 1900s, the cheerful chap was made welcome in every house on Bumchums Row. He was well fed, well clothed and well loved. Everybody wanted to hug and cuddle the diminutive sprite who, according to the aunts, was said to have been found under a toadstool by the canal. He radiated joy and gave pleasure to all.

Nobby spoke fondly of the warm and friendly atmosphere of Bumchums Row.

"Doors were never locked and nobody knocked. Everybody knew everybody else. Those women were in and out of each others homes like yo-yos." He suddenly skipped a jig and sung a silly ditty about a yo-yo. "If somebody was took bad, they'd all muck in and help out with shoppin', scrubbin' and I don't know what. Wash day! What a palaver! More like a zoo than a wash yard. I use to watch bantams and rabbits running around Aunty Sally, sweating cobs, ponching that old dolly tub with her leg-of-mutton arms." He performed a quick impression of stout Aunty Sally ponching.

"Bantams and rabbits?" asked Simeon, in a desperate effort to bring the fool back to his subject.

"They all loved animals. If I wanted to cuddle a cat – straight round to Aunty Nellie with 'er big belly." Impression of a wobbling belly. "She had five cats. Dogs – now that was racy-tongued Edna. She looked just like her Bonzo. Massive dog! I could get lost in its dense black coat. Bonzo loved to be snuggled, he did. If you didn't know he was soft, you'd take him as the *Hound of the Baskervilles*. It was *Edna* to watch, never mind t' dog. She'd an acid tongue had Edna! I loved Bonzo but couldn't abide Aunty Mae's nasty cockerel which had a *vicious peck*. Ooo, it were keen! I've ran many a mile to keep out of its way. That bastard bird 'ated my guts! *And* it lived to a great age just to spite me! Now then!"

"Did you have a favourite aunt?" asked Simeon to head off a cockerel impression.

"Well, Aunty Gertie. She were a good-hearted old soul. Great swollen varicose vein legs, she had. And then there were that boring tortoise. Boring because it didn't *do* anything. It just wasn't there. Sad really. I used to pick it up – and, do you know, you could see straight through! Now then! It either died or left its shell before I was born. She was always talking to it. I tried to tell her. 'Aunty Gertie', I said 'It's GONE!' I said. But she wouldn't 'ave it. No, she wouldn't 'ave it."

From the first Thursday to Saturday of each October, the little gnome would be absent from his seven homes causing no concern. On the contrary, the seven jolly aunts went to see him enjoy the thrills and spills of the medieval Nottingham Goose Fair. Much to the irritation of the toad, the gnome acquired his ability to get a free ride in life during those boyhood days on the Forest Recreation Ground north west of the city centre. In 1903, the travelling fun fair people were enthralled with the supernatural appearance of the charming little chap kitted out in his hand-made medieval attire. They made Nobby an honorary member of the Showmen's Guild which came with the privilege of free rides for life.

Encouraged by these good travellers who were quick to detect an inclination and talent to entertain; each October, Nobby developed his funny little dance which, many years later, became legendary. Also acquired were his juggling skills and dexterity for performing magic tricks. Such skills were practiced and honed to perfection in his various homes during various parties organised by his various aunts. Most of these women were illiterate save for Aunty Lil who was able to give little Nobby a rudimentary education. Accordingly, at the age of 12 he was able to read and write.

Simeon listened to this early biography with great interest. It was a tale which contrasted sharply with his own, often miserable childhood. Nobby – a small boy untroubled and happy – was wanted. Simeon was never wanted. Nobby never went to school. Simeon was coerced to a school which showed no mercy. Nobby enjoyed halcyon days in a run-down ghetto which was branded immoral and corrupting. Simeon endured brutal days in a respectable but heartless Church of England junior school which nearly destroyed him.

Nobby's aunts were proud of their charming, elfin child. Simeon's parents and sisters were ashamed of him. Nobby enjoyed whiling away the time exploring the canal and the river. Simeon stayed in and contemplated suicide.

Nobby grew up to be tolerant and forgiving. Simeon did not. Throughout Nobby's life in the lavatories, he sustained a number of unpleasant and violent incidents. He was once physically lifted off the bowl, manhandled out of a WC and thrown on to the public pavement by a homophobic thug. Not long afterwards he came across the same thug and, consistent with his good-natured disposition, gave him a cheery greeting. The thug was impressed. They had sex. They became friends! Simeon was amazed.

A similar example occurred when Monks maliciously stamped on Nobby's hand when it appeared under the WC dividing wall. At a later date, Monks was rudely squatting in a different WC. He allowed, nay, *welcomed* a similar, anonymous, sensitive hand to enter his private space. Naughty fingers gently caressed, wantonly stroked and gave exquisite pleasure to that yob's erogenous areas to the point of a powerful ejaculation which anointed the mystery hand. Monks was embarrassed and ashamed to discover that this particular hand of bliss was attached to that same old gnome – Nobby the Gnome – no less. Nobby knew that it was Monks, the teenage tearaway, who was in residence next door. It mattered not. The Gnome had forgiven Monks. Simeon was amazed.

Rewind to the early days of the 20th century. The teenage Nobby had a faint memory of some sort of happening which caused a fuss in his street. Somebody had died and somebody else was being acclaimed. Simeon suggested this event could be the death of Edward VII in 1910 and / or the Coronation of George V in June 1911. Nobby agreed. He recalled buntings, a street party, bright warm sunshine and his aunts raucously celebrating with a wild knees-up.

Also, he recalled during that time, that he had already been cottaging for 'a few years'. Taking all the evidence into consideration, Simeon suggested that his pal was probably born in, or near to, 1895. The naughty gnome estimated that his first 'spunk' had occurred about three summers before that party. For some extraordinary reason, he associated that first cum with the popular songs *Oh Oh Antonio* and *Shine on Harvest Moon*. He also remembered a man taking him to a structure of corrugated tin roof called the Tin Truck. It housed an amazing contraption called a bioscope. His own research had revealed that those songs and the Picture Palace were popular in 1908 when Nobby would be about 13 – old enough for his first ever orgasm.

The ever smiling, jolly Nobby enjoyed all seasons of the year. Simeon was spellbound by romantic descriptions of thick fogs of November which held strong sexual connotations for the teenage gnome. Fuelled by the onset of adolescence, after tea, he would politely trot out to one of his aunts a familiar mantra – 'Please may I leave the table'. Rough and raucous, they may have been, but these spinster fish wives took their parenting responsibilities very seriously. The courtesy and consideration taught by these good ladies to this budding gentleman served him well throughout his long life.

He left the cheer, the warmth and the light of one of his several addresses and stepped on to dark, damp cobbles which lay below the murkiness of a thick mist, so characteristic of the damp Meadows at that time. In that low area between the canal and the river, the smoke of a thousand chimneys mixed with ground level cloud to form a spectral vapour consuming the dreary silent streets of dreary silent rows of houses.

Notwithstanding, the crafty gnome with his distinctive gait skipped his way over those cobbles under the dirty, amber gas lighting. That same haze also blurred the ghostly outline of shadowy, secretive men as they silently drifted towards the local urinal seeking out other strangers who also seemed to float through the thick, dirty fog.

Nobby became familiar with these dowdy, secretive strangers with their flat caps and hobnail boots. Quiet, still and anonymous, they lined up at the urinal always pleased to see the regular visitor, the aptly named little gnome of 'oh so nice touch'. In secret silence, he would play with those 'big mesters'. The same skills which could make small objects appear and disappear could also make other things get bigger. He worked with competence and flair. Soft, sensitive, naughty little hands sought out the special favourite places of those big men who had developed a taste for a naughty little gnome. Fumbling, fondling fingers explored the nooks and crannies of bliss which could make subtle changes to a man's face, his breathing and his posture. Nobby's deft little digits, wet and gooey with excited dribble were too clever, too cunning in technique to bring matters to a conclusion too soon. No. *This* naughty gnome knew how to make big masters beg. He knew how to make men moan, how to bring urgency to a voice which was already breathy and pleading and – eventually – inarticulate.

After he had 'spunked' the big man, occasionally he was rewarded by a few pennies or even a sixpence. Then he would move to the next big man for another sixpence – and so on. Nobby was pleased to have his efforts and talent acknowledged in this way, but, truth to tell, money had never been important to him either at this early stage of his life or in old age. The aunts had little money to spare, but they always had enough for their simple needs and the needs of little Nobby. Like osmosis, he seemed to absorb the values of these contented, cheery women. It was this very lack of materialism which enabled the legendary vagrant to be pleased with his gypsy-like lifestyle in Derbyshire; a lifestyle which, up to 1966, had lasted for more than half a century.

CHAPTER 30

Narrations of a Naughty Gnome

It was getting late. Mavis had cleared the table, washed the pots and bade toad and chicken a sharp 'good night' which sounded more like a grunt of contempt. Still absorbed with tales of Nobby, Aubrey pressed Simeon for more information about gay life before the Great War.

"I really must try to cultivate his friendship. Tell me, when did you hear all this?"

"Last summer when I was cycling around. With the gnome, it's a case of whenever you happen to meet up with him," replied Simeon. "We had a real humdinger heart to heart one August afternoon; in fact it was August 23rd when I came across him sitting in the gardens of Nottingham Castle. I've good reason to remember that date."

Nobby was in pensive mood on the slopes of that one time medieval fortress when, in a pleasant moment of serendipity, the cyclist greeted him. For a while they sat in contemplative silence surveying the southerly panorama of a mid-20th century city which had changed little in the previous 50 years. It was a comforting view for a homesick boy who had been isolated in Detroit. It was so English, so nostalgic. To the west, lay The Park. In the early 19th century it was a *real* park. The 1965 view was a forest of Victorian roofs and smoking chimneys which fell away in serried ranks, nicely decorated by the occasional mature tree. To the south, there was a distant vista of the meandering River Trent which encircled the poorer rows of roofs in The Meadows. This dreary picture, soothing and calming, was complemented with grime and grit. Beyond, moving east, there was evidence of commerce, industry and pollution. A distant train whistled. It painfully puffed and clanked slowly over the Nottingham Canal, under Abbey Bridge and, eventually, out of sight and out of hearing.

Simeon savoured the quality this very British, very East Midland moment. Why quality? Some years later, feeling trapped and irritated in a Detroit traffic jam, he returned to that moment in an attempt to find calm. He analysed the ingredients which constituted a zone of such comfort which was so very nice. It had to be said; the scene before him was quite scruffy, so how did that add up to quality? Dirty scruffy kids were having a great time chasing each other around the flower beds, but the yells and squeals were no problem at all. On the contrary, they were a welcome part of the scene and added richness to the total picture. A scruffy old man who had slowly struggled up the hill, thankfully, rested himself on one of the several benches. Like Nobby and Simeon, he stared out across the plain seeing into infinity. The old and the young: *that* was the difference. In the murder capital of the USA, you seldom saw the old and the young. It was ill advised, too dangerous. They stayed inside where it was safe.

It was a still, but rather dull, grey day. Simeon seemed to be seeing it all in shades – as if he were viewing a black and white film – and he wondered why? Then it came to him. He had seen all this five years before watching *Saturday Night and Sunday Morning*. Set in Nottingham, it portrayed the working class heterosexual 'kitchen sink' existence of boozing, brawling and bedding so graphically evoked by Alan Sillitoe. All this existed dangerously close for homosexuals. Perilously, they tried to make contact their own kind as they struggled to snatch their own special pleasures in the big City of Nottingham. There were numerous undocumented casualties. And nobody knew this better than Nobby the Gnome who had the scars to prove it. Was he thinking of these perils now?

In an attempt to read the old man's thoughts, Simeon studied his profile. Nobby had a nice if rather gnarled face. The once cute turned-up nose, as sweet as a button, was now turned down and slightly bent to one side. A fact once cruelly observed by an irritated high and mighty Hoadley after the lowly creature had dared to address him outside of Derby Cathedral. True, the ancient gnome *was* misshapen. He was worn by years of lavatory living and long exposure in the howling wilderness winds of North Derbyshire. But Nobby was not so old or as hideous as the Belper Goblin. Nobby had nothing of the leering, fish eyes of that crooked old crone, or any of the knobbly carbuncles which disfigured the countenance of the weather beaten Toby Jug. And knobbly Nobby was totally innocent of the lust infested, fat, stubbled, slobbering face of Guzzly Granddad. Moreover, he certainly had no trace of that twisted look inflicted on the repulsive face of Becksitch Betty by a life time of sustained, spiteful thoughts.

"A penny for your thoughts," said Simeon to Nobby.

"I'm thinking about my friend Ron. It's his birthday," replied the gnome, sadly, still staring out over the wide Vale of Trent.

"That's nice," said Simeon, gently, treading carefully, mindful of deep waters. True to form of all gay men, Simeon asked [as Mr Toad would say] – 'the eternal question'.

"How old is Ron?"

"He would have been 72 today," said Nobby in a voice which was steady – but only just.

"Would you like to talk about it? encouraged Simeon.

The years between 1908 and 1911 were happy years of frequent visits to Nobby's local latrine. This quaint, Victorian urinal under an ornate cast iron gas lamp, was conveniently situated at the end of Bumchums Row. It was a feature in a cheery but limited existence. The pre-pubescent lad in the years prior to 1908 had already investigated other active lavatories by the canal side and by the river side. Nobby often nostalged to Simeon about erotic activities involving groping hands in the seedy, dark suspension bridge cottage and wild adventures on Queens Drive where he often came into conflict with the pushy toad.

Although he never knew it, in 1911, Nobby was 16. By that time he was well acquainted with every toilet in Nottingham. Instinct, caution and good advice from the aunts had protected him from bad experiences in dangerous places such as Narrow Marsh and Broad

Marsh. He avoided the rowdy and often violent scenes which were common on Saturday nights near public houses at closing time.

But anonymous sex in the ubiquitous gentleman's urinal always beckoned. In Nobby's opinion, the best one of all was situated at Canning Circus next to the General Cemetery. It was a visit to this notorious cesspit of sin in the summer of 1911 which was to change his life.

It was a warm August afternoon. As usual, there was a selection of motionless figures, all guilty, all lined up before the ornate Victorian porcelain in a tension of repressed excitement. The chirpy gnome toddled in, quickly surveyed the field and selected a vacant stall next to a chunky figure. He was a powerfully built young man with a handsome well bronzed face which nicely contrasted with a fair complexion. An untidy shock of wild golden hair was distinctive in an age where 'short-back-and-sides' was the norm. Instinctively, Nobby knew that the roughness of this youth was more rural rather urban. He was dressed in a shabby Harris Tweed suit; clearly a hand-me-down, one size too small emphasising tempting well-proportioned buttocks. It had given several owners good service and seen better days several decades before. The stranger towered at least one foot over little Nobby who, in spite of his mid-teen status, could easily have been taken for a boy of twelve but, was in fact, several weeks older than the Adonis in scruffy garb.

With many bad experiences still before him, the young gnome was fearless. Brazenly, he placed himself next to the young hunk who had been given a wide birth by the other men. If appealing, the eyes of this newcomer were hard and cruel. One seemed dark as if recently blackened. Those eyes were intently focused on the porcelain and a somewhat brutal expression said – 'keep clear; approach at your peril'! On the other hand, an impressive erection, proud as punch, mischievously straining to reach as high up the ceramic stall as possible, was giving a different message. It said – 'touch me, tease me, tickle and taste me'. Naughty Nobby preferred to heed this second message. Enthusiastically, he threw caution to the wind. He got stuck in to the job busily loosening constrains of belt, buttons and tweed to gain free access to all erogenous areas, employing considerable dexterity of both hands.

It was a risk. Cottaging was always a risk, but, on this day, Nobby had pushed his luck to the very brink of imminent hazard. Even on a warm, sleepy summer afternoon, there was always a fair probability that a heterosexual might casually answer the call of nature and be utterly outraged by the rough and ready sight before him. This scene would include a rough youth standing with his trousers in a scruffy heap around his ankles. Next to him, a notorious gnome who was always ready, conscientiously tending to the obscene sight of excited genitalia – part erect, part dangling and part hidden in a little place where the sun never shines. And to complete the picture, the hapless intruder would be gobsmacked by the sight of a half dozen wildly excited, furiously wanking voyeurs.

On this occasion, Nobby got away with it. The venture paid off because they were not interrupted by police or public. If not audible, the ruffian's concluding moments of ecstasy were signalled by evocative body language. An arching of back, a bracing spasm of joy gripped the youthful body. It all complemented an open mouth which issued a silent scream of rapture from the very foundation of his impressive masculinity. This was the instant when the little chap was usually content to be rewarded by the familiar gush, the milky issue of his skills. This ruffian, however, was different. He was valued as high quality. In this case, Nobby was not prepared to see his partner's seed wasted. He would not allow it to shoot out, to spill on dirty stone flags in a common public lavatory.

No. There was only one place for this precious seed and that place was deep inside Nobby. As with so many previous anonymous encounters, the gnome had learned that he was unlikely to see this gorgeous youth again.

Having no further use of Nobby, without a word or a look, the stranger abruptly pulled up, pushed his big bum back into his trousers and stomped off down Derby Road – with the gnome in hot pursuit! This ill-advised chase was as much as a surprise to the small chaser as it was to the stomping youth clomping along in his hobnail boots.

"Fook off, ya dirty bastard!" threatened the lout.

"I've got bread an drippin'!" yelled out the lad, on automatic pilot, desperately trying to make contact.

"Don't want ya dirty bread an drippin'. Piss off ya little runt! Yol get this down ya gob ole!" warned the irate hunk, brandishing his fist and still in complete denial of what had just passed between them. It is hard to believe that these bellicose words were the first of a loving relationship.

Nobby the Gnome was not prepared to let this one go. He was fired by a combination of lust, love, longing and semen in his belly. The latter gave energy which sustained a fast walking chase through the Old Market Square up to Goose Gate, up Heathcoat Street and all the way up to St Mary's Rest Garden in which there were several large stone memorials. Both combatants were breathless as they collapsed on separate headstones glaring at each other. After a minute, the beggarly runt with dirty face dug into his shirt and retrieved a squashed, brown paper package stained by something moist from within. Both boys looked sadly at this crumpled mess when, cautiously, Nobby approached the other and held out his peace offering. It was accepted.

It should be mentioned that teenage boys, as well as being randy, are also often ravenous. This rustic ruffian, accustomed to the standards of the basic working class world of 1911, was not inclined to be too fussy when he uncovered the gnome's half eaten lunch of squashed sandwiches of bread and dripping. Like a cow, he slowly munched through the mess with the same curious expression of a cow. When all had been consumed, he stared at his unsolicited companion as if to say – 'now what?' Nobby answered the unasked question by moving closer and, warily, he reached out his naughty hand to feel and fumble around a tempting bulge between the other's legs. Having a good long grope and noting a hard result, the small fumbler, wearing a pathetic expression, looked into the unfriendly, hard, handsome face which had now registered assent. Tip of tongue appeared between full lips to show that the stranger was ready for more action.

They looked around for an area of concealment and noted a nearby thicket in the corner of the memorial garden. Seconds later they were well cloaked by a dense tangle of midsummer foliage as; once again, the naughty gnome struggled with belt and buttons to uncover his prize. Silently, he guided his new friend to a rude position on all fours. With one tongue well trained for anal ecstasy, together with eight, busy, wetted fingers; the scruffy runt sent that moaning, squirming hunk into seventh heaven for the second time in one hour.

They returned to the light, back to the place of stone memorials and, again, they looked at each other in a 'now what?' moment. In some frustration, the ruffian returned to his post orgasmic stance of aggression. Again, in a deep growl of adolescent croak, he threatened little Nobby with a shaking fist to lend emphasis.

"Watch it! Am tellin' ya! You – ya little turd! I'm dangerous! I'm like 'im. 'im there. 'e'd knock ya 'ead off! 'e would! 'e were a *lion*!"

The hunk was pointing to a stone lion resting on top of a plinth. Age and weather had almost erased an inscription which attracted Nobby's curiosity. He approached and knelt down for a closer inspection. This action, a demonstration of reverence, seemed to calm the bully whilst the gnome was able to decipher a few words –

'** ***ory o* W**liam **omp*on 'Bendigo' of Nottingham who died **gus* 23rd 1880 aged 69 **ars. In life always brav*, fighting like a lion. In death like a lamb, tranquil in Zion.'

The few words read were followed by a few questions asked. This was the beginning of a soothing dialogue which occupied the two boys for the next hour under a warming sun, gently mottled by the green leaves of a mature tree. The agitated bully, in a constant state of denial over his sexuality, now had something to talk about. Enthusiastically, he told Nobby all about his hero. In that conversation, this hulk, this ruffian, this bully – relaxed. He revealed his name. His name was Ron.

The butch, rough Ron was not articulate. Notwithstanding, he gave Nobby (a willing pupil with a desirable teacher) his first experience of geography, history and bible study. Bendigo the 19th century 'Champion of England' was a famous Nottingham boxer. His real name was William, but he took his professional name from the fact that he was one of triplets who were known as Shadrach, Meshach and Abednego [Bendigo] after the companions of Daniel, the Old Testament prophet. This was interesting instruction for Nobby on that day of August 23rd in 1911 and, equally interesting instruction for Simeon on August 23rd in 1965.

Ron was proud to announce that it was his birthday. And Ron's birthday fell on the same day as the death-day of his hero, Bendigo – the unbeatable of the Prize Ring. This fighter was also celebrated in verse by Sir Arthur Conan Doyle. Ron's name was Thompson, the same family name of William Bendigo Thompson. He drew strength and comfort from these remarkable coincidences which, according to his pious grandfather, were a favourable sign from God.

Ron rejoiced in berating the ignorance of the 'stupid squirt' who knew nothing of the 'good book'. He was lectured about a wicked king called Nebuchadnezzar who had destroyed Jerusalem and carried the Jews into Babylonian captivity. Shadrach, Meshach and Abednego refused to worship the king's golden idol and were punished by being thrown into a fiery furnace. However, solemnly, Ron informed his attentive pupil that God always smiles on the righteous and these good men were fireproofed and miraculously delivered from the flames! A similar miracle saved Daniel from a den of lions. More than half a century later, Simeon was also fascinated by these gnomal narrations about events which took place 600 years BC. Nobby spoke of Daniel interpreting the dreams of Nebuchadnezzar and recounted the mysterious appearance of doom laden 'writing on the wall' during a sacrilegious feast.

"Mind you," said Old Nobby to Simeon, "Ron told me that Daniel was a cautious sort of bloke – not one to push his luck. He left his cap in that den of lions, but didn't go back in to get it. Now then!"

CHAPTER 31

Man Shalt Not Lie With Man

Reverently, Ron placed his hand over the head of the stone lion. He explained that Bendigo underwent a religious conversion in later life and became a Methodist preacher. Suddenly he acquired energy, sprang into action forcing the small runt to step back for safety. Dancing around the memorial in aggressive excitement, jabbing the air with his fists; he acted out one notorious occasion when Bendigo interrupted his sermon and took a few minutes to 'lay in a heap' six disruptive hecklers. The little gnome watched respectfully and listened to the commentary in awestruck silence – until Ron had concluded his performance – sat down and fell into a pensive, sad silence. Eventually Nobby became uncomfortable and concerned. He broke the silence in an effort to encourage his new friend to further enthusiasm.

"Bendigo! Ooo, 'e sounds good! A rate good bloke! Bet *you* can look after ya self like 'e does. *You* got muscles. Bet you're *never* scared. *You're* a good un as well."

"No. No, am not good. Am no good," replied Ron, softly, in deep melancholia. With bitter shame, his face was out of view. He was downcast, resting his strong arms on his knees addressing a clump of dandelions at his feet.

After gentle prompting, Nobby was able to uncover the cheerless existence of Ronald Thompson. For the 16 years of his short life, he had been brainwashed and bullied by his devout bible bashing granddad known as Gramps. Grandfather Thompson owned a small, isolated farm some seven miles south west of Nottingham near the River Soar: a lonely, unpopulated fertile plane, described by locals as 'the middle of nowhere'.

Ron made a stumbling, awkward confession to his little friend. It was revealed that, for several years, he had dishonoured his Gramps and the memory of Bendigo by trekking the 14 mile round trip from Sedges Farm to Nottingham, answering the call of fleshly pleasures. He had lied to his Gramps and misused his occasional days off from agricultural labouring. True, he *had* looked in shop windows, desired all the wonderful things he would never have and he *always* visited St Mary's rest garden to pay his respects to the Great Boxer. But... the other visits? He never told Gramps about 'being rude' in public lavatories. Gramps was not told about all the strangers who had touched – nay – were *invited* to touch Ron's impressive private part – frequently inflated before porcelain in public view.

Guilt over sexual activity was totally alien to Nobby. He listened to this account with mixed feelings. He was sorry for his friend's torment, but had to hold back a sudden compulsion to laugh when Ron's face turned red. This was an unprecedented and difficult social situation for the little chap. Accordingly, in his usual cheery style, he blurted out the first thing which came into his little head.

"Well! Never mind! Nowt wrong with it – is there? I *like* ta be rude. I *like* strange blokes ta touch *me*. Anyway – ya granddad – 'e's old, 'e dunt know oat."

"'e does. 'e does know. 'e says am *dirty*," replied Ron.

During the 1960s, Simeon Hogg absorbed a wealth of information from all his quirky queer characters. Decades later this rich data would be recycled and ploughed into several titles dealing with local homosexual life. Between 2020 and 2032 several books would be published. *Nobby: True Tales of a Naughty Gnome* launched in November 2022 would prove to be a popular example of a social history based on the recollections of that colourful vagrant. Those days of creative writing came late in life for Old Simeon, but he was grateful for a keen memory and for the rough notes he scribbled down when inspired.

One such example was the poem often recited to Ron by his bearded, bigoted and overbearing grandfather –

"The idle and bad, like this little lad, may love dirty ways to be sure. But good boys are seen, to be decent and clean, although they are ever so poor."

Ron was made to learn and repeat this ditty many times whenever Farmer Thompson suspected that the 'dirty lad' indulged himself in any 'rude thoughts'. This 'punishment poem', a 'verse of shame', dated back to 1901. It was a painful occasion when he embarrassed his six-year-old grandson and a friend from another farm. The old man stumbled across the two lads in a corner of the cow shed, both fully exposed, enjoying an erotic experiment of 'touching tiddlers'. A humiliating, angry reprimand was a damaging experience for both boys who were never allowed to see each other again. Thompson had deliberately confused the Victorian virtue of 'cleanliness is next to Godliness' with his puritanical obsession with 'unnatural sin'. He began a sadistic reign of terror which included Bible readings with frequent visits to Leviticus 18.22 –

"Thou shalt not lie with mankind as with womankind; it is an abomination."

Nobby heard all about Ron's pain of deep shame which always followed a busy day in the wicked City of Nottingham. When sitting at table during the saying of grace, this hunk would colour up under the bayonet-like inquisitorial eyes of a stern Ayatollah. Those old, grey eyes seemed to be seeing a lascivious scene acted out just hours before. Was it possible that those suspicious eyes, hooded under bushy brows, could penetrate time and space? Could they see through an opaque door, clearly indicated as 'engaged'? Could he really see the coarse crush of four bodies within? Could he really see the grandson who was stretching up, mouth wide open, grasping an iron bar near the roof of that WC cubicle? Chin high up, young eyes focused to heaven were too ashamed to see the sins of Sodom below. They avoided the view of six sensitive hands and lively lips with three assiduous tongues taking full advantage of rising knees reaching up to chest in an obscene, suspended, foetal position. And Ron even attempted to deny, to blot out his own whispering voice. He pleaded with one of those clever tongues, applying itself to that very special place of great pleasure. He begged the tongue – 'don't stop'. He begged the tongue to go deeper and finish the job before the strength of his powerful arms failed him.

In the early hours of August 24th, Nobby – in love – in one of his several little makeshift beds on Bumchums Row – was tossing and turning. He was unable to find peace, let alone sleep. Ron had stomped out of his life. It was unbearable. He *had* to find his Ron. And this presented unprecedented problems because little Nobby had never been out of the big city of Nottingham. It had never been necessary – until now.

Aunty May's 'Nobby bed' was an old single mattress situated directly on the floor at the foot of her own brass bed. At such close proximity, she was roused by the unusual restlessness and moans from a boy clearly in distress. Concerned, she suggested a cup of tea. He was invited for a chat in the kitchen, already becoming lit by the dim greyness of an approaching summer morning.

Listening to this story from the lips of an old man, once again, Simeon was quite amazed. He was not surprised that Nobby was infatuated with a desirable youth and all the pain which came with that familiar condition. He was, however, shocked that any teenage boy was prepared to open his heart to an adult and admit to being in love with *another* teenage boy – effectively confessing his homosexuality. Simeon had been raised, surrounded and damaged by a solid, unforgiving, working class wall of rabid homophobia. Mrs Hogg had once told her son –
       "If I thought you were like that, I'd strangle you!"

As best he could, Nobby tried to enlighten Simeon about the mores of Bumchums Row. The accepted morals of the seven aunts in Nottingham: it was a different world from 'chapel every Sunday' in Horsley Woodhouse.
       "Well! They wouldn't be like to call me, would they? I mean – I wasn't daft. Blokes coming and going all hours, day and night! Beds creakin', moans and groans, smell o' spunk. Bloody 'ell, they'd stand some need to go on about *me*!" Nobby looked at Simeon. Simeon looked back at Nobby. "Didn't ya know? You've hear of Snow White and the Seven Dwarfs? Well then – why not Nobby the Gnome and the Seven Sluts?"

In his 2022 biography of Nobby the Gnome, Simeon's research had uncovered details about the seven aunts of Bumchums Row. At one time or another they had all been 'ladies of the night' with the possible exceptions of Sally Dilks and Nellie Duro who were probably lesbians. In 1911, the sisters May and Gertie Crump, at fifty-plus, were well past the age of 'active service' and the former [who made Nobby's clothes] had been a great beauty in her youth when she was also a skilled seamstress. In contrast, Fish Face Fanny Fowkes, quite a character, was able to joke about being 'the oldest and ugliest tart on the row'. She was 68 in 1911, but Simeon could find no record of her death. Scant information was available about the 'acid tongued Edna' who may have been Edna Orme born in 1869. 'Legs Up Again Lil', at the age of 22 turned out to be Lillian Stokes, a bright, cheerful spark who taught Nobby to read and write. He suspected (and rather hoped) that she was his real mother, but an age difference of six years made that impossible.

Lavished with love, little Nobby was adored by all seven women who expressed that adoration in different ways according to their different personalities. Apart from being non-judgemental, all seven, having graduated from the school of hard knocks, were well placed to guide the lad through his first major emotional crisis. It fell to the usually simpering and sweet Mae Crump to counsel and console. She listened carefully to a long account of the Ron Thompson saga and sympathised with all the anguish of young love. In a later conference with her friends and colleagues on the row, it was agreed that May had given their 'beloved little boy' exactly the right advice.

"Well, lad! You'd better wash your face, get dressed and go and find your Ron. You may never find another one like him or feel the same way ever again. If you can, get him away from that nasty old granddad, but at least you must *try*. If he'll come, bring him here to live with us until he gets his life sorted out."

An hour later, after a bowl of hot porridge and more tea, Nobby toddled out of the house and out of Bumchums Row in search of Ron.

CHAPTER 32

Frantic Run to Trent Lock

Which way to go? That was the question Nobby put to Aunty May. Wisely she responded with pertinent questions about her nephew's conversations with Ron. They revealed that it took the labourer about two and a half hours to complete his journey, so May guessed about seven miles away. He lived at Sedges Farm, a lonely spot near the River Soar and mentioned using the ferry at Trent Lock.

Neither Aunt nor gnome had ever seen a map, let alone read one. They had limited geographic knowledge and almost no concept of space or distance. There was Nottingham – all the other places where simply 'somewhere else'. May knew that the river near to her house was called the Trent. She had heard of the River Soar but was not sure where it was. The best clue was Ron's reference to Trent Lock. As young girls, the Crumps were occasionally taken to that popular summer playground which was about a seven mile walk from Nottingham through the old gravel pits and reed beds of the Attenborough pond.

Looking Nobby straight in the eye, slowly and carefully, to the best of her memory; May described the footpaths and byways which followed the river bank all the way to a place she recalled in the late 1860s as – '

"A gay scene in August! Eee it were! Picnics on the embankment wearing our pretty hats. Ooo it were grand! And then there were posh pleasure boats and we used to squeal with excitement and shout at white wings on the water."

"What?" asked Nobby.

"Fast boats with lovely white sails. I think they called them yachts. If you ask nicely, they'll be plenty of folk there to tell you about Sedges Farm – but you've to ask nice – remember your manners. And mind you have a good look round. It's a special place. It comes back to me – like what they used to say. It's where three counties meet... let me see... Leicestershire, Derbyshire and... yes – Nottinghamshire. And do you know, I think the River Soar is there also! Yes, I'm sure of it now. All sorts of rivers and canals meet at Trent Lock. And your Ron won't be far away either. Now then, you've got your sandwiches in your big pocket? And do you remember the footpaths like I told you?" The little gnome nodded. "Have you got a sixpence for the ferry man if you need to cross the river?" Nobby gave another nod. He had been a busy boy during the previous week and had several of those small silver coins.

It had been raining during that night which gave way to one of those delicious cool, clear August mornings when you could taste the air. As directed, the lad ran south to follow the road on the north side of the Trent. He noted the church tower of Wilford poking out over the river on the opposite east bank as per May's instructions – so far – so good. At all times he had to keep the river to his left. With a leap of joy, he found May's stile which took him from the road to a footpath along the bank. As foretold, the pretty area of Clifton Grove appeared on the opposite bank. It stayed there until the River Trent turned north to meet the start of the Beeston Canal and locks at Rylands. Nobby knew that a canal and a river were different, but was not entirely sure why, until his aunt explained.

"Well you see, our Nobby, a river goes where it wants to go. A canal was dug out by rough Irish Navvies. It goes where *you* want it to go."

Still following the wide water, the north bank path became a narrow strip, a sort of raised embankment with the water to his left and, as May had predicted, a large pond appeared on his right. She said it was a half-way point and suggested that the little fellow should seek a suitable log upon which to rest and perhaps have a nibble at his simple [once again squashed] lunch. But rest was not needed – Ron called. It was a kind of frantic wild madness which only young love can inspire. In the same way, 55 years later, Simeon was fleeing for his very life – yet – a less rational part of him wanted to flee into the arms of his lover, Ahmed.

Also in that year, Simeon followed Nobby's footsteps on what was then called the Trent Valley Way. In that very low and flat kingdom of dragonflies, the walker saw the *real* meadows which were tracts of lush grassland. This is how south Nottingham looked 200 years ago, long before the construction of Bumchums Row. As Simeon said in his book about Nobby the Gnome –

"Look at a map of Nottingham. Note the shape of the meandering River Trent. At the south of the city it forms the shape of a sink into which was crammed an appalling blight of dowdy rows to house the low and the rough of that city."

His first time out of Nottingham, Nobby was excited, enjoying his new discovery. It was a flat world with no building: an archipelago effect of many fragments of low lying marshy land along the slow, lazy river. This extensive waterlogged area stretched to the north and west, but southwards the gnome skipped and ran, down the path, following the river's smooth, swinging curves. He took it all in. There were lush growths of flowers and birds, he had never before seen, darting in and around rushes, sedges, reeds, alder and willow. With some pleasure he noted a church spire on his left and one on his right which confirmed that he was not lost – going the right way. Aunty Mae said the left spire was Barton in Fabis Church and the right spire was Attenborough Church which appeared to rise out of the water to the north.

A little way on, he came to an old, rickety wooden bridge. Mae mentioned a bridge which crossed a smaller river but could give no further details. It was, in fact, the confluence of the River Erewash joining the River Trent and Nobby was not aware that he had now passed into Derbyshire by crossing that old bridge.

The ever toddling gnome, making a gay progress with the occasional skip, did not notice increased turbulence and a rise in the river level. This ominous change was fuelled by overnight heavy rain over the Peak District which is drained by the River

Derwent. The Derwent flows into the Trent at a marshy area called Great Wilne, some two miles east of Trent Lock.

At long last he reached a canal on his right with locks to access the river. Looking at the canal and looking back at the river, Nobby noticed a difference which had slowly, almost stealthily gripped the big river. It had become a raging torrent! An old gentleman resting on the lock gate confirmed that he had reached the Cranfleet Cut and his final destination was barely half a mile along that tow path. But, a brief conversation with the old gent also confirmed that the gnome was not to see Trent Lock that day.

"Nay, lad! What's that you say? Pleasure boats? White wings on the water? Not for you! Not for you today, lad. Just look at it! Water's on the rise, lad – too fast – too strong for any boat."

Nobby explained that he wanted to get to Sedges Farm.

"Sedges Farm! Yes I know it. Not far from here. Just over there." Vaguely he swept a hand southwards to an area over the river. "But you'll not see Sedges Farm today, lad. Only way to see Sedges Farm is by ferry and the ferryman won't put to water today – or tomorrow – by the look of it."

Little Nobby – erstwhile so full of hope and joy – studied the man's moving lips and tried to make sense of his words as their full impact crashed in on his conscious mind. Immediately, deflated and devastated, his eyes – appealing for mitigation against such a harsh judgement – welled up with tears.

"Nay, lad! It can't be that bad! Dear, dear, dear. Now you come with me, and let's see what can be done."

The old man, unaccustomed to a weeping youth was discomforted by the sudden emotional scene and somewhat unsettled by those odd, watery eyes – much too close together. For the following ten minutes, silently, he led the boy along the Cranfleet Cut to the point where it goes under the main railway line.

"No promises, mind you," said the man, "but Jack has been known to help out in an emergency. Mind you – it had better be urgent! It *is* urgent – isn't it?" Now reasonably composed, Nobby stared up into the man's face, sniffed and nodded. He assumed that 'Jack' was the man he could see up in the signal box curiously looking down at them sensing some consternation. "Off you go, young 'un. Get up those steps and tell Jack all about it."

With some relief, the old man watched the gnome scuttle up the steps in search of Jack. Jack heeded the panicky cascade of inarticulate words which poured out of a child-like mouth. This jumble of dialogue said something about an important, long journey from Nottingham – but was more intriguing for what it did *not* say. It mentioned Ron and Ron's granddad without clearly explaining the necessity of the visit to a remote farm on the other side of the river. Puzzlingly, it completely failed to explain the relationship between the angst ridden oddity and members of the Thompson family. The signalman was cogitating on this tearstained curiosity when a loud bell rang out and shattered the peace! It forced him into immediate action: pulling several large levers in a certain order.

However, Jack Dakin did not have to cogitate for too long. He knew of old Thompson the religious recluse who lived alone with his strapping grandson Ron. And Jack Dakin (a man in his late forties with an interesting past) easily recognised the familiar dissembling convolutions of speech and explanation which were so typical of a queer life style. He had heard talk about the ultra butch Ron of Sedges Farm, who was said to be very shy of girls and would always be more comfortable in the company of blokes. Jack had heard this talk – and Jack had wondered. But this bachelor signalman, now well into his 'second life' had to be very cautious. In his 'first life,' twenty years before, as a bachelor shopkeeper in a quiet Derbyshire village, Jack had been denounced and exposed as a 'disgusting poof'. Effectively he had been driven out of the village. He had to re-locate and reinvent himself.

Accordingly, Nobby was in luck. Jack guessed the root of his distress, his turmoil and, obligingly, asked no probing questions, only suggesting solutions.

"Now then, little un," he said cheerily, "when the ferry fails, how do we get you over all this angry water?" As usual, full in the face, Nobby looked up at friendly Jack, unable to answer. "Simple," said Jack, "we break the law!" The little gnome blinked and sniffed. "You got handkerchief? Here, take this one. Keep it."

Another bell rang. More action, more pulling of levers.

"Now then, little un... how old are you?" Little un said he did not know. "Like that is it? Eleven or twelve I'd guess." Nobby protested that he was more. Jack looked at him and sighed. He then looked at a large clock on the wall. "In five minutes, an express is due." He pointed south over the river. "It'll race over that bridge, over the river, and into that hillside, through that dark tunnel. When it's gone – you can race after it – along the line." Nobby blinked. Jack looked at him. "Do you understand me, lad? You'll be breaking the law – and I'll look the other way. I've never seen you. Understand?" Nobby gave a single nod. "Don't be scared. It's inky black, but if you keep going into that dark hole, you'll see daylight at the end. Red Hill is not what you'd call a long tunnel. Just keep going. When you come out, climb over a fence on your right. Do you know your right?" Nobby indicated his right hand. "Good," said Jack. "You'll see a great rock in the middle of a field. Run to the rock and climb up to the top of it. It's not difficult. Stand with your back to the tunnel entrance and look down the railway line. A long way off you'll see the church spire of Ratcliffe on Soar. Turn a little bit to your right and, much nearer, you'll see a clump of big old willow trees... oh, about four fields distant." Nobby nodded. "Sedges Farm is hidden behind those trees." Nobby nodded with more enthusiasm. "Mind those fields! They can be very soft and boggy in places. And mind Old Man Thompson. He can be a cantankerous and nasty old sod."

Nobby was greatly cheered.

"Good luck, young un," said Jack in typical macho brusqueness which failed to disguise the strong emotion in his voice. But this tender moment was immediately shattered by earth shaking and the charging of a fire breathing monster. The roaring express abruptly ended that brief encounter between man and boy which might have concluded with an affectionate hug. Nobby shot through that tunnel without a single look back. He was running for his life – running for his Ron.

At a fast run, the black smoky tunnel quickly enclosed Nobby in darkness. Equally as quickly, it disclosed the light at its southern exit. In this dash into the hillside, he passed from Derbyshire back into Nottinghamshire and with youthful agility, the runner cleared the old fence with one leap. He mounted the tip of the rock with ease, located Ron's home and was running into the farm yard ten minutes later with the same energy and nimbleness as Romeo's eager ascent up to the balcony of Juliet. But, like Romeo, little naïve Nobby had not considered the dangers of entering enemy territory.

CHAPTER 33

The Scarecrow

It was like a tableau. An old, bearded bigot and two boys made up a static scene which could have been an evocative Victorian painting. It was the sort of picture you can spend a lifetime looking at – and yet, still detect a slightly altered nuance of stance, or a changed facial emotion. In a decrepit old farm yard, the younger boy had just screeched to a halt surprising the other two who were in the middle of a task involving the cutting and transport of an ancient fallen willow.

Nobby the Gnome was both exhilarated and apprehensive. At the sight of Ron he was ecstatic, but had been frozen to the spot by the glower of stern bullet eyes under full and fearsome eyebrows.

"Who the devil are you?" barked the autocratic ogre.

By disposition, Ron was a youth of slow thought, slow speech and inclined to caution. Notwithstanding, he knew his Gramps. Here was an emergency which required a quick and plausible response before the stupid gnome might blurt out an indiscretion bringing disaster down on that Victorian scene.

"He's the little runt from St Mary's Rest Garden! He was paying respect to Bendigo," he added to placate the pious grandfather. "What you doin' here?"

"I've come to see ya," replied Nobby with as much cheer as he could muster.

"You never mentioned any runt in Nottingham." growled Gramps, suspiciously studying the stunted peculiarity and observing simple features which could have been painted by a child. "This is a working farm!" he snapped. "You get back inside whatever hole you crawled out of. Get you gone!"

"We could do with an extra hand, Gramps," intervened the grandson, trying to sound reasonable and practical to appease the penny-pinching miser. "A funny sort, I know, but if the runt could help me with these logs it gives you chance to do fencing in middle field. Runt could be worth five hours! Then we give him a bit a supper for his trouble and send him off." Gramps uttered a grunt of contempt. "No point wasting him! Is there?" pleaded Ron to drive home his argument.

Ungraciously, the old man moved unwillingly to apply himself to the urgent fence mending. He muttered something about a –

"Goblin-like weakling! Huh! Sent by Lucifer. Couldn't lift one log. Not right. Not a proper lad. No good'll come from it."

"You've no business coming here! Getting me into trouble!" threatened the hulking labourer with shaking fist when the farmer was well out of earshot. Choked with emotion, the love sick Nobby was unable to respond. "What am I supposed to do with you?" he added in softer tones, having noted the onset of tears.

He also noticed that his friend was quite exhausted and in need of a sit down. They retired to an area of hay storage where Nobby groped for the handkerchief given to him by Jack Dakin. He wiped his eyes, blew his nose and smeared his little face. It was already messy from a five hour journey and recent run through the smoke filled, soot laden tunnel. With concern which might be shown to a younger brother, Ron remarked on this dirty face and was astonished to hear of adventures connected with gravel pits, raging water and trespass on the railway line.

"You could have been killed in that murk! Trains can't see a little lad, a lad like you! You daft, you are. What you doin' the other side of the river anyway? The path is *this* side of the river!"

On the previous day, Ron mentioned the Trent Lock Ferry several times in connection with walks to Derby, Ilkeston and Long Eaton – all necessitating passage over the River Trent. Nobby had *assumed* that the river crossing was also a necessary part of Ron's journey from Sedges Farm into Nottingham.

Like Nobby, indeed, like many poor children of the early 20th century, Ron Thompson was unschooled, barely literate and unable to read a map even if he had one of the area. However, his tyrannical guardian had granted him the limited freedom of occasional days such as the previous day, Wednesday, August 23rd 1911 – Ron's 16th birthday. Compared with the 'stupid runt' before him, young Thompson was quite well travelled and had acquired a reasonable local knowledge of the landscape. With the usual lack of teenage tact, he exploited his superior knowledge and castigated Nobby as a prize fool.

"You twerp! You prat! You only had to cross Wilford Bridge and follow the road until you see the footpath through Clifton Grove. What's a matter with you? It's easy. Through Burrows Farm, Barton-in-Fabis and Thrumpton and look out for the bridleway. Easy. You've walked a good two miles too many. Trent Lock! Red Hill Tunnel! You silly stupid little runt!"

Ron shouted a loud, raucous guffaw, pointing his finger to inflict the maximum humiliation on his undersized victim. At the same time, he laid his tongue to as many insults as could be hurled at the hapless lad who was ill-equipped to compose a reasonable defence. Since that inefficient trek had been inspired by great affection (as well as great lust) Nobby was hurt and angry. On the other hand, this situation had a complex chemistry and, in a situation of true love, sometimes there is a blurred line between hurt, anger and passion. Accordingly, in the firm belief that this gorgeous lover could never do any *real* harm to the little runt; the little runt decided to attack the offensive labourer. Runt selected a moment when a seizure of laughter caused Ron to fall backwards into the hay.

The recumbent, guffawing labourer was taken by surprise when little runt jumped on top of him. Runt was offended! He vehemently denied stupidity and stridently objected to the frequent appellation of 'runt'. In a childish tantrum, little arms flayed and rained down blows on the laughing hulk who was obliged to protect his writhing giggles with powerful sun kissed arms and large hands.

Two fighting boys struggling in the hay: but this was a mock battle, a scene which had been acted out many times before. In this case, it was a ludicrously unequal contest between the two combatants. As with many times before, when the combatants happen to be gay, during the boyish struggle there comes a decisive point. It is a moment of realisation. It is a moment of eye contact. Both boys freeze. Pleading eyes meet, the pretence of violence dissolves and suddenly, it is all very serious.

All muscles relaxed, but for that one special tumescence between the legs which is common to all healthy adolescents. Ron allowed Nobby to kiss him and, for the first time, Ron felt a desire to kiss Nobby. This was not brotherly love. Stirring within that erotic charge, there was the first suggestion of genuine affection. Alas, this tender moment of loving looks was suddenly interrupted by an intrusive thought in the head of the hunk which caused sudden panic. This delightful roll in the hay was taking place at Sedges Farm. Gramps was not far away! Urgently, Ron threw off his lover. He reminded him that work, hard work, was needed to cart, chop and saw the remains of a giant willow tree recently prostrated due to living beyond its allotted time. In one respect, Nobby, Ron and Gramps shared a common value. They took the view that an old tree should be treated with respect and never be condemned until nature herself had made that decision.

Nobby the Gnome had never done any hard work – until this day. He did not like it. However, working side by side with his beloved Ron went a long way to softening the blow. The bigger, stronger lad was mindful that the smaller boy, by necessity, should be given as much help as possible.

The biography of the gnome, written by Old Simeon more than a century after the events on that day, relied on a good memory from the original account of Old Nobby in 1965. Any history will focus on what the author considers most significant – and most significant by far – was the extraordinary reference to 'the scarecrow' in the middle field. Nobby noticed it standing near to what looked like a medieval, decrepit wooden fence undergoing repair by Gramps. Each time they passed near with another load of kindling, the old man ignored the boys, but seeing his first scarecrow, the younger was gripped with a fascination of horror. It was frightening, and at the same time, inspired pity. The melancholy expression on that dirty ragged face held a terrible look of despair as if the poor creature had been begging for its life. It seemed ill-used and somehow betrayed. Nobby was distressed and shared his anxiety with Ron.

"Don't you be daft! It's just my old clothes stuffed with straw and an old bag for a head. It's not me." Ron checked that the old farmer was not looking and gave his Nobby a quick reassuring hug. "Don't you worry, I'm all right. Come on, let's get moving."

The old man was also moving, getting on well with his fence repair and quite content to work well into the early evening, at the same time, extracting maximum boy hours from Nobby and his grandson. Consequently, a rough and simple dinner, as always prepared by Ron, was not on the table until the relatively late hour of seven. He was motivated to have his boyfriend with him and to spare him an unfamiliar seven mile walk in failing light at the end of a day of hard labour. Therefore, the grandson persuaded the grandfather to allow a small gnome the use of a tiny, uncomfortable truckle bed which was older than the old man himself. Ungraciously growling threats that 'the runt be out at first light', the bible basher clutched his black book, his candle and skulked off up narrow stone steps to the sparse, cold bed chamber in which he had slept and prayed all his life.

Nobby looked sadly at the inadequate ancient bedding which accompanied that medieval bed. It appeared to be utterly miserable and lost in a huge attic room with so much bare stone that, even in August, it still held on to the bleak midwinter cold. Ron was equally as miserable. He lay still, looking up at the ceiling, knowing his lover, just above, was as uncomfortable and as frustrated as he himself. It was unusual to have a guest in that ancient, isolated house. And such a special guest! This was a rare experience for the grandson who was beginning to think about the deathly silence in his grandfather's bed chamber. Gramps had always boasted of soundness of sleep due to a clear conscience: the heavenly reward for wholesome thoughts and good clean living. Soundness of sleep – deep sleep! Could Ron take the risk?

Nobby was not the least bit alarmed when a white figure silently drifted towards him through the chilly air of that long – wide – space. Moonlight diffused and weakened through small dirty windows illuminated a tatty nightshirt which probably once belonged to the grandfather of the grandfather. Such symbols of austere living mattered little to the gnome who was about to be guided in ghostly hush to his lover's bed. His heart leapt for joy because this night visitor was no spectre. A cold spirit does not enjoy the advantages of a warm, firm body under the shroud. Decaying flesh does not sport a burning staff with eager fiery head protruding from under the old shirt. Oh no. This was *living* flesh, straining at the bit, begging for delicious contact with little fingers and clever tongue to quench the flames, to obtain sweet release. Oh yes! Here was more to do with life and nothing at all to do with death.

It was in two parts. The first amorous play, rather brief, took place in the attic. It was similar to previous incidents. The childlike boy did all the work – and did it gladly. On the other hand, the manlike boy had lost something of the contempt which characterised his earlier bullying attitude. This was a modified Ron, less guilty, more relaxed, more affectionate and more inclined to reciprocate with kisses and cuddles.

The second part took place in Ron's bed. The amorous play, much longer, was characterised by cooperation between a hard working hunk and a more passive gnome yielding his maidenhead, conceding victory to the dominant partner. An observer might well have challenge the word 'passive' at the voluptuous sight of a naked posterior – pure and white as snow – bounding, wriggling, twisting and jutting out in a frantic effort to swallow up as much stiff stake as possible. In adolescence, such a state of inflamed ecstasy cannot endure for more than seconds. This romp was no exception. It was too soon concluded, when the rider, thoughtfully, gently, passed his hand underneath to explore the sensitive nether regions of his unruly steed. That helpful hand produced a milky spill and a deep groan of such resonance – such bliss – it surprised and delighted both parties who melted away in sweet delirium. Minutes later, two happy boys, safely locked into each others arms drifted into a peaceful slumber.

On the retelling of this tale many years on, in front of his computer keyboard, Old Simeon had great difficulty reconciling the natural progression of two lusty lads in love with the extraordinary event which followed.

The moon, full and bright, rose high over Sedges Farm and bathed the middle field in its silver light.

"It's like daylight," said Ron – who was now walking up the slight incline on that otherwise flat field. Suddenly, he realised that he was cold. Feeling damp grass beneath his bare feet, clad only in his old nightshirt – something was very wrong. The scarecrow! It was missing from its usual place. The supporting stake was there, but the sad looking chap was gone? He was fearful. Nobby had been scared and now, so was Ron. And this fear was an overwhelming dread of some appalling harm which had come to the poor scarecrow. Until this moment, Ron had felt nothing for the ragged dummy – had hardly noticed it.

Unwillingly, he lifted his eyes to the fence recently repaired by Gramps and then he saw it. It was the unfortunate scarecrow! It had been dragged from its comfort zone and roughly tied up to the fence for some unspeakable purpose. For a few moments, this appalling sight froze him to the spot. In trepidation he struggled to put one foot in front of another and slowly approached the sad, heartrending figure, its loose drooping head downcast and its silence so ominous. Some horrific cruelty had broken the spirit of this limp creature... some wickedness had...

And then, Ron Thompson, entrapped in an unreal situation with irrational concerns for a stuffed dummy; suddenly knew that he was confronted by an atrocity which was all too real. The shattered figure before him was no scarecrow. He reached out and gently lifted the chin to see a bruised and smashed face. It was a boy like himself. Before being badly beaten by despicable persons unknown, he had been a handsome boy – perhaps a beautiful boy. That beauty was now marred by clear evidence of torture. There were lacerations around the face, neck and head which was now a bloody mess of mattered hair and dried blood. His clothes – bloodstained, slashed and torn by a sustained attack without pity – covered a body brutally distorted by savage, unrelenting kicking. His poor arms and hands were cut, scratched and gashed in a pathetic attempt to defend himself from this hateful homophobic attack. Oh yes, it *was* homophobic! Ron *knew* this boy was homosexual and knew the victim had endured his agonies because of his homosexuality. And something else... Ron *knew* that, in some way, the poor lad hung from that fence and suffered for him – Ron Thompson – and for all other people who were like him.

Overwhelmed by the emotion of such an iniquity inflicted without mercy on one of his own, Ron reached down deep inside of himself to find a voice to scream out the pain which this boy must have endured. In that dry throat he tried to roar outrage into that silent, bright, night sky... but no sound could be found until... until the slumped, tied-up wreck of humanity showed a slight indication that it still lived. The boy was still alive!

This was *not* good news. Ron had taken some small solace in the fact that his fellow homosexual was dead – beyond suffering. That flicker of life at the very door of death was felt as agony compounded on agony. It was this impetus which released the pent up rage of howl, of fury and despair. Ron found his voice. Ron bellowed and wailed a wail which roused and nearly stopped the heart of his sleeping partner Nobby. Worse – it also roused his grandfather.

CHAPTER 34

Nightmare

Simeon Hogg first heard Nobby's account of Ron's nightmare in 1965. It was disturbing in the extreme, but he would have to wait another 33 years before the budding author felt the full impact of that dreadful crime and come to understand its true significance. After the first hearing, he found the story of the boy tied to the fence, puzzling and intriguing. At first sight, the scarecrow had prompted both fear and pity in the gnome. These irrational emotions were immediately rubbished by the farm labourer who had hardly given the dummy a thought. Yet it was Ron who woke up screaming having suffered the vivid, terrifying dream. And it was Ron who empathised so strongly with the suffering of – as he put it – 'one of his own.' Nobby made it quite clear that his lover had not experienced a premonition of his own violent death.

"No! He went on and on about that lad in every particular. My Ron was gorgeous – but he was rough with it. Ya know, sort of... big – hunky and chunky. One of Ron's eyes was always dark, like, sort of, he'd been in a fight. His other eye had a cruel squint. He was tough. No, this lad was different. In the nightmare he wasn't like *my* bloke. He was – well – smaller, slight and more delicate like. Even years on, Ron told the *same* story over and over. He never budged an inch. Now then! He was haunted by that face. It was a trusting, innocent face. Ron felt that he knew the lad. He could see those pretty eyes like they were *before* the beating. He was a lovely gentle trusting sort who had gone off with nasty types – queer bashers. And another thing – I'll tell ya something else; that poor sod had been tied to that fence for hours and hours! He was barely alive and died some hours after Ron had found him. Ron never got over that dream. He spoke of it... for the rest of his life." said Old Nobby as his voice trailed away in private grief.

"Did your Ron offer any explanation for the dream?" asked Simeon, gently. "I mean, did he think the boy may have been a ghost of a tragic scene from years past?

"Ron always said that poor lad was real – but miles away – somewhere else – begging for help."

Nobby continued with his story of dramatic events in the early years of that century when he tried to comfort a distressed youth who had just let out a scream which could have woken the dead.

It woke granddad! He was a big man, slightly stooped in that ancient doorway originally constructed at a time when men were shorter. An alarming figure, he stood there in nightshirt and nightcap holding his candle. It could have been Scrooge! Indeed, when he laid eyes on two boys in one bed, his heart held about as much compassion as that same Dickensian miser. His stern scowl was set on a sullen countenance already deeply etched by decades of disapproving. That ugly face was now further disfigured from illumination located below; it emphasised a ghastly appearance. Terrifying, deep set, steely eyes were overshadowed by angry, bushy brows. A bony, accusing finger pointed to its victims after the style of a maddened John Knox who once harangued Mary Queen of Scots. Hateful words, when they finally came, spat out from his lips.

"SIN! WOE! Woe to those who succumb to the sin of Sodom! Ya no better than the beasts of the field an ya'll burn in hell the two of ya – burn for eternity."

Expecting more, both sinners froze. Ron was mortified at this invasion of his private space. Nobby blinked. The old man trembled in fury and was struggling to find further words of sufficient damnation when he spotted Ron's bible on a rough stool near his bed. He lunged; seized the black book and deftly thumbed to the chapter of Leviticus. Having located 18.22, with insane fury, he began to splatter out that same spiteful passage. It had been chanted several times, aimed at the grandson, since the time lewd suspicions had been conceived some years before.

As the condemning words rang out into the quiet of that night, Ron's usual fear of the old bigot was subsumed by the rage of injustice which still filled his heart; a rage inspired by the recent nightmare. He had reached the age when a young man can feel the intensity of passions such as anger, lust, love and the sheer wrongs of prejudice and discrimination. As with many other fiery young men before him – those who were pushed beyond the point of reason – Ron snapped! Anger turned to violence in its demand for overdue revenge. Accordingly, he sprung out of bed, charged at the ranting preacher, grabbed the tome of hellfire and damnation, ripped out the offending page and screwed it into a tight ball.

At this unprecedented attack on his authority and dignity, together the shock of a violation to the good book – the old man opened his toothless mouth wide in horror – only to receive that tight ball of Leviticus suddenly, painfully, slammed into that open orifice.

"Eat, eat. Eat it!" demanded the grandson in a fairly calm quite voice which had the effect of disquieting both his gramps and his lover. "Eat it."

Muffled nasal moans seem to be pleading for mercy as the broken spirit collapsed to his knees, struggling against the strength of a long, abused young bull now savouring his moment of triumph. Nobby jumped out of bed. He was disturbed by this startling scene, the ill-treatment of an elderly gent. Heretofore, it was an experience completely unknown to this lad who had spent most of his short life giving pleasure rather than inflicting pain.

As the inarticulate sounds of distress continued against a grip of powerful arms, Nobby realised that the old fellow was frantic for more than his freedom – he was gasping for breath – fighting for his life.

No, Ron! No! It's not right. It's ya granddad, Ron. Please Ron. Please! Let him go. Let him be!"

Little Nobby was too weak. Pathetically, he grappled against the murderous muscles to no avail – because – at this moment – Ron Thompson had murder in his heart. A quiet, controlled rage, a malevolent force had taken command and was waiting for that expected moment when all resistance would cease. He was waiting for the writhing to diminish, waiting for that moment when the old body would become limp, the moment when old gramps would be at peace with his evil god, with Leviticus stuffed down his evil throat.

Just in time, a moment came when the pleading little voice was heard and heeded – a moment when love triumphed over hate. As the defeated old theocrat fell to the floor in a moaning, gasping slump; together, they walked out of that room and into a new life.

It was a good new life. It started when Ron gathered up a few items into his well-worn kitbag, and they walked out of Sedges Farm just as there was a deep maroon glow of promise in the eastern sky. Hand in hand like a big brother caring for the smaller – they never looked back.

The seven aunts looked on indulgently, smiling admiration, giving Ron Thompson an enthusiastic, unconditional welcome to Bumchums Row. Nobby had come back, had won back his young man. He still looked like a little boy – and nobody was sure of his age – yet, somehow, this triumphant return had enhanced his adult status. A hundred years later, everybody would have spoken of them as 'an item'. It now seemed inappropriate for Nobby to be itinerant, wandering from home to home as he had always done before. Consequently, all aunts gave pressing invitations to stay with them. However – it was Aunty Mae who had urged her precious charge to retrieve his heart's desire – so Aunty May claimed the couple for herself. Their lives were idyllic.

An incident occurred in the middle of a cold, dark night in the spring of 1912. The boys were in bed. They were locked together, arm in arm in cuddly love when, suddenly, they were stirred by unusual sounds from over the street. Little Nobby pressed his button nose up to the window pane for a better look. Shadowy figures were stealthily moving around in the darkness carrying objects out of Freda's house. In Bumchums Row, everybody knew everybody else and all the women were in the same business. But this was different. Why were these people taking things out of a neighbour's house and loading them onto a hand-cart? On closer inspection, Nobby recognised two of the three men doing all the work. They were regular customers to the row, nice men, not burglars. The lusty lad often wished they would go to his latrine for some fun – but it never happened.

"We should stop this!" whispered Ron.

"Don't you do any such thing," whispered a voice behind them. This was Aunty May who had silently crept in for a view to the front. She went on to explain that, from time to time, some of the women got behind with the rent and had to do a 'moonlight flit'. A fourth person joined the flitting party who was identified as Freda herself. One man pulled, the other three pushed and, slowly, the heavily laden cart began to move. When it was out of sight, Nobby showed concern for the woman who – like all women on the row – was considered family.

"Where will she go? What will she do?"

"Yes! What will happen to Freda?" asked Ron in some alarm. May put her arms around them in a gesture of comfort.

"Don't you worry none. Freda's got friends on Northcote Terrace. They'll be there in a few minutes. They're expected. She'll be looked after. We all look after each other. Now then – you two love-birds snuggle ya self back into kip. Don't fret none. Freda'll be all right. And her loss might be your gain!"

Indeed, the following day was a very good day for Ron and Nobby. But, according to breaking news recalled by the latter, tragic news sweeping through Nottingham; it was not a good day for many unfortunate passengers on a certain big ship called the Titanic.

The vacancy over the road became a love-nest for the two love-birds. They took possession of their new home at the standard rent of four shillings a week for the basic standard of a two-up-two-down terraced house in The Meadows. Ron walked into a leisurely life-style long enjoyed by his partner in which money, up until this day, was never an issue. Everything had been provided by the seven aunts.

Ron's interest in public loos declined in married life, but Nobby was a highly charged, promiscuous nymph who continued to make regular visits to his favourite place – the gas lit local urinal at the end of the row. Unlike his aunts, he never considered making a professional charge for his services which, increasingly, became more popular. By way of a tip, he was always pleased to accept a few pennies, once in a while, a silver joey, or the occasional sixpence. In spite of this, these small amounts never added up to four shillings per week – and now, four shillings a week was a requirement every week.

It was the young attractive (and most active) Aunty Lil who saw the potential for Ron Thompson as a rent boy and suggested his earning power in Nottingham could well be counted in pounds rather than shillings. As it turned out, Ron sometimes *did* earn more than two pounds a week – as a window cleaner. Like Nobby, he was uncomfortable with the idea of selling his body, but, unlike Nobby, he was never afraid of hard work. Impressed by his enterprise and enthusiasm for the idea, collectively, the women bought him a ladder, bucket and shammy-leather. He made an offer to pay them back out of his earnings, an offer which was firmly refused.

Furthermore, on the fine sunny day of Tuesday, April 16th 1912, without invitation or request, all seven women – Sally, Nellie, Edna, Lil, Fanny with sisters May and Gertie – entered the new love nest and scrubbed floors, walls and the stairs to a standard which had never been seen by Freda. They were in and out all day long putting up curtains and laying down mats. Pieces of furniture, pottery, cutlery, bed clothes and towels were all gifted and gratefully received. It took a lot to make Ron cry, but, overwhelmed by such unaccustomed generosity, on this special day, he gave way to strong emotion.

And so this idyllic situation continued year in, year out. Nobby and Ron were very happy together living in their own home opposite Bumchums Row with nearby loving aunts and kind neighbours. The window cleaner went out each morning and conscientiously built up his business. In a weak effort to become a house boy, the gnome made a half-hearted attempt to acquire the rudiments of cooking and cleaning but, over the road, Mae continued to wash the clothes and most meals continued to be consumed in the other homes. Whilst Ron spent his days running up and down his ladder in various parts of the city, Nobby spent *his* days at his usual stall in his favourite latrine. He conscientiously polished up an already considerable anatomical knowledge of the male body. With special and enthusiastic attention to the location of the erogenous zones, his little paws investigated ever new erotic titillations and wonderful ways of how such areas could be further stimulated to ever greater ecstasy. Both boys were very successful in their respective lines of enterprise.

Ron did not mind. This will surprise and perhaps even offend heterosexual sensitivities. But Ron Thompson truly understood the lascivious nature of the boy he had come to love dearly – and, that love was unconditional. He was tolerant. Ron accepted the whole package which included a sparkling sense of humour, dancing, juggling and magic tricks as well as numerous anonymous encounters with dozens of different strangers every day in a public lavatory. After a hard day in the bog, Nobby always had plenty of energy left to give Ron a 'good going over, a good tongue bath ta get rid o' ya dirty water.'

CHAPTER 35

He Suffered For Us

The idyllic years continued as 1912 pleasantly melted into 1913, and then into 1914, which was Ron's last year as a teenager. The same applied to Nobby, but the occasion could not be celebrated without a birth date or, indeed, any clear idea of his true age. For Ron and the aunts, this enduring mystery was endless fodder for raucous humour and ribald comment. Indeed, Ron relished his status as the older, big tough guy, frequently demonstrating his seniority by hoisting the little gnome up on his shoulders or throwing him up in the air and catching him as a playful dad might frolic with his small child. This 'child', on the other hand, had changed hardly at all over their contented three years together. He was often teased over his sparse display of pubic hair. On one humiliating occasion, Aunty Lil interrupted bath time which was taking place in the rude, primitive kitchen, in the shallow stone sink.

"E our Nobby! Just look at *you*! Poor little sprite! Eee, lad, nature's not been generous to thee as she? A reckon Ron's 'ad your share."

The gnome had grown up with this banter which typically ended with hoots of laughter. He played up to it, and parried with clever wit.

"If Ron's got it, he's welcome – and it's more for me! You're just jealous, our Lil. I'm good. I'm a worker. I don't need to be big up front. These are my tools." He waggled soapy fingers and stuck out his naughty tongue at the giggling girl.

The residents of Bumchums Row had little interest in world affairs. Accordingly, the assassination of an Archduke and heir to the Austro-Hungarian throne on the Sunday of June 28th 1914 – did not even register. The 'Clap of Thunder over Europe' [headline of *The Daily Chronicle*] was not heard by Ron cleaning his windows, or by Nobby, very busy in his stall. Yet those two shots fired that day (by a youth of the same age) started a process which would eventually cost ten million lives during a titanic struggle involving many nations. Indeed, Old Nobby told Simeon that he was surprised that he had no recollection of the famous Balkan murder which was to tear apart their Elysian existence.

It did not happen at once. The rest of 1914 passed without incident, as did 1915, with the exception of the day of Ron's 20th birthday. It marked a triple anniversary which had been celebrated each year since August 23rd 1912. He and Nobby made their annual visit to the stone lion at St Mary's Rest Garden where they would stand for a few minutes in meditative silence and pay their respects to Bendigo. That day, always sunny, was the famous boxer's death-day. It also marked the four happy years they had enjoyed together. Leaving the garden, a smiling woman approached and presented Ron with a white feather.

"Ooo! Isn't that nice," cooed Nobby looking up to his lover.

"Is it?" responded Ron, twisting it round with finger and thumb. He studied the feather with a puzzled expression. She returned to a small group of other women, quite well dressed, all looking over to assess his reaction. They were different from the ladies who had now become family, the seven aunts who had been so kind, who had made him so welcome in The Meadows.

"I don't like those women," murmured Ron, responding to an instinct that all was not well.

In answer to a question about the 'best known face in Britain' in 1915, Nobby declared that he had absolutely no memory of a stern moustached man accusingly pointing his finger at young men who had yet to don uniform and serve King and Country. On the other hand, he recalled a little ditty which was doing the rounds –

"O! why the deuce should I repine and be an ill foreboder? I'm twenty three, and five foot nine, I'll go and be a soldier."

An ominous development came early in the following year. On January 6th 1916 the Government introduced what was known as 'the call up' – conscription. That date was not really significant because Ron and Nobby were still blissfully ignorant, but in February it became clear to everybody that single men, fit for service, were being recruited in Nottingham, and the aunts were alarmed to hear of several boys in nearby rows who had no choice – no choice at all – they had to go. And the dreadful news of carnage, blood and guts was filtering through from distant lands. Those accounts reached even into Bumchums Row. Those boys taken – they had gone to hell.

Even at this point, Nobby was hopeful. And that little gnome was a crafty little gnome. He was becoming aware of his status of anonymity – no records of his birth or parentage. Officially, Nobby was invisible. He rejoiced in that advantage. He was a child. He was small, scrawny, puny, underweight and looked like a child, although he would become 21 in July – but nobody knew that – not even Nobby, and Nobby was happy not to know. Nobby enjoyed being twelve-years-old.

Nobby was also hopeful for Ron. He hoped that, on the occasion his hunky lover had walked out of Sedges Farm, nobody knew where he had gone. The women agreed. At an impromptu conference, Fanny, the oldest aunt, pointed out that Ron might have lost a considerable inheritance when he assaulted the old man and marched out on him with no intention of returning.

"If he's chucked all that, nobody will expect him to be at a place like this with the likes of us!"

"And they'll be more than one Ron Thompson," chipped in Edna.

Sally and Nellie (the only two of the seven who always seemed to be more interested in each other than in other men) were more cautious. The former reminded them –

"It's common knowledge round these parts; a young window-cleaner's living in t' same 'ouse with a little lad. And another thing, Ron's name's on t' rent book."

As it turned out, Ron was discovered via a more malicious agency. We often forget what we have inadvertently told people. During conversation, Bumchums Row was mentioned over the dinner table at Sedges Farm. Whilst in a taciturn and surly frame of mind, the old man did not close his ears to the sparse few words which passed between his grandson and his very odd visitor on that evening four years before. After hearing that soldiers were sorely needed at the front, Old Thompson informed the authorities where one strapping lad might be found. He did not see this as an act of spiteful revenge. He saw it as his Christian duty to frustrate unnatural sins of the flesh and to make sure that his nearest relative did *his* duty to bring honour to his country and honour to the Thompson family name.

"It was like a sudden death," said a tearful Old Nobby to Simeon at Nottingham Castle in 1965. "We never even said goodbye. You see – I wasn't there when they came. When I got back, Ron was gone."

Very gently, Simeon probed. It seemed that Ron was 'not a great one for writing' so there were no letters. Nobby was inconsolable. His world had fallen apart and he fell into a deep depression. He was not clear about what actually happened over the next few years. Old Simeon had to piece together all the remembered fragments from the sparse sources available. But the gist of it was as follows: on a day in late February 1916, the day Ron was taken; the little gnome toddled out of Bumchum's Row and was never seen again by the ladies of easy virtue, the women who had loved him dearly since his very earliest memories. Having lost both of their boys on that same day, they were heartbroken.

Nobby himself would not, or could not supply any details. Simeon suggested a loss of memory, a nervous breakdown, mental illness or all of those things. Nobby shook his head. He simply did not know or would not say. It was also difficult to establish any accurate dates from members of the Derbyshire / Nottinghamshire gay community as to when the character of Nobby the Gnome was first recollected. In 1965 he was already a popular old curiosity, a legend in his own lifetime. Everybody agreed that the famous 'old tramp' of medieval appearance was frequently seen, out and about, rambling in the Peak District, Derbyshire and Nottinghamshire well before the war in the 1930s. Some would claim they had seen the vagrant wandering through the dales and mounting hills during the early years of that decade, but nobody could be sure. Some claimed to have had a sexual encounter with an old vagabond who was known to doss in public lavatories. But 20th century Derbyshire was well supplied with eccentric, elderly homosexuals who inhabited the murky world of the cottages, all eager to give good service.

It seemed reasonable to suppose that he could be described as an 'old tramp,' even as early as 1930, given that 'gentlemen of the road' are often much younger than their outward appearance would suggest. An itinerant, sleeping rough, worn, battered and weathered by 14 Derbyshire winters might well look decades older than his 35 years. The cute little gnome – cherished and coddled in early years – held on to his charm and childlike image up to the point when his world was shattered by the worst possible disaster of losing the one person who was all the world to him.

"But could you be *sure* that you really *had* lost your Love?" pleaded Simeon. "*If* he was dead, surely there would have been a telegram to your old address to confirm that Ron Thompson was killed in action? Didn't you – just once – go back to those goodhearted souls, generous women who thought so much of you? Surely an official communication confirming his death would have reached one of your aunts?"

The unspoken answer from this somewhat inarticulate old man was a profound silence and stillness followed by more silent tears running down his cheeks. It communicated to Simeon an overwhelming despair and an acute helplessness. The articulate answer to the question, not obvious to a young Simeon, became all too clear to the older writer who, over the years, had grown to understand how heterosexual culture with its homophobic rules and values had systematically negated the rights of homosexuals. Nobody knows the address Ron gave after his induction into the army. It could have been the one in the Meadows or Sedges Farm. Officially, only the latter would have been recognised if old Thompson had given contact details for his grandson. Indeed, in the fullness of time, in fact in the late 1990s, Simeon's research uncovered the record of a telegram which was delivered to a Mr Harold Thompson of Sedges Farm. Couched in the customary mendacity and euphemism of the day, it assured the grandfather that Pte Thompson died quickly and bravely on July 1st in the Battle of the Somme.

Ron Thompson was one of 47,000 British boys who had been killed or wounded, in that massacre, on that day, as they slogged on with rifle and pack to a ghastly slaughter. Simeon was put in mind of one bitter soldier who wrote –
        "You smug-faced crowd with kindling eye who cheer when soldiers go by. Sneak home and pray you'll never know the hell where youth and laughter go."

And then, he recalled the scarecrow. Simeon remembered the boy who was tied to the fence. That beautiful young man, at first sight mistaken for a scarecrow, horribly wounded, hung and suffered there for many hours before he died. He recalled another young man. In the smoky shell shocked craters of the ragged trenches, there was a terrible account of one lad who, seconds after going over the top, was shot. Not dead, he was conscious. He was caught up in a barbarous tangle of barbed wire, caught fast, beyond the reach and help of his comrades. In agony – he hung there and suffered for many hours – moaning through the night – before he died. Was that Ron? In that nightmare, had Pte Thompson foreseen his own death? The question had been put to Old Nobby, but he was certain that his beloved did not die in that excruciating manner. He insisted that the beautiful boy who suffered in the bad dream was quite different.

If there were common aspects to that apparent premonition, common sense suggested a coincidence and Simeon tended to this view for many years – until the year of 1998. On the night of October 6th – October 7th of that year, it was reported that an unspeakable sadistic act had taken place in a remote rural area near Laramie, Wyoming USA. Without pity, two youths indulged in savage gay hate. To no avail, their chosen victim had begged for his life. The beating was so severe that the only areas on his face that were not covered in blood were those where his tears had washed the blood stains away. Matthew Shepard was found tied to a fence 18 hours later by Aaron Kreifels, who, at first, thought that the boy – was a *scarecrow*. Matthew had been robbed, pistol whipped, tortured and left to die. The 'scarecrow' with his severe injuries – lacerations to head, face and neck – remained unconscious for five days before he died.

The brutal homophobic murder of this beautiful 21-year-old had a profound effect on Simeon. He was beginning to look back on his life, a life blighted since adolescence by 41 secret summers in which he was compelled to suppress his secret lusts, secret desires, secret fantasies and, worst of all, his secret loves. The Matthew Shepard atrocity focused his attention on all the other Matthew Shepards who had lived and suffered without the benefit of positive publicity which had been generated by good parents like Dennis and Judy Shepard. Their sustained and valiant efforts over the years helped to frame the Matthew Shepard Act which was vetoed by President Bush in 2007. Following his election in 2009, President Obama stated that he was committed to passing the Act.

A few of Ron's words had always made an impact on Simeon. 'That poor lad had hung and suffered – for me. He suffered for all folks like me'. It reminded him of something familiar. Sometime later, he made the connection between words spoken by a farm labourer and the central core of the Christian message which had been drilled into a young Simeon during those dark, despairing years at Mundy Street Boys School – 'Jesus hung and suffered there for us.' Simeon had learned to despise religious indoctrination served up with daily cruelty from sadistic theocrats. Suddenly, in 1998, he received an inkling of what Christianity might be all about. Following both of those 'executions', good had come out of bad. The savage murder of Matthew Shepard outraged the global gay community and galvanised heterosexual public opinion on the side of justice for an oppressed minority.

It *could* have been a coincidence. It was certainly all very intriguing. In 1998 it was not possible for Simeon to discuss it with Nobby who had long since disappeared. For that magical little chap, 'disappeared' seemed a better word than dead. The legend of the gnome faded away in much the manner as it had originally materialised. From time to time he was seen and, for some, delightfully experienced in the 1970s, but less frequently in the 1980s. He had completely vanished before the end of that decade.

In the conclusion to his book *Nobby: True Tales of a Naughty Gnome*, which would be published in 2022; from accounts of the multitude who had remembered the little legend with affection, old Simeon summed up the general feeling.
"Nobby the Gnome, a fairytale character, appeared to be a natural work of art. He seemed to have morphed out of the very elements of Derbyshire. Long after he was gone, his face could still be seen in the gnarled, knotted, writhing and twisting trunks of ancient trees depicted with more skill and imagination than any human artist could achieve. At any moment, his head might poke out of a hollow old oak, a suitable home for such a character. He could be seen sitting in the coils of choking ivy, or in the pocked and rotting recesses of an ash tree recovering from a long hard winter. The imagined representation of that old gnome was as invisible as the hidden gay underworld in the Peak District itself. Throughout most of the 20th century, the illusive sprite had always been there one minute, and gone the next. Now he has gone forever. He has reunited with other bizarre elements of Derbyshire homosexual history. They have all passed away, gone to that Great Cottage in the Sky. We will never see their like again."

CHAPTER 36

Manchester Milk Train

Returning to the Tuesday morning of May 10th 1966 – two World Wars later – a more equal and affluent Britain was at the height of the 'Swinging Sixties.' Moral panic voiced by Mary Whitehouse contrasted with Mary Quant who was pushing at the heterosexual boundaries with her mini-skirts modelled by cavorting, chic, waif-like Cockneys with huge eyes. But not in Belper! That old mill town was still very much in a post war time warp. Here we had the repulsive Mr Toad in an ill-fitting Harris Tweed suit with huge sad eyes bidding farewell to his chicken who could be delayed no longer.

An early start made for a long day. Over the pleasant haze of thin cloud, a weak but strengthening sun gradually took the chill off an enthusiastic ride out of Belper. He pressed on up the A6, up Via Gellia and climbing higher to several attractive Derbyshire locations – Winster, Elton, Youlgreave, Over Haddon, Ashford and, on up, to the greater heights above Great Hucklow where he noticed a public phone box of the old style with button A and button B. This was a reminder that Simeon's most important friend had asked to be updated on all developments. Accordingly, following careful instructions, he gave the operator the barrister's phone number and the number of the phone box from which he was calling. He specified a 'person-to-person' reversed charge long distance call to Martin Harcourt QC from Sam Clifton. After a minute, Martin was heard to say that he'd accept the charge. The operator said –
"Go ahead, Mr Clifton."
"Martin?"
"Sam! I've made a note of your number from the operator. Hang up and I'll ring that number."
Another minute passed. The public telephone in the middle of that remote quiet Peakland village suddenly proclaimed its existence with an embarrassing shrill report. Martin's rich tones came back in an unexpected, higher level of clarity.
"Martin! This is a *much* better connection. You sound like you're speaking from the next village."
"That's because it's a secure line, Simeon. We need to be careful. Each time you ring me, always give your number, and I'll ring you back."
Feeling reassured, Simeon unburdened himself of the trauma (and a few of the pleasures) of his four hour Sunday afternoon adventure in the dark caves on High Tor. Mr

Harcourt listened to the full story in stony silence. To Simeon's dismay, this brought forth from the barrister, a stern reprimand.

"That was very foolish, young man! Plain *stupid* might be a better word. How can I protect you if you insist in putting yourself in harms way?" In a choked haze of hurt, there was no answer. "You *must* try to be more careful, Simeon," Martin added, a shade softer. "I know your motive was honourable – concern for a friend. You went in there for the best of reasons but the toad should have stopped you. Those caves are run by lewd Chesterfield elements known locally as the Third Camp. It's a sort of dustbin for any homosexual who is not one of us, in Nottingham, or any of Hoadley's pretentious nodding heads in Derby. Monks and Muckles! My God! That really *is* scraping the barrel. Young and desirable certainly – but *dangerous* – absolutely – without doubt! OK – I can understand the temptation…"

"Sorry Martin," interrupted Simeon, timidly.

"I rest my case. You were quite right to tell me. I need to be properly briefed if I'm to be useful – and on that subject, I've already set in place several lines of enquiry. *Now* I'll have to find Gary Mackenzie."

"Do you think he'll be all right?" asked Simeon anxiously.

"God knows! For what it's worth, my best guess is that he snagged something quite desirable and went home with it."

Replacing the receiver, Simeon was a touch miffed after receiving the sharp edge of Martin's tongue. He had already endured a lecture from Hoadley about the important need for vigilance and security in the twilight world of queers. Now he had been instructed to avoid the so called 'undesirables' of Chesterfield!

It seemed so unjust. In a world where all sexual deviants were condemned by a bigoted majority, self-styled 'respectable' homosexuals in the professions should cast out boys like Monks and Muckles and treat them as pariahs. In the previous year, Simeon had stayed at Guzzly Granddad's Chesterfield house and met his amusing and colourful collection of freakish friends. However, the older Simeon came to understand why that exciting gaggle of rough trade and silly queens, so despised, so feared, were also threatening to older professional men who had a great deal to lose in a homophobic society.

In the late afternoon, Simeon found rest, food and accommodation at the Castleton Youth Hostel. He requested an evening duty to facilitate another early start on the Wednesday morning. The enduring high pressure up in the High Peak produced even more mist after a cold night. It condensed to patches of thick fog lurking along the roads through Hope, Thornhill and ascending to Ladybower Dam. He turned off the A57 and climbed a steep country lane leading up to Strines Moor. In due course, the fog melted into mist and a weak sun made its first appearance near the summit, as Simeon pumped up to enjoy views to the east over Sheffield. And then down to Dale Dike Reservoir where, briefly, he recollected the drama of Sheffield Sam before cycling through Low Bradfield, Wigtwizzle, Midhopestones and finally into Holmfirth where he found cheap accommodation at a private terraced house.

Thursday morning dawned much brighter. After an adequate breakfast with a second pot of tea, he paid his fifteen shillings to the lady, mounted and launched down a pretty road which paralleled the meandering River Holme. Gravity aided the cyclist and the water, as both rushed into the Colne Valley, entering a Lowry landscape of weed-infested, craggy cobbled roads, all well-trodden by generations of clogs. A forest of chimney stacks rising from woollen mills announced the gothic setting of Huddersfield. It cried out to be explored. Such interesting investigation, however, came at a price – it soaked up most of the morning.

His aim was to reach Harrogate that evening which was some 35 miles further on, but Simeon had not reckoned with the delaying attractions of Bradford where smoke grimed wool mills meant great wealth. Amidst the impressive façade of giant Corinthian columns, he could feel the very heartbeat of industrial Yorkshire. He empathised in Victorian pride. Here, a century before, there had been confidence and boasting. To please the eye, there were plenty of flamboyant arched windows, pinnacles and stone embossments.

Not far from the city centre he cycled down narrow terraced streets not unlike the Nottingham rows described by Nobby the Gnome. Simeon was impressed to see women on their hands and knees scrubbing doorsteps and whole sections of pavement in front of their house. He fell into conversation with a man who looked just like Andy Capp from the *Daily Mirror,* but Mr Capp was doubtful when asked about bed and breakfast. Kindly, he had a quick word with 'the missus' and suggested the cyclist might share a simple meal and stay the night. A man of few words, he ignored the boy's offer to pay the standard fifteen shillings.

Simeon reasoned that a city the size of Bradford could support at least one gay pub – possibly more than one – but, especially in 1966, a warning instinct prevented him from putting that question to Mr and Mrs Capp over the dinner table. Accordingly, after the repast, he consulted at the nearest homosexual Tourist Information Centre – the local cottage.
        "The Junction! It's at the bottom of Leeds Road. That's where *you* need to be," said a chatty chicken with a cheeky smile known as Fluff. "I'll take you there." For an underage drinker, this sexy number was surprisingly well informed. "It's really old, seventeen something. The atmosphere in there is fantastic! You never know who is going to walk through the door. In Victorian times it became a regular haunt for actors. So, as usually happens, it became a haunt for queers," continued Fluff, flashing another enticing smile. "Cora, she's the landlady, well, she's *very* stern – but fair. She always manages to keep order. Hey! Listen." He stopped and faced Simeon. "Bet you can't guess how she keeps order?"
        "I'm all agog," said Simeon. "How does Cora keep order?"
        "Cora's got an artificial tit! It's hard, black an' heavy like a discus. If somebody's a nuisance, she'll chuck it at them to sort them out!"

Simeon, who preferred tea shops to pubs, was beginning to wonder if he really wanted to patronise The Junction with its ambiance of raucous laughter, rough company – not to mention the hazard of flying tits. He considered returning to the cottage. It *was* a very busy cottage! On the other hand, it seemed rude to detach himself from this enthusiastic youth who was clearly enjoying his role as a Bradford tour guide. They marched swiftly past a cinema proclaiming the main feature, *A Man for all Seasons* before arriving at the old hostelry.

Like most queer pubs, The Junction was noisy, crowded and smoky – even on a Thursday evening. As in most queer pubs, Simeon hated being pierced by those staring, leering eyes each time he made an entrance into any homosexual venue. He rationalised. Two chickens were likely to attract more attention than one chicken. Moreover, at least these cheery Yorkshire folk were not the sneering, leering eyes of the Derby Friary snobs. And another thing; Bradfordians shared something of the camaraderie he had enjoyed in the cramped Derby Corporation Hotel passageway.

Simeon hated squeezing through a density of humanity to reach the bar for an orange drink he did not really want; so, sensing that young Fluff had no money, two half crowns were pressed into his sweet, soft chicken hand with an instruction to purchase two drinks. Fluff was surprised at Simeon's choice of a soft drink.

"Truth to tell, I'd prefer a pint mug of hot tea. You know, the sort you'd get in a transport café."

"If you don't drink, why ask for a pub in the first place?"

"I asked for a *queer* pub. Anyway, I had to say *something* to get you out of that cottage, didn't I?"

A common feature of a gay pub is one dominant personality who holds court. In The Friary it was Claud Hoadley. In the corporation it was Dolly. In The Junction it was a boastful queen, complete with bad teeth, known as Hetty Howitt who sported an odd sort of hair style, a bizarre zigzag effect which intrigued the observer from Derbyshire.

"It must be a wig!" he said to Fluff who had returned.

"Oh no," replied the soft, downy chicken under his own mousy hair, beginning to look tempting and cuddly. Their hands touched, lingered, for longer than was required for the passing of a drink and change. Both boys held eye contact… until sheer embarrassment triggered a question.

"Not a wig?" asked Simeon, wistfully, studying the adolescent fuzz on the other boy's chin.

"Oh no," said Fluff, again, more softly. He lowered his eyes and slightly craned his neck to better enjoy the effect of Simeon's bottom, nicely filling out his close-fitting jeans. He stirred himself. "No, not a wig. It's all his own. Know what," he added warming to his subject, "he's *bald* except for the back and sides. He's let it grow long at the back and drags it over to cover the top. It's held in place by a half tin of lacquer. Hey, know what? I saw him walk down by the Wool Exchange – it was windy. Fascinating! It started to lift – just like a pedal bin!"

Both lads giggled. And in that giggle, mindful of the crush giving a modicum of privacy, naughty Fluff felt free to feel, and made free with Simeon's backside as Hetty's bragging increased in volume, fired up by the recent purchase of his new Sunbeam Talbot.

"My dear it's a *dream* on wheels! I insist! You must all go out and admire it. All of you. It's stunning! You'll all drool. It's beautifully finished in black and gold."

"Very nice," drawled an acid queen next to Simeon. "It'll match her teeth."

Fluff and Simeon went out with the multitude – but *not* to admire a new Sunbeam Talbot. Unobserved, they crept down a scruffy but interesting old cobbled lane – hand in hand. Past nine and getting dark, the cobbles were quiet, the only thing left of a one time neighbourhood of slum housing, probably cleared after the war. Crossing a rough recreation ground, they broke hands after catching sight of a few grubby kids playing with a football. A few minutes later they stood in front of a council house, one of many on that estate.

"Mam's at the pub. Hey! Come in and listen to my records."

At this, Simeon expressed concern about finding his way back to the Capps residence, in order to return at a reasonable time, as is courteous for a B&B guest. At best he could spend no more than an hour with his new friend. Fluff was miffed. He did not agree that it was necessary to 'check in' before 11.00pm. Simeon parried.

"I'm careful about my sleep! And I need to be in good shape to cycle to Harrogate tomorrow. As long as I'm back at that cottage by half ten... it's only a few minutes from there. Promise you'll guide me – please?"

The promise was given. Moving through a depressing miasma of musty smells, they entered into a cheap, tacky atmosphere, clomping up stairs barely covered in thin, worn carpet. Fluff's small bedroom, his little world, was equally in bad taste in terms of lurid colour and shoddy furniture, probably purchased from Woolworths circa 1959. But this was his little world. It was all he had, and it *was* clean and tidy, an attribute common to most gay boys.

The window overlooked 'the rec'. Scruffy kids were still raucously yelping, laughing and kicking around an old ball in near darkness. It was even darker in Fluff's little domain – time for a cuddle. It was an interesting cuddle because Simeon was overwhelmed by a strong, yet sad affection for this vulnerable child in his arms. It was a gentle feeling, as if, gingerly, holding a young fluffy bird. Once again, it amused him to note that his bum was an area of erotic fascination receiving more strokes, more caresses from those sweet fluffy hands.

Simeon pulled back. His own hands, somewhat less naughty, cupped fluffy pale cheeks which had seen little sunshine. Sad eyes met sad eyes. Words were not spoken, but thoughts were thought. They said –

"Don't go back to the Capps. Stay with me. Stay here all night. Don't go to Harrogate. Let's be together – always."

Fluff broke the silence with an enthusiastic reference to his room decorated in brash radical contemporary patterns. Books, with garish covers displaying images of Roy Rodgers, Gene Autry and PC 49, competed with a few *Eagle* comics and an intriguing poster of a handsome man with cap and black beard.

"Who is that? asked Simeon.

"Che Guevara, replied Fluff.

"A pop star?" pressed Simeon.

"Don't think so. Hey! Look at this! It's only second hand, but it was 11 guineas new! It's got *four* speeds! Dansette's one of the best record players. It's got an Italian styled cabinet!"

Only one speed was required – 45 revolutions per minute. Fluff went over to a rack of records and selected one which he considered to be romantic enough to suit the situation. It was a catastrophic failure! Simeon begged him to remove it from the turntable *immediately* on the grounds that he detested *Tears* by Ken Dodd. Something by Jim Reeves was offered. Simeon responded with a look of horror but *Don't Worry Baby* by the Beach Boys was very acceptable and played several times. With feathers slightly ruffled, Fluff suggested that Simeon's wholesome insistence on early-to-bed, eight-hours-of-sleep might be spoiling his fun in life.

"Bet you've never been on the Milk Train. You've got to be up late to catch the Milk Train."

The next ten minutes were given over to an exposition of Fluff's exciting Saturday night adventures in Manchester. He described wild escapades with his mates from Leeds in The Union at the junction of Princess Street and Canal Street. The Rembrandt and The Trafford Long Bar were also mentioned. These well known gay pubs of Manchester were familiar to Simeon because he had been carted around them by the notorious Dolly of Derby in the previous year. Tongue in cheek, Fluff explained that 'chucking out time' coincided with Simeon's bed time – 10.00 pm – but carnal activities continued in the nooks and crannies of alleyways, jitties, tow paths and toilets until five minutes to midnight when the last train departed from Manchester.

"I expect you were one drained, worn out Fluff dragging yourself on to that train!" with a slight edge of concern.

"Not always. Sometimes we were a right bunch o' sluts! We deliberately missed that last train and *extended* the evening!

"Extended! No wonder you're thin and pale. You can't possibly keep on having seedy sex after midnight. Well, for starters, it's not safe."

"Manchester's full of excitement into the night. Come and join us sometime. You'd like it. You could be nuzzling up to dodgy chickens in that sleazy all night café in Dale Street. You'd love it."

"No I would not!"

"Yes you would! You could drink yourself silly at a shilling a time downing big pint mugs of tea. And getting gobbles all night long in that grotty lavatory at the back."

"How did you know that's what I like?" responded Simeon, more softly.

"Saw you in the cottage didn't I? Bet you like *this* licking don't you," continued the lascivious chicken in gentle tones, his hand returning to the erogenous regions at the rear end. Delicately, Simeon removed that hand and gave it a tender kiss.

"And you shouldn't be doing that either, little boy; you could catch hepatitis."

Playful tickles and a big hug followed. They both fell on to a lumpy little bed and Fluff fumbled to release the prisoner he had been waiting to service. It did not take long. In due course, a satisfactory conclusion to yet another conquest had been achieved and the two boys lay quite still, silently, side by side, staring at the ceiling. The satisfaction was physical. Simeon was never hypocritical about sex. He enjoyed it, but in this instance the experience had left him... troubled. He reasoned that there must be thousands of Fluffs in West Yorkshire who claim to be having a great time each weekend, out late, 'on the piss', 'burning the candle at both ends' and doing themselves little good with such an unhealthy life-style. Simeon knew that Fluff was unhappy and, abruptly, Fluff broke into these brooding considerations with an unexpected suggestion, an echo of his previous thoughts.

"Let's be 'an affair'!"

'An affair' was common parlance in mid-20th century homosexual English circles for a relationship / partnership. Simeon was more accustomed to the American term 'lovers'.

"No kidding," he insisted, "let's go steady. I... I love you."

Simeon looked at Fluff as an older, wiser person might look indulgently at a child. Emotionally, Fluff *was* a child and, quite simply, Simeon, not much wiser, did not know what to say to him. He considered reaching for the usual clichés such as – 'Aren't you confusing love with desire?' or 'Where would we live, we have no money.' or 'We have very little in common.' On the other hand, Simeon respected the boy's sincerity and was far more sympathetic in contrast to the callous cynicism recently voiced by the sneering and envious Claud Hoadley.

"I expect you think you're Prince Charming," said Fluff, slightly tearful, but miffed by the delay in receiving an answer to his heartfelt proposal.

"Actually, I'm running *away* from Prince Charming."

Having articulated the reality which now controlled his life, coupled with the passion for Ahmed which still obsessed, Simeon's countenance clearly registered the anguish of his deep feelings and Fluff, with alarm, noted that sudden pain.

"What's a matter? Are you in trouble then? What's wrong? Tell me. Please tell me."

Simeon, feeling that, at the very least, he owed his new friend an explanation gave a brief and discreet outline of his escape from America.

"Why Harrogate?"

"Why not? It's a nice place. It'll do for a few days. I just have to keep moving to keep safe. Oh yes. I can see it in your face. It *does* sound like a tall story, but it happens to be the truth. Take it or leave it." He looked at his watch and gave Fluff a kiss. "Sorry. Time to go. Remember your promise?"

They walked across the rec, now deserted and cheerless, in sad silence. At the far end, the gloomy tension was eased when Simeon remembered Fluff's earlier absorbing reference to the Milk Train.

"Oh, that!" he brightened. "They've got the right name for it, haven't they! Spunk everywhere! Slipping, sliding and that old train jolting and lurching – it's a wonder I don't break my neck. On some Saturday nights it's a right gangbang. No, Sunday; because it pulls out at four every Sunday morning."

He was describing the early Sunday newspaper and parcels train. It left Manchester with one ancient passenger coach which had no corridor. After missing the last train, just before midnight, Fluff and his randy friends had to wait four hours before boarding the Milk Train.

"It's like this – you walk down the platform, along side the carriage and check who is in each compartment. If you see something nice, something you fancy – well, you get in with them. As soon as the train moves, you're completely cut off because there's no corridor, so nobody can catch you at it! Great! You can get cracking. You can get down to it. I've had fantastic rides in that lovely old ramshackle train! Last month, it was heaving; there were six of us going at it hammer and tongs! You'd love it."

"No I would not! Don't get me wrong. I *like* orgies. But a *mobile* orgy! In the middle of the night!"

Eager to secure as much time as possible, Fluff walked Simeon right up to the Capp's front door at the entirely acceptable time of a few minutes past half ten. Simeon yarned, Fluff did not. Simeon was sad. Fluff was heartbroken. He broke down into heavy sobs as Simeon tried to say goodnight. Alarmed, he pulled the tearful chicken into a side entry and, for a few minutes, comforted him as best he could with hugs, kisses and tender words.

"You need love, not Milk Trains," he whispered.

"I love you," moaned Fluff, miserably.

"You *will* meet Prince Charming," said Simeon, pretending to be wise, pretending to be strong – a strength which was necessary for them both at that moment. "But don't expect him to *look* like Prince Charming. Life is full of surprises."

The few minutes turned into about a quarter of an hour before Simeon could extricate himself from his pitiful friend. The hardest part for both parties was the grim prospect of no further contact, save that they *might* meet again, sometime, by chance. But they never did. Simeon's own heart was breaking as he gave a last wave to the sweet, slight, fluffy lad who looked alone – so very alone – just before he turned the corner and went out of sight – forever. Just for a moment he hoped that Fluff would turn and run back. Simeon would say – 'The hell with the Capps! I'll get my bike and we'll go to a hotel and cuddle all night. I'll hold my pretty little Fluff and never let him go'. But Fluff did not come back and now it was Simeon's turn to hide his wretched face, give in to the spasms of despair and weep in that dark, lonely entry, somewhere in Bradford.

CHAPTER 37

Bradford Cathedral

Halfway through a good fry-up breakfast on Friday, May 13th, Simeon was in a pensive mood. He was thinking about his tears in the Capps entry the previous night. Had he fallen in love with that sweet, sexy tempting chicken? No, of course not. He was still in love with Ahmed. He was puzzled and could not adequately explain that grief-ridden drama until the passing of 42 years.

The older Simeon realised that he had formed a bond of affection for this one-night-companion. He was crying for *all* the Fluffs out there in the lavatories, alleyways, seedy pubs and milk trains. Against the odds, many gay youths were searching to discover love, to lead a decent fulfilled life against a background of fear, disapproval and insecurity.

For much of the next four decades, Simeon had hardly thought of Fluff. But that painful parting came back to mind, one particular day, under a perfect autumnal blue sky, the day of Derby Pride / Derby Goes Pink on Saturday, September 27th, 2008. It was a heartbreaking irony! At the same moment when hundreds of people were happily celebrating the culture of gay life, one vulnerable gay teenager, like Fluff, not far away, was suicidal. Far above a jeering crowd, baying for blood, he was standing on the roof of Westfield Centre car park, threatening to jump, to kill himself. Seventeen year old Shaun Dykes, did just that; he plunged to his death at 5.30pm. Two well-trained police officers had tried to help Shaun, but they were outnumbered by despicable, taunting ghouls who had flocked to see death, after the style of a public execution.

Shaun and Simeon had much in common. They were both gay, had both attended school in Heanor, had both been very unhappy to the brink of jumping from a high place. Tragically, Shaun jumped. Simeon did not. He went on to write autobiographic books which explain the problems of being homosexual in a society which is often very homophobic.

He did not know Shaun. He was not familiar with the circumstances which drove him to commit suicide. Hopefully, the students at his Heanor Gate School treated him more kindly than some of the more savage pupils of Mundy Street Boys School who subjected Simeon to a daily routine of physical and psychological torture. In 1957, Simeon's typical day started with prayers and hymns and ended with a desire to be dead. In the autumn of that year, with the assistance of a sadistic schoolmaster, head bowed and eyes downcast, he had reached an advanced stage of humility and obedience to the bullies who had... broken him. It was the end. On one particular day, 51 years before – Simeon had become Shaun Dykes.

Like Shaun, he was looking down to a pavement below. Not Derby, this was a Heanor pavement at Red Lion Square, beneath his top bedroom window. Unlike Shaun, nobody was there to help Simeon, neither was there anybody to taunt or humiliate. That was an everyday occurrence at his Church of England school. However, on this day, Simeon's pain felt like the wording of a medieval ordeal – 'As much as you can bear, and greater'.

The details of Shaun's pain were not well publicised. However, one of his inner circle said he was 'ordered out of his home' after 'confessing' his homosexuality, only to be followed by a devastating rejection from his partner. In a homophobic community still heavily ingrained in a football-mad-macho-coalmining culture, even in the more enlightened days of the early 21st century, all of Shaun's support had evaporated. His fragile world had collapsed around him. And just for a short poignant time, Simeon had been invited into the fragile world of a poor Bradford boy known as Fluff who was desperately seeking similar support. Alas, Simeon was unable [or unwilling?] to provide that support.

Simeon was touched by Yorkshire kindness and consideration. Mrs Capp had insisted on washing and ironing his small bundle of dirty laundry – socks, pants, an extra vest and an extra shirt which were re-crammed into his saddle bag. After profuse thanks and a fussy send-off with several neighbours looking on, Simeon mounted and waved cheerio to the good hearted Capps.

It was rather warm, a touch humid and he felt no great urgency to seek the road to Harrogate. Accordingly, he slowly pedalled towards the city centre and soaked up more of the interesting architecture of which he knew nothing. The Yorkshire Penny Bank caught his eye. He was impressed, but not able to describe the profuse decoration which was French / Italian Renaissance. Neither could he articulate his enthusiasm for the entrance vestibule with its mosaic-tiled floor and iron gates. He just knew that he liked it. It was different.

Presently, he came across more iron gates framed by a stone Tudor archway. They were open and inviting. Wide stone steps took him into a darkened enclosure formed by an intrusion into the side of a hill. He was climbing up, approaching some mysterious destination, perhaps a medieval castle? The adventurer passed several landings adorned by elaborate Victorian gas light fittings and decorated stone finials. Eventually, he emerged into brilliance. He was dazzled by sun and the colour of a beautiful garden. Was this still a public place, or was Simeon trespassing? He looked around for a castle – in vain – but found himself in the agreeable precincts of a cathedral – Bradford Cathedral, situated on a rise overlooking the city.

He made good use of this fine vantage point from which to appreciate the townscape and terrain of that metropolis – a splendid panorama of pinnacles and finials. Most notable was the distinctive Italianate clock tower of the City Hall and the ornate Venetian Gothic parapets and pinnacles of the Wool Exchange. They reminded Simeon of an ancient fairy tale castle. A busy city, and yet here, just a stone's throw from that vibrant centre – such peace and beauty! He had arrived in a tranquil garden of ornamental trees, shrubs, bluebells, red roses, lupins, bird song and dappled sunshine. One convenient tree provided a suitable resting place for his bike giving him more freedom to explore.

As ever, the fascination of foliage and deep shade called Simeon to the west and south of this Cathedral where mature trees dominated. A leafy path taking a route in front of the great tower revealed an entrance on the left made all the more grand by a rockery of heathers and low spreading conifers on each side. The entrance beckoned; an impressive portal, carved into that old, substantial stone tower.

Once inside the great nave, the atmosphere was immediately different. Simeon had exchanged sun and singing blackbirds for the hushed peace of an ancient serene space which, like the outside, was completely devoid of humankind. His eyes adjusted to the dimness and instinctively followed the high timber roof supported by carved angels. They came to rest on the red and purple stain of the West Window with its illuminated lights appearing to paint several women in biblical dress.

On exit, he was enveloped by the fragrance of rowan blossom which came from the left, as he turned left and left again to investigate the south side which was heavily shaded by two beautiful copper beech trees. Here indeed in the midst of a great city was a 'secret garden'. Underneath the deep gloom of their boughs, on such a warm day, the cool felt good and Simeon entertained the idea that he was being protected by tree spirits. As a breeze stirred the leaves, he watched the dapples of sun dancing on the old headstones which had been laid flat to facilitate a high quality paving – *Farewell my friends and children dear, I am not dead but sleeping here.*

He noted weeds struggling to grow between the slabs and raised his sight to look due east, through the rusty leaves, glimpsing a narrow street adorned with tall quality buildings of a highly distinctive character. This intriguing street was level, but connected with others on a steep slope: just the sort of area he enjoyed investigating. Simeon had discovered Little Germany, an enclave of Victorian charm.

He retraced his steps out of the south side 'secret garden', around the tower and back to the warmer, sunny north side with its open lawn which inclined upwards from west to east. After checking the bike, he selected a comfortable bench which gave him a pleasant view of the city and, just opposite, several Georgian houses with pleasing symmetry.

The emotional turmoil of the Fluff incident had robbed him of quality sleep and now, alas, at nearly 11.00am, the cyclist, pleasantly tired, was in no mood to cycle. He closed his eyes and bathed in the sweet music of a dozen blackbirds, the scent of bluebells and the sunshine which felt good on his legs. Very slowly, it all dissolved into the pleasant sedation of Elysium Fields until, one sleepy Simeon, fell into the arms of Morpheus, the god of dreams and sleep.

It was a dog! Friendly, fussing and smiling; it had licked him into wakefulness. In response to this lavish affection, characteristic of all dogs, Simeon kissed and cuddled the rich brown head of this delightful chocolate Labrador which, sadly and abruptly, was called back by an owner, anxious to make further progress on his walk. That retreating man was the first person he had seen in this tranquil Cathedral Close of St Peter; the second was the boy sitting on the other bench, on the lawn, quite close, just a little way up the incline.

Still dozy, bleary eyed, taking in sweet scents born on gentle zephyrs; Simeon saw those beautiful blue eyes in soft focus. Unreal! Was he still dreaming? From a fading smile on a face of calm intelligence, it appeared that 'blue eyes' had been amused on overhearing Simeon's special 'doggy talk'. This particular gobbledygook was an emotional response, an attempt to communicate with dumb animals so affecting and so loving. That said, a conversation with a Labrador, chocolate or otherwise, was private, causing this well licked youth to be somewhat miffed and slightly embarrassed.

But not for long. The boy, who appeared to be about Simeon's own age, retreated back into his ring binder which, according to the cover, was about somebody called *Maurice*. Hiding behind a shield of apparent 'no eye contact', Simeon was able to study the boy. Strong blue eyes perusing the text were, indeed, quite easy on the eye. A strawberry blond Beatle cut complemented neat attire, fitting a desirable body.

Suddenly, those blue eyes were on Simeon! He was being 'looked at'. To avoid further embarrassment, he abruptly focused on the pleasing proportions of a handsome horse chestnut tree just above the object of his desire. That object was now smiling for the second time and annoying Simeon for the second time. With no intention of continuing with this silly game, the cyclist rose and boldly approached the reader of *Maurice* – whatever *that* was.

"Good book?"

"Excellent!" smiled blue eyes. "But this is a manuscript. It's not a book until it's published."

"What's it about?"

"It's about Maurice."

They both laughed. And that welcome mirth immediately knocked the sharp edges off Simeon's suddenly acquired butch act and enhanced the warmth and sincerity which came across in the confident, but soft, well-modulated voice of 'pretty blue eyes'.

"Tell me all about Maurice," said Simeon, seductively, dropping an octave to a daring purr. He sat down and sidled nearer to pretty blue eyes who, eventually, introduced himself as Paul.

Furtive lust soon dissolved into intense interest as it became clear that Paul was not only a kindred spirit, but an intelligent, articulate university student who was not prepared to accept the bigotry, prejudice and discrimination which, in the 21st century, would come to be known as homophobia.

"*Maurice* is set in the Edwardian period," said Paul. "I've read it three times and each time it's been upsetting, very emotional, very hard going. At a point where a character is set up and arrested for 'gross indecency' by agents provocateurs, I became quite distressed."

Paul was frequently interrupted by questions. He had to explain to Simeon that 'agents provocateurs' were undercover police who tempt homosexuals to commit a 'crime' and that 'gross' indecency simply referred to sex between men. Indecency between a man and a woman was, presumably, neither indecent nor gross! Paul admitted that he gave up on the novel half way through the first reading and was reprimanded by his English professor. He was a friend of one of the selected friends of the author, one of the few who had access to a manuscript.

"You should have stayed with it," remonstrated the professor. "It all turned out well in the end. No matter how harrowing, this powerful work makes powerful points. It has a happy ending."

"Try to understand, Simeon," continued Paul. "I'm not sure I have the skill or impartiality to effectively analyse the full extent of total horror evoked in my queer soul by E.M. Forster's story line. Reading *Maurice* is like watching a process of brainwashing. It is heterosexual society continually *succeeding* in breaking down the spirit of gay men. It shows society being successful in the act of destroying the natural inclinations of a homosexual creature, leaving behind a form of zombie. This element of defeat is so unendurable, so painful, so devastating for me. Having been beaten into submission by all the formidable powers of the heterosexual establishment, the zombie gets married, produces children and leads a cabbage-like meaningless existence, following a path to the grave. I'm determined *that* will *not* be me! Take Clive Durham, a close friend of Maurice in the novel; he is a sickening example. The heterosexual majority had triumphed in this book, and I just wanted to scream out my rage from the rooftops."

Paul came to a halt and looked at the boy who was just inches away from his face. Simeon blinked. He half understood what had been said to him. He had *felt* these things described by pretty blue eyes, but was mesmerised by skills of eloquence and an ability to express a lucid argument with such precision.

"Perhaps," continued Paul, "E.M. Forster was also screaming out *his* rage when he set out these atrocities. But he was scared. He wrote this book for himself. This manuscript, one of just a few copies, is never to be published in his lifetime – only after his death. Isn't that awful! After his *death*! On the other hand, an author can also be God and God can put things right – as he does at the end of this excruciating story."

"Oh," replied Simeon. He was moved by the argument, but not sure what else to say. Paul smiled.

"It's educating as well as painful. Over the years, Maurice Hall fights his way through obstacles which include fear of discovery, fear of blackmail, fear of insanity, the odious baggage of biblical instruction, internalised hate, unrequited love and ignorant aversion therapy which amounted to torture. Hearing of a man's homosexuality, George V was once heard to say – 'Good God! I thought fellows like that shot themselves.' And many did. However, in spite of all the disapproval, prejudice and bigotry – at the end of this novel – the spirit of Maurice is *not* broken. So the professor was right. I *should* have sweated it out – to the end. And what an end!"

Paul leaned nearer and lowered his voice.

"Listen, there's one wonderful moment when a *gorgeous*, rough gardener climbs into Maurice's bedroom in the middle of the night. He gets in bed with him! Wow! It's a Damascene vision when Maurice realises that if the soul can't be true to itself, then life is simply not worth living.

"At the end," continued Paul, "Maurice and his lover go off into the sunset and you *know* that they really do 'live happily ever after'. What a pity that E.M. Forster is too terrified to share his masterpiece in his own lifetime. A book like this could do so much good in the campaign for homosexual equality."

"What's homosexual equality?"

"It's a motif we're hearing more and more. Not here in Bradford and not in the mainstream press, but in London and especially in San Francisco where homosexuals have their *own* newspaper! It's exciting!"

"Well?"

"Well what?"

"What about you? So far I've done all the talking."

Simeon took this opportunity to unburden himself. Martin Harcourt had said tell nobody. But, already he had forgotten about Sam Clifton and had revealed his real name. So much for tight security! Like the waters which burst through Dale Dyke Dam, he gave vent to a deluge of pent up truth about his affair with Ahmed Hamah. He started with the Windsor Bath House, describing his 'golden cage', unknown chickens appearing in the Great Bed, the rules and the death threats, his suspicions regarding child sex, gay on gay abuse including rabid racism which was just one example of the persecuted turning on the persecuted. He struggled to articulate the painful incompatibility with that foreign American of Arab extraction, the uncomfortable silences when there was nothing to say and the good silences, after sex, when the Englishman was snuggling inside the American's jacket, foetal like, listening to his heartbeat. All this, he told Paul.

Paul was listening. He listened carefully to Simeon's puzzling contradictions – an articulate intelligent lover who, at the same time, was rumoured to be dishing out punishment beatings, possibly involved with contract killers! This was the same guy who spoke of 'that chaos we call love, the big chaos that is worth the risk – an enterprise worth embarking on'.

"Sounds like a fantastic man! No wonder you're smitten," said Paul with genuine enthusiasm.

"He was fantastic. He talks poetry. I'd never really connected with poetry until Ahmed spoke it."

Simeon took a moment to recall the exquisite richness of Ahmed's deep base tones when those words of profound meaning were first quoted. He tried to say them to Paul.

"Something like… 'We can die for love'…"

"We can die by it, if not live by love. And if unfit for tombs and hearse, our legend be, it will be fit for verse," corrected Paul.

"That's it!" said Simeon, all excited to hear the original. "Probably Shakespeare."

"No."

"No! What do you mean – 'No'?

"Not Shakespeare. You have the right period, the wrong poet. It was John Donne."

"Oh! Well… come to think of it, Ahmed never actually said *who* it was. Did this same bloke say something about… 'let's have a good feel'? And then end up saying what a great place American was. Ahmed was *always* ramming that one down my throat – USA marvellous – UK rubbish."

Paul's face broke into wreaths of smiles and he shook with laughter. Politely he composed himself, apologised and quoted.

"License my roving hands, and let them go, behind, before, above, between, below. O my America, my new found land."

"You're quite right about a 'good feel'" explained Paul, "but Ahmed was talking about exploring your *body* when he mentioned America! In the same way, the colonies were being explored for the first time when those lines were written 400 years ago. You see, Simeon, Ahmed was paying you a tremendous compliment when he quoted Donne. He was honouring you. He was making a statement about love – and especially his love for you."

Paul noticed the emotional effect on Simeon who was now staring out over the skyline of Bradford, and on much further still, with moist, melancholy eyes.

"Stick with it," whispered Paul, gently. "It's not easy. I have issues with poetry. It seems so personal and exclusive to the writer."

The far away dreamy eyes came back to the lovely Cathedral garden and rested on the blue eyes of his young teacher. Somewhere in his mind he heard the plucking of pizzicato strings. He heard a light adolescent voice sweetly singing out a fragment of lyric, popular a few years before.

'Pretty blue eyes – please come out today – so I can tell you – what I have to say...'

"What?" asked Paul, puzzled by Simeon's sad smile.

"Nothing. I just caught a few words of a Craig Douglas record I use to play. Some lines seem to capture special moments of our lives – and keep bringing them back to us." He looked up at the smiling sun and took a pleasurable deep breath. "Sunshine! It's been a wonderful summer."

"And yet, you and me, Simeon, we hide in the shadows. Just as *you* are hiding now, hiding from...you're not sure what. In the queer world we're disabled by a lack of accurate information. We only know what we are told in this secret world. We stumble around in ignorance. It grieved me in *Maurice* when Clive Durham tells his lover that they are finished! He is giving up – getting married to a woman – surrendering to the majority. The most distressing line in the novel is when Durham says – 'Don't you realise how *easy* it is for *them*' – meaning easy for heterosexuals – easy to be open and above board. Sorry, Simeon. I'm being morbid again. Too much *Maurice!*"

"It's OK, Paul. No sweat. You're an educator and I need to be informed. Christ! It's already gone one o'clock!"

"Harrogate?"

"Yes, I have to keep moving."

"I must be gone and live, or stay and die," said Paul.

"Pardon?"

"Now that *is* Shakespeare!" laughed Paul. "It was Romeo tearing himself away from Juliet after their first, and last night of love."

The garden was still quiet and deserted, so they risked a quick cuddle and a goodbye kiss.

"Take care of yourself, pretty blue eyes. You're needed, you're the future."

"We are *both* the future." replied Paul. "And if we all stick together and work together – we can make it a better future."

CHAPTER 38

Harrogate Royal Baths

The distance between Bradford and Harrogate is a little over 20 miles. A rural route along country lanes had been planned which made the cycle ride a length of about 30 quality miles, including a visit to the 12th century Kirkstall Abbey set in leafy grounds with sycamores sloping down to the banks of the River Aire. It was not quite the idyllic setting the cyclist had anticipated due to a build up of glowering thunder clouds from the unseasonal warmth of mid spring.

Under these threatening, blackening billows and bereft of recent company from Fluff and Paul – Simeon was overtaken by an onset of loneliness. He felt the need for a friendly familiar voice. A GPO Public Telephone Box near the abbey tea shop was a welcome sight. It was one of the new STD [Subscriber Trunk Dialling] contraptions which took a little time to understand. Eventually, he heard the urgent pips and pressed in his silver sixpence to hear leaping excited zeal, the sound of Butch, the sexy black houseboy.

"Simeon! What ya know, sweet meat! Give me ya number before ya change runs out and then hang up, baby." In seconds the phone rang and the cultured strains of Martin Harcourt QC made the magical leap from Nottingham directly into a lovely Yorkshire valley which was about to get very wet. Pleasantries were cut to a minimum in an exchange of data which took on a serious business-like tone.

"I have bad news about your friend Gary Mackenzie."

"Oh God! What?" said Simeon, looking through a rain spattered pane and beginning to feel cold.

"It's usually said that 'no news is good news'. I'm not so sure. Information received suggests that Gary has disappeared off the face of the earth. As you probably know, *my* information is of the best quality. It's not good, Simeon. Gary should have returned to the toad. He didn't. He is not with any of our lot, the Nottingham Camp. He's not contacted or been with any of the Chesterfield low life. Same with Dolly, the Goblin, the Crone, the Gnome, the Jug, the Pig, the...

"The what? I've never heard of 'the Pig'!"

"Good! Keep it that way. He's something to do with Guzzly Granddad. As I gather, a disgusting gloop of obese slime whose main passion in life is to replace toilet paper. A waddling health hazard. Stay away."

Simeon immediately made a link between the bleak Dickensian institution described by Muckles and this character known as the Pig. He would conceal himself in a dark 'pig hole' and make grunting noises to amuse the lads before using his tongue. Martin continued to explain social divisions of the homosexual community in his locality.

"Of course, last year you met examples of the freakish riffraff we refer to as the 'Third Camp' – the *lower orders* as Hoadley would have them described. I have my spies in all three camps. Gary has not returned to the Professor, the one they call 'the skull', or any other member of the 'so called' elite Derby Camp. I've made sure that neither Hoadley nor Hawley are hiding him. He's not turned up at any other homosexual watering hole, neither has he left the country."

"Can you be sure of that?"

"Yes. You'll recall I have a connection with the Special Branch and the Foreign Office. Of course, it's a two way process. We're useful to each other. Mackenzie has not returned to his parents. I mention all this to confirm my credentials. On the other hand, I've failed to crack the security of your Pink Mafia in Detroit and the mystery men, the ones who were enquiring about you. They have completely disappeared."

"Well! *Are* they contract killers, as you suggested? Or are they just private eyes?"

"The fact that they're untraceable proves that they are more than your average sleuth. As to their objectives, murderous or otherwise, it's impossible to say. My original advice to you last Saturday was based on the best available evidence from a number of sources. I stand by that advice. Keep cycling from location to new location. Even if I had you here in *my* house, you would not necessarily be safe. The man who asks to read the gas meter – he might calmly shoot you in the head using a silenced gun which would sound like a sneeze. Nonchalantly, he walks out with a cheery 'thank you'. Make no mistake, Simeon, the people who maintain the security shield of organized crime are ruthlessly efficient and carry out their duties without conscience or pity. Detroit is one of the most dangerous cities in the world and its criminal subculture has everything tied down tight. Your Ahmed Hamah exists alright, but there is absolutely no criminal record or anything at all out of the ordinary which we can trace. On paper, he *appears* to be an all-American, clean cut, blameless, conscientious *student* at Wayne State University!"

"And Gary?"

"Probably still in those caves."

"Dead?"

"I said probably. There is no certainty. You have to face the fact that he *should* have returned to the toad to retrieve his money – quite a large sum of money. He hasn't done so. The Firm, the people of the Detroit criminal underworld have no real reason to eliminate Gary Mackenzie."

"A mistake? They thought they had dealt with me?"

"They don't make mistakes. I was cross with you for entering that world of darkness, a dangerous place with the possibility of encountering dangerous people. It's entirely likely that Gary's been attacked or suffered some accident down there. Who is going to rescue him? Will respectable ambulance staff descend to save a slimy sodomite who loiters in public urinals? If your friend has been badly beaten, will a self-righteous copper lift a finger to bring a gay hating thug to justice? You already know the answer to those questions, Simeon. I don't know where Gary Mackenzie is, but I *do* know that he inhabits a world which regards him with deep disgust, an affront to decency, a pest which should be eliminated. My job and your job, Simeon, is to challenge those evil attitudes.

We must make a better world for gay boys who can love openly in the sunshine. We shouldn't need to descend into an abyss. What's that noise?"

"Heavy rain pelting the phone box."

"You'll be soaked! Where is your next overnight stay?"

"Harrogate."

"Harrogate! Good. Great! Go straight to the Royal Baths, the famous Turkish Bath of Harrogate on Parliament Street and ask to speak to the manager. Don't forget to give your name – Sam Clifton. Jason's a friend of mine. By the time you arrive; he'll be expecting you and he'll know what to do."

"What will he do?"

"First he'll put your bike in a safe, dry place. Second, he'll take one bedraggled, sodden chicken and take off *all* of his wet clothes! Third, he'll place that cold damp chicken in the beautiful, mosaic Moorish steam room to bring you up to an erotically charged temperature. When nicely warmed through and through, you'll be ready to yield to the exquisite ministrations of the legendary Big Bill of Harrogate."

"Who?"

"He's *always* there. He *lives* there! Actually, he lives in a suite at the Old Swan Hotel just across the way…"

"Yes?"

"Sorry, Simeon. I'm just thinking something through. Listen, instead of the Youth Hostel, or your usual basic B&B; how would you like a few nights in a top quality 'old world' hotel, beautifully half hidden by Virginia creeper, renowned for its charm and gracious living?"

"I'd love it! Just two problems, Martin; I forgot to squeeze a dinner jacket into my saddle bag and I'm trying make £250 stretch to a cycling safari as far as possible, and as long as possible. Something tells me that the establishment you describe will soon make a big hole in my precious £250!"

"Don't worry. Your luxury break will be on me and Tommy. You'll dine with Big Bill in his suite. A dinner jacket will not be required. The main advantage – it will be *safe*. In fact, we can risk it for a full week. Who knows, by that time, I may have got to the bottom of this God-awful business. Anyway, what was safe enough for Agatha Christie should be safe enough for Sam Clifton."

Simeon, who was now feeling very cold and a touch miserable, did not wish to show his ignorance by asking questions about a favourite author. However, he was most intrigued by the character called Big Bill who was 'always in a steam room'. Martin assured him that he and that 'mountain of flesh' were practically made for each other.

"You'll find that Bill Bulman is *very* good! He's up to the standard of Guzzly Granddad and that obese American you call Droopy. Bill is distinctive, quite a personality." At this point Martin, using a deep gravelly voice, roared down the phone his impression of a thunderous fat cowboy. 'I'M A LANDMARK IN THESE PARTS!'"

"He's an American!"

"From the Deep South, but an anglophile to boot. Says there is only one place in the world for him – Harrogate – fell in love with it after the war. You'll love him, and he will certainly love you!"

Exiting the phone box, Simeon braved a fast flowing stream which, minutes before, was a dry country lane. He struggled against the wild wind and driving rain to don a rain cape which was pathetically inadequate for the cheerless journey ahead – a journey which would now be as short as possible along main roads. Several thundershowers merged to keep Simeon well soaked under an endless torrent of heavy rain. He pedalled on through the deluge all the way – all two hours of the miserable way – right up through the columns of the impressive portico which announced the grand entrance to the Harrogate Royal Baths which first opened its handsome Victorian doors some 70 years before.

The kiosk lady recognised the drenched chicken as soon as he made an entrance. Self-consciously dripping an embarrassing mess, soggy Simeon paddled through his own puddles which he had brought into the grand foyer, resplendent with mosaics and eastern arches.

"Mr Clifton? Hold on," she said with some urgency, "I'll get Mr Fuller here as soon as possible."

Jason Fuller did not look like a manager of the famous Harrogate Royal Baths. Casual, cosy and comfortable, he looked more like the 'man next door' on any Sunday morning. He asked a passing worker in a boiler suit to move a waterlogged bicycle to the boiler room.

"And that's where these wringing clothes are going," he added. "They'll be bone dry in a couple of hours." His warm voice, sincere and reassuring, held a gentle intonation with no trace of affectation. When you are wet and cold, Jason is the ideal man to meet – a thirty-something with friendly, light brown puppy-dog-eyes on a round smiling face which gave him an appealing child-like innocence and modesty.

Simeon was escorted into the delicious tropical warmth of the main bath, a Palace of Saladin redolent with gentle fragrance of Eucalyptus. As Martin had foretold, he was stripped and grateful to be guided into a medieval Moorish alcove. This small place was home to a Jules Verne like contraption – an ornate complication of plumbing – effectively a cage of pipes giving water jets vertical, horizontal and even a few at 45 degrees, together with one massive rose producing a flow of Niagara proportions from above. It took some time for Jason to open and close all eight valves giving Simeon the best hot shower of his life. Self-effacing and unpretentious he may have been, but this manager was proud of his splendid Cecil B DeMille set. He gave his guest [now decently clad in a large warm, white towel] a brief tour through various decorative rooms which had the feel of an ancient Eastern temple dedicated to the god of pleasure and sensuality. There was the richly tiled Plunge Pool, together with Hot Room Chambers – Tepidarium, Calidarium and Laconium. They entered the dry area and padded over soft, thick pile carpets and progressed through exotic, tranquil halls. These areas of rest beds were resplendent with crafted wooden partitions sporting occasional Arabian motifs to complete the fantasy for recumbent fat bathers – all of them retired with all the time in the world. These were the guilty ones, the soft, flabby, shapeless, old men who furtively observed the only firm body in that plush silence, that serene restfulness which could have been a gentleman's club in London. Much was hanging in that humid air, but little was said.

Simeon knew the rules. Like Derby, the Harrogate Baths were open to the general public – caution and discretion were the watch words. According to Kinsey's figures, 5% of the population are exclusively homosexual, but the reverse was almost always true inside any British Turkish Bath where perhaps one in 20 male bathers attended exclusively for the pleasures of hot steam, relaxation and therapeutic benefits. For many decades before the advent of 'the gay bath house', poorly paid bath attendants gladly accepted big tips to look the other way should they stumbled upon any illegal activity.

Jason and Simeon passed elaborate oaken cubicles with luxurious maroon curtains before they turned back into the wet area and came to the entrance of the steam room.

"I've had a word with our Mr Bulman. A regular fixture and a fine gentleman! He can be abrupt! Don't mind him too much. He can be fierce with a rough manner, but very popular with the staff. Underneath a hard shell, he's really quite courteous and always generous. Anyway, he's expecting you. You'll find him in his usual place, right at the end on the right. A big man, you'll not miss him," said the manager with a twinkle in his puppy-dog-eyes. "Be careful, the steam is quite dense at that end and the lighting's very dim," he added with some unspoken significance.

Pushing on the heavy door, Simeon was hit by an angry, gurgling hissing which seemed to emanate from the subterranean depths of Harrogate. Gingerly, he moved into an opaque blinding fog of hot steam with visibility further limited by inadequate, low powered, amber bulbs. Carefully, slowly, step by step, his eyes gradually became accustomed to the nebulous atmosphere. A cavern was discerned, longer than it was wide, occupied by occasional lumps of flesh, Lords of Lard who silently lurked on stone benches, in dark Turkish recesses on either side. He selected a vacant seat and sat down. The heat felt good. The shower was great, but after two hours of cold rain, these lovely minutes of hot haze penetrated deep into his cold bones. Warmth and relaxation brought him to a point where he closed his eyes, drifted into a lethargic reverie and, for a few minutes, came very close to sleep.

A sudden the touch of flesh! He looked up to see a fat face smiling encouragement to engage in... well, Simeon was no innocent. It reminded him to progress further. He was expected in deeper, denser steam and had yet to reach his objective. That bench, with its uninvited guest, were abandoned and he advanced into an even darker section of the long, dimly lit chamber of erotically charged vapours. The first indication of an oversized bather was the faint glint of something shiny and metallic leaning next to the mosaic wall. On closer inspection, it resolved into the top of an expensive, stout, walking stick – silver, in the image of a bull's head.

Peering into the vapours, he could hazily discern the vague outline of what appeared to be two figures. The first was no fat man and, unusual for that establishment, he was anything but soft. It was the rear view of what Simeon usually described 'a real, solid bloke'. A well-tanned hairy torso was well supported above perfectly formed muscular buttocks. Strong tattooed arms suggested a rough working man, the sort often referred to as 'hairy arsed miners' by coarse, drunken slags who staggered over Heanor Market Place in Simeon's early teenage days. He never thought he would see such a macho bloke, standing to attention, mouth wide open, intoxicated with carnal delight. The voyeur drew closer and was excited hear a deep purring of mounting rapture. At the same time, this real rugged bloke started to arch his back, surrendering his manhood for the delectation of another macho man, a big man, who was seated. Two hands, big hands with pleasure giving digits were busy, wantonly stroking those firm beautiful buttocks. They wandered further, around dangling genitalia and sought out secret places out of sight. Also out of sight, hidden deep inside a fat throat, was a stiff cock. It was begging for release inside a salivating grotto, complete with an experienced muscular tongue, greedily extracting drops of dribble before the final bliss – that final, creamy jet of completion.

The rough workman, now with fast beating heart, breathing steadily, stood still and made no attempt to unsheathe his weapon from a head which seemed fused onto a great pile of blubber. That head was slowly slurping and, for a moment, it looked like 'rough bloke' was staying put, staying in for a second session. Eventually the great gape of Bulman opened and released its spent prisoner, a satiated glistening member – visibly exhausted – in decline, bobbed its way to take rest on a nearby stone bench. Almost at once, Simeon, very close, waiting his turn, felt the pleasure of a big hand cup his bottom, pulling him into that well practiced grotto of ecstasy where his seed would soon join the seed of many who has gone before.

CHAPTER 39

The Old Swan Hotel

He felt dizzy. He stumbled and grabbed at a fellow bather who, concerned, called to the attendant. The dazed patient was sat down. Both men were uneasy, hovering, fussing and twittering solicitously.

"Now then! What's all this? Are you alright?" asked the attendant.

"Too much steam, I should say," said the bather.

"I'm OK. Really! I'm good. No sweat," remonstrated Simeon, feeling embarrassed by all the attention.

At that point, he saw a third man, a very large man, a mass of blubber painfully waddling with the assistance of a strong staff topped with a silver bull's head. This was his first good look at Big Bill Bulman who was slowly approaching, completely naked because no towel was large enough to cover his nakedness. Nude, yet this fat man was completely decent. A meaty apron hung down to his knees covering any genitalia which, presumably, lurked below. He was reminded of Droopy the sad man of the Windsor Bath House with his sad begging eyes. But this was different. This was Bulman, the big man of big voice and big confidence.

"What gives?" he bellowed in deep based gravel in Confederate tones. "Why! Weren't you the little critter arr see in the steam just now?"

"He fainted!" said the bather.

"I didn't!" denied Simeon with some indignation.

"No stamina! Can't take it." responded Bill shaking his great hulk of a head. He looked closer and continued in husky, harsh mode, more akin to reprimand than any bedside manner. "Why – you'll be Sam! You'll be the friend of Martin Harcourt from Notting-*ham*. You got here on bicycle didn't ya? You're pale! When did you last eat, boy?" he barked, brandishing his walking stick.

Simeon lifted his eyes to an elaborate clock on the wall. A few minutes past 6.30pm was indicated. He had completely forgotten to eat since consuming a feast of a breakfast (cereal, full grill with several slices of toast) nearly ten hours before in Bradford.

"Miles and miles pushing pedals up hill and down dale in pouring rain! An hour in hot steam – and you go an *starve* yourself, boy! Why – that is the *dumbest* thing arr ever heard!" He leaned closer to Simeon's face. There was a hint of conspiracy and a twinkle in the eye. When the big man spoke, an element of compassion softened the raucous bawl. "You bin over-doin' it, little guy. Take it easy. I got ta feed ya. Put somethin' back in ya."

This was a coded reference to the lascivious union which had just taken place. A coupling which, having extended past *two* orgasms, had completely drained the 'little guy'. Accordingly, the big guy roared out his demands to the attendant. He ordered the largest item on the Royal Bath menu which was gammon, egg and chips to be served as soon as possible in Mr Bulman's double cubicle which was located at the far end of that plush hall of curtains.

Bill Bulman was the nearest thing to Tennessee Williams' fictitious creation – Big Daddy. He looked and sounded just like that bombastic plantation owner – but Bill also had much in common with Ahmed Hamah. They were both macho homosexuals with a voracious appetite for other macho homosexuals. They both hated effeminate men and harboured an aversion to Negroes. They were also wealthy and unwilling to disclose the source of their considerable wealth. Bill, a man who could have been anywhere from 50 to 70 years old, had many more years of secrecy to conceal.

However, Martin's prediction came true. Simeon and Bill were well matched sexually and well complemented in temperament. Despite his basic white-trash-education and coarse, plantation-field-hand speech, Bulman was not your average redneck. He was a self-taught man aiming for culture. In adult years he discovered England, art and was horrified to find that Simeon, a self-confessed lover of Derbyshire, had never even heard of Joseph Wright, the famous Wright of Derby! The ravenous cyclist eagerly tucked into his large grill and learned a great deal. From a man born in the Mississippi Delta, Simeon heard all about an 18th century artist who was born at number 28 Irongate in Derby. Bill waxed enthusiastically on the skills of this painter who created beautiful contrasts between darkness and light. He raved about moonlight, flames of candles, fire and furnace. In graphic detail, he described 'An Experiment on a Bird in an Air Pump', a disturbing scene which illustrates Wright's skill portraying a range of emotions on the faces of those watching. Simeon, an animal lover, was not impressed. He parried with his knowledge of Derbyshire and the different towns visited. However, the big man was disappointed that the cyclist had never explored his favourite Derbyshire town.

    "Why – you missed the best one!" he bellowed. "Wirksworth is fascinating! Old, *really* old with a wealth of history. Aint ya seen the Puzzle Gardens? You should. Intriguing. Why – quirky miners' cottages, tiny tiny homes perched perilously on the hillside. Yad think they'd all fall over! They're linked by... how would you say... rabbit warren-like walkways. We don't have in the States. You have a name for them...ginnys?"

    "Jitties and ginnels?" suggested Simeon.

    "Right! *That's* what they call those things. Arr can hardly get through them!"

In the days which followed, Simeon enjoyed exploring all the fascinating nooks and crannies of Harrogate. Over dinner in Bill's suite, this student made sure he would not be caught out by embarrassing ignorance of that celebrated Victorian spar, beautifully built in the sombre dignity of dark Yorkshire stone. Weather wise, Saturday, May 14th was like day following night. A cool front had crossed the country clearing away all the rain, all the cloud and all the oppressive humidity. Sparkling sunshine illuminated Valley Gardens, the sheltered park lying in a natural dell which almost reached the handsome frontage of his new home for the week, the Old Swan Hotel. He ambled under the vine covered Sun

Colonnade walkway, and took in a relaxing view of carefully manicured lawns and shady trees – so much nicer in fresher air.

It seemed to Simeon that Harrogate was a town of old folks. He liked that. He warmed to the relaxing tranquillity; an atmosphere of old buildings, old mineral springs with healing virtues where time seemed to have stood still. Some gay people [like Fluff] met their own kind in public houses and city alleyways late at night. Simeon preferred the 'Harrogate method' – sauntering around a scene of dignified architecture, enhanced by mature trees, banks of flowers and well planned parks with wide open spaces of grassland. Rough elements such as queer bashers were not attracted to this sedate environment where older homosexuals could live in peace. Apparently innocent old men, cautiously mooched from park bench to park bench. They admired carefully tended beds of spring flowers with one eye, whilst keeping the other eye alert for another man of similar inclination. In this gentle land of the elderly, Simeon had the advantage of close fitting shorts and a face which deducted several years from its true twenty. His daily strolls tended to attract older, friendly, dawdling gentlemen who were keen to demonstrate their oral skills in well secluded leafy retreats – of which there were many from which to choose.

But Big Bill was no fool! He was a jealous 'mountain of flesh' and managed to thwart the dawdlers by being – Big Bill. It was simple. He kept his chicken constantly drained – eternally empty. From the onset, he made it clear that Simeon was expected to be with him for breakfast, lunch, afternoon tea at the Royal Baths and dinner back at the Old Swan which was always ordered for 7.00pm. Simeon, who was grateful for a regular milking of the highest quality, was more than happy to agree to these strictures.

Indeed, the big man's throaty conversation was informative, thoughtful, cultured – and yet, curiously at odds with his gruff manner. In thick and crusty tones, Bulman was able to deliver intelligent comment on a range of diverse subjects. After dinner on the Wednesday of May 18th, it transpired that he was a regular visitor to The Junction in Bradford and was occasionally appalled by the outrageous and garrulous conduct of Hetty Howitt. That flamboyant queen admitted to 45, but Fluff had been complimentary, suggesting that Hetty, well preserved, could get away with late thirties. Simeon's private estimate was middle fifties. Bill, however, was more experienced, less kind with a sharp eye. He let rip an explosive guffaw.
        "That ol' queen? Forty five! Why, that mendacious bitch! Why, he's a painted *hag*. He done put the clock back some 20 years. When you're there next time – look again. You'll see more art than nature. Check out the little haggard lines at the corners of his eyes. And those eyebrows! Why, they're more black than a nigger's ass; more black than nature ever intended. Huh!"

Bill possessed a curious mixture of innate racism and, for 1966, a progressive attitude to homosexuals. He passed judgement on the actor Alan Bates who had twice stayed at the Old Swan Hotel.
        "Didn't ya know? Why, sure. It's true. He's as queer as a three dollar bill but he don't like it. No, sir. He's paranoid about his lover Peter Wyngarde. Peter told me so himself. 'I have to walk two paces behind Alan. If we go to a party, we can never arrive together. I have to go earlier – or later.' Shit! I wouldn't stand for that! No way. I've been in this place for years and I seen it all. It is so sad. Dirk Bogarde. He's been here

with his boys but… shit… creepin' around the corridors obsessed with secrecy, caution an God knows what! I don't say to shout it from the rooftops but if folks like us could just find the courage to acknowledge friendships… Shit! We should face the world as we are."

He went silent for a moment, staring at a nearby squirrel just the other side of his large window. Bulman was on the western side of the hotel, located on the first floor. His suite was adjacent to a garden deeply shaded by a massive horse chestnut tree, the leafy limbs of which almost invaded his space.

"Would you be ashamed to be seen with me, Sam?" asked Bill in somewhat pleading manner – a sudden step change to soft tone and quizzical appealing countenance. The question came as a surprise. Apart from the baths and in the lush public rooms of the Old Swan, the friendship of 'Sam' and Bill had never been exposed to public gaze in the five days they had now been together. Up to that point, physical contact had been limited to one standing and the other sitting. Simeon now felt it necessary to leave his seat and reassure the big man who was opposite, reposing in his extra strong, custom made, oversized dining chair. At that moment, sensitive and vulnerable, old Bill Bulman basked in the warmth of an affectionate embrace and several kisses from his toy boy. He was assured. Toy boy made it perfectly clear that he would be proud to be seen with such an erudite and cultured gentleman. On another level, Simeon was rebelling from the cruelty of his fellow Detroiters, the discriminatory S&C Coffee Bar chickens who despised the old, the fat and the ugly. As with the toad, in many ways, Simeon found older people much more interesting.

This tender smooch gradually activated the fondling qualities of wandering fat hands. It was like a conditioned reflex which kicked in after several days of so much pleasure from the touching and stroking skills of those fat arousing fingers, now fumbling to release the clasp of his dining partner's trousers. Bill was doing what he did best, playing with his toy boy, arousing a fire in the erogenous regions to extract the last course of what had been an excellent dinner. First dribbles and finally the full flow of seventh heaven as Simeon, pressing high on tip toe, peered through the window into a leafy world of increasing darkness. As if by sheer embarrassment, it sent the squirrel scurrying away along one of the many aerial highways in that great tree.

Conversation following Thursday morning breakfast was more subdued since they both knew that the cyclist would have to vacate his room, leave Harrogate and cycle on to explore fresh pastures. Martin Harcourt had sent the manager of the Old Swan a cheque to cover seven nights in a double room with adjoining private bathroom. As Mr Bulman's guest, the cost of meals, room service, laundry and all other miscellaneous expenses had been settled on his account. Simeon's room, quite opulent, was situated next to the apartments which for the past 20 years had become known as the Bulman Suite. He had enjoyed the same lovely outlook onto the same horse chestnut tree and had made friends with the same squirrel.

It was a sad occasion for man and boy, but the latter reflected with some satisfaction on the huge improvement of his circumstances in this year of 1966. Simeon started life in Horsley Woodhouse, a rough colliery environment of open coal fires, gas lighting in a primitive terrace of tiny draughty cottages. By contrast, the Sultan's Palace of Palmer Heights had been the pinnacle of sumptuous splendour. However, here in England, here on home ground, the Old Swan Hotel was luxurious comfort set within a culture of which he was familiar. Here was something a million miles away from a basic Skegness boarding house. Here was a top notch hotel of high repute, a building as old as the grand old chestnut tree which nearly came through his window. It had character, history and romance. The hard nosed utilitarian ambiance of Detroit could never achieve that level of quality.

A very correct waiter in smart livery deftly cleared the table and respectfully addressed Mr Bulman's guest.

"Compliments of The Manager, sir. Would Mr Clifton kindly spare him a few minutes this morning?"

Worried, Simeon took the thickly carpeted steps two at a time at breakneck speed to get down to Reception to hear what news may have come from Martin Harcourt – the only person who knew he was there. The Manger, tall, perfectly attired with gleaming hair plastered down firmly in place with the power of Brylcreem – imparted extraordinary information.

"Good morning, Mr Clifton. I hope you've not started packing yet?"

Considering the few worldly goods which filled Simeon's small saddle bag, it was a specious question, albeit courteously put. The ragamuffin was in no doubt his presence had been tolerated in this elite establishment at the request of the rich American. It was made clear that the cyclist would dine, at all times, in the Bulman suite. Whilst not exactly encouraged; shorts and casual dress in the public rooms were not actually banned. In addition, the Old Swan was always pleased to fill one if its many vacant rooms and could not afford to displease prestigious and valued customers such as Mr Martin Harcourt QC or the well heeled, if brash Mr William Bulman.

"Should you wish to remain with us," said the manager in haughty manner, "I have good news for you, Mr Clifton. A gentleman has offered to prolong your current accommodation for an indefinite period – on the strict condition that he remains completely anonymous."

It took several seconds for this intelligence to sink in. Eventually, Simeon looked up to the manager and asked him to explain the word 'indefinite'.

"It means a period with no definite end. You could be here for a few more days – or indeed, a few years! Mr Bulman has been a resident here since the November of 1946." He gave the youth before him a superior smile and added – "Quite a dramatic development isn't it? Shades of Miss Havisham – don't you think?"

Having not read Dickens or seen the 1946 film *Great Expectations*, any intended clue was lost on Simeon. He did, however, twig that this camp manager might be gay and quickly twigged that the identity of his mysterious benefactor was as plain as a pikestaff. He liked Big Bill. He liked him very much and had been very happy in Harrogate this past week. Climbing the steps more slowly, he decided that, at the very least, his big friend with big generosity was entitled to know the full truth. He decided to tell Bill that Sam was really Simeon. Then he stopped. No. That would not do! He recalled Martin's comment about the gas man – an innocent looking bloke who might have a deadly sneeze. Yes. He was still under threat of death. Anyway, Bill had said next to nothing about *his* past. How did he become so wealthy? And another argument seemed to come out of the ether from Gary Mackenzie – alive or dead? Gary would certainly say –

"Get real, Kid! Two tons of gloop is besotted with you, puts you right back on cushy cushions in Saladin's Harem; but this time you are the only one! And this time *it is safe*. And what do you intent to do? You are going to tell old fatso all about ravishing

Ahmed! The beautiful young hunk you are still crazy about! That is *real* smart. How will
Big Blubber take that? Will Bill still be inclined to pay the bills? Go ahead – tell the old
cock sucker, but plan to leave the grandeur of the Old Swan Hotel – plan to push real hard
on those pedals through more soaking rain, right up to the next youth hostel. Oh, yes – and
don't forget – do your hostel duty!"

By the time he reached the Bulman Suite, Simeon was back to being Sam and Sam told
him the good news about a mysterious benefactor. Bill acted his part very well. He came
over as genuinely surprised and his delight was absolutely genuine. Toy boy took the view
that – if Big Daddy wanted to play it that way – well, why spoil a good game?
        "It has to be Martin," bawled Bill. "I guess he wants you to enjoy a longer
vacation. Why! If I could – without damaging this dear old building – arr'd surely jump
for joy!"
        "Which brings me to a request, Bill," asserted Simeon, firmly, now boldly
renegotiating a new contract. He had thoroughly explored all the lovely corners of
Harrogate, but had been impeded by Bill's insistence that he must attend lunch and
afternoon tea. This rule curtailed more ambitious ranging such as a visit to Harlow Car
Gardens and a hike to Birks Crags which, he explained to the man with the money, he
would like to do today. Bill was enthusiastic in granting this request. As a man with
limited mobility, he rejoiced in Sam's youth, his health and energy. In bullhorn bellow he
ordered him to –
        "Get right back on that bicycle. Yeah. Scout around York-shire. Enjoy the
summer." Those words shot from Bill's mouth had a positive effect on Sam, who would
now plan several cycling excursions.

In contrast, the large lascivious tongue which stealthy followed those words was silent,
but it had a powerful libidinous effect. It stopped Simeon in his tracks. He was frozen to
the spot. It was Droopy all over again. But this was the big seductive tongue of Big Bill,
a clever tongue which could send Simeon into an orbit of ecstasy. Perhaps that luscious
tongue was the *real* reason to stay in Harrogate. These fat kings of fellatio, Big Bill,
Droopy, Guzzly Granddad – they were a breed employing the same technique. Bill's rude
tongue was big, glistening, promising pleasure. Stuck out – it was obscene – it tempted
– beckoned and mesmerised like a cobra as it had done so often before. And, as so often
before, Simeon subsumed his shame and the abasement of this gross act and released the
dribbling beast with no conscience. It anticipated the rapture of grunts and the sensuality
of slavering slobber. Without uttering one word, that tongue called and its quarry stood
to attention. It moved forward. It yielded to the exquisite delights of an accomplished
master of his art; a master who was going to make very sure that, by the time he released
and drained his victim, there would be very little left for any other rival.

CHAPTER 40

The Ghost

Since the welcome freshness of the previous Saturday, the weather had been an interesting mixture of sunshine and showers. Simeon was entertained by magnificent billows of brilliant white clouds which looked like fantastic castles in the sky. Those castles were even more impressive on this Thursday when the temperature dropped to unusual low levels for late May and forced the hiker to don his warm jacket. For communion with the elements, he retained close fitting white shorts. A north wind seemed to blow him up the Valley Gardens and further still into the Harlow Moor woods where he fussed lots of friendly dogs with lots of friendly dog owners taking the cool air. Harlow Car Gardens on Crag Lane looked interesting, but would have to wait for another day.

He turned into a deepening ravine carved out by a beck which abruptly changed direction to the north east. This was a fascinating landscape of silver birch, ash and oak struggling up between grit boulders which became ever larger – ever higher. Tangled root systems exposed by years of erosion fired Simeon's imagination in the same way as aerial castles far above his head, far above a fairyland of nooks and crannies which might be inhabited by elves, sprites, pixies and imps. The wind picked up, made eerie music through the branches as he pressed on along an enchantment of holly, heather, bracken and moss. Eventually he beheld a gigantic boulder leaning against the hillside, precariously perched on the edge of a great drop to infinity below. This, indeed, was something to rival his beloved Derbyshire! Simeon scrambled up and over this gritty mountain and achieved a westerly grandstand view. It gave on to an endless panorama of purple woodland seeming to dissolve into a distant purple mist, a haze alternatively illuminated by sun and then darkened by fluffy cumulus cloud.

This exhilarating moment was crowned with the triumph of an extraordinary phenomenon for the month of May. It started to snow! It started to snow in brilliant sunshine. He was warmed by the sun – yet cooled by swirls of gleaming, scurrying snowflakes attacking his face and bare legs. This brief blizzard came directly from the threatening black base of one humongous celestial mountain above him. Simeon stood proud and elated enjoying this masterstroke of nature.

His was a solitary safari, up until, looking down to the south, he noticed a dark hooded figure make a brief appearance between the trees, on the rough track, some distance back in the woodland. The rambler was a few minutes from reaching this impressive viewpoint. Accordingly, Simeon decided to wait until the mysterious figure had caught up and would himself want to ascend Birks Crag. Judging by the masculinity of stride and gait, he was keen to have a closer look at this 'hood'.

But the hood never arrived? And this was most strange! Where else could he have gone to? He could not go left unless he fell into an abyss of thorny foliage. He could hardly go right and risk scaling the forbidding and dangerous ramparts of massive grit stone. He did not retrace his steps. A full half hour of watching made sure of it. It was a mystery.

The walk eventually ended in the prosperous residential area of western Harrogate. Using a street map, he navigated around wide and leafy well-to-do roads until he emerged at the Cornwall Road entrance into the Valley Gardens where a public call box caught his attention. Martin Harcourt had to be updated on all developments and received the news of a 'secret benefactor' with mixed feelings.

"I don't like it Simeon! Very nice, plush and comfortable perhaps, but staying in one place? Not too good. It *will* compromise your security. You certainly seem to have turned Bill's head. In the years we've known him, he must have emptied and worn out thousands of dishy dinner guests, but has never actually invested in a resident paramour before. Well..." The barrister went silent for a moment. Simeon could hear him tapping his fingers. "Ok – I won't press you to leave your pleasure zone... for the moment. Keep being Sam and keep vigilant. By the way, how many post cards have you sent to the toad?"

"Just the one from Bradford"

"Good. That must be his last."

"He'll worry!"

"No. He's often a foolish toad but not entirely stupid."

"You'll tell him that I'm safe – won't you?"

"*I* don't tell toads anything! Notwithstanding, I promise you this: toad will be told three things: Simeon is comfortable, Simeon is well but, for the time being, Simeon has been advised to be silent. You've already explained to him your predicament. He'll understand."

After replacing the receiver, the weary hiker made slow progress through the Valley Gardens back to his hotel and wondered if he should have mentioned the mystery of the black hood.

The following weeks passed very pleasantly. Years later, Simeon looked back on these happy Harrogate days as an idyllic interlude to be savoured. His relationship with Bill remained warm, affectionate and erotic. On a few occasions his 'slave state' streak of racism raised its ugly head such as after dinner on the Saturday of May 21st.

"Niggers have ruined the fight game!" he bellowed. "Arr see that Cassius Clay has beat the shit out of your Henry Cooper today. Bad. Real bad. That Ubangi! Why, he was dancin' around that ring braggin' an' thumpin' his black chest like King Kong!"

Not wishing to confront the bigot directly, Simeon changed the subject to Nobby the Gnome. He spoke of his past, his adventures in an effort to draw a parallel with racism and the discrimination suffered by homosexuals. Bill did not become a convert, but he was impressed with his friend's zeal and his ambition to write a gay history, to set down what had, heretofore, never been set down. This led to the surprise appearance of a new typewriter in his room on the following Monday, with several reams of paper. The enthusiastic author spent several days tapping away to an intrigued squirrel, making notes, recalling Nobby's words and using the resources of Harrogate Library to fill in the gaps. The resulting work of many pages contained references to Sheffield Sam, the Dale Dyke Dam disaster, the Meadows of Old Nottingham and Nobby's tragic First World War love affair with Ron Thompson. These pages, read with interest by the encouraging American, became the inspiration and foundation for *Nobby: True Tales of a Naughty Gnome* which was eventually to be published 56 years later in 2022.

On the Friday, June 10th, during a wet morning of research in Harrogate Library, Simeon had another curious experience akin to the incident of the black hood. He was in the reference section, searching out information on Dale Dyke Dam, looking for books which might mention Sheffield's Victorian water supply. Scanning tomes along the appropriate shelf, suddenly, he came upon a gap giving on to the next aisle. In that gap was a face! It was a familiar face! It was a black face, more black than the self-proclaimed 'pretty face' of Cassius Clay and more African in its features. This face had the classic features of the quintessential Negro – wide nose, big round eyes and big thick lips which, for this white boy, had a powerful aphrodisiac effect. After barely a quarter second, the face moved away to the right. Simeon moved to the right. As fast as the fastest walk could move him, he shot to the end of that wall of books to confront the face and its owner. Nobody there! There was no one in the aisle. He checked the other five aisles – nobody at all! It was all very quiet. The librarian at his desk had seen no one. The other guy on that floor, reading at a table, said the same. As a last ditch attempt, Simeon rushed to a window with a view down on to the street and, unsurprisingly for Harrogate, saw only white faces. After several thoughtful minutes, he made a slow return to a table cluttered with books and sheets of scribbled notation – now being perused by a youth in tight jeans under a mop of untidy sandy hair.

"Oh! Sorry! Sorry to be so cheeky. I'm intrigued! I've been reading your stuff about," he looked down at the paper, "Nobby the Gnome," said the guy who had just been questioned.

"No problem," said Simeon, cautiously, embarrassed because association with the antics of Nobby the Gnome would certainly damage his 'straight' credentials.

"Too bad I couldn't help you find that Negro. Friend of yours?"

"Yes…" said Simeon hesitantly. That is, he *was* a friend, if he's still alive."

"I don't understand. You just told me and the librarian you saw a Negro?"

"Sorry to be vague. Laurent may be a ghost. Although, of course, that's all nonsense," replied Simeon, more to himself than to the youth. "I *thought* I saw him at Birks Crag, about a fortnight back. He was wearing a black hood. It was his walk. You know, the way he moves. But… he disappeared…"

In the emotion of the moment, Simeon found himself telling a perfect stranger about Laurent, his association with the Detroit mafia and fears for that young man's safety.

"It could be your imagination? The mind sometimes plays tricks. And we do worry about our friends. It sounds to me like you were quite good friends," added the youth, significantly, as they both sat down.

This signalled a change in the conversation. When two gay boys come together in these circumstances, each has to be very careful. Society is hostile to sexual deviation, making it necessary for each party to send out feelers testing for reaction. Each party tries to read body language, maintains eye contact to gleam any friendly or unfriendly messages subtly communicated by minute changes in facial expression. The boy offered Simeon his hand and his name – Mark. Simeon played safe and stayed with Sam. The hand was warm, delightful to the touch, and maintained that sweet touch for several seconds, longer than would have been normally acceptable. Tête-à-tête – closer than would have been usual for two boys – Mark, an upbeat teenager, did most of the talking and all the messages from those enthusiastic dancing eyes were very encouraging – very friendly.

A year before, Mark was living with his typical middle class parents and two older sisters in Leeds until one chance remark changed all their lives and inflicted horrendous damage on that family. Responding to a newspaper item, one sister said –
        "Dirty sod! He should get more than that. Two years is no good. Corrupting the young! It's terrible. It's these teenage lads experimenting with sex together. That's what it is. It turns them queer. You see if it doesn't."
        Mark was incensed by an unjustified draconian punishment inflicted on a teenage boy for committing an act of 'gross indecency' with a younger teenage boy. Unknown to his sisters and mother, they were Mark's friends, consenting partners who were deeply in love. During an impassioned drama, he attempted to reason with these three ignorant women who ganged up on him, shouting him down with outraged bigotry. At the height of the fury, Mark attacked his family using his most potent weapon. Aiming directly at that brick wall of prejudice – he fired a missile – his own homosexuality. He told them he was queer. Into the stunned silence which followed, this intelligent and articulate student tried to educate, tried to explain the reality of being a homosexual.
        "If teenage boys can be 'corrupted' to be homosexual, then why wasn't *I* corrupted into being a heterosexual? Don't you understand? I was *born* a homosexual in the same way that the girl next door was born a redhead and the chap at the corner shop was born with dark skin. All my life I've seen boys kissing girls and men marrying women. Why hasn't that turned me?"

With his back against the wall, Mark had nowhere else to go. His earnest appeal failed to produce the understanding and tolerance for which he had hoped. It did have one effect. It made him homeless. Not at once – there followed further recriminations during which he was urged to seek medical 'help'. He refused. Simeon was horrified to learn that Mark was kicked out of the house he has lived in for 18 years. He spent months of vagrancy on the streets of Leeds during which time medieval 'bible bashers' in the Salvation Army, taking full advantage of his emotional weakened condition, nearly broke his spirit with the repeated mantra – 'You can't help what you *are*, but you can help what you *do*'.
        "It was so insulting! But that was last winter," said Mark. "In February I met Edward. He gave me a home, work, self-respect and love. We're very happy together, in spite of an age gap of 25 years. Hey! I'm *really* excited about your Nobby the Gnome stories and your friendship with the Negroes of Detroit. You see, Edward... well, it's like this: he's a senior lecturer at Leeds University and he's researching a thesis exploring all this stuff which is going on now."
        "What 'stuff'?"

"Stuff like civil rights, women's lib, free love, Swinging London, the King's Road in Chelsea, hippies, Twiggy, Mick Jagger, Bob Dylan, Joe Orton – it's all happening, man!"

"Is it?"

"Look I'm trying to explain…" Mark was interrupted by a warning shush from the librarian. He continued sotto voce. "Edward thinks that something really big is happening and we, the queers, are going to be a big part of it. The hippies don't care if we hold hands and cuddle in the park and I read in the paper that 63% of Britons are in favour of abolishing the law against us. Did you know that it carries a maximum penalty of life imprisonment? Just for a bit of sex! Anyway, Edward says the 'baby boom' generation are coming out to play – and that is *us*, Sam – you and me – hip young homosexuals seizing the moment – on the move – it's a social revolution attacking stuffy traditions – burying the bigots…"

"I *must* ask you to keep your voice *down*!" said an angry librarian who was now menacingly standing over them.

"Sorry," said Mark, a touch miffed as they were the only two on that floor. "What I'm *trying* to say is this: Edward is investigating connections between all these things. If women and black people can make progress, then so can we."

Simeon caught sight of an enraged librarian who was now close to evicting them. Quickly he gathered his work and returned the books from whence they came. The two new friends left the building and walked down the street to the wide open space of West Park. Here, under big skies, there was room for more enthusiasm and more volume about Swinging London. It exploded from the exuberant Mark.

"This is *our* decade, Simeon! I can feel it. It's the world capital of toleration and liberation. You should get down there. Same in New York and San Francisco – old attitudes are being thrown out like old clothes. I just want to do cart-wheels!!"

Down Prospect Hill he nearly did! Fortunately the magnificent terraced flowerbeds outside Betty's Tea Rooms calmed Mark down. Simeon said he would like to have invited his over-wound pal back to the Old Swan for lunch. But, he too lived with an older man, a *much* older man who may well be jealous. Or worse, he might even roar out a demand for sex! An instinct told Simeon that slim, sexy Mark would *not* be excited at the sight of the flowing fleshy folds of blubber which comprised the massive bulk of big Bill Bulman.

CHAPTER 41

Leeds

The sadness of parting was mitigated when Simeon accepted an invitation to stay with Mark and Edward three weeks later during the weekend of July 1st returning to Harrogate on July 4th.

"I'd have you over tomorrow, but it's the first free weekend we have and I'd like to show you around Leeds – my hometown – I love it!"

"Leeds? That's about 20 miles. I could cycle it in about three to four hours."

"It's nine miles. You could walk it. I often walk to Harrogate. We live *this* side of Leeds, in Harewood."

"You live in Harewood House!"

"Not so grand as that," laughed Mark, "but Edward has a very nice home. We live in Harewood *village*. It's just outside the park of Harewood House. Here's the address. Arrive at about five, dinner's at seven."

There was a pause. In half smile, both boys looked at each other. To Simeon's surprise, Mark blurted out –

"*I'm* not ashamed of my sexuality."

"Nor I," responded Simeon, in defiance.

"In London, boys kiss boys."

"Really!"

"It's illegal you know – kissing boys. Homosexuality is supposed to be an illness."

"Nonsense!" barked Simeon.

"And the police treat us like criminals," added Mark checking his watch. "Anyway, you'd better not keep your friend waiting for his lunch. Know what?"

"What?"

"Let's throw caution to the wind!" At this, to Simeon's horror, directly in front of dozens dining at Betty's; Mark lunged at his new pal enveloping him in a big hug and pressing one powerful kiss. With fleet of foot, typical of athletic youth; he ran up to the War Memorial, stopped, looked back, waved and blew a second kiss. Simeon was stunned! Conscientiously, he avoided eye contact with the proper and decorous senior citizens who were resting on benches in the terraced gardens. Equally, he steered clear of shocked expressions which might be seen on the faces of the sedate and the serene who were politely nibbling and chatting in the prestigious Betty's on his left. Slowly, with dignity, he walked down towards the Royal Pump Room Museum en-route to the Old Swan Hotel and lunch with Big Bill.

Simeon was also conscientious about cycle routes. On Friday, July 1st he pedalled up Valley Drive and thereafter made best use of all quiet country lanes through Harlow, Burn Bridge, Kirkly Overblow and into Harewood village set out in the 18th century with terraced houses of dark grey stone. The exception was his destination. A more experienced observer of that mellowed ivy-clad facade would have said – 'Oh yes, Jacobean'. And he would have been wrong. It was a fine example of Jacobean *style*. Nevertheless, Edward's house, built by his grandfather in 1907, possessed many admirable features including a handsome stone fire place, a rich panelled staircase lighted by a two storey large leaded window which Simeon found as delightful as the secluded garden. The tranquillity of this quiet backwater, eminently suitable for Simeon, was a contrast to Mark's animated personality and his passion for 'Swinging London'. As he put it –
    "The place to be, man – hip and fast – celebrating the present – not the past."

And Edward was certainly a contrast to Mark. He was a prematurely grey forty-something, gracious and friendly, sharing his lover's optimism in the NOW and the future, but at half the speed. With impeccable courtesy, he steered the after dinner conversation around areas of agreement.
    "I'm with you there, Sam," said Edward in a refined voice. "This stubborn culture of effeminacy in homosexual circles has never sat well with me. Your macho friend at the Old Swan, well; he sounds like quite a character. The Old Swan! And you a writer! I do hope you're not parading under an assumed name in an effort to escape a doomed love?" Simeon's face contorted into an expression of horror. So much so, his host became quite alarmed. "My dear boy! What did I say? I assumed that you must have seen the plaque in the hotel lobby?"
    "What plaque?" croaked Simeon, so hoarse that he made a second attempt to improve clarity. "Sorry – I said – what plaque?"
    "It simply commemorates the fact that Agatha Christie was found there in 1926, a few weeks after she went missing. Loss of memory it was claimed, but it's never really been explained to *my* satisfaction. Following the discovery of her abandoned car, at great expense to the tax payer, there was a nationwide police hunt. It was interesting. She *claimed* to have no recollection of how she'd travelled from Surrey to Yorkshire, yet she signed in as a Miss Neele? Neele was the name of Colonel Christie's lover! I find that rather suspicious. What do *you* think, Sam?"
    "I don't know what to think!" said Simeon, trying not to sound too defensive. He knew exactly what to think. At lease it explained Martin's cryptic reference to that author, but his own odd behaviour: that was another matter. It alerted Edward to the fact that 'Sam' might have something to hide. The academic, thoughtfully stroking his chin, was studying and reappraising his weekend guest when Mark cheerfully broke the tension with encouraging praise for Sam's entertaining Nobby stories.
    "You should read it, Edward. What a find! A destitute little queer with a wealth of oral history in his head!"
    "I must say," said Edward, grateful for the change of subject, "it's an inspired idea, telling our story through the eyes of an indigent gnome. Well done, Sam."

After a leisurely start to Saturday, they arrived in Leeds in time for lunch at The Flamenco, a coffee bar situated not far from the River Aire and near to the Corn Exchange. From the outside, the café looked a touch seedy. Inside it was clean and patronised by a preponderance of respectable looking male diners who, with interest, noted the entry of the three newcomers. This informed Simeon that he was in a gay venue. *In Thoughts of You* by Billy Fury was playing on the juke box when they sat down. Hearing that very special voice, an emotional link with his adolescence, coupled with the painful memory of Ahmed's cruel act of vandalism, put Simeon into a nostalgic, melancholy brood. Mark broke through that moody haze with an enthusiastic commentary.

"It's good fun, good food and very popular with gay men 'cus the owner's gay. We're lucky to get a place by the window. There're usually all taken," added Mark with a cheeky grin.

"I like to look out at the world," said Simeon, musingly.

"Mark is trying to tell you, Flamenco customers, particularly, have a special interest in that part of the world which is just over the road," smiled Edward.

Simeon was puzzled. He looked over at a monolith of Victorian engineering, huge stone arches which supported a railway line above them. Each of the semi-circular structures housed several down-at-heel shops, one scruffy garage and a cobbling business.

"He hasn't seen it," said Edward.

"The hole in the wall," whispered Mark with a little giggle. "You must tell Nobby the Gnome about it. Once in, you'd never get him out! That whiffy urinal is well over a hundred years old. Very busy. Very *active*. Some of them sit in here all day long keeping an eye on potential trade."

Over a tasty lunch, lots of men passed in and out of the notorious 'hole in the wall'. One caught Simeon's attention – a well-built teenager, rough, common with dirty blond hair. Suspiciously, he was in and out for the best part of half an hour. With an enticing cruel squint and the other eye looking as if it had been recently blacked, Simeon was reminded of Ron Thompson as described by Nobby. But the men best remembered in Leeds on that summer afternoon were to be seen in Thornton's Arcade. Robin Hood, Gurth the Swineherd, Richard Coeur de Lion and Friar Tuck were part of a very interesting old clock – the first two figures striking the quarters and the second two striking the hour.

Edward's lucid knowledge and Mark's zeal presented Leeds in its best possible light. Simeon did not expect it to be a beautiful city, but beauty was shown and explained. He was taken to the 'pride of the city', the impressive but blackened Leeds Town Hall.

"Completed in 1858," said Edward, "It needs a good clean. The original stone work, biscuit-colour, was quite attractive. You're looking at decades of industrial grime."

Very kindly he was treated to dinner at The Royal, paid for on Edward's new Barclaycard, Britain's first credit card which had been introduced just days before. This old coaching inn on lower Briggate, discreetly equipped with a 'gentleman only' bar, was the oldest homosexual venue in Leeds. Leaving the restaurant and entering the male only preserve, Simeon expected to step into Yorkshire's answer to The Friary in Derby, effectively an exclusive 'gentleman only' zone for staid suits of sneering snobs. Here in down-to-earth Yorkshire, he was pleasantly surprised. The Royal held a licence for music and dancing making it attractive to young people. Cramped into a small space called the 'rock an roll' floor, about 50 men were twisting and writhing to exciting strains coming from another juke box. By coincidence, someone had selected a record which again evoked a heartrending memory of Ahmed. It was the same record by The Ronettes, the same thrilling vibrato voice which had filled Sam's car and filled Simeon's eyes with tears two months before. On the line –

'And would I die, if you should ever go away...'

Once again, he was nuzzling under the shirt, into that magnificent torso, breathing in that body scent, protected by those powerful arms, enveloped by that controlling forceful love. And again, utterly miserable in a place where he was supposed to be happy.

This atmosphere was picked up by Edward and Mark who were patient and kind. Something was wrong; they were not sure what, but were tolerant and compassionate. Years later, Simeon could stand back and analyse that situation. His mood was triggered by a combination of longing for Ahmed and, at close quarters, empathising with a successful relationship between two self-sufficient contented men. Mark and Edward were a good example of a stable couple. They were bonded by, not just the cement of love, but also a shared passion to improve the quality of life for all homosexuals. They moved in a world often dysfunctional, a world often promiscuous, and yet, against all the odds, appeared to rise above the unsettling chaos of that world.

A visit to the feisty and raucous Hope and Anchor was suggested. This was an old lesbian pub in a quaint, if seedy Victorian area, near the river. It was managed by two women who were friendly to gay men and hostile to unwanted heterosexuals who occasionally came in to 'take the piss' as Mark put it.

"Don't cross Punch! That's the butch one. She uses a truncheon to drive out the yobbos. Judy's more of a lady: the landlady actually, but her tongue can have a nasty edge when called for. Let me show you the river."

Simeon was guided through a back door into welcome fresh air, into a space where several men stood drinking, chatting looking over the water. It was already quite late, minutes before closing time, and quite dark. Beyond a short stretch of long grass, glinting silver under sharp moonlight; the river looked very black indeed – but Simeon was not looking at the river. The grass was more interesting. It moved! It moved because of illicit activity such as the rise and fall of bare buttocks, pink globes which caught weak light from the open back door. The boys became mesmerised by several bottoms making similar appearances above that grass.

"I thought it might cheer you up," laughed Mark.

It did. Sunday passed delightfully in a local walk along the River Wharfe, all the way to Wetherby and back, following a pub lunch. On the Monday morning after breakfast, an affectionate farewell included embraces and heartfelt good wishes. Simeon cycled off, was waved off, until out of sight.

CHAPTER 42

We can Die by it, if not Live by Love

It was good to be back at the Old Swan. In reception, Simeon was greeted by a humongous vase bursting with fresh expensive flowers and, as ever, the fat clock on the chimney-piece ticked with a heavy comfortable regularity. Here in the large chairs there would always be time to relax, to escape from the cares of 1966 to a past world decades before. He located the famous plaque commemorating the Agatha Christie incident of December 1926. Perusing those words, suddenly, the peace of the old hotel was shattered by a loud elation! A great roar of welcome resounded through the adjoining public room from a great fat man reposing in his favourite easy chair at the far end. They all looked! Big Bill, thrilled to have back his chicken, took leave of his customary caution. No matter, Simeon was equally thrilled to have been so missed.

After lunch he was even more thrilled. That big welcome home was consummated in noisy, coarse, corporeal form in the privacy of the Bulman Suite. Protected by a giant custom-made napkin from neck to knee, Bill was a ravenous and messy eater. It was a deep dark secret, well hidden in the depths of Simeon's psyche. He would never admit it to respectable friends like Mark and Edward, but when it came to 'afters', Simeon swallowed his shame and *encouraged* Bill to make a pig of himself. Those disgusting grunts, moans and slurps sent the young man into a spin of euphoria, so welcome after such a well-mannered celibate weekend.

For convenience, Simeon had fallen into the habit of phoning Martin Harcourt from the rather sumptuous public telephone glass closet situated between reception and the main public room in the Old Swan. Martin knew something of Edward's valuable work and was pleased the weekend went well. However, he continued to express concern that Simeon, already resident at the Old Swan for over seven weeks, may well be a 'sitting duck' for any hostile element who may have a murderous duty to discharge.

"Don't think that I haven't agonised over this, Simeon. Some days I tell myself that you're in the safest place of all. Who the hell is looking for Sam Clifton at an antiquated hotel in a quiet backwater of Old England? My man tells me you are fine..."

"What man! Is he a black man?"

"Sorry. I shouldn't have said that. That's the problem! The longer this thing drags out, the more chance that we make mistakes. Anyway, he's not *my* man. He's an agent watching over you and you mustn't start getting paranoid about every man you see with a turban and long black beard."

For various reasons, Simeon had never mentioned the incidents of the black hood and the black face in Harrogate Library. In that split second, he could not be positive about the identity of any face. Many Negroes shared Laurent's African features and Simeon was too embarrassed to admit the possibility of ghosts to an eminent down-to-earth QC.

"Don't worry about it," continued Martin. "See him as a guardian angel."

"I don't see him at all."

"Good. That means he's doing his job well. Regarding the Old Swan: let's agree to split the risk. You can stay until the end of the month. Then you must cycle on as before, B&B to B&B, throughout the month of August returning to your present home in September. What do you say?"

"I say Bill will never stand for it! After this weekend with Mark and Edward, absence has certainly made the Bulman heart grow fonder. He's already announced a treat for this coming weekend: a chauffeur driven ride down to London from July 8th returning on Monday 11th."

"That'll be nice for you. Educational too. Of course, you must be prepared for a very slow waddle around all the main art galleries."

"That – and Mrs Shufflewick at the Black Cap in Camden Town."

"That's Bill! A mixture of high culture and low life. But seriously," continued Martin, "after breakfast on the Sunday of July 31st you *must* tell Bill that you need to leave for at least one month. Tell him that you need a change – a cycling holiday in Scotland – you need to be alone – you have certain business to attend to. Anything – but you *must* follow my instructions. I've been discussing this with my colleagues. After a further month, September at the Old Swan; we feel that you will *probably* be clear. It's not a certainty, but, likely as not, you'll be safe as Sam – or – even as Simeon."

"Assuming, of course, that Bill will continue to pick up the tab in September! Martin! Tell me this. Why do you come to this... consensus... conclusion – it will be 'probably safe'?"

"We don't know, Simeon! That's the truth. But it's odds-on that the Detroit elements are not going to search for you forever. Even Ahmed's gang wouldn't be able to afford that. Our agent is not just looking *at* you; he's also surveying the field *around* you. There's not been the slightest hint of any surveillance whatsoever. That activity probably ended in Derbyshire and Nottinghamshire. If true, it's good news. The August cycling trip is a precaution. If this thing ends badly, *I* need to know that I've done all that I can. Promise you'll do as I ask."

The promise was given. After replacing the receiver, Simeon went into a brown study. He stared out over the plush reception area with unseeing eyes. Martin had used the term 'agent'? MI5? MI6? Special Branch? Secret Service? With a twinge of guilt, he considered the expense of an 'agent' watching over him for seven weeks – not to mention the weeks to come. He recalled Edward's comment about Agatha Christie being a burden on the taxpayer – and all for nothing!

The following weekend was another success. Simeon learned more about paintings and was intrigued to be entertained by Mrs Shufflewick in the flesh. There were no televisions in 1950s Bog Hole row in Horsley Woodhouse, but on at least two occasions, Simeon saw this amusing woman. It was on a one hundred guinea PYE 17inch 'Luxury Console' in a more affluent area at the top of the village. As Mrs Shufflewick was Simeon's first experience of television, he was shocked to learn [from of all people, a man of the Mississippi Delta] that Mrs Shufflewick was *not a woman*! After the show, Bill proudly introduced his toy boy to Rex Jameson, the drag act who created Mrs Shufflewick. Of course, the boozy dame of Camden Town ten years on was a far cry from the comedienne who appeared before millions on the solitary BBC television channel. Lines like – 'After the boat race, I was taken to meet the team and kissed their cox' – would have been wasted on Simeon the child.

TV was also much in mind when the impressive proportions of the Bulman Suite were graced with the appearance of a large COSSOR. It was a handsome set housed in a walnut veneered cabinet. The Old Swan had a designated TV lounge, but Bill was not prepared to share the forthcoming World Cup football match of England v West Germany with anybody else. As usual, Simeon and Simeon's seed were required for lunch – but, thereafter on that Saturday afternoon of July 30th – the big man was not to be disturbed under any circumstances short of a life-threatening fire. Damaged by painful memories of humiliations on the Heanor Town Ground pitch, Simeon had a horror of football and was not at all offended when ordered to keep well away from that all important match.

On the contrary, the cyclist was rather thoughtful, rather sad. He was wondering how to break the news to his friend that he must cycle off to undisclosed destinations for the month of September, which would begin on the Monday. Back in his room, he picked up a photograph recently signed 'Sincerely, Rex Jameson' (Mrs Shufflewick). There were three men looking out of that glossy black and white effort – Simeon Hogg, Rex Jameson and Bill Bulman. It was Simeon's only photograph of his friend Bill. On the back, in an unsteady hand, he had written –
    'For my dearest and best friend, Sam Clifton. In fond memory of the happiest weekend of my life. Old, ugly, but I'll always be <u>your friend</u>. Faithfully with affection, Bill Bulman.'
    He took the photograph over to the window and placed it carefully, reverently on the windowsill, slowly lifting his head to the great tree to locate the squirrel. It was not there. Indeed, not much could be seen of the boughs and leaves through a vale of tears shed for a fat man who trusted him – loved him – an essentially decent man who had been lied to, shamefully deceived. He looked again at Bill in the picture, and it occurred to Simeon that he did not possess one single photograph of Ahmed. Considering his line of work, perhaps that was to be expected. On the other hand, there were no photographs of Ahmed and Simeon *together* – and that was more than sad, it was tragic. The most important love of his life – and no photographic record of that great love.
    He sniffled, needed to dry his eyes, blow his nose. He went to the drawer to get a clean handkerchief and noticed a sheet of paper inscribed with a few lines of familiar handwriting.
    "We can die by it, if not live by love. And if unfit for tombs and hearse, our legend be, it will be fit for verse."

Simeon recognised the unmistakable, strong, bold handwriting of Ahmed Hamah.

CHAPTER 43

Figure in Deep Shade

He stared down at this paper for many seconds. He seemed to be looking through it, in a fruitless effort to locate more information. At that moment, the reader desperately needed to unlock the meaning of a conundrum, first heard up a beech tree, from the lips of Ahmed in the early spring –

"We can die by it, if not live by love. And if unfit for tombs and hearse, our legend be, it will be fit for verse."

Now, with pantheistic instinct, he was staring into the midsummer richness of a massive, horse-chestnut tree, desperately trying to extract comfort, reassurance, from that big-leafed world of deep green. Those enigmatic words, first spoken in a distant tree, came over as threatening. And yet, a boy with beautiful blue eyes in the garden of Bradford Cathedral had given quite a different interpretation to the words of John Donne. Paul had said that Ahmed was honouring Simeon. He desperately wanted to believe Paul, because, at this moment, another interpretation was possible. Was Ahmed mad with love? This note: did it announce his arrival? He might step out of the shadows at any time! He might smile, take the fugitive in his arms and give one last cuddle and perhaps one last kiss before extinguishing the life of a renegade. It was also possible to reconcile both interpretations. A fiery Arab may wish to honour his lover with poetry just before making sure that no other person will ever taste his flesh again. If Ahmed was in the Old Swan, he would know about Bill – and that infringement of 'the rules' would never be tolerated. Such went the thoughts of Simeon who now felt quite defeated.

Through the open window came a fat man's roar from the adjacent suite. Had Bill been executed? No. More likely a goal had been scored. He looked back at the sheet of paper. It was certainly not there before lunch. The staff treated Simeon's room as an adjunct to Bulman's domain. Gratuities were regular and generous. They ensured a superior level of service from waiters and especially chambermaids who were thoroughly conscientious. Each day after breakfast, Simeon's accommodation was serviced, left spotless and severely tidy. That note had been placed on that surface when Simeon was eating with Big Bill.

He felt the need to get out. He rushed down the stairs, through reception, past the beautiful cut flowers, through the main entrance and turned right along the front of the building which was covered by mature, extensive Virginia creeper, now in full glory. To his left, there was a blaze of colour from neat flower beds. Beyond, smooth well-tended lawns ran down to where York Road blended into Swan Road. It was all brilliantly illuminated by the well-remembered summer sunshine which kissed England on that famous day of English triumph.

But round the corner to the west side of the Old Swan; it was different. Here was the domain of the squirrel, an area of deep shade underneath the Bulman Suite which received less attention from the team of gardeners. Entering this pleasant coolness, Simeon felt safer. Perhaps he would commune with the tree spirits – the dryads, soliciting their protection from harmful elements in a far away concrete jungle. As usual, it was deserted, quiet and peaceful. Even more so today, since the world was indoors watching television. He followed the dark damp path underneath the great horse-chestnut and came to the edge of an old bowling green, more moss than grass, beautifully decorated with dancing flashing sun mottles intruding into the gloom. Just beyond, a neglected pond reflected sun dapples glinting and sparkling around shimmering limbs of dark trees. He looked hard, looked down deep into that earthy mirror. There he saw a parallel world with a dark blue sky, a tempting world, deep below to which he might try to escape. Simeon looked up, and turned round to take in the view of laurel and holly shrubs beyond the span of the big tree, when he noticed a figure standing in the blackness of deep shade. Blinding dapples and sun speckles became even more excited when stirred by a light breeze high in the horse-chestnut canopy. To avoid the glare, Simeon took a few steps forward and identified a man. It was Ahmed Hamah.

A strange moment: he thought he would be frightened, but Simeon was relieved. Whatever was to come was here now. It was over. Cool intellect told him that he was in danger. His heart told him something else. He was elated. It felt like that moment back on January 8th when he was seized, shaken like a rag doll, yet, did not struggle *too* hard to escape from the arms of a beautiful young man. He had thought of paradise then. Perhaps now, *this* garden had indeed become paradise.

It was a bizarre situation. Simeon ran. Simeon ran into the arms of that beautiful young man who may well have received orders from higher authority to execute him. But now, he was taking advice from John Donne – if you can't have that one great prize of love, then life is simply not worth living. Maurice had said the same – if you have to live a lie, you may as well be dead. And with these thoughts giving comfort and courage, Simeon's whole mind and body surrendered to that stunning stud, that raw masculinity which had dominated his consciousness during the previous seven months. He buried his head, nuzzled it up into that powerful, firm torso of such perfect proportions and drank deep of the familiar warm body scent. He yielded into incarceration, submitted to the superior strength of those masculine arms. In the emotion of the moment, a very expensive shirt was smeared with silent tears of relief from melted eyes, firmly closed with embarrassment.

On this warm summer's day, there was no need to cuddle up inside that bomber jacket as had happened on the night of May 2nd / 3rd in the State Bedroom of Sultan's Palace. On that that terrible, lonely night in Detroit, Simeon was seized with a paroxysm of grief and despair. On that night he was desperate. From that empty jacket; he tried to draw in some spirit, some actuality and some essence of the man he loved. Now he had the real thing. Now he was composed. He showed his face and looked up into those familiar deep pools which were also moist from emotion. They were slowly twinkling to a smile, when another obese roar escaped from the open window above.

"We're winning, Booby!"

"Are you on our side?" asked Simeon, in an unsteady voice.

"I've always been on your side," he said gently. I've been at your side from the moment I first laid eyes on you. I've never stopped loving you – and I'm real sorry I scared you." He motioned to a seat next to the mossy bowling green. They sat down. "I've had a bad press, but can't complain. That 'bad press' has been encouraged. Fear has been useful. It's served The Firm well. We need fear. We need discipline. Know, Booby; we're branded as criminals anyway. Our love is illegal. You knew that! A man, right here in England, last week; he's been put behind bars for two years because he sent a love letter to another man. I call that immoral, barbaric."

Ahmed was at his very best – softly spoken, suave, gentle, diffused sunlight enhancing his stunning good looks.

"Know something else," he continued, "immoral is not always the same as illegal and illegal is not always immoral. Sure, my company use heavy handed tactics, but it's for the greater good. We're like an ants nest. Ants look after their own. We use pheromones for communication. Sort of, like, we're individual brain cells making up one big brain. And I do mean big! We're international. We can get anywhere."

Simeon popped the obvious question.

"Is that how you found me?"

"Finding you was very difficult. I have to hand it to Mackenzie, if I ever catch up with him… well, I might just offer him a job. He's good. How did he get you out?"

"Catch up with him! I thought *you'd* got him already – killed him even."

"No. Not guilty. But if he gets there first, *Howard* might waste him."

"Howard! What's Howard got to do with it?"

"He stole Howard's money – a *lot* of money."

Ahmed went on to explain that Howard was often careless about large sums of cash kept in his house. Indeed, Simeon recalled the concerns of Olga the bouncer when she remonstrated with Marie for leaving the office unlocked.

"One of these days, one of those chickens is going to wander into that office and help himself in a big way."

At about 7.00am on Tuesday, May 3rd, about $40,000 in one hundred dollar bills was stolen from Howard's office. Ahmed and Simeon returned from New York on the Sunday evening of May 1st. The latter woke up alone in the Great Bed on the Monday morning. He discovered that Ahmed had to leave earlier on urgent business. Dale seemed anxious. All was not well. On arrival at the university, Laurent had been replaced with an intimidating guard who looked like Lee Van Cleef who said –

"Bad move, kid, stickin' ya dick in a nigger's maw! Worse for the nigger!"

"Hell yes!" said Ahmed, indignantly. "I picked Laurent out of the gutter. I gave him a good job with The Firm to prove to *you* that I was not prejudiced. I did it for *you*. And what did you guys do? You did me dirt! I was as mad as a hornet."

"Was Laurent beaten – murdered?"

"I fired his black ass. And then later..." He moved closer. Tenderly he took his lover's hand and became affectionate. "Booby... I fell to pieces when you left me. I was no good to anybody. I'm no good without you. I spoke to Barney. It was a steep learning curve but... well, he didn't tell me anything that I didn't already know. He reminded me of the rules – not *my* rules. Those were unreasonable restrictions I imposed on you. Barney reminded me about the reality of gay life in Detroit. Guys are horny. Guys are tempted. Sex is casual, anonymous. It becomes a kind of sport. You have to get more dick than the next guy and boast about it. I've taken what I wanted. I took you. I paid the price."

"I know that I've not been fair with you," continued Ahmed. "I'm a bully. I've abused my power. I frightened you – tried to control you – found that part of you which was vulnerable. And I expected too much of Laurent. All that time you guys were together and I expected him to keep his black paws off... off the best thing that ever happened to me. And... I *did* listen to what you said about that racist stuff. I *should* have shown Laurent more respect. Beat on Laurent? *Murder* Laurent? Is *that* the way to get you back into my arms? In the middle of one sleepless night I lifted my miserable face from a tearstained pillow and made a decision. I went back to the gutter, found Laurent, doubled his pay, and kicked his black ass all the way to England with orders never to show his face in Detroit until he found you. He found you. So I gave new orders – guard Booby well."

"Then it *was* Laurent that I saw?!"

"The library? Sure, he's not perfect. But he's done good and sent back lots of material. I enjoyed reading Nobby the Gnome."

"From the library! He *couldn't* have made copies without me knowing!"

"Easy. He photographed the sheets from your hotel room when you were out. He's been right here, in the Old Swan, watching over you for weeks. More diligently, I might add, than Harcourt's spook who spends most of his time in the bar."

"How could you possibly know about that?"

"Laurent is a good negotiator. He has an arrangement with that slimy queen with the plastered hair who runs this place. Don't look so surprised. *His* moral fibre isn't so great. He's cheap – easily bought. This place pays peanuts so they get a monkey manager. He's offered more nuts and agrees to keep his mouth shut and ask no questions. I'll tell you, Booby; you were so right about Negroes being as good as us. Laurent is a bag of tricks, has so many skills, not just sleuthing. He's a whiz at phone tapping. He's recorded every call you made to that lawyer from the call box in the lobby. Sorry, kid, we know everything. So much for a secure line!"

"What about the two guys asking questions in Derby and Nottingham," asked Simeon thoughtfully, "they were white, but must have been your men?"

"Howard's men. But it's the same thing. You must have guessed that Howard is a wheel in The Firm. At that point, he was just trying to get the money back. That's why Barney put two guys on the job."

"Surely you didn't think that *I* stole any money!"

"No, Booby. I know you're honest and I know why you flew the coop. You were scared and homesick, but mostly scared – scared by Olga and Mackenzie – especially Mackenzie. Not to mention all the disinformation we put out to keep the kids in line. People call *me* a criminal, but I never took anything which wasn't mine. Eventually, Laurent located your toad. Oh boy! Bulging eyes, groping paws – the poor guy really earned his bread on that day, wheedling out data and at the same time fighting off a sex mad reptile. Anyway – he got lots of useful information about your afternoon in the caves and Gary's disappearing act."

"ACT!"

"Oh sure. We know Mackenzie better than *you* know Mackenzie. Howard wants me to put him in hospital. But I say put him in charge of one of my units. Much more sensible. I'll make you a deal, Booby. Tell me how Gary got you past all our security and I'll explain his conjuring trick. Deal?"

CHAPTER 44

Truth

It was a deal. Simeon outlined his abrupt exodus from the USA, the adventures from May 3rd to May 6th. Careful not to mention the young chauffer's name, he described the road trip along the I 94 Freeway, the best part of 100 miles *east* of Detroit Metropolitan Airport, all the way to an isolated airfield not far from Battle Creek. At that moment, he was surprised to discover that Gary was also travelling to England. They boarded a chartered flight to Buffalo in a light aircraft. They transferred to Allegheny Airlines, a scheduled flight to New York and then on to Prestwick Scotland, via Icelandic Airlines.

Ahmed was smiling with admiration. It was clever audacity, going west when The Firm expected them to head east. The convoluted complications of that route from Detroit to Derbyshire would have challenged any manhunt. Ahmed's few questions elucidated Gary's careful preparation for a plan to steal money and use Simeon's escape, to cover his *own* escape.

During March, Simeon's domestic problems were reaching crisis point involving several sadistic incidents compounded by at least three thinly veiled death threats. His solution was a plan of escape, an emotional insurance if the strain became too much. All this was confided to his street-wise friend at one of Howard Mueller's parties.

Tempted by an easy target, Gary Mackenzie had toyed with the idea of robbing Howard for sometime. From selling his own body, he had savings as was suggested at Toad Hall, but not enough to account for the large sums splashed around up until he vanished inside High Tor in Matlock Bath. Mr Toad, Simeon and even Martin Harcourt had totally underestimated the wealth of Gary Mackenzie. He had nearly quadrupled his money after the theft from Grosse Point which took place early on the Tuesday morning of May 3rd. Simeon's problems presented an opportunity for Gary to plan and realise a recently acquired ambition; to defect from the Detroit scene and vanish into the English countryside with enough capital to live comfortably for many years. If invested wisely, perhaps for a lifetime.

Over the time of his friendship with Simeon, Gary Mackenzie had heard glowing reports of English life, especially the *quality of life* as opposed to the material standard of living clearly superior in the United States. It was during that conversation in early March with a fearful homesick Simeon, when Gary conceived a design in which he might be able to appropriate a large sum of cash from the mob and, in a haze of confusion and misdirection, get out of the country quickly under cover of an entirely different suspect. A few chickens, including Gary, knew about Howard's money. If not well protected by a safe, that treasure trove enjoyed the protection of fear. In Detroit it was common knowledge: if you valued your good looks, your ability to walk, to see, to be alive; you would not cross any officer of The Firm. As well as Ahmed, Howard Mueller was such a man.

Gary had neither taste nor skill for burglary. He reasoned that the best time of access to the cash, was early morning when Howard and Olga were soundly sleeping. Marie, the early rising effeminate houseboy, would be cleaning or preparing breakfast. A suitcase was needed for the haul. However, arriving at that prestigious Grosse Point address at 7.00 in the morning, unannounced, with a suitcase – how could this be explained to Marie? The solution – pornography. Gary had often boasted about his collection of obscene photographs, so many, they had to live in a suitcase. Marie was intrigued by this alluring collection of hunky men doing naughty things to each other.

"When do *I* get to peep, honey?"

"You'll have to do *your* looking early, very early, before your boss or the bodyguard gets up. My pictures are too precious. I don't want them disappearing into *his* greedy hands. I'll stop by one morning."

Shortly after Gary lent his sympathetic ear to Simeon's tentative plan to abscond; this crafty seed of salacious smut was planted into the rather scatty head of Marie.

Gary was fond of Simeon. It would be wrong to say that he hatched his self-serving scheme with a total disregard for this friend's welfare. He genuinely believed that the First Boy of Ahmed's Harem was in real danger – mortal danger. He also knew that Simeon's simple exit strategy was amateur and doomed to failure. In dangerous territory, Gary, the hardened hustler of sharp wit and superior experience, was confident that he could deliver success to this very tricky operation – which, of course, he did. He also knew that, in the unnerving circles of Ahmed Hamah, it would be only a matter of time before something would alarm Simeon and trigger the plan of escape. Gary Mackenzie had only to bide his time and wait for that trigger, that opportunity which came on the Monday morning of May 2nd when Simeon made his frantic phone call from the university.

On the following morning at 7.00am, Gary arrived at Howard's house at the side kitchen entrance with a suitcase full of rude pictures. Marie was delighted, more delighted when Gary emptied his load of indecency on to the kitchen table and said he would return for them at a later date. Bidding a hurried goodbye, he left the houseboy who was, as expected, totally absorbed sorting through the pile of forbidden erotica. As expected, Marie was too busy to notice that Gary had not returned directly to his car, out of sight, in the driveway. With an empty suitcase, he went straight to the most important room in that impressive house, Howard's private office.

Howard had always taken the view that anything valuable was most safe when it was in *plain* view, disguised as something else. Up to 7.05am on May 3rd 1966, that strategy had served him well. Two walls of quality bound books, dark leather easy chairs and a great gothic desk made Howard's study an impressive place of serine silence. Six shelves up on the wall facing a massive floor to ceiling window, 30 volumes of the Encyclopaedia Britannica blended insignificantly into a background of similar tomes to everybody – except the master of the house – or so he thought. Some two years before, his flamboyant servant, mincing around with feather duster, had accidentally discovered the secret of this, very expensive set of books. One year before, in a depressed drunken stupor, that chatty little queen accidentally revealed this secret to a young man who was lending a shoulder to cry on.

"Know, Gary, sometimes I think I should just 'up sticks' and get the hell out of here. I will! I'm not kidding – and I'll take that fuckin' encyclopaedia with me for the pension I'm due. That'll teach the old bastard. I'll do it! I will! See if I don't!"

Gary Mackenzie was to remember this captivating reference to an encyclopaedia which was worth a pension. And now he was standing in that office-cum-library, looking intently at those 30 tomes. He dragged over a coffee table, reached up to examine a volume which disappointed. It turned out to be – just a book! He put it back and decided to be methodical. He started at Volume One which was also disappointing, as were volumes two, three and four. Volume Five – jackpot! It was hollowed out containing dozens of $100 bills. Intermittent volumes at random concealed close on to a haul of $40,000 quickly stuffed into the suitcase which, until minutes before, had been the resting place of the nude, rude and lewd. Casually, he strolled out of the house and drove back to Allen Park where he lived uneasily with his respectable middle class parents who had no idea that Gary would be leaving the family home for a very long time. The money, heavy, and filling about half the suitcase, left plenty of room for other vacation needs. Items of clothing nicely protected the cash from any check at customs, which, fortunately for Gary, did not happen. Customs officers at Prestwick were more interested in the rucksacks on the back of Gary and Simeon. In the mid-1960s, rucksacks on the back of teenage boys were regarded with suspicion due to the growing epidemic of drug use.

Gary had packed his case and donned his rucksack just in time for the arrival of little Sam in his big car. The 1960 Chevrolet Impala with the distinctive rear gull wings, never failed to impress Simeon. It all went to plan. All three left Wayne State University at 9.30 prompt.

At some point after a few days with toad, Gary knew that he had to disappear and to be *seen* to disappear by witnesses. Meeting 'the professor' in Derby on the Friday evening of May 6th was an unexpected bonus. He told Gary about the caves on High Tor in Matlock Bath where gay men congregated for sexual activity. On Saturday, the professor and a couple of unsavoury characters known as Monks and Muckles took their attractive American guest to Matlock Bath for a tour of those caves. For Gary, this was an exercise in reconnaissance. It was the foundation stone for the conjuring trick he performed so successfully the following day.

"Laurent did his best," explained Ahmed, "but he couldn't get to the bottom of how Gary made an exit from that god-awful hole in hell. He felt sure that these hoods 'Monks and Muckles' knew something about it, but, well, low-life like that; they're used to keeping their secrets. After *that* trail went cold, it was all guess work. Of one thing I'm sure, Booby, Gary *did* get out of that maze. He's too careful of himself to fall into a bottomless pit."

"What's your best guess?" asked Simeon.

"He's not like you," said Ahmed, thoughtfully, slowly. "I don't think he would bury himself in some Cornish village and live quietly on the interest of his loot. Gary Mackenzie needs the energy and stimulation of the big city. So, look for a big spending, dark haired kid in London."

"Dark haired!"

"Right. Blonds can make the change more easily than we could. But we'll find him. Oh yes, baby! It may take months, even years. We'll find him. Yes, sir. We'll find him."

Ahmed was right and wrong. He was right about Gary being careful of himself. He had no intention of confiding his plans to Monks, Muckles or the professor – or any other living soul. He always played a lone hand. Neither did he have any intention of trying to navigate through an unknown labyrinth in total darkness. The scouting trip had shown the solution immediately. Subtly, in conversation with Simeon and toad, he established a 'waiting point' out of sight of the cave entrance where toad could sit down with Simeon and spend the half hour suggested. Simeon, trusting as ever, would see Gary go into the entrance and *appear* to descend into darkness in pursuit of carnal pleasures. In fact – he hardly penetrated more than five foot – where he waited a few minutes for Simeon to re-join the toad. Under cover of shrubs and fern, he stole out and descended the wooded hillside and back into Matlock Bath where he purchased a large rucksack. He took a taxi back to Belper, entered Toad Hall through a decrepit cellar door which was never locked anyway, and went to his untidy room. The mess was a help. The removal of a few items to get him through a few days would never be noticed. Leaving £230 in his old rucksack would, to Englishmen of average means, make it look as though he had vanished from the face of the earth. Gary knew that, even Simeon, who had lived in the US, could not conceive the sums of money circulating around the gay mafia of Detroit. With regard to stealing Mueller's money, Mueller's 'petty cash' to buy chickens, Mackenzie had little conscience. Mackenzie knew that forty grand was a fraction of Mueller's worth.

When Gary exited Toad Hall with his well stuffed rucksack, as instructed, the taxi was still waiting. Ahmed was wrong about the blond turning into a brunette. It was not necessary. But Ahmed was right about the relocation to a capital city – not the capital of England – the capital of France.

Simeon and Ahmed looked at each other. Another hearty rumble drifted down from Bill's open window suggesting a goal or, perhaps, a near miss.

"So. How *did* you catch up with me?"

"I followed your inclinations," replied Ahmed, leaning forward and touching the tip of Simeon's nose. "I told Laurent to stop wasting time in the bars. Follow the vapours, I told him. 'North, south, east or west?' he asked. I suggested north. After Derbyshire, Booby is obsessed with Yorkshire. We highlighted the most likely baths, or Turkish baths as you call them here. We checked out reputations. Not too many of them. That made it easy. Not much in Sheffield but Manchester looked like a sure bet – a place called Sunlight House near the Opera House – big, dirty and very active. Laurent made himself agreeable with some of those horny bathers. He chatted about a cute chicken on a bicycle, staying at Youth Hostels. He drew a blank. So he moved on. In Leeds he struck gold! He heard about an antiquated but spirited bath house in a sedate town called Harrogate. Not only that, but *this* bath house had an experienced blob of blubber, a permanent fixture in the steam room who kept the punters really happy; *so* happy, the guy at the front of the line would go right to the back of the line for seconds.

"In this country we call it a queue," said Simeon with dead pan expression.

"Queue or line, I told Laurent – check it out. It sounds like Booby's idea of heaven. If anyone can find a fat man like *that* – Booby can! Don't look so glum. I've done a lot of thinking. I accept you as you are. I don't blame you. Once we'd found the best cocksucker this side of the Old South, I knew you wouldn't be far away. Hey, listen up – I had a *great* time in that hot fog. *I* was standing in that same line – sorry – queue – last Saturday – all afternoon. And I'll tell you, it was a pleasure meeting him. A cultured fellow countryman: he's good conversation. If I can ever wrench him from that television, I intend to thank him for looking after you so well."

"He's been very generous to me."

"And *you've* been real generous to *him*," said Ahmed with twinkle.

"No," replied Simeon in sheepish embarrassment, "I mean, I've grown fond of him. He's been paying the bills here for the last two months and more."

"Has he?"

Something in Ahmed's gentle and ironic tone made Simeon look up sharply. Ahmed's eyes were full of love.

"After Harcourt stopped paying, *I* picked up the tab. I needed you to keep still. I wanted you to stop cycling around, to be at the Old Swan, to keep an eye on you. I needed time to sort out my ideas. That greasy manager gave you a clue. He mentioned Miss Havisham. For years, Pip thought Miss Havisham was his anonymous benefactor. In fact, in *Great Expectations* – it turned out to be somebody quite different."

Ahmed looked at Simeon and Simeon looked at Ahmed. Seconds passed as Simeon absorbed the significance of this new intelligence: the knowledge that for many weeks Ahmed had known everything, had been paying for everything. These seconds were filled with silence because neither could think of anything to say until the stronger partner made positive comments about Bill's encouragement.

"One thing, Booby; when it comes to exposing social ills, you and Dickens are sure driven by 'fire in the belly'. Old Bill did good buying you that typewriter. I guess we have a whole history which hasn't been told – and *should* be told. *You* taught me that about the Negroes. Remember? You said they'd been written *out* of history."

"I'm glad you read the Nobby stuff. Back in Detroit you never wanted to hear about him. One of my freaks, you said. You said all of my Derbyshire friends were freaks."

"Not all. I've come to respect the Nottingham lawyer. He's an honourable man doing his best. But you have to admit… well, I mean…*gnomes, toads, goblins, crones*… and those snobs! Laurent thought he'd stepped into a Restoration comedy! He'd never seen anything like it! So contrived, counterfeit… it was all sham. They're not just freaks but *fake* freaks. Look… I want us to look *better* than that. If the heterosexual majority – a 95% majority, I remind you – if they are going to read about our history, I'd rather them hear *less* about Nobby the Gnome and *more* about Alan Turing."

"Who?" said Simeon, genuinely puzzled.

"There you go! 'Who?' you say. You know all about a Gnome who haunts urinals and nothing about a gay man who helped Britain win the war. If it were not for

Turing, you might be speaking German today. He was a mathematical genius, the founder of modern computing, a brilliant guy who cracked Nazi military codes."

"Was he?"

"Yes he was. A few years back: 1952, I think, Turing got mixed up with a younger guy who'd been stealing his money – giving him a rough time – stuff like that. He told the cops. He *expected* justice, but it all came out. Turing could *not believe* that a bit of fun, mutual masturbation, would be so important compared with theft and harassment. He had admitted to committing an '*act of gross indecency*'. That is the law's description of sex between two men – two *consenting* men! It is a crime. But, hey, listen Booby – where is the victim? What Turing did with that guy, is *exactly* the same as a man and a woman getting intimate. But, know what, that is *legal*. That is OK! *And you have never heard of Alan Turing!* That is sad, Booby. He was a war hero, a *gay* war hero who has been written *out* of history."

"OK," said Simeon, sitting straight, rising to a challenge. "Go out and find him. Find this mathematical brain. *I'll* talk to him. I'll interview him in the same way that I interviewed Nobby. He can tell me his story. We'll tell the world about it. We'll shout it from the rooftops!"

"Too late, Booby. Turing killed himself. An apple laced with cyanide. After his arrest and conviction, it was all downhill. He lost his job, self-respect and everybody despised the man who saved England from the Third Reich. It was a crucifixion."

These words hit Simeon hard. Just for a moment, he felt the pain of Alan Turing. He was back in the playground of Mundy Street Boys School suffering the humiliation of jeers and pig grunts. The hog had to be taught a lesson.

"It was either jail – or some kind of hormone treatment," continued Ahmed. "I guess you know what happens to people like us who go to jail. It's no surprise that Turing chose to take the treatment, a form of chemical castration. It was supposed to 'cure' his homosexuality. It drove him to depression... and suicide."

CHAPTER 45

Happy Ending?

That down beat, one gay man defeated and dead, triggered its own reverential minute of silence. As if to end the silence, Ahmed did, what he did best. He took the initiative and embraced his lover. In that embrace, the warmth of body, heartbeat and vitality of youth underlined the fact that these two gay boys were *not* defeated – were not dead. Theirs was the future. And that reality, like osmosis, seemed to percolate through both bodies which were locked in that big hug. Words were not spoken. Words might have spoiled that ineffable, overwhelming physical and emotional moment. It was not spoiled, it was ended by an extraordinary phenomena.

The Great Spreading Chestnut Tree, and its tranquil domain, was suddenly transformed by spontaneous whoops of joy from the open hotel windows. A gaggle of yelping revellers could be heard around the corner at the entrance. All exultation blended into a more distant thrum of celebration, emanating from the heart of Harrogate. The nation was now buzzing with the excitement of triumph – a replay of VE Day.

"An omen?" asked Ahmed, releasing his lover, looking him directly in the eye. "Let's consider it a good omen." Gently, he stroked Simeon's cheek with soft fingers. "Know, Booby – little boys like you – you're too naïve, too trusting. You only know what you're told. You tend to believe what you're told. It isn't always so. In the gay world especially – so secretive – lots of hearsay – lots of gossip."

The carnival jollifications continued in the background. Simeon was silent. He was snared with emotion, affection and admiration in the presence of such a powerful personality. Ahmed moved his lips within inches of his besotted boy. The latter surrendered. He bridged the gap to affect a gentle kiss.

"I came back, not to kill you, not to punish you, in any way. I came back to love you. You've been rejected by your parents and family – but I loved you, and do love you. I'm not perfect. I've desired many, had many, and boasted about it. It's part of my make up. But I've loved only you. I need to care for you. I need to cherish you. Please come home. I *ask* you to come home. I'm no good without you. It's hard; I know it's going to be hard. But please… let's try again. Let's give it another go. I'm a proud man, Booby. Don't make me beg."

He talked about a future together. Ahmed talked about Simeon's need to get back to university, the need for the student to be encouraged in his writing. There was a general re-negotiation of the unwritten contract of their partnership. Ahmed made concessions which took account of the realities of homosexual life, especially the promiscuity of that life, along the lines of – 'as long as you always come back to *me*'. All his life, Simeon held to the belief that any gay relationship had the best chance of success if it was an open relationship. Ahmed did not need a verbal response. He could see his answer in Booby's eyes – because it was *his* Booby. It had always been and always would be.

In a speech which was obviously rehearsed, there were generous concessions regarding the thorny issue of Simeon's homesickness. Ahmed suggested the two of them should have an annual vacation, the whole month of May, in England, in Harrogate, at the Old Swan Hotel. He also ceded the month of December and the New Year, every year, in a top notch hotel in London.

Ahmed swept on. He concentrated on common ground. He drew attention to the ideals which tied them together, the need for his partner to write a gay history, their mutual zeal for social justice and resistance to what would be termed homophobia 40 years later. He emphasised the practicality of returning to Detroit. It was the home of The Firm, the source of wealth to fund Booby's education, wealth to fight for the gay cause and wealth would buy pleasure and make life very comfortable. Wealth would make it possible for Simeon and Ahmed to travel through life – first class – every time. The latter focused on the alternative. A teacher's salary of twelve pounds a week in England would condemn that teacher to relative poverty with no power to advance the argument for homosexual equality.

Ahmed, pushing on an open door, came to a rest with his re-claimed property looking at him with wide-eyed, hero-worshipping, dreamy, starry eyes. In a small part of his rational mind, Simeon noted his conqueror had carefully circumvented troublesome matters of a moral nature. He had tiptoed around contentious subjects, such as, young boys in a criminal network and the violence and fear which maintained that organisation. He had avoided the serious issues of incompatibility which were still lurking in the shadows. Nothing had changed. They still laughed at different things and would seldom laugh together. Social communication would continue to be difficult with big gaps and long silences – evidence of a profound gulf in ethnic and social background. Such reservations, however, were not allowed to interfere with the euphoria of that special moment of reconciliation. The conclusion of Ahmed's spiel was followed by more physical activity – kisses and cuddles – which in turn was followed by a warm, comfortable silence, eventually broken by Simeon.

"So! Where do we go from here?"

"*You* go to Room 304," said Ahmed, using the tips of his fingers to gently toy with Simeon's lips. "It's the age of Black Power and one black stud is thirsting for one Little Booby. It's been too long. Laurent deserves his reward. He's guarded you. He's waiting for you."

"And you?"

"Hector's found a new playmate! I'm taking him to the Bulman Suite to celebrate. Hector likes a good tongue. You know, one that teases. He wants sport, frolic – the usual stuff. Just for an hour; we need to look after our friends. Listen Booby, we have the rest of our lives to look after – to cherish – each other."

Go forward half a century. Simeon is 71. He is indulging in nostalgia. He often did this; an attempt to make sense of his life. He looked back over the decades to the adventures and the characters of his youth – the toads, gnomes, crones, goblins – the old and the ugly. And then there were the chickens… beautiful boys… but only one Ahmed Hamah. Simeon had penned several books and often considered writing about his secret summer of 1966 which witnessed the love of his life – his one great love – the gorgeous American of Arab extraction. Friends were encouraging.

"… but it *must* have a happy ending. Everybody wants a happy ending."

Shelagh Delaney was criticised for the 'unsatisfactory' ending of *A Taste of Honey*. It was seen to be both sad and, somehow, incomplete. She argued that it simply reflected real life which does not always turn out as we would wish. In composing a novel about *his* great love, Simeon was faced with the same problem – if they want a happy ending, where should it end? Along the continuum of life, there are days when we are happy and days when we are not. On Saturday, July 30th 1966, the nation rejoiced in victory, but three months later on Thursday, October 27th, it mourned the death of 116 children who were buried alive under a slag heap which wiped out a generation in Aberfan.

Real life is like that. And Simeon always wrote about real life and real people. He might have preferred that he and Ahmed had been 'strangers in paradise'- lovers who meet in a lovely garden, under the whispering leaves of a mulberry tree, as did the Caliph and his true love in *Kismet*. The hard fact of meeting in a gay bathhouse in 1966 did not make Simeon's great love any the less great or less fulfilling. The actuality of Nobby and Ron meeting in a urinal in 1911 did not diminish that life changing, profound relationship. Real life is like that.

On Saturday, July 30th 1966, Ahmed and Simeon were ecstatically happy. If his love story was ever written, Simeon decided it would end on that day of blissful reconciliation and delightful reunion. The book *could* have ended on October 27th when, in mid Atlantic, on the old Queen Mary, the two boys heard the tragic news about the sliding Welsh coal tip. On *that* day, *Secret Summer* would still have had a happy ending. The authorial voice could truthfully describe Ahmed and Simeon, smiling, blithesome, in good spirits sailing west into a magnificent sunset of brilliant red, purple and gold. It was cold on deck, but they cuddled together to keep warm. It made an all-important physical connection which continued to weave its magical spell – continued to keep them together.

The narrator might be tempted to reach for the traditional ending to a fairytale love story, such as this one – Ahmed and his Booby. But in their case, the old cliché – *and they lived happily ever after* – would have to be *implied* rather than spoken, if the author was to be *completely* honest.

Notwithstanding, on October 27th 1966, Simeon and Ahmed *did* sail into the sunset and they *were* blissfully happy.

ABOUT THE AUTHOR

Narvel Annable's first book *Miss Calder's Children* (1997) described his early post-war schooldays in Belper, a quaint Derbyshire mill town. His second book, *Heanor Schooldays* 1998, was also autobiographic, covering his unhappiness in a grim, gas-lit, Dickensian, Church of England junior school from 1955 to 1958. Adolescence and the move to William Howitt Secondary Modern School, "A culture of kindness" in September 1958 was a dramatic improvement, graphically retold in the second half of the social history.
In 1963 he emigrated to the United States and arrived in Detroit on the day before the assassination of President Kennedy. The next seven years saw him in a variety of jobs which included labourer, lathe-hand, bank messenger and camera salesman. In 1975 he graduated from Eastern Michigan University (magna cum laude) and taught history for a year at St Bridget High School in Detroit.

In 1976 he returned to Derbyshire to help organise and launch 'Heritage Education Year 1977' at Sudbury Hall. From 1978 to 1995 he taught history at the Valley Comprehensive School in Worksop in Nottinghamshire. Seizing retirement at the earliest opportunity, he started to write historical and educational articles for the local Press and has been interviewed several times on BBC Local Radio. *Death on the Derwent* – A Murder Mystery set in Belper 1949, his first novel, was published in 1999. His fourth book, *A Judge Too Far* – A Biography of His Honour Judge Keith Matthewman QC of the Nottingham Crown Court, was published in 2001.

Inspired by his early gay experiences during adolescence at school, Narvel's second autobiographic novel *Lost Lad* was published in 2003. His third autobiographic novel was published in 2006. *Scruffy Chicken* follows his adventures during an extended English cycling vacation in 1965 where he uncovers a hidden world of repressed homosexuality in deepest Derbyshire. *Secret Summer*, a fourth autobiographic effort is a gay love story set in Detroit and Derbyshire in 1966. It was published in 2010.

Narvel lives with his partner Terry Durand in Belper, Derbyshire. In September 2010 they celebrated their 34 years together.

Lightning Source UK Ltd.
Milton Keynes UK
UKOW031629170812

197686UK00005B/62/P